THE DARK HOURS

DAVID J. GATWARD

WEIRDSTONE PUBLISHING

The Dark Hours
by
David J. Gatward

Copyright © 2023 by David J. Gatward
All rights reserved.

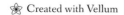 Created with Vellum

To everyone at Cockett's Bakery and Butchers

Grimm: nickname for a dour and forbidding individual, from Old High German grim [meaning] 'stern', 'severe'. From a Germanic personal name, Grima, [meaning] 'mask'. (*www.ancestory.co.uk*)

CHAPTER ONE

CARL WALSH ARRIVED AT HIS DESTINATION EARLIER THAN HE had expected that Thursday afternoon. The planned stop on the way, which was only a mile or so from where he was now parked, hadn't taken as long as he had expected. He'd scuffed his knuckles a little, and cut a finger, but that wasn't an issue. So far, everything was going according to plan. And now here he was, smug at the genius of it all, of his own awesome mind, and staring up at a large house sat just a few miles beyond a hamlet going by the name of Marsett.

The journey from home had been a joy, a smooth ride in luxury, driving a 4x4 with the speed of a sports car. When he'd pulled up in front of the house, parking next to a solitary white Volkswagen campervan, the smile on his face had been close to becoming a permanent fixture, not just because of the vehicle, but his confidence in his plan.

The vehicle was top spec. At least, that's what he'd been told in the sales room by a young man in a tight suit, who was so thoroughly doused in aftershave, Carl had tasted the stuff at the back of his mouth for days after. And that suit had been the stuff of nightmares, tight in all the wrong places, with a lining so bright it didn't so much catch the eye as burn itself permanently into the retina.

The whole thing had been quite the impulse buy; a sunny day, nothing to do, and a fat bank account that needed emptying burning a hole in his pocket. At first, the salesman hadn't taken him seriously, focusing more on the cost of the cars on display, the large deposit, the finance, than what such a car was like to drive and own. His aim had been, Carl assumed, to dissuade him from the folly of a purchase so clearly beyond his means, and to have him leave as quickly and quietly as he could politely ensure. So, Carl had done the exact opposite. Because he could.

Admittedly, Carl hadn't helped matters by turning up in a pair of scruffy jeans, and a jumper that was more a collection of holes than a guard against cold weather. However, once he'd given plenty of evidence of his finances, things had changed considerably. Coffee had been provided, and a lovely comfy chair, while brochures were presented. The manager had come out to greet him personally. And so had the assistant manager. He'd even been offered a Danish pastry; warm, too, which had both surprised and delighted him. That he could afford a Porsche at all was a joy, though perhaps not a surprise. He had done a lot to get to where he was now, and he was damned well going to enjoy it.

Top speed, engine size, model, none of that had really mattered to Carl. It wasn't like he was about to treat himself to track days, or go crashing through the speed limit on the motorway. All he had really wanted was a car that didn't just make him feel good, but let everyone else know that he was doing more than okay for himself, thank you very much. To hell with anyone telling him it was a midlife crisis. For a start, he was a few years and a couple of notches on his belt beyond that anyway. And frankly, this was no crisis; he knew where he was, how and why he had got there, and the view was bloody marvellous. Also, it wasn't like he was going to have the vehicle for long, was it?

The car was black, and climbing up into it was like opening a door in a splinter of the darkest of nights. The interior was all cream leather, and the driver's seat seemed to reach out and embrace him as he sat down. Once fired up, the growl of the engine was almost preternatural, the sound both musical and haunting, something conjured up from another place out of time.

Carl had worked damned hard his whole life, not just to be able to afford a car such as this, but to live the rest of his life in quiet, unadulterated luxury. He had taken risks, done things few would ever understand, and even fewer would ever know about. But that was the thing about secrets; it wasn't just about keeping them, but knowing their value and how to use them, and right now he was staring at a mere fraction of their worth and reaping the rewards.

That everything was soon about to change bothered him a little, but he'd gone through things, if not worse, certainly similar, and everything was planned. Also, this time? He was wealthy beyond the reckoning of most people. And although money didn't necessarily make you happy, the amount Carl had squirrelled away in various offshore accounts and investments, certainly gave him a warm fuzzy feeling inside. It also gave him one hell of a safety net.

A fierce gust of wind pulled Carl's attention away from his car, nearly knocking him off his feet. There was ice in that wind as well, chill teeth gnashing at his skin as he dashed around to the passenger door to grab a jacket. The wind came at him again, seemed to grab the door and push, turning the simple act of trying to get warm into a battle against the elements. Yes, the weather was about to take a turn for the worse, but in all honesty, it was only going to work in his favour. He was prepared for it, better than anyone would ever know.

Jacket retrieved, Carl let go of the door and the wind slammed it shut, then he grabbed his luggage and headed over to the house. Of the two bags, one was light enough to carry over his shoulder, while the other, which had sat beside him the whole way as a passenger, was large and heavy and needed to be dragged across the parking area to the door, leaving tramlines in the gravel as it went.

The house was, in many ways, very simple; a large front door of oak sat dead centre, a small window, like an eye, staring out at about head height. On either side of the door were pairs of bay windows, and above it a further five windows, all spaced equally from left to right. The house and all those windows reminded Carl of a giant stone spider, staring out at the valley below it with a well-worn and rather superior air. The roof was slate, the edges of which were crusted, not only with frost, but a garland of thick icicles, some of which hung down low enough to reach from an open window.

Booking the place had been based on a number of factors. First, he'd wanted to find somewhere that was cost-effective, but at the same time sufficiently grand to give the weekend just enough wow to impress the guests.

And they were guests in a way, weren't they? Carl thought.

Yes, this was the first course he had ever put together, but it was also to be the last. However, referring to them as attendees had felt a little too commercial. He wanted them all to believe that he thought they were special, that by paying a not-inconsiderable amount to come along and listen to him talk, to take part in the sessions he had planned, he was fully behind the idea that they were more than a step above the average Joe on the street.

How little they knew. He smiled. It would also add to the story he was trying to spin, though perhaps the magician's distraction was a better comparison; the sell had to be very, very convincing.

Carl had also wanted to find somewhere that was more than just remote; he had wanted accommodation at which mobile signal was, even on a good day, truly awful. In fact, it was so bad, that the house, which had no land line, had an emergency shortwave radio set up in an outhouse, just in case, though just in case of what, Carl wasn't really sure. Still, a bad phone signal would add to the isolation. It would also give him another edge if he needed it.

Pausing now in front of the heavy front door, Carl reached up and hefted the iron knocker against the wood, the sound dull and hard.

He waited, glanced back at his Porsche, then when no answer came, reached up to knock once again, this time harder.

The door opened on the third tap to reveal a young man with a shaved head and piercing grey eyes. He was wearing black trousers and the white top of a chef. His sleeves were rolled up to his elbows, and he stood at the same height as Walsh himself, a good six foot, give or take. He was slim, Walsh observed, built like someone who either lived on their nerves or did far too much exercise, perhaps both.

'Oh, sorry,' said Carl, plastering his face with that devastating smile he'd used so often to such good effect. 'Wasn't sure if you'd heard, but here you are!'

'The kitchen's right at the back of the house,' the young man said, a little out of breath. 'I was just in the middle of prepping some beef; didn't think it would look too good if I welcomed you with bloody hands, holding a knife, if you know what I mean.'

Carl gave a laugh and introduced himself, holding out his hand, which the young man gave a firm shake.

'You must be James Acton.'

The young man shook his head.

'Sorry, James is ill,' he said. 'I'm Jack Miller.'

'Ill?'

'Hungover, probably,' said Jack. 'Birthday party last night, or something like that, anyway. Don't worry though; I'm a better chef, I can promise you that. Anyway, you're earlier than I expected. Thought you'd be here closer to teatime than lunch.'

'So did I,' Carl said, hiding his concern about the sudden change in staffing. 'But I was up earlier than I thought I'd be. Never been a believer in just hanging around, so here I am.'

Jack stepped back into the house, opening the door further.

'Get yourself in, then,' he said. 'You must be hungry.'

'Very.'

'Then follow me.'

Stepping inside, Carl heaved the heavy bag up a deep doorstep behind him, relieved to be out of the cold winds chasing each other around the house like brawling banshees. Not that the house was all that warm, but the scent of burning wood certainly gave the promise of heat, even if he couldn't feel it quite yet.

The hallway was wide, and presented a number of doors left and right, and a large staircase rising to a windowed landing, before turning back on itself to make its way to the first floor. The walls were hung with paintings of the local landscape, soft watercolours showing drystone walls, barns, and sheep.

Following the chef, Carl smiled to himself. The house was perfect, he thought. Now all he had to do was make sure that Jack was all his confidence said he was. The other chef's CV had been superb, so Jack needed to impress.

'Sit yourself down,' Jack said, pointing to a large dining table in the centre of the kitchen floor. 'What would you like?'

'What would you suggest?'

'Well, there's plenty of cold stuff you can start on; meats and pies, that kind of thing. Or would you like something hot?'

'What about an omelette?' Carl asked.

Jack gave a nod, then set to with a pan and a few eggs.

Carl sat back, watching him work. He'd read somewhere how an omelette was a good way to check on just how competent a chef was. It was the kind of dish that was as simple to do as it was difficult to perfect. It also gave him a chance to watch him work, check Jack's body language, get a feel for the person beyond just his voice and some fancy clothes.

A couple of minutes later, Jack presented Carl with a plate and some cutlery.

'Omelette with grated parmesan and black truffle,' he said. 'Easy.'

The omelette glistened like wet gold, the smell rich and intoxicating.

Carl picked up the knife and fork and tucked in.

'Bloody hell, that's delicious.'

'It's supposed to be.'

Carl said no more, words losing all meaning as he carved his way through something that he was fairly sure had no right to be so tasty.

'Thanks,' he said, the omelette gone in barely a couple of minutes. 'Best omelette I've ever had.'

Jack took the plate and placed it in a dishwasher, while Walsh wiped the corners of his mouth with his fingers and sucked off the crumbs he'd found.

'I passed the test, then?' Jack asked.

Carl smiled.

'And what test would that be?'

Jack leaned against the kitchen cupboards, his arms folded.

'You could've asked for a sandwich, but you asked for that. Trying to catch me out, right?'

'Just needed to make sure,' said Carl. 'And yeah, you passed the test.'

He stood up, patted his stomach.

'Course I did,' Jack said. 'Though I'm not sure what you'd have been able to do if I hadn't.'

'Must be a takeaway nearby,' said Carl, though not in any way seriously.

He saw Jack's eyebrow rise just a little as he let out a quiet laugh.

'You've not been here before, have you?' he asked. 'The area, I mean, not this house specifically.'

Carl shook his head.

'Well,' Jack continued, 'I know there's a takeaway, but it's at least twenty minutes away, probably closer to half an hour if the weather's bad. And it looks like it's certainly going to be this weekend, doesn't it?'

'Does it?'

Jack's raised eyebrow dropped swiftly into a frown. He folded his arms.

'You've not looked?'

Carl shook his head as convincingly as he could.

'Probably best you don't, then,' said Jack.

'It's that bad?'

'Depends on what you mean by bad,' Jack replied. 'You brought skis, right?'

Carl laughed at that. No, he hadn't brought skis, but he had brought something else, and it would most definitely come into its own soon enough, no matter how bad the weather got.

'You know, the last time I saw serious snow was too long ago to even remember it,' he said. 'And if it does snow, it'll be nothing more than a dusting, I'm sure, and a lot of panic in the news, that's all. You know what the tabloids are like; always foretelling the hardest of winters, deep snow, and power cuts.'

'Well, we'll just have to see, won't we?' said Jack. 'We've plenty of food, the woodshed is well stocked, so we'll be good regardless, even if we do get snowed in and cut off for a while.'

Carl made his way to the door.

'Right, I'm going to get myself settled in,' he said. 'There's a bar in the lounge, isn't there?'

'There is,' Jack said. 'Fire's been lit a while as well, so it'll be nice and cosy in there, I'm sure.'

'That sounds just perfect,' Carl said, then turned to leave the kitchen.

As he did so, Jack called after him. Carl turned around to see the chef holding an envelope in his hand.

'Sorry, nearly forgot; this arrived for you earlier today. Probably from one of your guests telling us they're a vegan or lactose intolerant or something.'

Carl took the envelope.

'Do you need a hand with that?' Jack then asked, nodding at the large suitcase Carl had dragged through the house.

'No, I'll be fine,' Carl said.

'Seems heavy.'

'That's because there's a body inside,' said Carl, then laughed, perhaps a little too loudly.

Jack smiled, then turned back into the kitchen to get on with his work.

A few minutes later, with his heavy luggage stowed in a

cupboard under the stairs, and the other bag deposited in the largest of the bedrooms on the floor above, Carl was sitting in the lounge in front of the fire and sipping on a very generous single malt.

Despite what he'd told the chef, Carl knew all about the weather forecast for the weekend. In fact, all things considered, it would probably play in his favour, he thought. There was still some planning and sorting to do, for sure, but for now, he was quite happy to sit back and relax.

The envelope Jack had given him was on the coffee table in front of the fire. Carl had a good idea as to the contents, but reached for it anyway and opened it. Yes, he thought, no surprises there. Which was good, because the sender had no idea at all themselves, did they?

Carl folded the letter up, slipped it into a pocket, then leaned back into the sofa to drain his whisky, only as he did so, an icy draft cut through the room from a gap under the door and he dropped the glass, shattering it on the wooden floor.

For the next few minutes, all Carl could do was stare at the pieces.

CHAPTER TWO

LATER THAT SAME DAY, AND WITH EVENING CRAWLING ITS WAY across the Dales, huffing and puffing cold harsh winds as it went, drinks were being enthusiastically poured in another house.

Marina White was sitting at the dining table in a very shiny, new kitchen and she was already tipsy, but that didn't stop her from taking a hefty gulp of the fresh gin and tonic she had just been handed by her husband.

'You trying to get me drunk?' she asked, looking at him over the top of her glass.

'Perhaps,' Harvey replied, himself sipping on his favourite cocktail, a Bloody Mary, strong and spicy enough to sting his lips. 'It has been rather a long time, hasn't it?'

'Too long,' she said, eyes wide over the rim of her glass.

'And yet here we are, after all these years, still together.'

As Harvey leaned in for a kiss, Marina reached over to meet him halfway, and somehow managed to slip off her chair. He caught her, causing them both to laugh.

'So strong,' Marina said.

'Not bad for someone touching sixty, right?' Harvey said. 'There's bugger all to do in prison other than go to the gym, so I made good use of the facilities. Kept me out of trouble as well.

Which is saying something, isn't it? And it's not like the food they serve is going to have you put on weight.'

'You sure about that?'

Harvey flexed his rather impressive biceps and Marina had to admit that being inside had actually done him rather a lot of good, though she hoped the changes weren't just physical.

Harvey raised his own glass.

'God, that tastes good,' he said, taking a gulp to leave behind a thick red moustache.

Marina reached over and wiped it off with her thumb, taking another sip of her own drink in the process.

'I can't believe it's been eight years,' she said. 'How did we manage to survive on nothing more than visits and phone calls?'

'Nothing can break what we have,' said Harvey.

'And what's that, then?'

'True love!' Harvey laughed. 'What else?'

Marina shook her head, rolled her eyes, but deep down knew his point was well made. They'd met as teenagers, Harvey the dashing young man in a shiny car, her as a girl just trying to make enough money to pay the rent by working two jobs, waiting tables and serving behind the counter at the local chippy.

It had been his eyes that had caught her attention, grey and calm and strangely bright. Every Friday he'd visited to put in the same order—a portion of chips and scraps—always putting his change in the tipping jar.

Their first date had been a simple affair of a trip to the cinema and a shared box of popcorn. To this day, she couldn't remember what the film had been, so preoccupied had she been with wanting to make the right impression.

A year later, they had married, and Marina had never questioned where or how Harvey had earned his money. Those rare occasions where she would find bruises on his body, or when he would come home with bloody knuckles, well, they worried her. But she trusted him, too, and decided early on it was better and easier, to ignore it. She loved him and she knew he loved her, and really, that was all that ever mattered, even now, so many years, and a prison sentence or two, later.

'So, as these are my first days of freedom, what do you have planned?' Harvey asked, pulling Marina from her thoughts and memories.

'Very little, actually,' Marina said, then looked around them at the room they were sitting in. 'This place is as new to me as it is to you, so I didn't see the point in putting together any trips out.'

'A weekend in, then?'

'I'm afraid so.'

'Sounds absolutely perfect.'

Following Harvey's instructions, which were never anything less than meticulously detailed, Marina had used various ways and means to purchase the house under a new name. Now, here they were, strangers in a strange land, with a view of a lake and hills all around, both hoping to live happily ever after, and with as little disturbance as possible. Harvey had more than enough stashed away to keep them happy and secure for more years than either of them had before them, and his old life, they were both sure, would never come knocking. He'd burned a lot of bridges, done his time, and now it was time to relax.

The doorbell rang.

'Expecting someone?' Harvey asked, the brightness of his eyes dulling for a moment.

'The only person I was ever expecting was you,' Marina said, unable to hide the sound of shattered glass in her voice as a shiver of fear broke it.

'You're sure about that?'

'Of course I'm sure,' Marina said, and she was. 'No one knows we're here. Hell, even we don't really know we're here, do we?'

'Then who the hell is it?'

Marina thought for a moment.

'My guess is that it's a neighbour,' she said. 'I bet that's exactly who it is. Probably just popping round to welcome us or something. Yorkshire people pride themselves on their welcomes, don't they?'

Harvey said nothing, placed his now empty glass on the table, and headed out of the kitchen and along the hall to the front door. Marina knew that he was naturally suspicious, even more so considering everything they had both done to disappear.

Marina followed and watched as her husband checked on a small screen to the right of the door to see who was standing outside. She leaned in and saw the image of a man wearing a uniform and carrying a parcel.

Harvey opened the door.

'Evening,' the man said. 'Sorry to bother you. I've a parcel here for you, I think.'

'No, I don't think so,' Harvey replied. 'We've only just moved in and we're not expecting anything.'

'You sure about that?'

'That we've only just moved in?' Harvey said. 'Yeah, fairly sure.'

The man stared at the parcel, then showed the address label to Harvey.

'This is you, right? Well, not you, but here; this house, I mean.'

Harvey read the label.

'That's our address, yes,' he said, then he seemed to notice something.

'Something the matter?' Marina asked.

'There's no name,' Harvey said. 'Just says *The Owner*.'

'Which is what you are, isn't it?' said the delivery man. 'You just told me that yourself.'

Harvey gave a nod.

'Maybe it was for the previous owners,' he said.

The man at the door shrugged.

'You can refuse delivery if you want,' he said.

'Really?'

'It's up to you. It'll just end up back at the depot on a shelf before it's then returned to the sender.'

Marina watched as Harvey took the parcel, turning it over in his hands. There was weight to it, she could see that from the way he held it, then he shook it and she heard something heavy inside moving a little.

'There's no sender address,' Harvey said.

'Well, if there's no address inside either, then whatever that parcel contains will either end up binned or being taken home by someone at the depot,' the delivery man said. He leaned in conspiratorially, his head close to Harvey. 'You'd be amazed at some of the stuff no one claims that we get our hands on. Not all of it legal either, if you know what I mean.'

'No, I'm not sure that I do,' Harvey said.

Marina reached out and gave Harvey a tug on his sleeve.

'We may as well take it,' she said, though she could tell immediately that Harvey wasn't so sure.

'Something about this just doesn't feel right,' he said.

'Don't worry about it,' the delivery man said, taking the parcel back, and stepping away from the door. 'I'll just take it back to the depot. Might end up with whatever it is myself in a week or two. Knowing my luck, it'll be bin bags.'

Harvey called the man back.

'It's fine, we'll take it,' he said.

'You're sure?' the man asked. 'I mean, it's no bother at all.'

Harvey gave a nod and a smile.

The man held out his phone.

'Sign here, then,' he said.

Harvey etched a scribble on the screen and then took the parcel.

'Nice place you've got here,' the man said. 'Looks like you've done okay for yourselves.'

Harvey gave a nod and a smile.

'I've done okay,' he said, then swished the door shut, and turned to face Marina.

'You sure you've not been doing some online shopping?'

Marina shook her head, then followed Harvey as he walked back through to the kitchen and placed the parcel on the table.

'Well, are you going to open it, then?' Marina asked.

'You're sure no one knows we're here?' Harvey asked.

'Not a soul,' Marina said. 'I followed your instructions and here we are. Harvey and Marina White no longer exist. We're the Taylors now, like you said; Harold and Karen. And that parcel doesn't have a name on it anyway, does it? It's harmless. Has to be.'

Harvey sat down at the table and opened the parcel. He pulled out a bottle of whisky.

'Well now,' said Marina. 'That's a turn up for the books, isn't it? Is there a note? Something from the sender?'

Harvey didn't answer. He was staring at the whisky, eyes wide, trying to stop his hands from shaking.

Marina sat down beside him and reached out a hand to rest on his arm.

'Love? What is it? What's the matter?'

Harvey blinked hard, and when he opened his eyes, he saw Marina staring back at him, her eyes filled with the warmth of a summer's evening.

'Nothing,' Harvey said, and before Marina could stop him, he ripped off the foil from the top of the bottle, and pulled out the cork.

Marina quickly grabbed two small glasses from a cabinet behind where they were sitting.

Harvey poured two generous measures, then handed one to his wife.

'To us,' he said, raising his glass.

'Always,' Marina said.

Outside, the man who had delivered the parcel climbed into a black van and pulled a phone from the glove compartment. Putting in a call, he waited for the answer by lighting a small cigar, the rich scent of tobacco filling the air with the aroma of wood and old leather.

'Well?' said the voice at the other end.

'Yeah, it's him,' the man said, then killed the call, puffed out a thick grey plume from the cigar, and drove off into the night.

CHAPTER THREE

GRACE BLACK WAS OUT WALKING A FEW FIELDS ON ONE OF
the larger farm estates she worked for. Her gun was open and
unloaded under her arm, and Jess, her dog, was happily bobbing
along at her side. Friday's morning was trying to break, but the heat
from the rising sun was doing little to crack the ice, and the green
fields and fells of Wensleydale were blanketed in a hard frost.
Grace stepped into a puddle and the frozen surface squeaked as it
gave way, thick mud the colour of chocolate oozing through.

She'd headed out about an hour ago, and though her belly was
warm and full, thanks to the porridge she'd eaten for breakfast,
Grace's hands were cold because she had forgotten to bring along
her pocket warmers. Heated by slim sticks of lit charcoal, their
smell was as comforting as the heat they gave off, sending her back
to the wintery days of her childhood and fetching the bus to school.

She still had the same ones that she had saved up her pocket
money for all those years ago, sneaking out one lunchtime to pop
into the gun shop in Leyburn to buy them. But the memories
weren't really as effective as the real thing. Blowing on her painful
fingers to warm them, Grace was sorely tempted to send a few
cartridges down the barrels of her shotgun just so she could then
use them to heat her hands a little.

Stepping through a stile in the wall, Grace pushed on through to the next field, her hands deeper in her pockets, her breath condensing in front of her, little ghosts playing in the dawn. Freshly dug mole hills dotted the field, steam rising from the dark soil. The same was true of the holes dug by rabbits and foxes, the steam huffing out into the day as though it were the hot breath of the Earth.

As ways to make a living went, hers was a tough one, but it was also one she wouldn't change for all the money in the world. But then, if she had been the kind of person to whom money was important, being a gamekeeper would not have been high on her list of dream jobs, that was for sure.

Her life was a hard one of long days spent outside in all weathers, and for little financial gain. And yet, even as the cold wind bit into her cheeks and gnawed at her fingers, as she reached down to rest a hand on Jess's soft head, the smile on her face only grew. Her office was not a desk in a room where the air was stale, the view little more than concrete and glass. She had the dales as her workplace and the air was so rich you could eat it. Breathing it in this morning, though, set her teeth on edge and froze her throat.

The reason for the morning walk was twofold. One, was get the dog up and out, give her a proper run before a day of being in and out of the back of the old Land Rover. Jess was clearly enjoying herself, bouncing along at a slight angle as though tacking against the wind, tongue lolling, hot breath forming a permanent cloud in front of her face. The other reason was rabbits, which was why Grace was carrying her gun.

She wasn't expecting to finish the walk with her bag full; walking fields with a shotgun wasn't exactly the most efficient way to bring the numbers down. To do that, she would be out in a hide and there she would stay, eyes on her quarry through the scope attached to either her FAC-rated air rifle, or the .22 rimfire she'd purchased a few years ago. A legal limit air rifle, the kind anyone could own, was all well and good. For her line of work, however, Grace knew that more power and increased range were vital. And if she didn't fancy doing that, there were always the ferrets. But today was cold, and they were snuggled up warm in their pens back at her dad's place, and it had seemed unfair to disturb them.

Today was more of a recce. At least that was how Harry had described it when Grace had told him what she was up to. He would often fall back on a military term, the soldier he had been so long ago still just a scratch away beneath the surface.

The rabbit season was generally regarded as early November to late February, though being classed as vermin meant they could be taken at any time of the year. And although rabbits were plentiful early in the season, Grace, like many others experienced in keeping their numbers down, chose to wait until either snow or a hard frost made it easier to follow their tracks.

She was out to see just how busy the warrens were, and with the frost on the ground white as icing sugar, she was given a clear view of where the rabbits had been most busy. She saw other markings, too, of deer and fox and hare, and wondered for a moment if she was now being spied on from afar, thin eyes staring at her from beneath branch and bush.

Moving slowly and carefully into the next field, one she knew had a large warren under the wall at the far end, Grace moved slowly, carefully, quietly. Her eyes were now accustomed to the light and far off she spotted a number of brown lumps in the frost, like flotsam floating in sea foam, rabbits were filling their bellies on the rich meadow they called home.

They were too far off for her to be sure of a clean kill, and Grace prided herself on only ever taking a shot if she was absolutely sure of making it. She had met other shooters in her time who gave less care to the craft, who didn't respect the animals they were hunting. Most times, she avoided them, but there were occasions where callous idiocy and dangerous gun craft had caused her blood to boil. She had no problem throwing paying guests off expensive shooting days, and had done so on more than one occasion.

As one particular memory drifted across her mind, Grace

spotted a dark line of tracks along the other side of the field. The
frost there had been well disturbed, though by what she wasn't
sure, at least not from this distance. So, forgetting the rabbits, she
headed over, always keen to ensure that she knew what was
happening on the land she worked.

About halfway across the field, Grace heard an engine sparking
to life, quickly followed by another, neither coming from the direction of the road. Instead, they were further on, over where the fields
were cut by an ancient track, the line of which had scarred the
landscape for centuries, though its origin was now lost to history,
and perhaps even the fells no longer remembered.

The grumble of the engines was harsh in the early morning
quiet, and it was soon joined by barking and the angered shouts
of men.

Grace paused, closed her eyes, held her breath. Turning her
head, she homed in on the voices, trying to make out words, but
they were lost over the distance. The barking was broken by a yelp,
and then the shouting grew in volume and venom.

With a fair idea as to where the noise was coming from, Grace
marched to the other side of the field and to a gate. On the way, she
crossed over the line of tracks she had spotted, a mix of boots and
paw prints and the unmistakable tracks of a hare.

Through the gate, Grace's pace was close to breaking into a jog,
anger already lighting her veins with the fire of adrenaline. The
engines and shouting were louder now, and she heard doors being
slammed. Then movement caught her eye as, in the distance, she
saw the rear ends of two vehicles, a white van and a red four-by-
four, racing off down the old track.

Grace's jog became a run, Jess enjoying the increased pace.
They arrived at the track just in time for her to see the vehicles
disappear around a bend. She cursed that she was too late to catch
sight of a number plate.

Heading around to where the vehicles had been parked, Grace
soon found evidence of what she had suspected on seeing those
tracks on the other side of the field. The ground was a mess of paw

prints and boot marks. A cigarette end was resting on an iced puddle and still smouldering. There was blood, too; not much, but enough to tell her that the hare the dogs had been sent to chase was no more.

Grace swore through gritted teeth and pulled out her phone, took a few photos of what she had found, then called her dad.

'Now then, Gracie,' Arthur said. 'Everything alright, like?'

'No, Dad, it bloody well isn't,' Grace replied, breathing hard.

'I said you should've taken the ferrets, didn't I?' Arthur said.

'No, it's not that,' said Grace, then explained what she had found.

When she had finished, Arthur was silent for a moment. 'And you think racing across a field to chase after them is sensible, do you?'

'What do you expect me to do?' Grace replied. 'Just let them get away with it?'

'I expect you to have a little bit of common sense,' Arthur said, his voice rising.

Grace, though, really wasn't in the mood.

'Don't you go lecturing me, Dad,' she said. 'I can look after myself. And it's not like you're one for talking, is it?'

Arthur laughed, but Grace heard no hint of amusement in it.

'Is that right?' he said. 'Look after yourself, can you?'

'You know exactly what I mean.'

'Oh, I do, right enough, like,' Arthur said. 'But you've no idea who they were, where they were from, what they're like, have you? No, you haven't. No idea at all, lass!'

Grace shook her head, sighed. He was right, she knew that. She just didn't want to be told right then, that was all.

'I didn't call you to have my ears burned off,' she said.

'No, you called me hoping I'd understand,' said Arthur. 'And I do, Grace, of course I do. And you should know that better than anyone, because if you don't, then what bloody use have I been as a dad, eh?'

Grace was tempted to kill the call, but that would only serve to make things worse.

'I'll tell you this for nowt, lass,' her dad said, still going, 'one thing's for sure, whoever they were, they're not the kind of people you just walk up to of an early morning in the middle of nowhere and give a bollocking to.'

'They were gone by the time I got there,' said Grace.

'And what if they hadn't been?' Arthur asked, love and anger in his voice. 'Then what?'

'It doesn't matter anyway, does it?' Grace said, stung by her father's tone. 'They're gone, and that's all there is to it.'

'No, it isn't all there is to it,' Arthur continued. 'That hot head of yours, it'll get you into trouble one day, that's what worries me, Grace. Always has. Always will.'

Grace laughed.

'My hot head? Says the man whose knuckles aren't covered in scars just because he's a little bit clumsy.'

'That's different.'

'Is it, now? And why's that, then? Because you're a man, is that it, Dad?'

'It just is!'

A moment of silence allowed Grace and Arthur time to step back from the sudden argument.

Arthur asked, 'So, what do you want to do, then?'

Grace kicked a stone, sending it down the track to skid across the glassy surface of a frozen puddle.

'Well, there's nowt I can do, now, is there?' she said. 'I didn't even get a number plate. They're gone.'

'You saw the vehicles though, right?' Arthur said.

'White van, and a red four-by-four.'

'Anything else?'

Grace was about to say no when she spotted something. A single set of tracks, paw prints heading away, and not in the same direction as where whoever they were had been chasing hares.

'There was a lot of shouting,' Grace said, dropping down to

look a little closer at the paw prints. 'I heard a dog yelp. I think one of their animals might have done a runner. There's tracks here heading off. I'll go and have a look, see if I can find anything.'

'You be careful,' Arthur said. 'If it's hurt or panicked, it won't be in the mood for company. But you're right to go look. I'll join you.'

'No, Dad, that's not necessary.'

'I wasn't asking for your permission, lass,' Arthur said, then hung up.

Grace went to stuff her phone in her pocket, then paused, and sent a text to Harry. She was fairly sure there wasn't much he could do, but if falling for a detective chief inspector didn't allow her to at least ask for his help now and again, then she'd be having words with him later, that was for sure.

Text sent, Grace called Jess to heel, then headed off to follow the trail of a lost dog. A few minutes later, she checked her phone, saw that Harry hadn't yet read it, so sent another one, just to wake him up.

CHAPTER FOUR

DCI HARRY GRIMM WAS ALREADY AWAKE AND STARING INTO thick darkness when his phone buzzed itself right off the bedside cabinet and down onto the floor. Something was niggling at the back of his mind, something important he had to do, though right at that moment, he had no idea what it could actually be.

Maybe whatever my phone is buzzing about would clarify things, he thought. So, he rolled over to reach down the side of the bed to grab it with his right hand, and instead managed to flick it further under the bed.

'Bollocks ...'

The phone now silent, Harry rolled back across his bed and pulled the duvet up to cover himself again. He had no idea of the time and he didn't want to know, either. Not yet, anyway. A morning as dark as this wasn't exactly inviting. And neither was the sharp sting in the air so gleefully betraying the harsh temperature beyond the warmth of his duvet, which was noticeably colder than when he'd headed to bed.

A huff from the bottom of the bed made Harry laugh, as something pushed itself closer to his feet.

'Morning, Smudge,' he said, rubbing a foot through the duvet against the warm bulk of the dog. 'Made yourself at home again, I see.'

Having moved into his new home in Gayle just over three months ago, Harry was still getting used to the old place. Built around a couple of hundred years ago, the small cottage had its own creaks and drafts, its own smells. The walls had stories to tell, he was sure. Sometimes, when he walked down the stairs, he had an almost comforting sense of all the others who had lived there before him, as though each wooden step held within it an echo of times past.

The bedroom door, though, definitely had a life all of its own. He had fixed the damned latch numerous times, and always made sure each and every night that the slim, panelled door was shut. And yet still there were mornings when Harry would wake to find the door wide open, and Smudge once again curled up and a little too comfortable at the bottom of the bed. It was as though the house responded to the weather, to changes in temperature, stretching and contracting and breathing, just enough to allow the door to fall open.

The phone buzzed again, and Harry tried once more to reach for it, stretching as far as he could without having to get out of his bed, but the darkness had swallowed it, leaving him little choice but to get down onto the floor.

Crouching, and shivering against the cold, Harry ended up halfway under the bed before he found the phone. He was tempted to then just jump back into bed, but he had a feeling that would be a bad idea. He was up now, so better to just face the day.

Stumbling around the bed to head to the bathroom, and leaving Smudge curled up behind him, Harry pulled up two messages from Grace, reading them through bleary eyes. He was a little groggy still, but managed to understand them enough to call her back.

'Did I wake you?'

'Yes,' Harry lied.

'Sorry about that.'

'You sent two messages,' said Harry. 'The second one said, *Get up, you lazy arse.*'

Grace laughed, though Harry heard stress in the cheery sound.

'So, what's happened, then?' he asked. 'Your message said something about courting hens, though I'm fairly sure that's not what you meant.'

'Bloody auto-correct,' said Grace. 'Hare coursing, not courting hens. Why the hell would I be doing that, whatever it is?'

'That makes more sense. Where are you?'

'Out the back of West Witton.'

'And what is it you've found, exactly?'

Grace explained, and Harry listened.

'You know it's probably a good thing you didn't actually catch up with them, don't you?' Harry said. 'People like that, they're not the type you want to go confronting with their misdemeanours, if you know what I mean.'

'Don't worry, Dad's already given me the exact same dressing down,' Grace replied with a sigh. 'And he's on his way over now, would you believe?'

'Yes, I would,' Harry said, smiling.

'I think that whoever they are, one of their dogs ran off, and they just buggered off and left the poor thing to fend for itself. So, he's coming over to help me try and find it.'

'Why would they do that?' Harry asked.

'Because people like that, the ones you've just pointed out I shouldn't go confronting, they don't give a toss, that's why,' Grace said. 'And I'm not about to abandon it to freeze and starve to death, or to be knocked over on a road.'

Harry yawned, then turned on the shower to allow the hot water to run through the system and steam up the bathroom, and stepped out and closed the door to speed up the process.

'I'm in work after lunch,' he said, 'but I'll have someone over to you earlier.'

'No, there's nowt to rush over for,' Grace said. 'Hardly crime of the century, is it? And it's not like we need your forensics team crawling all over the place looking for DNA.'

'Still ...'

'It's just some arseholes getting a kick out of terrifying animals,' Grace continued. 'They had a van, a white one, and a red four-by-four. And there are plenty of tracks here, tyres, footprints, and a cigarette butt. That's not much, I know, but it's no reason to be sending someone racing over.'

'I'll send one of the team out as soon as I get in, then,' Harry said. 'How's that?'

'That makes more sense,' said Grace. 'Gives me a chance to get on with a few things as well. I can always leave dad here, can't I, to keep an eye on things? What's that name you give to someone who checks everyone going into and out of a crime scene?'

'Scene Guard,' Harry said.

'Exactly that. That's what I'll tell him he is; he'll love it.'

Harry heard the laugh and warmth in Grace's voice, but he wasn't sure just how serious she was about having her dad sit on the site until someone from the team turned up.

'You okay to have whoever it is give you a call, sort out how to find you?'

'Of course,' Grace said. 'I'll just arrange to meet them here.' Then she added, 'Well, looks like Dad's just arrived. Unbelievable.'

'Hope you find the dog,' said Harry.

With a quick goodbye, behind which Harry heard the voice of Arthur calling, Grace ended the call.

Leaving the bedroom in the safe care of Smudge, Harry headed back to the bathroom. Stepping into the shower, and aware that the phone call hadn't done anything to deal with the niggle that had woken him in the first place, he braved the sting of the hot water against his chilled skin.

Leaning his forehead against the cold tiles and closing his eyes, he lost himself for a moment to the heat, only to find himself stumbling through flashbacks of the past couple of years, still unable to fully grasp the reality of where he now was. Good things had

THE DARK HOURS   27

happened, and bad, and some part of him felt sure he should have been considerably more affected by it all. But he wasn't. Because, no matter how he looked at things, the good far outweighed the bad. How else could he explain that he was happy to live in a house where, just a few months ago, his own father had been murdered?

In many ways, it made little sense. He was fully aware of the fact that an event such as that would have hit with such force that the shockwaves from the impact should, by rights, go on for years. Yet all Harry felt was a sense of calm. It wasn't that he was cold-hearted, or that he was simply pushing things deep down and ignoring them. It was perhaps more that the past, *his* past, no longer had a hold on him.

His present was now so full, so rich, that sometimes he found himself smiling. He couldn't help it. Just a few years ago, life had been colder, harder, mean-edged, and he had been moulded by it. It had made him into the detective he was now, for sure. Now, though, since moving to the Dales, those edges had been smoothed off a little.

Though he would be the last to ever admit that he was content, Harry was damned certain that he was what could best be described as happy, a state of mind he really wasn't used to at all. As he stepped out of the shower and back into the cold air of his house, he was smiling, not least because, sitting on the landing outside the bathroom, Smudge was now staring at him and thumping her heavy tail on the floor.

Dressed, and with breakfast done, Harry was about to head through to the lounge to do very little indeed, other than enjoy the few hours before work just relaxing, when a knock rattled the front door.

He ignored it, and made to continue through to the lounge.

The knock came again, harder this time, determined.

Harry turned back into the hall and opened the door.

'Morning,' said the far too smiley face staring up at him. 'You ready, then?'

Detective Constable Jenny Blades was standing in the open

doorway in front of Harry, dressed in her running gear. She was bouncing from foot to foot to keep warm.

'Clearly not, no.' Harry frowned, seeing ice crystallising the grass of the small garden, which led from his own front door down to the edge of Gayle Beck.

Jen stopped bouncing.

'You've forgotten, haven't you?'

'Forgotten what?'

Jen gestured at what she was wearing.

'Surely this is enough of a clue?'

Then the niggle at the back of Harry's mind turned into the blaring alarm of a quarry siren, and he remembered. Something about him saying how he was still feeling the effects of eating too much and not moving enough over Christmas. Then something else about Jen persuading him to sign up for a five-kilometre race and promising to help him with his training.

'Sorry,' Harry said. 'Didn't sleep well last night. Must've slipped my mind.'

'Then best you unslip it sharpish,' Jen said. 'I didn't get up early and drive over here on my morning off just to have a chat with you on your doorstep. Get your trainers. We're off.'

'We are?'

'Yes.'

'You do remember that I'm your commanding officer, don't you?' Harry asked. 'I was going to have a lazy morning; I'm not due in till later.'

Jen cocked her head to one side and just stared.

Harry leaned out to look at the day as a gust cut down past the front of his cottage sharp enough to rip the skin off his nose.

'And I've already had a shower.'

'I'm quite sure you'll survive being decadent enough to have two showers in one day,' said Jen. 'I've done it myself and I've never once been struck down from on high.'

'Can we not just skip it?' Harry asked. 'Leave it till tomorrow, maybe?'

Jen folded her arms.

Harry sighed.

'Shall I take that as a no, then?'

'Probably for the best.'

'What about Smudge, though?' Harry asked.

'We're not going to be out long,' said Jen. 'And as, like me, you're not in work till later anyway, you'll have plenty of time to take her for a walk. Or she can come with us.'

Harry had a sudden image in his mind of getting himself tangled up in Smudge's lead and ending up on his face, then being dragged down a path slick with mud by an excited Labrador.

'Give me five,' he said, and stepped back inside, Jen following.

Harry headed upstairs, spent a few minutes swearing at his chest of drawers as he tried to find his running gear, then headed back downstairs to grab his trainers from a cupboard in the kitchen.

Giving Smudge enough time to deal with a quick call of nature in the front garden, he left her inside the cottage, curled up on her bed in the kitchen, then headed out at Jen's side, down the path at the front of his cottage to turn right over the bridge. Striding over, he gazed down at Gayle Beck and noticed ice had formed at the water's edge, a thin, milky-white crust that creaked and giggled as the waves passed beneath.

Leaving the bridge behind, they then headed down Old Gayle Lane. The road was quiet, the surface glassy enough to force him to focus hard on his feet, though he wondered if a slip now wouldn't actually be too bad a thing, if it meant the run was cut short.

'How are you doing, then?' Jen asked.

Harry was very aware of how Jen's own running style seemed effortless, which was only magnified by the fact that every step he took himself seemed to make the ground shake, his body shuddering and wobbling in places he really wished that it didn't.

'Oh, I'm just fine and dandy,' Harry said, his breath painful, his body moving with all the grace of a hippo running out of control down a hill.

Jen slowed the pace to a fast walk.

'The first few runs, you just need to ease into it again, okay?' she said. 'Run, walk, run, walk. You'll be back into it in no time. You were a Para after all, weren't you? Your body will remember soon enough.'

Harry wasn't so sure, and even less so when the fast walk once again became a jog. It was a couple of decades ago since he'd been in the Paras and fit as a butcher's dog.

Having thudded his way past the back end of the auction mart, Jen eventually led them through a stile and across a field, into the top end of Hawes. They slowed down for another brief spell of walking, then were jogging again, heading back into town and along the cobbles, past Cockett's and into the marketplace. The dark morning was still murky, as Jen led them up the path alongside the church, then across the old flagstone path, which followed Gayle Beck out of Hawes and back up to Gayle.

When they finally arrived back at the cottage, Harry was fairly sure that if they'd gone on for much longer, he'd have coughed up a lung. Jen, however, didn't look like she'd been out for a run at all, though her face was red now from the brisk, wintery air.

Harry opened the front door and felt like falling through it onto the floor.

'Wasn't so bad, now, was it?' said Jen. 'How are you feeling?'

'About as bad as I look,' Harry answered, trying but failing to control his breathing.

'Well, it was probably a good thing you got out now rather than later,' Jen said.

'Why's that, then?'

'Ignoring how cold it is right now,' Jen said, 'you've seen the forecast, right?'

Harry frowned. Yes, he had seen the forecast, but for the last few weeks, all it had really promised was more of the same; more cold, more rain, more of everything being deeply unpleasant. Yes, it was certainly colder today, but then it was February, so that was to be expected.

'Have I missed something?' he asked.

'Snow,' Jen said. 'And lots of it. Looks like there's a storm on the way. It's been promised all week, and seems like it might actually arrive today. You can smell it in the air. Running in snow is fun, like, but only once it's stopped falling.'

'I'll believe it when I see it,' said Harry.

'Well, my advice is to get yourself into town for a sledge,' Jen grinned. 'There's a good chance you'll be needing one. You've a pair of snowshoes, right?'

'Snowshoes? Of course I haven't got any snowshoes!'

'Anyway,' Jen said, cutting Harry off before he had a chance to say anymore, and stepping away from his front door. 'I'll see you later. Like you, I'm not on duty till this afternoon. See you then.'

As Jen headed off, Harry called after her.

'You're sure about this snowstorm, then?'

'We'll just have to wait and see, won't we?' Jen called back.

'Say hi to Steve for me,' Harry said, then Jen was gone, jogging back down the path.

Back inside, his legs stiff, his feet sore, his skin stinging from the cold, Harry made his way to the stairs, then headed up once again to the bathroom for a shower.

The water was hot enough to sting, and soon his skin was bright red. Then, as he was about to get out, he remembered what Jen had said about the weather. The thought of falling snow was more than enough to have him enjoy just a few minutes more, so he ducked his head under the water again and closed his eyes.

CHAPTER FIVE

'BLOODY HELL, WHAT'S HAPPENED TO YOU, THEN?'

The question was from Detective Sergeant Matt Dinsdale, the only member of the team at the office at the community centre when Harry arrived. Midday had passed, so Harry fully expected that the rest of them were out on various errands, grabbing lunch, or both.

Harry ignored the question for a moment and shuffled through the door, unclipped Smudge from her lead, carefully eased off his jacket to avoid any sudden movements, then slumped down in a chair. Somehow, he managed to groan with the agony of a broken man.

'You're walking like you've got piles the size of a bag of satsumas hanging out of your arse.'

'What a thoroughly delightful and specific observation,' Harry said, stretching his legs out in front of him.

The walk from Gayle, back across the footpath to Hawes to give Smudge a run, had been agonising, each step as though walking on bones made of splintered glass. Harry's second shower of the day had gone some way towards easing the aches and pains from the run, and he'd had a good stretch after as well, but as the day had worn on, the pain had grown to the point where he'd popped into the chemist to grab some painkillers. Hopefully, they'd kick in soon, he thought. As yet, though, they clearly hadn't.

'So, what's the problem, then?' Matt asked. 'Have you pulled a muscle getting out of bed or something?'

'I've pulled all of my muscles,' Harry replied, 'including plenty I didn't even know I had.' He rubbed his thighs and then looked up at the DS. 'Jen turned up at my door before even the good Lord himself woke up, to take me for a run. And there was me foolish enough to think I'd be having the morning to myself.'

Matt shook his head.

'As I've told you before, exercise, it's not good for you,' he said. 'Not that kind of exercise, anyway. Never seen the attraction.'

'I used to be a fairly decent runner,' said Harry. 'Back in the day.'

'And I used to have a thirty-two-inch waist, and could drink ten pints and get up fresh as a daisy the next morning,' said Matt, 'but like yourself, I'm not twenty anymore.'

Matt tapped his stomach to prove his point.

'And neither am I an octogenarian whose idea of a good day is to manage a trip from the sofa to the kettle and back,' Harry said.

Matt frowned.

'Did you really just use the word octogenarian?'

Harry shrugged.

'I've no idea where that came from either. The pain in my legs must've caused a short circuit in my brain.'

Matt walked over to the small kitchen area in the office. Early January, the old kettle had finally given up the ghost, so the team now had a slightly more reliable urn instead, providing a constant supply of hot water for the copious mugs of tea they drank throughout the day. And they had all taken to it with considerable enthusiasm. Matt returned with a steaming brew for Harry.

'You'll have seen the forecast, like,' Matt said, the words a statement rather than a question.

Harry shook his head, clasping the mug between his hands.

'Jen mentioned it, though,' he said. 'Snow, apparently.'

'Well, there's no apparently about it,' Matt said, sitting down beside Harry. 'Not now, anyway. It's all been a bit uncertain for the past few days, right enough, but as of a few hours ago, we're all on standby with the mountain rescue team.'

'Really?'

Matt gave a nod.

'Call's gone round that it'll hit sometime later on this afternoon. It'll be sporadic to start with. Blustery, I think they said, but then it looks like it has the potential to get worse. A lot worse.'

'It's serious, then.'

'Very much so,' said Matt. 'Obviously, there's always the chance the storm will sweep past, but to be honest, this looks like we're in for a rough few days. That's why the whole team is on alert. So, as you can imagine, Jadyn's more than a little excited.'

'Jadyn?' Harry said, then remembered. 'He joined after Christmas, right?'

'He did that,' said Matt. 'He fairly flew through the interview as well, and he's completed his half-day hill navigation assessment with one of the team. He's on probation now, which he thought was very funny, seeing as he's a police constable. A little too funny, really, but there you go.'

Harry laughed at that.

'Is that it, then?' he asked.

'There's a lot of training left for him to do,' Matt said, 'but he's already got himself a first aid qualification, so that's useful. And he's more than fit enough, as you know.'

'But doesn't he need to actually live in the area?' Harry asked. 'I mean, he's over in Catterick, isn't he?'

'Well, he was, yes,' said Matt.

'Was?'

'He's moved.'

Harry frowned.

'Why do I feel like this is information I'm aware of but have completely forgotten?'

'Like I said, you're getting old.' Matt laughed.

'I'm not exactly at death's door, am I?'

'Well, you've been busy enough with your own life this past while, haven't you?' said Matt. 'Settling yourself in up in Gayle, so your mind's been busy. Anyway, he's renting himself a little place in Reeth, over in Swaledale. Moved in last weekend.'

'Really?'

'It's temporary, bit of an impulse I think, but that's Jadyn, isn't it? I'd hate to have him know I think this, but now and again, that enthusiasm of his, it's almost inspiring.'

'Why Reeth, though?' Harry asked, smiling at Matt's comment.

'Close enough, but not too close,' Matt said.

'To what?'

Matt raised an eyebrow, and Harry remembered.

'Ah,' said Harry with a nod. 'Jen, right?'

'Right,' said Matt. 'But none of us talk about that, do we? Because they don't either. And we don't know anything about what's going on. Even though we do. Because it's so bloody obvious. Certainly from Jadyn's side of things, anyway. That lad couldn't lie if his life depended on it.'

Harry smiled. They'd all noticed something going on between the two constables, but were leaving them well alone for now and just standing back to see what would happen.

'So, what will he be doing with the rescue team now, then?' he asked.

'It's all down to experience really,' said Matt. 'Attending call outs and being supervised while he's on them, doing more training in climbing and rope skills and caving, though that one he's a little unsure about.'

'You've not taken him down Crackpot yet, then?' Harry asked, remembering his own experience of that particular cave with Matt back in the early days of his time in the Dales.

Matt shook his head.

'Plenty of time for that,' he said, then rested a hand on Harry's knee and added, 'And you can come with us if you want, seeing as how you loved it so much last time.'

'I can, but I won't,' Harry said, shuddering a little. He still wasn't sure he'd entirely forgiven the DS for the experience. 'Must be busy for the team if there's heavy snow, though.'

'If it comes in hard and fast, roads soon close, folk'll end up stuck trying to get home,' Matt said. 'And there's always one or two out on the hill who end up needing help, no matter how well-equipped they are. Once, we even had to dig out a couple of cavers, would you believe? The silly sods had gone for a quick explore underground, only to find on their way back out again the entrance was blocked.'

Harry heard the office door open and turned to see Liz Coates and Jim Metcalf, his two police community support officers, stroll in, both wearing hefty winter coats and warm hats, clearly ready for the promised snow. Except it didn't look so much promised, now, as something that was happening, as Harry spotted flecks of white on their hats and shoulders.

'Where's Fly, then?' Harry asked, seeing that Jim was without his dog.

'Out helping Dad,' Jim replied. 'His old dog, Jip, is a bit under the weather, so Fly's out with him, bringing the sheep down into the lower fields. We've most of them down anyway, what with the threat of the storm all week, but there's a few stragglers hiding up beyond the Roman road, as always. Fly will be having the time of his life, I'm sure. The snow's coming in now, too, so they'll be busy.'

As he was speaking, Harry watched Smudge head over to Jim, clearly confused by the absence of her furry friend. Jim gave the dog a scratch, then Smudge turned and headed back over to where she had been lying on a bed in the corner of the room, next to a radiator.

Jim and Liz hung up their coats, snow falling to the floor to melt into the carpet.

'How's Ben?' Harry asked.

It was a few months now since his younger brother had moved in with Liz, and though they still caught up as regularly as they could, this past while, Ben had seemed to be rather more busy than usual. Though with what, Harry had no idea.

'Forgetful,' said Liz.

'How's that, then?'

'Left his lunch at home. I only found out when I was halfway here myself from a walk around over in Leyburn, when he called to see if I could pick it up for him.'

Harry laughed.

'You made him go back for it, then?'

Liz shook her head.

'It was no bother for me to fetch it for him. But he owes me, and I'm thinking Chinese tonight, to make up for it. He can pop over to Leyburn for that when work's done.'

'I've not seen him for a good while,' Harry said. 'Always seems to be busy.'

'He's on with a big project at work, I think.'

'Must be important, then.'

'I think so, yes,' Liz said, then headed over to the urn.

'He's been on at me to swap out the old Rav4,' said Harry. 'Not sure for what, though. And anyway, it's still going fine.'

With a mug of tea poured, Liz turned and smiled at Harry.

'That'll be Mike,' she said. 'Ben's mentioned how he's pushing him to do a bit of sales stuff as well. Ben prefers to be under the bonnet and covered in oil, though. He's not a fan of customer-facing stuff, selling, that kind of thing.'

The office door swished open. Harry looked over to see Detective Inspector Gordanian Haig stride in. She wasn't in uniform, and the dark blue down jacket she was wearing had a dusting of snow on it, just like with Liz and Jim.

'Well, it's certainly starting to come in,' she said. 'So, I won't be staying long.'

'You shouldn't be here at all,' Harry said, remembering that Gordy was now on leave and heading to the Highlands for a week away with Anna, her partner and the local vicar.

'I know,' said Gordy, also brushing the snow off her jacket, 'but I came to drop these off. And, judging by the weather, just in time.'

She then held up a set of keys.

'What are those, then?' Harry asked.

'Keys,' Gordy said.

Harry said nothing, waiting for a bit more of an explanation.

'I've been pestering for a very long time that we need a decent four-wheel drive up here,' Gordy said. 'And we've finally got one. It's not as new as I'd like, as you'll soon see for yourselves, but it'll do the job.'

Gordy dropped the keys into Harry's hand.

'There's in the nick of time and then there's this,' said Matt.

'I had no idea one was even available,' said Harry.

'It probably wasn't,' said Gordy. 'Like I said, it's not exactly new, but it'll do the job. Best you come and have a look at it first, though, before I head off.'

Harry stood up with a groan.

'Goodness, man, what on Earth's wrong with you?' Gordy asked.

'He went for a run with Jen,' Matt explained.

'Serves you right, then,' said Gordy, barely able to disguise her smile.

Grabbing his coat, Harry followed the DI outside, the rest of the team trailing on behind him.

When he'd arrived at the office about half an hour ago, the air had been ice cold, the sky still dark. Now, however, the day was brighter, but it was an eerie glow that lit the town, as the sky filled itself with snow, the flakes falling slowly to the cold ground.

'Here you go,' Gordy said, directing Harry over to where Anna was parked up.

Harry waved to Anna, who was sensibly staying inside her warm car, then stared at the vehicle parked alongside.

'Well,' he said, standing back to really take it in, 'I'm not really sure what to say, if I'm honest.'

The vehicle was an old, long-wheelbase Land Rover Defender.

How old, Harry wasn't really sure, but it had certainly been through the wars a bit over the years. The official livery of the police force was scratched in places, faded in others, and completely absent on the wings, as though they'd spent most of their time getting stood on. Which explained why an aluminium chequer plate had been riveted on both sides, he thought, and for good measure on the bonnet as well.

'You'll want to sit in it, then,' Gordy instructed.

'Will I?' Harry asked. 'I'm not so sure.'

'Trust me ...' said Gordy.

'I've sat in vehicles plenty of times to know what to expect.'

Gordy's response was a hard stare Paddington Bear would've been proud of.

As the team looked on, Harry walked around to the driver's door, unlocked it, and yanked it open.

The smell that hit him was a rich and funky mix of oil, diesel fumes, damp, and wet dog, behind which other aromas hid, and for that he was thankful. The steering wheel was trying to hide under a leather cover which, when Harry stepped up into the vehicle to sit down, he found to be sticky to the touch. He slipped the key into the ignition and kicked the engine into life, surprising them with how smooth it sounded. The seats were held together by numerous strips of black tape, the roof lining was sagging enough to touch his head, and, like his own Rav, the entertainment system comprised a tape player.

Harry pushed the eject button and a cassette tape popped out.

'Best TV Themes,' he said, reading the faded sticker on the cassette.

Matt broke away from the rest of the team, walked over, and opened the passenger door.

'Didn't think it would have central locking,' Harry said.

'Oh, it doesn't,' said Matt. 'I just figured, looking at the state of the thing, that the locks probably don't work. And they don't.'

'But this is a police vehicle,' Harry said. 'Surely locks are crucial, all things considered.'

'Apparently not,' said Matt. Then he tapped the dashboard and added, 'You know, this isn't half bad.'

'Isn't it?'

'I've seen worse.'

'So have I,' said Harry. 'But only when one of these was hit by an RPG or two.'

Matt laughed, glancing over into the back of the vehicle.

'It's well kitted out, anyway,' he said.

Harry looked over his shoulder to see a couple of shovels, a large waterproof bag, and a first aid kit lying on the seats behind him.

'What's in the bag?' he asked.

Matt jumped out and opened the rear passenger door. He unzipped the bag.

'Blankets, that kind of thing,' Matt said, then peered over the passenger seats into the rear. 'We've got rescue boards and a tow rope too. And I noticed there's a winch up front, too. It may not look like much, but we've struck gold here. Well done, Gordy!'

'It runs well, too,' Gordy said. 'And that's what matters. For now, anyway, particularly with the weather coming in like this.'

Harry spotted another face now with the team, Police Constable Jadyn Okri having obviously just arrived.

He gave Harry a thumbs up, then called out, 'Sweet new motor, Boss!'

Harry smiled, turned off the engine, and slipped back out into the snow, which was now starting to bluster around a little, twisting and turning in small swirls at his feet, like tiny spectral ballerinas.

Gordy dropped herself into Anna's car.

'Best we get going,' she said. 'We're stopping half away, some small country hotel in the Lake District, then heading off first thing tomorrow. Don't want to be snowed in with you lot when there's the faint promise of some skiing up in Glencoe.'

'People actually ski in Scotland?' Harry asked.

'You'd be surprised,' Gordy said.

'I am.'

'You can also go tubing, which is great fun,' Gordy added. 'Just drop yourself in a large inflatable doughnut and throw yourself down the slope.'

Anna leaned over Gordy and said, 'There's a great café, too. They do the most amazing hot chocolates!'

'You have a safe journey now, the pair of you,' he said. 'And don't even think about coming back having decided to put in for a transfer to Police Scotland.'

Gordy laughed.

'If you can, bring us back some of those Tunnock's Caramel Wafers,' Matt called over.

Harry closed Gordy's door and Anna reversed her car away, then with a peep of her horn, headed off up through the marketplace.

'Let's get inside,' Harry said. 'Before we all end up looking like snowmen.'

Back in the office, Smudge greeted everyone with a few thumps of her tail, but refused to move from her warm spot by the radiator and didn't even raise her head. Harry headed to the front of the room and waited for the rest of the team to take a seat. As they did so, he found himself staring through the window at the weather coming in. The snow was getting heavier by the minute and the glass was now mottled with it, making the room just a little darker.

'Told you, didn't I?' Jim said, looking over at Harry.

'Told me what?' Harry asked.

'At the Christingle, on Christmas Eve if you remember. Having snow then as we did was a sign that we'd be in for it again sooner rather than later.'

'Fortune teller now, are you?' Harry said.

Jim shook his head.

'I'm a farmer,' he said, then tapped the side of his head. 'We know things ...'

'Good,' said Harry, looking around him. 'Then perhaps you can tell me where the Action Book is?'

CHAPTER SIX

From the moment he'd left his drive very early that morning, retired Detective Chief Inspector Peter Jameson, Pete to his friends, had been tempted to just turn around and go home, back to bed. The journey was enough of a deterrent in itself, as were the all too numerous, and somewhat soul-destroying, call-of-nature stops along the way.

And yet, here he was, a couple of hundred miles north, bladder once again telling him it was full, even though he'd not drunk a damned thing for the past two hours, hungry despite the pile of empty sandwich and crisp wrappers in the passenger footwell of his car, and crawling through the snow. Snow! What the hell was that about? And the only reason, really, that he was there in the first place was because he was bored.

If only Ellen could see me now, he thought, shaking his head with a smile born as much from sorrow as it was from the warmth of the love he still felt for his wife all these months later. Months? No, it was longer, wasn't it? Almost a year ago now. God, he missed her.

With only a few miles to go, Jameson had decided to park up and just have a moment. He'd managed to navigate the narrow, slush-covered lanes without mishap, the landscape around him as beautiful as it was bleak and foreboding. The cold and the snow were turning the green fells of the Yorkshire Dales into a pastoral scene of winter's hard beauty, smoothing off the edges, covering walls, and no doubt turning streams into frozen scars freshly sewn into the peat.

Staring out through the windscreen, he saw the dark shape of a lake in the valley below. Even from where he was sitting, he could see white-tipped waves galloping across its surface, breaking into each other, and throwing themselves against the shore. It only made him feel all the colder. He turned the heating up a notch, then sat back, shaking his head.

Closing his eyes, Jameson let out a long breath he'd not even realised he'd been holding. He felt himself sink a little deeper into his seat. Tiredness then slipped over him, warm and comfortable, so he turned off the engine, leaned the seat back just enough, and gave into it.

Memories flooded his mind, spilling out the last four-and-a-bit decades like a photo album bursting on impact after being dropped on the floor. He allowed the images to cascade, and soon they were moving through him so fast he could barely keep up. There was no order to how they presented themselves; the years were mixed up, and recent memories joined hands with those from the days when he'd had a fuller head of hair. And still they came, racing past, a torrent of moments so precious he wished he could just drown in them.

Jameson opened his eyes and realised he was gripping the steering wheel, his knuckles white, his arms solid. He forced himself to relax, took a few deep breaths, then leaned forward to rest his forehead against the back of his hands.

What the hell am I doing, Ellen?

The words slipped quietly from his lips, but they echoed long and loud in his mind.

It was a fair question, though, because his actions were not those of a man who had prided himself through his many years in the police force on not only always knowing what he was doing, but also why. It was one of the many reasons he had always loved the job, even though it had given him high blood pressure, a backache, nightmares, PTSD, and a few too many scars, both inside and out.

This, though; the reason why he was, for the second time in three months, in Wensleydale? Well, it was nothing short of desperation, he was sure of it. But then, what else did he have left? He'd tried hobbies, but had found the whole notion of doing something to just pass the time both frustrating and pointless. He knew all the arguments, from learning new skills and doing something you enjoyed, to stress relief, decreasing boredom, and making new friends. Trouble was, he wasn't really sure what new skills he wanted to learn in the first place, which didn't help. As for making new friends? He wasn't entirely sure he liked many of the ones he already had, so the last thing he wanted to do was add more to the pot.

First, Jameson had tried pottery, and had taken to it like a duck to tennis. A few coil pots and an egg cup or two later, and he had realised that turning grey mud into things of glazed beauty just wasn't for him.

Then there had been swimming. It was something he had never really done at all, but had agreed with his doctor that it was good for fitness and perhaps even relaxing. Having joined an over-sixties group, he had quickly discovered it was neither of these things. Swimming was in fact very difficult, very frustrating, made him short of breath and very sweary, and when you put all of that together wasn't really all that relaxing, either. The last straw had been managing to get into an argument with a middle-aged triathlete who yelled at him for hogging the lane. The look on the man's face when Jameson had pushed him back into the pool had been worth the ban he'd received from the leisure centre that same day.

Golf, he had never given serious thought to and never would. Yoga had only led to an embarrassing hour of lying on a mat on the floor and discovering, in front of a dozen others his own age, just how farty he was when told to do downward dog or give salutation to the sun.

He'd tried other things, too, from a local rambling group to fishing, even a film club. The rambling had been fun right up until the moment he'd set out in all his shiny new gear only to find that walking en mass across a muddy field, with people gleefully discussing their aches and pains and very successful offspring, was about as much fun as putting his hand in a blender.

Fishing? Well, it looked good on television, that was for sure, but in reality, for Jameson at least, a whole day sitting in the rain by a river, staring at a fat swan, and slowly eating his way through the global surplus of egg mayonnaise sandwiches and a pork pie or two, had been excruciating.

And as for the film club? He hadn't even managed to stay long enough to watch the film, deciding within the first five minutes of meeting the rest of the club that if he stayed any longer he'd have made more enemies than friends. And he didn't exactly have that many friends to begin with.

So, here he was. And he was fairly sure he could hear Ellen laughing. That thought in itself was enough to make him think that, seeing as he was here, he may as well just get on with it. He'd paid for it, after all, and not a small amount either.

He knew a little about Carl Walsh, but only from what he'd read about the man in various crime magazines that had belonged to Helen. He was a private investigator whose podcast had a huge following, and whose long-running series of novels, though hardly the best written, were certainly entertaining.

Jameson had signed up for the weekend after an evening spent on his own listening to one of the episodes of the podcast, and consuming the better part of two very good bottles of red wine. Cheese had had something to do with it as well, he was sure, but the blame lay with him in the end. The following day, he had been tempted to ask for a refund, but his hangover had been bad enough to keep him in bed long enough to not give a damn.

Another thought occurred to him then, and Jameson reached over to the glove box to grab his phone. He pulled up a number, ready to make the call, but hesitated. He had, after all, kept his visit private, deciding it was probably best to not tell a soul where he was going, or what he was doing. So, would telling a certain other DCI really help at all? All he'd probably get for it would be laughter and disbelief, and he'd given himself enough of that, for sure, as well as a slap or two.

Jameson placed the phone back in the glove box. With a stretch, and deciding that it was better to hold in the urge to have a piss until he arrived at his destination, as the weather looked cold enough now to freeze parts he'd rather keep safely zipped up, he started the engine, slipped the gear lever into first, and was off.

The lane ahead fell at a steep angle, and it was hard for Jameson not to imagine losing control of his car at the sharp bend just ahead, clearing the wall, then rolling and tumbling all the way down to the bottom of the valley, no doubt to end up upside down in the lake. And then drown. But he managed to navigate it safely, and a few minutes later, with the lake now disappearing behind him in his rearview mirror, he found himself driving by a collection of houses and buildings that looked as though they had been just dumped there by the wind from a couple of centuries ago. He didn't stop, intrigued as he was by the lonely red phone box standing on the rutted village green, because surely there was no way that it still contained a working phone.

Beyond the village, the road narrowed, if that was at all possible. Jameson leaned forward over the steering wheel, as though being an inch or two closer to the windscreen would help him spot any oncoming traffic just that bit sooner through the snow.

When the house finally came into view, Jameson bladder seemed to contract. The pain made him grit his teeth, and he parked up as quickly as he could, pushed open the driver's door, then ran over to the house, dodging around the campervan and the Porsche Cayenne, also parked outside. He managed to catch his ankle on a tow hitch sticking out of the back of the Porsche, which made him yelp. The front door was shut, snow covering it, and Jameson hammered the heel of his fist against the wood, while at the same time rubbing the growing bruise at the bottom of his leg.

The door was opened by a man a few years younger than himself, with considerably more hair, the shiniest teeth he'd ever seen, and eyes bloodshot to hell, like he'd not slept in days; it was the PI, Carl Walsh, in the flesh.

Walsh steadied himself against the door.

'Everything okay?' he asked, staring down at Jameson, who was still crouched over his ankle and giving it a good rub.

'Yes, I'm fine,' Jameson said. 'Just knocked myself on that bloody tow hitch there.'

'That's my fault, I'm afraid,' said Walsh. 'Sorry about that. I should've reversed in.'

Jameson shook his head.

'Don't worry about it; I should've looked where I was going.'

'Well, you're the first here,' Walsh said, then reached out a hand. Jameson noticed the expensive watch clasped around the man's wrist, and a couple of plasters on his fingers. 'The others shouldn't be too long.'

'Nice to meet you,' Jameson said, and shook the extended hand. Then he pushed past into the house, adding, 'I'm also dying for a piss and if I don't go, you'll be scraping bits of my exploded bladder off the ceiling. Sorry ...'

'Just down the hall,' directed Walsh, 'second door on the right.'

'Thanks,' Jameson called back over his shoulder, not really listening, and ran.

'I'm Carl Walsh, by the way,' the man called out after him.

'Peter Jameson,' Jameson called out in response, turning into a door and stumbling into a large suitcase hard enough to make him swear. He reversed out, bumping into a shelf with his head and knocking a torch to the floor.

'Which door was that again?' he asked.

He bent over and picked up the torch, which had rolled over by the suitcase and over some scratches on the floorboards from where it had been pushed inside.

'The second door,' Walsh answered.

Shutting the cupboard door behind him, Jameson raced on, a hand clasping his crotch. As first impressions went, he thought, it wasn't exactly the best.

CHAPTER SEVEN

With the Action Book found, the first thing on Harry's mind was Grace's call that morning. However, there was always plenty to be going on with, especially with a weekend ahead, so he gathered the team to run through not just what was recorded on the pages in front of him, but anything else that they were dealing with. He was about to start talking when a call came in, which Matt answered.

'Traffic incident,' he said.

'Where?' Harry asked.

'Buttertubs Pass.'

Harry did a double take, but said nothing further until Matt had finished the call.

'So, what have we got?' he asked.

'Two cars blocking the road over the pass,' Matt said.

Harry shook his head in disbelief.

'You mean people still try to drive over that in weather like this?'

'Of course they do,' said Matt. 'And it's not exactly bad yet, is it? Nowt but a squall.'

'Isn't it?'

'Goodness, no,' said Matt. 'You can still see the fells for a start.

If there's a whiteout though, that's when things get a little hairy, like. And those barriers weren't always there, you know, the ones that line the side of the road when you roll down past the Butter-tubs. At one time, it was nowt more than a wooden fence. Not scary at all. Glad I'm not old enough to remember that. Or maybe I am, and the horror of it I've just forgotten.'

Harry asked, 'Any idea of what happened? Any injuries?'

'Someone probably just lost grip in the snow and experienced their whole life flashing before their eyes,' answered Matt. 'No serious injuries, though, and Emergency Services are already on their way. But they'll need us over there, too, if only to help direct traffic and be nice to people.'

Harry turned to the team.

'Any volunteers?' he asked, then added, 'And whoever it is will be the first of us lucky enough to drive our shiny new four-by-four and give it a good test run.'

'I'd go myself, like,' said Matt, 'but probably best I keep myself back in case there's a call out from the mountain rescue team, seeing as how it's only going to be getting worse out there.'

Harry saw Jadyn sit up at this and stare over at the DS.

'You mean there's a chance we might?' he asked, a little too much excitement in his voice. 'I knew we're on standby, but I wasn't thinking it was like, urgent or imminent or anything.'

Harry understood Jadyn's eagerness, though; it wasn't excitement at the thought of someone getting into trouble, but the adrenaline at being at the sharp end of a rescue and helping someone get home safe.

'Always possible when the weather gets like this,' said Matt. 'Walkers can be caught out by the weather turning, no matter how experienced or well-equipped they are. And the land can look very different covered in snow; doesn't take much for someone who knows the area well to trust their vehicle and local knowledge a little too much, make a wrong turning, and end up in trouble.'

Jen raised her hand.

'I'll go,' she said.

'Yes, and so will I,' said Jadyn, raising his own hand a few seconds after. 'I'll go. With Jen. Two officers. Standard procedure for something like this, isn't it?'

Harry hid his smile well. Whatever was going on between them was obviously serious enough for Jadyn to up sticks from Catterick to Reeth. At some point, though, keeping it quiet wasn't going to work for them, that was for sure, not with the way Jadyn was approaching things, anyway.

Harry was about to tell them about Grace when another call came in.

'This doesn't bode well, does it?' Matt said, reaching over to answer.

Harry, like the rest of the team, waited patiently as Matt once again spoke to someone on the other end of the line while jotting down a note or two.

Call over, the DS turned back around to face the team.

'Right then, we've a situation out beyond Marsett,' he said. 'Seems like a farmer's teenage son has gone and buggered off. It's the Cowper family. Not had any dealings with them myself. The lad's called Thomas.'

Harry recognised the name of the place, but wasn't immediately sure why.

'Remind me where that is,' he said.

'Marsett's out beyond Semerwater,' said Jim. 'Little hamlet, not much there at all, really. Just a farm, a telephone box, and a Methodist Chapel.'

'You've been there,' said Liz. 'It's a while ago now, though. That case with the doctor and the death of his sister who drowned one winter, back when they were kids.'

Harry frowned, quickly sifting through memories until he found the right one.

'I remember,' he said, then looked at Matt. 'So, what's happened, exactly?'

Matt said, 'There's been a family bust-up, or that's what it sounds like, anyway. Probably nothing, and no doubt we'll get there and the lad will be back, tail between his legs. Best we go check it out, though, obviously.'

'Parents call it in, then?' asked Jen. 'Must be a worry when your kid runs away.'

Matt shook his head.

'No, it wasn't the parents, actually,' he said. 'It was their neighbour who called it in, a Mrs Mason.'

'That doesn't bode well,' said Harry.

'She heard shouting, but that's normal, apparently,' explained Matt. 'Then there were a couple of gunshots.'

Harry held up a hand to stop Matt before he said anything else. 'Wait,

who was shooting at who here?'

'Not sure,' said Matt. 'Again, the neighbour reported that this is also quite normal, seeing as the farmer is often seen out with his gun; no law against that, after all. So, she's not sure if that's anything or not.'

'I'm hoping it's not,' said Harry, concerned now that he should race over to the farm right away, just to be on the safe side.

'The farmer's often out clobbering rabbits,' Matt continued. 'But this time, Mrs Mason saw their young lad race off on a quad bike, only he was being chased by his dad, who was apparently holding a shotgun at the time.'

'Bloody hell,' said Harry, with a twist in his gut telling him they were already into a Friday that had all the potential to be one that would be hard to forget. 'Is anyone hurt?'

'We've no report of anything like that at all,' Matt said. 'Only what I've shared just now, which isn't much, I know. There was some kind of family row and the lad, clearly having had enough of it, shot off up into the hills. My guess is that this happens more than we ever hear about round here, don't you?'

Harry said, 'Still, it sounds like we need to head over there sharpish.'

Matt agreed.

'If the weather's like this here, then it's going to be a whole lot worse up there, that's for sure. And I don't like the idea of anyone being out in it, least of all a frightened kid.'

Jen was already on her feet and grabbing a jacket, ready to head off up to Buttertubs Pass.

'Wait,' Harry said, then turned to the rest of the team.

'Jen, you'll be off up to the traffic incident, as we've just agreed. Like I said, take the Land Rover; I don't really like the idea of you heading up the Buttertubs Pass in weather like this in anything else, if I'm honest, not with how bad it's supposed to get. And Jim, I want you to go with her. Something like this, I think it's better to have two of us there than just one.'

'I'll make a flask of tea to take up as well,' said Jim. 'Keep their morale up if it takes a while to sort things out.'

Harry was impressed with Jim's thinking, then he saw Jadyn's eyes widen, so before the young constable had a chance to speak, he turned to him and said, 'I need you to speak with Grace. Here's her number.'

Harry flipped his phone around for Jadyn to see Grace's number on the screen.

'But—'

Harry raised a hand.

'She's found evidence of hare coursing,' he explained, giving Jadyn no chance to reply, 'and whoever it was out doing it, it sounds as though they've also gone and abandoned one of their dogs. I need you over there this afternoon to talk with Grace about what happened, find out what she saw, collect any evidence you can. Maybe even find the missing dog. Grace will have been out looking for it already, and so will her dad, so if they've not found it, you can help have another look.'

Jadyn raised a hand to interrupt, but Harry held him off with nothing more than a look.

'You're a police constable,' he said, voice calm but firm. 'You've more power than a PCSO, more training. And I don't need two constables at a traffic incident; this is a much better use of your skills.'

Harry noticed Jadyn's chest swell at that a little.

'My view on it,' Harry continued, 'is that we've probably got a few idiots from out of the Dale coming in to have their fun, before buggering off back home. And I'd prefer it if they didn't get to do it again, if you know what I mean.'

'You want me to try and catch them, then, Boss?'

'I think it's only fair, don't you?'

'I'll give Grace a call now,' Jadyn said, and copied the number.

Harry turned then to the remaining two members of his team.

'Matt, as you and Jadyn are both on standby for the mountain rescue, I'm inclined to agree with what you said earlier, that it's probably best if you stay here for now. That way, we have a central point of contact, and you can head off if necessary. Just let me know if that happens.'

'Agreed,' Matt said.

'You can also keep officer Okri informed if anything comes in from the mountain rescue. If a call out comes in and you're both needed, I need to know, sharpish.'

'And me?' Liz asked.

'I'm assuming you came over on that police issue off-road bike of yours?'

'Of course I did,' said Liz. Then added with a wry smile, 'You're not wanting a lift, are you?'

'God no, once was enough,' Harry said, recalling being on the back of the bike as Liz raced up the old Roman road from Bainbridge during another case. It had been exciting, for sure, but not something he had any interest in experiencing again. 'We'll head over to Marsett together, you and I, but I'll be in my own vehicle, if it's all the same with you.'

'No problem,' said Liz.

'If this kid really has headed off into the hills on a quad bike, and if we can establish where he's gone, then you'll be better equipped on your bike to go and try to find him, than just on your feet.' Harry glanced down at the Action Book, then handed it over to Matt. 'Best you keep a hold of this,' he said. 'Sounds like we've enough to be going on with now, anyway, and all of it urgent. But have a look through it anyway and follow up on anything if you need to.'

Matt took the book from Harry, who then turned to face the rest of the team.

'I know I don't need to tell any of you this, but be careful. Our job is difficult and risky enough as it is on a bright sunny day. But with the weather turning on us like this—' He gave a nod at the window, beyond which the snow was falling even harder '—it only gets more difficult. Now, are there any questions, before we all head off into what is very much looking like the beginnings of a storm?'

The team all stared back at Harry, eyes keen, voices stilled.

'Good,' Harry said. 'Perfect answer. Then let's get cracking.'

CHAPTER EIGHT

WITH SMUDGE SECURELY CLIPPED IN BEHIND HIM, HARRY reversed out of the marketplace and headed east, rolling out of Hawes and past the cemetery. The Rav4 was permanent four-wheel drive, but he could still feel the snow on the road, the surface already slick with it.

The storm itself wasn't yet quite at full strength, and Harry hoped that this was as bad as it was going to get. However, there was already enough snow falling to make things interesting, to keep people on their toes when out and about, but hopefully not enough to start sprinkling the day with danger.

Those thoughts were soon shattered when, as Harry left Hawes, another car coming to the junction just by the cemetery lost grip and slid far enough over for him to have to take evasive action to avoid a collision.

Sitting for a moment, if only to calm his nerves, Harry looked over to stare at the driver of the other car. The man at the wheel looked terrified and mouthed *I'm sorry* back at him. Harry jumped out of his vehicle and headed over, knocking on the window.

'You alright, there?' he asked.

'The car ... it just went,' the man said. 'I ... I wasn't going too fast, I really wasn't.'

Harry hadn't seen the man before, and his voice had a southern twang to it.

'Heading anywhere important?' Harry asked.

The man shook his head.

'It's the snow, you see. I'm a photographer. Just up for the weekend. Thought I'd pop out and take a few shots.'

'My advice is you pop right back to where you're staying,' said Harry.

'I'll be more careful, I promise.'

'Oh, I know you will,' said Harry. 'Because you'll be back inside, thinking just how lucky you are that you didn't end up in a serious accident with the local police.'

The man opened his mouth, but shut it again just as quickly.

Harry tapped the roof of the man's car, then climbed back into the Rav and headed off once again.

Behind him, Liz was keeping up easily on her motorbike, and Harry had a feeling that if it wasn't for the helmet she was wearing, then he would see a huge smile slapped across her face. She rode the thing with ease, as though it was little more than an extension of herself, though that didn't make him any less pleased to not be riding pillion.

About a mile outside Hawes, Harry turned right to head up the steep hill into Burtersett. The Rav had no problem at all with the climb, the snow on the road giving it little trouble. Not yet, anyway, Harry thought.

Jim lived just out the other side of the small village, and having navigated his way through the narrow, winding street that the buildings clustered around, Harry spotted the PCSO's father walking down through one of the fields by the house. Jim's dog, Fly, was with him, effortlessly herding sheep in front of it, and he couldn't help but be impressed.

Usually when he saw the dog, he was playing with Smudge, rolling around on the floor play fighting, or enjoying a chase, and yet at that moment, he was a focused tool of a good farmer, helping bring in the sheep out of the snow. He gave the man a wave as they drove past and saw the gesture returned.

A few minutes, and numerous turns and dips in the road later, Harry crossed over the intersection with the old Roman road. The ancient thoroughfare headed up from the village of Bainbridge, which itself was home to the striking remains of an old Roman fort, which rose above the place to stare down impassively. The road itself, an ancient thing worn by centuries of use by foot and hoof and cart and wheel, cut a straight line upwards, tucked tightly into the whitening slopes of Wether Fell.

Harry slowed down as he drove past, staring up the road into the snow. The dark line of the track soon faded from view, erased by swirling snow tossed across the hill like the scattered wings of giant gulls. The wind was certainly stronger up here and it buffeted the Rav. Harry was pleased that he had no need to head up the rough, stone-strewn track, and couldn't help but be filled with renewed respect for the farmers who, like Jim's own father, would brave such weather for their flock.

Soon, the road crested a rise, and a valley opened below. Staring down, Harry was able to just about make out the black surface of Semerwater. He had swum in those waters himself, though on a marginally warmer day than this. Right now, the water looked ominous, an oily hole threatening to suck in the surrounding valley, and being encouraged to do so by the excited cries of the wintery gale.

At Countersett, Harry turned away from the road that headed on down to the lake's frozen edge, and pointed his vehicle towards Marsett. The road was already grey with slush, the markings of other vehicles clear before him in the snow.

He remembered now heading out this way before, and how this small valley seemed darker than it had any real right to be. It wasn't so much that the vale itself was creepy, more that it held deep secrets it wouldn't tell. Whether the trees were trying to whisper those secrets to him as he drove past, Harry wasn't sure, but the wind through their branches certainly made them look agitated, as they bent over the road, reaching for him as he sped past, the tips clattering against his windshield.

Marsett welcomed Harry with deep puddles of slush and mud and heavier snow. A solitary phone box stood like a lonely sentry on guard duty, standing silent on the edge of a tiny green, now all but white. Beyond this, great shadows of hefty farm machinery moved in and out of focus in the snow, and beyond these were houses, huddled tightly together as though trying to share their warmth.

Harry pulled up on the green, and Liz came alongside, snapping her visor up. He dropped his window into the door just enough to be able to speak to her.

'That was fun, wasn't it?' she said, the corners of her eyes crinkling with the smile hidden inside her helmet.

'Well, that's one way to describe it,' Harry said.

'Bit of a close miss, too, outside Hawes. You did well to not hit him.'

'Before and after the moment he nearly crashed into me,' Harry said.

Staring out through his windscreen, the wipers swishing away a constantly replenishing covering of snow, he asked, 'So, where's this farm, then?'

'Just out beyond the chapel,' Liz said, pointing with a gloved hand. 'You may as well follow me.'

Harry followed Liz through the village. He spotted the chapel as they passed it on his right. It was a squat, almost black-stoned building, held back by old iron railings now wearing a soft armour of snow. The windows were formed of different sections of coloured glass, but despite this, there was an austere air to the place, as though frivolity was to be frowned upon.

Liz pulled left and parked up, tapping the kickstand down into the snow. Harry parked alongside, the Rav sliding just a little.

Leaving Smudge in the warmth, he climbed out into the early afternoon, swearing under his breath as the harsh wind from the fells greeted him with its icy embrace. Snow chased its way down his neck and he shivered.

'Bugger me, that's cold,' he said, stomping over to Liz, blowing onto his hands to warm them. 'Let's get out of it quick.'

Liz led the way and soon they were at the door of a small cottage that looked about as impressed with the weather as Harry felt. The front of the building, like those around it, was already draped in threadbare sheets of snow. Smoke rose from a chimney and he could see warm flames through a downstairs window.

Liz removed her helmet and then gave the door a knock. It opened almost as soon as her knuckles touched the wood.

'Mrs Mason?' she said, as a slim shadow stood in the space vacated by the door.

'You must be the police,' said the shadow. 'Come on then, get yourselves in out of all of that before it follows you inside and I'm having to dig myself out of my own kitchen just to get to my lounge.'

Almost as though it had been listening, a thump of wind pushed Harry forward and he followed Liz as she stepped into the house, snowflakes buzzing around them like bees.

As he entered the house, the shadow took on the shape of a small woman in brown corduroy dungarees and a deep red cardigan. She reached out to give him a helping hand and pulled him inside, heaving the door shut behind him so quickly that it gave his backside a cheeky tap.

'Through there,' the woman directed, pointing at another door, and Liz opened it to lead them all into a room bathed in the warm, orangey glow of a wood burning stove.

'Tea? Of course you want tea. Well, sit down, then. Can't have you both just standing there like you're about to leave, now can we? You've only just arrived, and I do pride myself on giving a good, warm welcome.'

Harry hadn't yet had a good opportunity to see the woman who had swept them both inside, and only now, in the firelight, was he able to. She was about the same height as Liz, so neither tiny nor tall. Age wise, he guessed she was in her late sixties. Her hair was as white as the snow falling outside the front door, and was pulled back gently into a short ponytail. She had bright, happy eyes and a relaxed smile.

Harry looked over to see Liz staring at him and smiling and they both slumped down onto soft chairs.

The room was small, cosy, and tidy, in a sort of controlled chaos kind of way. On either side of the fireplace were two sets of shelves stretching from floor to ceiling, each stuffed full of books. The wall directly opposite the only window in the room was populated by a collection of art, which seemed to be impressive more in terms of its quantity than its quality. Not that Harry was one for being the art critic, but what he could see left him more than a little baffled; all colours and swirls, as though whoever had painted them had done so with wild abandon and not too much skill. In the centre of the room sat a coffee table groaning under the weight of yet more books, and to the side of the wood burning stove was a basket of logs.

Mrs Mason came back into the room carrying a tray.

'Well, move those books, then,' she said. 'Come on.'

Harry quickly leaned forward and picked up a pile of books as Mrs Mason bent over to place the tray down onto the table.

'You'll be having cake.'

It was a statement rather than a question and a small plate appeared in front of Harry on top of which was a very generous slice.

'Thank you,' he said, impressed by the weight of what he had just been handed.

'No cheese, though,' Mrs Mason said. 'Hope you don't mind.'

'That's not a problem,' said Harry.

'Thank goodness for that, because frankly, I can't stand the stuff,' Mrs Mason replied.

Harry nearly choked on his first bite.

'Everything alright, there?'

Harry gave a nod, his eyes watering a little.

'I was under the impression everyone around here loved cheese,' he said.

'Well, I don't,' Mrs Mason said. 'Never have. Hasn't stopped folk from trying to persuade me otherwise, mind. But do I listen? Do I knackers, like. They can try and force it on me as often as they want—and they do—but I'll be having none of that muck in my house, I can promise you that.'

Harry laughed again, though thankfully this time his mouth was empty.

'I felt the same myself when I first arrived here a couple of years ago,' he said. 'But I think I've just been worn down.'

'Didn't think you were from around here, not with that accent anyway.'

'Somerset,' Harry said.

'Cider country,' said Mrs Mason. 'Now that, I am partial to.' She then eyed him quizzically and said, 'I knew a lad with similar injuries. A few years ago, now. Son of a friend, he was. Never really got over it. What happened, I mean, when he was over in Afghanistan.'

'It takes time,' said Harry, impressed with the woman's tact, though he had guessed what it was she had been staring at.

Mrs Mason sat herself down next to Liz, and opposite Harry. Then she leaned over and tapped his knee with a hand.

'Never mind,' she said through a faint smile of mischief. 'Now, you'll be here about the idiots next door, yes? Well, one idiot anyway.'

'We are,' Harry said. 'This is PCSO Coates, and I'm DCI Grimm.'

'Oh, I know that,' said Mrs Mason. 'And I'm Patricia, but you can call me Pat.'

'I'm Harry,' said Harry.

'And I'm Liz,' said Liz, and then added, 'Lovely little place you've got here.'

'It'll do,' said Pat. 'Moved here twenty years ago from Preston when my husband died.'

'Sorry to hear that,' said Harry.

'Don't be,' said Pat. 'It was a blessed release, trust me. He'd been ill for a while; the pain was terrible. He was young, but we still had a good few years together. All these books, and that god-awful artwork on the wall, it's all his. His hobby was painting, though I wish it hadn't been. I miss him, but he's with me every day still, because of it all.'

'What are the paintings of?' Harry asked, staring over the heads of Liz and Pat at them.

'I haven't the faintest idea,' Pat said with a shrug. 'But they make me smile, and when I see them, I can hear his whistle still; he always whistled when he painted, so I'm not about to be rid of them.'

Harry finished his cake and reached for his tea.

'So, Pat, about what happened,' he said. 'What can you tell us?'

'Simply that the mad old bastard needs arresting, that's what,' said Pat, and Harry saw a hard shard of flint glint in her smiling eyes. 'An awful man, he is, just awful.'

Harry pulled out a notebook.

'Perhaps it's best if you just take us through what you saw and heard,' he said.

He was conscious of the fact that Mrs Mason had reported a teenager as missing and they'd driven to Marsett as quickly as possible. Now he just needed as many facts as he could glean before heading off to speak with the family. There was every chance that the missing teenager wasn't missing at all and had just zoomed off to hide in a barn somewhere, out of reach from his family. He may even have already returned home. But racing off into the hills themselves to try and find him without having the facts straight wouldn't help anyone.

'There was a fair amount of shouting,' Pat said. 'But there's always shouting, so I didn't think much of it really.'

'How do you mean, there's always shouting?' Liz asked.

'That man,' Pat said, 'it's all he does. I swear he's only got one volume; bellowing.'

Harry asked for the family names.

'Brian,' Pat said. 'Brian Cowper. Wife's called Jane, and their son is Thomas. Don't see him around much and I don't speak to them either, really. Not for lack of trying, but that Brian, he's just rude.'

Harry jotted the names down as Pat continued to speak.

'All he does is shout at his wife, at his son, at the poor bloody animals he has locked in those ramshackle sheds he calls a farm. And if he's not yelling at his family, then he's screaming at a cow or a sheep, or trying to kick one of his dogs. Doesn't seem to have a decent bone in his body. Drinks, too, I'm sure of it.'

'Cows and sheep?' Harry said, reeling a little from the character assassination Pat had just performed on Mr Cowper.

'He keeps a small herd of beef cattle,' she said. 'And he's plenty of sheep out on the fells, though he doesn't seem to care two hoots about any of them, judging by how every time I see any of them, they're half lame.'

'So, you heard Brian shouting,' Harry said. 'Then what?'

'At first I wasn't even listening,' said Pat. 'Like I said, I'm used to the rows and I've kind of learned how to tune it all out, if that makes sense. I hear it, but I don't. Only this seemed louder, and there was a lot more swearing than usual, and that's saying something, believe me. Then I heard Thomas and Jane joining in. And then there was this bang. No, it wasn't a bang, it was more of a muffled boom.'

At this, Harry leaned forward.

'A boom?' he said. 'Can you describe it?'

'It was very loud, and sounded a bit odd, dull, muffled, like I said,' said Pat, 'but the second one a few minutes later? That was definitely a gun.'

'You're sure about that?'

Pat gave a firm nod.

'I didn't just hear it,' she said. 'I saw that mad sod race out of the house after Tommy and shoot the damned thing over the lad's head! Well, up in the air, anyway. I don't think he was actually shooting at his son. At least, I'm fairly sure he wasn't.'

'Where was this, exactly?' Harry asked.

Pat pointed out through her lounge window.

'I heard the shouting, like I said. Didn't think too much of it until I heard Jane and Thomas joining in. Usually, it's just Brian, you see, just ranting and raging at everything from a tractor to a dog to a barn door, like it's the world's fault he's such a bloody awful farmer. Anyway, like I said, I heard all of them arguing, really going for it, too, and then I hear that first boom, and I look out of that window, but there's nothing there, so I'm about to sit back down again, when the shouting starts up again. Only it's even louder. I look outside and I see him, Brian I mean, chasing Thomas, Jane coming up behind him, and she's slapping him and slapping him, but he's just ignoring her and pushing her away.'

'And he has the gun with him?' Liz asked.

'Rarely see him without it,' said Pat. 'Old thing, it is. I don't know much about guns, by which I mean nothing at all. It's got two barrels next to each other and makes a god-awful racket when it goes off. Looks ancient. He was out there, waving it around like some mad warlord. Wouldn't be surprised if he doesn't even have a licence.'

'Oh, I'll be checking that,' Harry said. 'What happened then?'

'Well, Thomas is away, you see,' said Pat. 'He's fast, like a ferret up a trouser leg, or a hare racing across the fields, and he disappears into one of those old sheds you can see on the other side of the lane.'

Harry had a quick look over the road to see where Pat was talking about.

'Next thing I know,' Pat continued, 'out he comes on that quad bike they have, and he's off, heading up the lane like the thing is jet-propelled, into the falling snow, two fingers raised high and proud to his dad. I cheered when I saw that. And Brian lifted that great big gun of his as his son was buggering off and he pulled the trigger. Bang! Then, he just turned around, pushed Jane to the ground, and headed off back towards the house. I mean, what kind of father does that? What kind of person at all?'

'You'd be surprised,' Harry said.

'Surprised? I'm absolutely bloody disgusted, is what I am,' said Pat, the flint in her eyes now being joined by venom on her tongue. 'I've seen how he is, and he's not a pleasant man at all. But that? I've never seen him like that. I've no idea what's happened, but whatever it is, I thought it best to give the police a call to go round there and sort it out.'

'That was the right thing to do,' said Liz.

Pat then said, 'I went round there myself actually, but no one answered the door.'

Harry shook his head, rubbed his eyes.

'Pat, can I ask, please, that you avoid doing that again?'

Pat sat up, indignation writ clear on her face.

'You can ask, but I can't promise.'

'Okay, then,' said Harry. 'Let's say I'm not asking, I'm telling. It's never a good idea to intervene.'

'I'm not one for just standing by and doing nothing.'

'I'm just concerned for your safety, that's all,' Harry said. 'Especially after all that you've just told us.'

Liz said, 'Like I said, you did the right thing by contacting the police, though. We always advise the public to do that instead of getting involved in something themselves. It really is for your own safety.'

Harry stood up.

'And right now, I think it's best we get next door.'

Liz rose to her feet and stood next to him.

'You're going to arrest him, then?' Pat asked. 'I can't wait to see the look on his face when you do. Might even fetch my camera.'

Harry said, 'What we're going to do is head next door and find out everything we can. Thank you for calling us out, Pat. You did the right thing.'

'The right thing would be to go round and boot that man firmly up the arse!' Pat said. 'That's what he needs. That, and a broken nose.'

Harry stared at Pat for a moment.

'You're quite something, you know that?' he said.

'I'll take that as a compliment,' said Pat.

'That's how it was meant.'

With their farewells said, Harry and Liz were once again standing outside in the snow. The wind had died a little and the snow, though still falling, was gentler now. Around them, however, the world had been transformed into a magical dreamscape, with the fields and fells, and the walls connecting them, being slowly tucked in beneath vast, undulating pillows of the softest white.

'So, what now, then?' Liz asked.

'Well,' said Harry, 'what I'm going to do is head over for a nice chat with Mr Brian Cowper who we've been hearing so much about.'

'He sounds a delight.'

'Doesn't he just.'

'If you're going on your own, I'm assuming then that I'm heading off after Thomas, yes?'

Harry looked up the lane, then crouched down close to the ground.

'The snow's almost covered the tracks,' he said, pointing at some markings in the snow at his feet, 'but not enough. Look ...'

Liz dropped down beside him.

'Looks busy, doesn't it?' she said.

Harry had to agree. The marks made by the quad bike were clearly visible, their distinct pattern like row upon row of Lego bricks in the snow. However, there were also a number of other tyre tracks in the snow, all heading up the lane.

'What's at the end of this lane, then?' Harry asked.

'Just a big old house,' said Liz.

'Of course there is. Can you be slightly less mysterious?'

'I think it's a holiday home. Too big for a family, from what I remember. More like a place you'd hire for a party, that kind of thing.' Liz pointed at the quad bike tracks. 'I'd best get following these before the snow covers them up.'

Liz pulled on her helmet.

'Doubt he's gone far,' said Harry, 'but go careful. The last thing I want is to have to call out the mountain rescue to come pull you off the hill.'

'Jadyn would love that, wouldn't he?' said Liz.

'Exactly,' said Harry. 'Now get going, before the snow starts falling heavily again.'

Harry didn't wait for Liz to answer. Instead, he turned away from the lane and headed off towards the large, weary-looking house owned by the Cowpers. He was already looking forward to meeting Brian ...

CHAPTER NINE

HAVING FOLLOWED HARRY'S INSTRUCTIONS AND SPOKEN WITH Grace before setting off, Police Constable Jadyn Okri had headed out of Hawes and down dale a few minutes after Harry and Liz. The drive had been exciting at points, the road slippery and the snow buffeting all around, but he made it to West Witton without incident and parked up on the main road, his vehicle facing out of the village towards Leyburn.

Climbing out, he caught sight of The Fox Inn on the other side of the road. The door was open and warm light spilled from it onto the pavement outside. Walking past it, the snow driving into his face, Jadyn was sorely tempted to pop inside for something warm to eat, but he forced himself on.

Following a thin path, which threaded its way between the houses and out onto the fields, he soon found himself trudging through snow already a few inches deep. As yet, the fields weren't completely covered, and grey-green patches of grass and scrub were still visible. With the way the weather was, however, Jadyn wondered just how long it would be before everything was covered.

The path across the field was hidden, but Jadyn was able to spot a stile in the wall ahead and made his way towards it. Huddled under the shelter of a wall, he saw a small flock of sheep, their fleeces wearing a cloak of snow, the ground beneath them clear. They all stared as he walked past, their heads moving as one.

Over the stile, Jadyn found himself on what had obviously once been an old cart track. Each side was lined with walls of stone, built by hands skilled and hardy. In places the walls were so tumble-down that they jutted from the snow like the fossilised teeth of some great, long-dead beast.

Turning right along the track, which was a rock-strewn thing broken by the roots of trees and the passing of livestock, Jadyn was struck by just how old the landscape was. Wherever he looked, history seemed to stare back, and he was struck by how different the place was from where he had grown up, and also from where he had been living only a few weeks ago.

The decision to move from Catterick had been a little impul-sive for sure, but work-wise, it certainly made sense. He was closer to the office for one, but he would also be able to get to know the area, and the community that inhabited it, a little better. Of course, the other reason was Jen. He wasn't exactly sure where whatever it was that was happening between them was going, but he was fairly sure that being closer, rather than further away, gave them a better chance at having a good go at finding out.

They were keeping it very low-key, very quiet because neither of them wanted it to get in the way of work. Though, Jadyn was finding doing so increasingly difficult, mostly because he'd never been all that great at keeping secrets. That wasn't to say that he was untrustworthy; quite the opposite. More that he had always lived his life by being open and honest with those around him, so not letting on, well, that wasn't easy when presented with the kind of questioning looks someone like DS Dinsdale could give.

He was a little miffed that Harry hadn't sent him off with Jen to the traffic incident over the Buttertubs Pass, but thinking about it, it was probably for the best. This way, they could both get on with the job, and he, for one, wouldn't be distracted. And if there was one thing that was certain, it was that he found Jen very, very distracting.

After a left dogleg bend, the track went to the top of a small rise, then down the other side, on towards a small number of spinneys, the trees of which seemed to cluster together against the snow. Jadyn spotted two old Land Rovers parked up a couple of hundred metres ahead.

Arriving at the vehicles, Jadyn found Grace and her dad, Arthur, sitting together inside the first. In the back, two spaniels were curled up together on a pile of hessian sacks.

Arthur, who was sitting in the passenger seat, swished open his window.

'Now then,' he said, and held up a battered old flask. 'Bovril?'

'What?'

'Bovril,' Arthur repeated. 'Weather like this, there's no other drink comes close, trust me.'

Jadyn frowned, not entirely convinced.

'But isn't Bovril just liquid beef?'

'It is.'

'Like, for making gravy, I mean.'

Arthur, clearly not listening, unscrewed the flask, poured some liquid as black as the strongest coffee into a mug, then held it out for Jadyn.

'There you go.'

'No, I'm fine, honestly,' Jadyn said.

'Get it down your neck,' said Arthur. 'Go on, trust me. It'll do you a world of good. Warm you from top to toe and put hairs on your chest.'

'But I don't want hairs on my chest.'

Behind Arthur, sitting in the driver's seat, Jadyn saw Grace battling with a barely suppressed laugh. He caught her eye, hoping she would intervene, but all she did was shrug.

'Don't let it go cold, now,' Arthur said. 'Drink up, lad, come on.'

Jadyn lifted the mug to his lips. The steam rising from it drifted up his nose, bringing with it the meaty scent of salty gravy. It was a smell that he associated with a good roast dinner, Yorkshire puddings, and roast potatoes. Not a mug.

With Arthur looking on, Jadyn took a sip.

The taste was two things all at once, both of which tumbled over each other to confuse him even more. The drink was the most revolting thing he had ever tasted, and also the most delicious. It made no sense, and Jadyn could feel his brain short-circuiting as it tried to find some way to categorise exactly what he was consuming.

He took another sip, only this time it was a gulp, and the beefy drink slid down his throat, warming him, or so it seemed, all the way to the ends of his toes, just like Arthur had promised.

'See?' said Arthur.

Jadyn handed the mug back through the window.

'That was actually brilliant,' he said.

'You should try it with vodka, a splash of Tabasco, and a squeeze of lemon juice,' Arthur said. 'Nectar.'

'Alcoholic beef?' Jadyn said, the thought of it screwing up his face. 'I'm not sure I should.'

'We'll see ...'

Grace climbed out of the Land Rover and came around to stand beside Jadyn.

'Lovely day for it,' she said. 'Thanks for coming out.'

'It's my job,' Jadyn said. 'Harry's told me a little about what happened, but if you could run me through it again, that would be useful.'

'Probably easier if I just take you there,' said Grace, and pointed down the track, towards the spinneys of trees.

Leaving Arthur and the dogs behind, Jadyn walked alongside Grace. The wind, he noticed, hadn't yet made up its mind as to whether it wanted to be a full-on, in-your-face, ripping-your-skin-off gale, or a gentle thing that did little more than turn the snow into little dancing whirlwinds spinning off gleefully across the fields.

'How's Jen, then?' Grace asked.

'Er, she's fine, I think,' Jadyn answered, rather taken aback by the abruptness of the question.

'That's good,' said Grace. 'I don't know her really, but she seems like a lovely lass.'

'Yes,' said Jadyn. 'I'm sure she is.'

'You're not very good at this, are you?'

'Good at what?'

Grace laughed.

'Exactly,' she said. 'Anyway, we're here.'

Grace stopped walking and pointed over at the wall on the right.

'You can still see a bit of blood over there,' she said. 'That'll be from the hare they'll have caught.'

Jadyn could see a few spots of pink bleeding through the white of the snow.

Grace then explained what she had seen and found earlier, and about the two vehicles.

'I didn't get the number plates, though,' she said.

'Harry mentioned something about a missing dog?'

Grace pointed off, further down the track.

'I followed the tracks,' she said, 'but I didn't find anything. Poor little bugger, must be terrified, wherever it is.'

'And you're sure one ran off?'

'The tracks headed off down there,' Grace answered with a nod, pointing further down the ancient roadway, 'but there were none coming back. So, I reckon if it's anywhere, it'll be in those trees, sheltering out of the wind and the snow. I know that's where I'd be. For all I know I walked straight past it and it's just too scared to come out.'

Jadyn looked along to where Grace was pointing, seeing trees not too far off, and the river Ure beyond.

'We could have another look if you want,' he said. 'Can't hurt, can it? And the river might have stopped it going too far.'

'If you're happy to,' said Grace.

'Once we're done, I'll go have a scout around the village,' said Jadyn, 'knock on a few doors. Someone might have seen or heard something. Might even be a camera or two that caught the vehicles you saw, you never know.'

With that agreed, Grace led Jadyn on down the track. The walls soon faded to nothing more than a thin trace of stones in the grass, but the track continued, the old furrows carved by so much use over the years they were still visible in the fresh snow.

At the first spinney, Jadyn followed Grace up and over some wooden steps into the trees. The wind which had chased them all the way there was now little more than a whisper in the branches. Above them, the snow caught in the upper fingers of the woodland was slowly shutting away the view of the sky, an icy roof built quietly by the invisible hands of winter.

Grace called out for the dog and Jadyn joined in, their voices louder and clearer than Jadyn had expected.

They walked through the woodland in a zigzag, splitting left and right to meet at the other side.

'Anything?' Jadyn asked.

Grace shook her head.

'Like I said, if it's here, it's scared and refusing to come out,' she said. 'We could do with something to tempt it out of its hiding place. Don't suppose you carry a few butcher's bones on you, do you?'

'Not usually, no,' Jadyn said. 'Sorry.'

Grace made to head off back through the trees when a thought struck Jadyn. Peering through the trees, he could see the two Land Rovers just a short walk away.

'I've an idea,' he said. 'Won't be long.'

Before Grace had a chance to stop him, he dashed off back through the woodland, over the wooden steps, and up through the snow to Arthur, who looked more than a little confused to see Jadyn turn up on his own.

'What are you doing, leaving Grace down there?' Arthur asked. 'Is she okay? Has something happened?'

'That Bovril of yours,' Jadyn said, ignoring Arthur's questions. 'Can I have it?'

'You've been converted, have you? It's the good stuff, right enough.'

'I need it.'

'And so do I,' said Arthur. 'There's not much left, so I'm saving the last bit for myself. Next time, you'll have to bring your own, won't you?'

'Actually, it's not for me,' said Jadyn. 'It's for the dog.'

Arthur's eyes widened.

'Dog? What are you on about?'

'The missing dog.'

'You've found it?'

'No.'

'Then how do you know it wants my Bovril?'

'A hunch,' Jadyn said.

Before Arthur could stop him, Jadyn reached in and grabbed the flask. Then he was off at pace, through the snow and back down the hill towards the trees. He heard a shout from Arthur, but decided it was best to ignore it and just explain later, assuming his plan worked, of course.

Once over the wooden steps again, he found Grace waiting for him.

'What on earth's got into you?' she asked. 'Why did you race off like that?'

'I went back for this,' Jadyn said, and held up the flask, quickly undoing the lid.

Grace shook her head in disbelief.

'Dad's Bovril?'

'Yep.'

'Well, he won't be happy you've taken that.'

Jadyn held up the now-open flask to Grace's nose.

'You can smell the beef, can't you?' he said.

Grace pulled her face away from the flask.

'Of course I can,' she said. 'I've grown up with that smell, courtesy of Dad's obsession with the stuff.'

'Exactly.'

'Exactly, what?'

'You can smell it ...'

Jadyn then set off through the wood once again, waving the flask around in front of him like a priest waving incense in church.

He heard footsteps behind him as Grace caught up.

'I have to say, I wish I'd thought of that,' she said. 'Very clever, Jadyn. Harry would be impressed.'

'Probably won't work though,' said Jadyn, the aroma of the Bovril all around them as they walked. 'But it's worth a try, isn't it?'

Jadyn walked on, wafting the steam from the flask left and right, as he and Grace called out in their best here-doggy-doggy voices.

The woods answered with the soft quietness only fresh snow can provide, deadening all sound, turning the world to the silence of slumber.

A few minutes later, they were almost back to the steps. Jadyn couldn't help but feel a little disappointed.

'I really thought that would work,' he said with a shrug. 'Sorry.'

'No need to be sorry,' said Grace. 'You didn't let the poor thing go, did you? They did, whoever they are.'

Then, as Jadyn went to answer, he heard something; a rustling in the fallen leaves and dead wood somewhere in front of them.

'What was that?'

The sound came again, clearer this time, and they both stared off at the same point in the wood, just a few metres away.

Grace pointed off to the right, deep into the trees again.

'It came from over there, didn't it?' she said.

'Here,' said Jadyn, and handed her the flask. 'You take this, and I'll follow you.'

With Grace in front, they both headed back into the trees. They would take a few steps, then stop and listen for the sound again, just to make sure they were heading in the right direction. It was a faint whine, so quiet that it was almost snatched away by the wind caught in the trees each time they heard it.

'This way,' Grace said, changing directions.

When the whine came again, it was louder and clearer. Then Jadyn saw movement.

'There,' he said. 'Over by that stump.'

Walking alongside Grace now, Jadyn headed over to where he'd seen a flash of grey fur.

'It worked,' Grace said, as from behind the stump, the small, grey head of a dog peered around at them.

It was shaking, Jadyn noticed, whether out of fear or the cold or both, he wasn't sure. He stood back, deciding it was probably best to leave this bit to someone who actually owned a dog.

Grace handed the flask back to Jadyn and then dropped herself low to creep closer to the clearly terrified dog.

'Come on, you,' she cooed, her voice soft and calm. 'Everything's okay now. There's nowt to worry about, I promise. You're going to be fine. We'll look after you. Come on, out you come ...'

The dog's head disappeared, only to reappear again a few seconds later around the other side of the stump.

Grace was close now, an arm's reach away. She stopped, held out a hand.

'Here,' she said. 'I found this. You'll love it. Come on ...'

Jadyn saw the broken end of a dog biscuit in her hand, something she must have found in a jacket pocket.

The dog hesitated, looked like it was going to duck away again, but then changed its mind, edging out from behind the stump towards Grace's outstretched hand.

'That's a good boy,' she said, the dog now fully in view. 'Come on then, come on ... Good lad, nearly there ...'

The dog sniffed the dog biscuit then reached up and took it gently between its front teeth.

Grace didn't move, just let him take it and munch it down. Then, almost imperceptibly, she reached out and stroked the dog's head. He jumped at first, but then settled down and came back for more. A couple of minutes later, he was in Grace's arms, snuggled in tightly, his thin tail wagging against her like a whip.

'No collar,' Grace said, bringing the dog over to meet Jadyn. 'Doubt he's chipped, either. Still worth checking though.'

'So we don't know what it's called then,' Jadyn said, reaching out a hand to the dog, which quickly turned its head to lick his fingers. 'He's certainly friendly.'

'He's a proper little darling,' said Grace, giving the dog a squeeze. 'Makes you wonder about some people, doesn't it? Why would you just abandon it? I don't understand it at all. And I don't want to, either.'

'So, what do we do with him, then?' Jadyn asked. 'Not sure this is quite in my remit as a police officer.'

Grace led Jadyn back to the edge of the woodland then up the track again, back to her dad.

'Animal Rescue,' said Grace. 'There's a local group, I'll give them a call. Give me a sec ...'

As Grace made the call, Jadyn stood with Arthur and they both made a fuss over the dog. It was still shaking, so Arthur grabbed an old towel from the back of his vehicle and wrapped the dog in it so that only its nose was visible at one end, its tail at the other.

'Seems to like that,' he said.

Grace finished her call.

'They've no space,' she said. 'Not immediately anyway. But they're going to ring around and see if any of the foster places they use can take the little bugger in.'

'So, what do we do with him till they find somewhere?' Jadyn asked.

'We can take him,' said Grace. 'I can't see Jess being too pleased, but she'll just have to suck it up.'

Jadyn gave the dog a scratch under its chin and it sent out a lick with the tip of its tongue.

'I could take him,' he said, almost as surprised to hear the words as Grace was herself, judging by the look on her face.

'No, it's no bother,' she said.

'I know it isn't,' Jadyn said, 'but I can take him back to the office, get him warm. There are no dogs there at the moment because Harry's out and Jim's dog is with his dad. We've got dog food at the office as well. And I can take him home with me if I need to; it'll be fun.'

Jadyn could tell from the look on Grace's face that she wasn't sure.

'Honestly,' he said, 'I want to.'

Arthur handed the still-wrapped dog over to Jadyn.

'Here you go, then,' he said.

Jadyn took the animal and it snuggled in under his arms.

'Hello,' he said.

The dog looked up at him, then leaned forward and licked his nose.

CHAPTER TEN

HARRY RAISED HIS CLENCHED HAND TO KNOCK ON THE DOOR, only to hesitate, as the house in front of him stared down through windows filthy with grime.

He had visited a good number of farms during his relatively short time in the Dales. Generally, they were ordered places, tidy, well maintained, with a place for everything, and everything in its place, even if sometimes that place was a crack in the wall. That was no easy task considering the fact that most of them were old buildings that required constant care.

One farm still haunted him though, and not just because the owner, John Capstick, had met a somewhat gruesome end under the wheels of a trailer. The place had been a mess, better suited as the backdrop to a horror movie, than a place involved in the good husbandry of sheep.

This house was definitely giving Harry a similar vibe.

Very aware that his imagination was working overtime, Harry couldn't escape the feeling that the grimy windows held some kind of deep-seated menace, as though whatever was behind them hated the world outside with a seething, roaring heat.

The stonework was dark. Thick lichen covered the walls in patches as though they'd been struck down by some incurable disease. Water spilled from the guttering as the falling snow melted on the slate roof, heated by a cracked chimney spilling thick smoke. Though the front of the house comprised a small garden, the iron railings on top of the wall surrounding it gave it the air of a prison, as though whatever was behind it was trapped, and for good reason.

Not much gardening had been going on for a good while, Harry thought, the small patch of ground bereft of any kind of greenery, and instead sprouted discarded springs and angular bits of metal. Rust bled into the soil, staining the falling snow a deep, orangey red.

Harry glanced up the lane just in time to see Liz disappear around a bend as she chased after the missing teenage boy. Whatever had happened to cause the lad to run, Harry needed to find out. He set his jaw, took a deep breath, and rapped his knuckles hard against the wood.

From somewhere deep inside the house, a dog barked, the sound strange, Harry thought, both angry and scared. He also heard scuffling, and something that sounded like the rattling of a chain.

No one came to the door. The dog continued to bark.

Harry knocked again, this time a little harder, and a little longer, rattling the door in its frame.

The dog barked once again, and there was more rattling. Then Harry heard a voice, harsh and mean, crash through the quiet on a torrent of swearing.

Harry waited. The dog's barking died, the swearing stopped. And still, no one came to the door.

In no mood for being ignored and left out in the cold and the snow, Harry gave up on what little tact he had and hammered the heel of his fist against the door hard enough to shake the hinges. Dark flecks of rust fell to the ground. That done, he then dropped his face to the letterbox, snapped it open, and called out to whoever was inside.

'Right then,' he said, 'this is DCI Harry Grimm. If you don't want me to accidentally kick this door off its hinges, then my advice would be to answer it. And quickly.'

Harry heard more barking, more swearing, then another voice joined in, this one a woman's.

Footsteps.

Harry stepped away from the door and braced himself for whatever was about to burst out of it. He grabbed a rusting length of metal from the ground to his left, just in case it was the dog he'd heard.

'Whatever it is you're here for, you can bugger off back to wherever you came from,' said a gruff voice from inside the house, the door remaining closed.

'I'm here about your son, Mr Cowper,' Harry said. 'Can I come in?'

'No. You can bloody well sod off, that's what you can do,' came the reply. 'None of your business, is it?'

'I'm afraid that it is,' Harry said. 'A disturbance was reported at this house and your son was seen leaving your property on a quad bike. It is my duty, therefore, to find out exactly what has happened.'

'Was it that nosy cow next door? I bet it was, wasn't it? Nowt better to do than stick her hooked, witchy nose into other people's business.'

'Mr Cowper,' Harry said, keeping his voice calm, but firm, which was already quite the challenge, 'you need to open the door and let me inside, so that we can talk this through properly.'

More swearing, at least Harry assumed that's what he heard, the gruff voice of Mr Cowper little more than a hate-filled rumble on the other side of the door.

At last, the door opened, scraping across the floor inside the house. There was no dog, so Harry discarded the length of metal he'd been holding.

The man standing in front of him put Harry immediately in mind of an angry mole. Mr Cowper was squat, well built, his head sunk into a non-existent neck. He was wearing scuffed denim trousers, a chequered shirt, and a worn, waxed waistcoat, which stretched beyond his hips. From a hole in one of the pockets, Harry saw the end of a shotgun cartridge poking through.

'You're not coming in, if that's what you think.'

Mr Cowper then fell quiet, squinting out from the gloom of the house, one hand shoved deep into a trouser pocket, the other braced against the door, no doubt ready to slam it in Harry's face.

'Thank you for coming to the door,' Harry said, ignoring what the man had said. 'May I come in?'

'Are you deaf?'

Harry said nothing, just waited.

'You got a warrant, then?' Mr Cowper asked. 'You need a warrant. Can't just come out here barging your way into my house, like, can you?'

'I'm here to ask you some questions,' Harry said. 'I don't need a warrant to do that.'

'I've watched stuff on the television. I know my rights. And what the hell's wrong with your face? What a bloody mess that is. You'll put me off my lunch.'

Harry paused before saying anything else, clenching and unclenching his fists.

'Mr Cowper,' he said, his voice as slow and measured as he could make it, 'I simply need to come in, sit down, and have a chat. That's usually the best way to get to the bottom of things like this and to find out what's happened. All that I'm really concerned about is the welfare of your son. So, if you wouldn't mind ...?'

Mr Cowper stared, cocked his head to the left, then slammed the door.

Or at least that's what he tried to do.

Stepping forward, Harry caught the door with a firm stamp of his foot and an extended arm, his hand gripping the door's edge.

'Oi! What the hell are you doing? You can't just—'

Harry pushed the door with considerable ease, opening it wide enough for him to step over the threshold and out of the snow, Mr Cowper sliding back across the floor as he did so.

'Very kind of you,' Harry said. 'Weather's getting a bit rough so it's nice to be out of it.' He then turned to glare down at Mr Cowper. 'Now then, where would you like to talk?'

'I don't want to talk,' Mr Cowper said. 'I want you off my property, that's what I want. Go on, sod off! I mean it. Who the hell do you think you are, Taggart?'

The reference to that particular long-running television detective caught Harry by surprise. Not only was it getting on for thirty years since it first aired, but the titular character was also one of the very few whom Harry had actually rather enjoyed watching.

'Do I sound like Police Scotland?' Harry asked.

'Well, your accent's not from round here, is it?' said Mr Cowper. 'You're like her next door, aren't you? Another bloody outsider moving in to tell us locals what to do, how to live. Well, not here you won't, not in my house.'

Harry didn't move. Instead, he just stood there, holding the door firm, staring at Mr Cowper. He felt pressure down his arm as Mr Cowper tried to move the door, but try as he might, there was just no way he was going to overpower Harry. The man's face grew more and more red as he pushed against it, trying to shift Harry, breath blowing out of his nose like an old bull with its head stuck in a gate.

As Mr Cowper continued and failed to close the door, Harry allowed his eyes to adjust to the murky darkness slouching around in the house beyond. Just along the hallway, he saw an open door leading into a kitchen.

'Perfect,' he said, and let go of the door.

Mr Cowper fell forward as the door raced to slam shut. Harry caught him before he ended up on his face.

'Watch yourself there,' he said. 'Kitchen's this way, I see? Don't worry about putting the kettle on or anything like that. Best we just get on with our little chat, don't you think?'

Harry didn't wait for an answer. Letting go of Mr Cowper, he headed off into the hallway.

The place was a higgledy-piggledy mess, piled high with lever arch files stuffed with invoices and bills, boxes of what he guessed from the names written on them were various concoctions for the animals on the farm, coils of copper tubing, and a couple of large, metal urns, much like the new one back at the office, and far too many pairs of Wellington boots. Harry waded through it all and on through the open door and into the kitchen beyond. Seeing a dining table in the middle of the room, he went to sit down, when a shadow leapt from the corner of the room with a snarl.

Harry stepped back, at the same time grabbing a chair from underneath the kitchen table to hold in front of him like a circus lion tamer, as a huge dog came at him, teeth bared, spittle flying.

'Bloody hell's bells!'

Expecting the dog to slam into him, Harry was shocked to see it jar to a halt in mid-air, a chain around its neck snapping it back and dropping it to the floor on its back.

'Down, Rex! Get down!'

The voice was a woman's and Harry watched as she emerged from a cupboard in the far wall, an extended finger pointing at the dog. In the cupboard, Harry saw the usual stores of flour and sugar and numerous tins, as well as plenty of jars of things floating in vinegar, and a good number of bottles filled with a liquid the colour of dark beer.

'Down! Now!'

The dog snarled some more, then backed away, slinking across the floor to drop itself into a bed made from what looked like the remains of a shattered pallet or two and a pile of hessian sacks.

Heart racing, and adrenaline burning his veins, Harry kept the chair up in front of him, just in case.

'Don't worry,' the woman said. 'He can't reach you, I promise.'

Harry wasn't convinced. The chain holding the dog back looked barely strong enough to take the weight of a bathroom plug.

Mr Cowper walked into the kitchen.

'He doesn't like strangers,' he said. 'Something we have in common.'

'Is he always chained up like that?' Harry asked, relaxing a little and resting the chair back down on the ground.

'Of course he isn't,' Mr Cowper said. 'Usually, he's outside, roaming around. Does a good job at keeping folk like you from nosying around things they shouldn't be, if you know what I mean.'

'Can't say that I do,' said Harry.

He sat down at the table, his eyes immediately drawn to the shotgun lying open across it. Beside it, were a couple of long sticks, one ending with a small metal brush, the other with a wad of oily rag, a gun slip, and sticking out of a pocket, a grubby-looking folded gun license.

'This is the wife,' Mr Cowper said, giving no name.

The woman smiled wearily at Harry.

'I'm Jane,' she said, introducing herself. 'Tea?'

Harry shook his head.

'I think it best if we just get to why I'm here,' he said. 'Your son ...'

'You don't need to be worrying yourself about our lad,' Mr Cowper said. 'He's always buggering off somewhere. Typical teenager. It's what they do, isn't it? He's at that emotional stage. It'll pass.'

'He's done this before, then, has he?'

Jane went to speak, but Brian jumped in.

'Even stays out overnight sometimes. Thinks he's Bear bloody Grylls.'

Harry pulled out a notebook, already beginning to think this was a bit of a storm in a teacup. Though what Pat had said about the shotgun disturbed him. And he really wasn't warming to Brian at all.

'I just need to confirm a few details first, if that's okay.'

Mr Cowper sneered.

'What, so you can put us into some database, is that it? Have our details on there forever, then send someone round to snoop on us, bug our phone, is that it? I know what you're up to and don't go thinking I don't.'

Harry wondered from what, exactly, Mr Cowper's paranoia grew.

'All I need are names, contact details, that's all. Nothing sinister in it at all, I promise. It's just normal procedure.'

'A policeman's promise?' Mr Cowper laughed, shaking his head. 'Like that's worth anything.'

He dropped himself down heavily onto a chair opposite Harry and folded his arms. The chair creaked alarmingly, but Mr Cowper seemed unbothered.

'Tea,' he said.

'The policeman said he didn't want any,' said Jane.

'Was I asking for him? Or course I bloody well wasn't.'

Harry watched as Jane turned away and took the kettle to the sink.

'So, your names, then?' he asked.

'I'm Brian,' said Mr Cowper. 'The wife's Jane, as you already know, seeing as she blathered that out as soon as she saw you.'

'And your son?'

'Thomas,' said Brian.

With the name confirmed and matching what he'd been told by Matt, Harry asked, 'And how old is he?'

'Fifteen,' answered Brian, then snapped around to Jane and said, 'Where's that tea, then?', the words spitting out of him like a spray of bullets from a Tommy gun.

Harry jotted down the names, then took their phone number, though Brian wasn't exactly keen on providing it. He then sent a quick message off to Liz, just to confirm the son's name.

Jane placed a mug of tea on the table and made to leave the room.

'I'm here to speak to you both,' Harry said, and gestured to another chair. 'Please ...'

Jane hesitated, her eyes glancing between Harry and her husband.

'Sit down. You're making the place look untidy,' said Brian.

Jane slid down onto the chair. Harry resisted the urge to reach over and ricochet Mr Cowper's head off the table for being such a revolting example of humanity.

'Perhaps you can tell me a bit about yourselves,' Harry said.

'Perhaps we can, and perhaps we can't,' Brian replied.

'What is it that you farm?' Harry asked.

'Sheep, what else?' Brian said.

'We've a few head of cattle as well,' said Jane.

'And I see you do a bit of home pickling, too,' said Harry, pointing at the still-open cupboard. 'And a bit of homebrew.'

Jane's eyes widened, and she dashed over to shut the door.

'The smell,' she said, sitting back down. 'The vinegar. Gets everywhere if you let it.'

'I've told you about leaving that door open,' Brian said, his voice a snarl.

'I know, I'm sorry.'

Harry watched as the Cowpers exchanged looks. Whatever they were worried about him seeing in that cupboard, he couldn't imagine. Not unless they had some particularly lethal pickled eggs hiding somewhere in the darkness. Which was entirely possible, he was sure.

Without mentioning where the information had come from, mainly because he wanted to avoid Mr Cowper going off on one again about their neighbour, Harry quickly outlined what he knew so far about what had happened.

'Don't know what all the fuss is about,' Brian said, once Harry had stopped speaking. 'Thomas has just buggered off in a huff, that's all. He'll be back, like I said. He won't be wanting to stay out in the snow, will he? He's not a complete idiot. But if he does, it'll serve him right, teach him a lesson.'

'I've actually sent one of my officers after him,' Harry said. 'If you're able to provide me with any details as to where you think he might have gone, I can call her now. It would be very useful.'

'I haven't the foggiest idea where he is,' said Brian. 'There's a woodland a couple of miles up the lane. Good luck finding him, mind.'

Jane said, 'He used to build dens up there when he was younger.'

'Perhaps you can tell me what happened, exactly?' Harry asked.

Brian took a sip of his tea, spat it back out.

'Where's the sugar, woman? How many bloody times ...?'

A look of horror ripped its way across Jane's face, and Harry watched as she leapt from her chair to grab a bag of sugar from a cupboard.

'Mr Cowper ...' Harry said, prompting the man to answer his question.

'What happened? I'll tell you what happened. He happened, that's what. Ungrateful little shit. Born into this farm he is, learning from me, and what does he want to do? Not farm, that's what. Beneath him, isn't it? One minute he wants to sod off to college, get a degree, like that's any use to me, next he's saying he wants to be looking after wildlife, game-keeping, hugging trees, all that bollocks. What use is that to us here on the farm? No bloody use, that's what.'

Harry noticed Brian's reference to a degree being of no use to him, with no thought as to what it might mean to his son. Which pretty much summed up where the man's priorities lie, he thought.

'So, am I to understand, then, that you had an argument?' he asked. 'Is that why he ran off?'

'I gave him a piece of my mind, that's all,' Brian said. 'He's always up in his room, always on with his music. Either that or he's fussing around with those bloody ferrets of his. Awful animals. The stink on them is enough to burn your eyes out of your skull. Well, I've had enough. He needs to pull his weight.'

'Music?' said Harry.

'He plays the guitar,' said Jane, and Harry saw the smallest of smiles threaten to cast a little sunshine into the grey lines of her face. 'He's very good as well. Very talented.'

'Well, there'll be no more of that now, that's for bloody sure.'

'Why?' Harry asked.

'I confiscated it, that's why,' said Brian proudly, the meanness in the man's voice razor sharp. 'Needs to get his priorities right. And playing that blasted thing isn't one of them.'

Harry was beginning to wonder why, instead of running off, the lad hadn't just battered his dad across the head with the guitar instead.

'What about the gunshots?' he asked, briefly imagining an unconscious Mr Cowper lying on the floor, a broken guitar across his chest.

'Gunshots? There was only one,' Brian said. 'And no, it wasn't me shooting at my son, if that's what you're thinking. And I'll be asking you to take that comment back.'

'Then perhaps you can explain what it was exactly?'

'Crows,' said Brian. 'Up on the roof. Don't want them nesting in the chimney, do I?'

'The information I have is that two shots were heard,' said Harry.

'Well, your information is wrong, isn't it? Because I only fired once. Don't believe me? Here ...'

Brian reached across the table to the shotgun and from a shallow box removed a spent 12-bore cartridge. He chucked it over to Harry.

'See? That's the one I sent down the barrel. Search me if you don't believe me. No need to lie about that, now, have I?'

Harry held the cartridge in his palm, but his eyes left Brian and he looked over at Jane.

'It was one shot, that's all,' she said. 'He only wanted to scare him, I mean them, I mean—'

Harry felt the temperature in the room drop as Jane cut her sentence in two.

'What, exactly, do you mean?' he asked. 'Scare who?' He looked at Brian. 'Just now you said it was the crows you were shooting it.'

'Of course it was the crows! What the bloody hell else would it be?'

'Mr Cowper,' Harry said. 'I think it's best to let you know that one thing I really don't warm to is the telling of lies.'

'It's not a lie. It was crows. There were crows outside. They scattered. That's what happened. Prove me wrong.'

'I don't want to prove you wrong,' said Harry. 'I want you to tell me the truth. It's easier that way, for everyone.'

Brian sat back, folded his arms.

'There's no law against shooting crows.'

'Where was Thomas when this happened?'

Brian's expression was one of both irritation and anger.

'Outside,' he said. 'Running away from his responsibilities yet again. Didn't like me taking his guitar. So, he goes and messes with my stuff down in the cellar, doesn't he? Buggers everything up. It's them ferrets next if he doesn't start helping, you mark my words.'

'What stuff, Mr Cowper?'

Brian shrugged.

'Just stuff that's got nowt to do with him, that's all. How would you like it? You wouldn't, would you?'

'You confiscated his guitar.'

'My house, my rules. Know your place, right?'

Tapping his pencil against his notebook, Harry realised Brian just didn't see the connection.

'So, you had an argument,' he said. 'Something about Thomas not wanting to work on the farm, if I'm to understand rightly, and you confiscated his guitar. In response, Thomas ran off. You chased after him. On the way, you saw some crows and just so happened to have in your hands this shotgun here. You then sent a barrel off at the crows at the very same time as your son was running away.'

'Stole my quad bike, too,' said Brian. 'That's the real crime here, isn't it? I need that to work the farm.'

'This is the story you're going to stick to, is it? Crows?'

Brian gave a nod.

'It is.'

'You do understand that when we find Thomas, we'll be asking him what happened as well?'

'You can do whatever the hell you want, for all I care,' Brian said. 'Wouldn't believe a word that lad says. Lies fall out of his mouth as easy as shit out the back end of a cow.'

Harry was tempted to press the matter, and he would've done, too, if he'd been alone with Brian. Trouble was, he had a feeling that he could trust the man about as far as he could spit. Jane, though? She had kind eyes beneath a worried brow, and something told him she wasn't lying. She hadn't said much, but she'd said just enough to give him cause to think that his next action, though no doubt unpopular, was very, very important.

'Well, thank you both for your time,' Harry said. 'It's been ... informative.'

'Off you go, then,' said Brian. 'About bloody time, too. Wasting my time when I've got things to be done.'

Harry reached over to the gun slip and removed the license from the pocket. 'I'm afraid I'm not quite finished.'

Harry noticed Brian's eyes follow his hand as he opened the license to give it a quick scan, then folded it again and tucked it into his jacket.

'What are you doing with that, then? That's my license. You can't take that.'

Harry stared at Brian.

'From our discussion,' he said, 'it is my opinion that this shotgun here may well have been used in a criminal act, and/or the breaching of the peace.'

Brian's eyes grew wide.

'What criminal act? That's bollocks, and you know it. Breaching of the peace?'

'I know the law,' Harry said.

'You know bugger all, that's what you know,' Brian replied. 'Give me that back. It's mine.'

Harry reached over for the shotgun.

'Don't you dare,' said Brian.

'Mr Cowper—'

'All I did was send a shot over his head! It was miles off!'

Inside, Harry smiled, but on the outside, he glared at the visibly livid little farmer in front of him.

'It is my duty, Mr Cowper, to confiscate your license, and whatever guns you have on the premises, while an enquiry into the incident is undertaken. Your license says that this is the only one in your possession, so it'll be coming with me.'

Brian was on his feet.

'You can't do that. It's not right.'

'I can,' Harry said. 'And I am.'

Brian reached across the table and grabbed the corner of Harry's jacket.

'You're not listening to me! Give me that back! Now! You're not having my gun!'

Harry, his glare fixed on Mr Cowper's mean eyes, rose slowly to his feet. The man held on, but when Harry was at full height, his grip gave way, and his hand let go of Harry.

From the shadows of the room, the dog growled.

For a moment, neither man said a word. In the silence, Harry took the shotgun and placed it in its case. He stood up and moved to the door.

'I can see myself out,' he said, then calmly walked to the front door and set himself once again against the snow filling the air outside.

CHAPTER ELEVEN

HAVING LEFT HARRY BEHIND TO FIND OUT WHAT EXACTLY
had happened to chase the teenager off into the snow in the first
place, Liz headed off up the lane on her bike. The rattling purr of
the engine was deadened a little by the snow as the studded tyres
pulled her on.

The lane was narrow, and the snow was settling just enough to
smooth out the edges between verge and tarmac. The wind was
blowing enough now to ensure that, rather than just settle on the
tops of the walls on either side, the snow was scalloped into small
drifts. Tufts of grass poked through like the ends of paint brushes
discarded by an artist halfway through painting the landscape now
surrounding her.

Adjusting her speed and her sitting position, Liz cut through
the beginnings of a drift, a sweep of snow sticking out from under a
gate like the giant tail of a white lizard, only to have the rear end
slip out from under her. She caught it just in time, bringing the bike
back under control, only to then have the front end catch in a large
pothole hidden by the snow, then skip to the right. The rear end
snapped out again and Liz dropped her right foot to the road,
quickly drifting the bike around a sharp corner ahead, and
narrowly avoiding crashing into a wall. Then she was back up on

both wheels, exhilarated, and grinning as much from the thrill of what had just happened as from the scare it had given her.

On she rode, deeper into the amphitheatre of hills that cast themselves around her, the white slopes cut by the zebra stripes of walls. The tracks from the quad bike were still visible, but only just, and a stab of concern for the missing boy caught her sharp. Then, with no warning at all, the snow died, the wind dropped, and Liz found herself riding out of the snow. She glanced over her shoulder and saw hanging from the sky a lace curtain of white draped behind her. Its surface fluttered in the breeze, and yet in front of her, at least for the moment, all was clear. Above her, she caught snatches of blue, as though some great, invisible god had slashed at the sky with a great knife.

Riding on, Liz realised she was humming to herself. There was no real tune to it, though there were snatches of choruses she knew in it, for sure, but the act was, above all, a clear sign that she was enjoying herself. And how could she not? She was riding an off-road bike she hadn't even had to pay for, trying to find a lost kid in some of the world's most glorious countryside, which was made even more so by the falling snow.

A few minutes later, she spied the straight edges of a woodland plantation on her right, probably half a kilometre away from the lane. The thickness of the trees seemed particularly dark against the stark white of the freshly fallen snow, as though any light attempting to pierce it would soon be swallowed. The plantation itself lay on the surface of the Earth as though weighed down and pushed deep into the land. There was a strange weight to the place, Liz thought, as though it had some faint gravitational pull holding it in place as well as drawing her towards it.

An open gate in the wall on her right welcomed the tyre marks of the quad bike, which turned off the lane and headed straight for the trees. Liz slowed down, turned off the road, then followed, lifting herself out of the seat as she did so.

From the corner of her eye, she briefly spied the large house at the end of the lane. Lights were on in the windows and grey smoke was billowing from the chimney. It looked warm and inviting and had she not been on such an urgent errand, she might even have tried to come up with a reason to stop by to soak it in a little.

Now away from the road, and standing up on the foot pegs, to Liz the bike seemed to almost come to life. Its traction had been adequate on the hard surface, but now, faced with soft earth and softer snow, the whole machine seemed to bristle with energy. She felt as though she and it were in tune, rolling across the undulating fields towards the fir trees ahead at a fair old pace. The bike bounced and Liz went with it, guiding it gently on its way.

Arriving at the edge of the plantation, the wall of trees seemed even thicker. Liz slowed, then brought the bike to a dead stop, dropping a foot to the ground. The tracks from the quad bike disappeared into the darkness before her, which hung from the trees like ripped cloth. She stared, narrowing her eyes in some vain attempt to help her see further and clearer in the thick shadows. Then she saw it, the quad bike itself, an alien shape painted red and hidden in the trees.

Kickstand down, Liz killed the engine and jumped off the bike, pulling off her helmet as she then stepped through the snow and onto the deep brown carpet of needles beneath the trees.

Where before the world had been quiet beneath the falling snow, under the branches of the trees the silence was deafening. Each step she made was a cacophony of snaps and cracks, as dead branches broke beneath her weight.

'Thomas? Are you here?'

Liz's voice hit the silence and died a quick death, the trees snatching it away to bury it deep in their branches.

'My name is Liz Coates. I'm the PCSO over in Hawes. You're not in trouble, but people are worried about your safety. Can you hear me?'

More silence, this time even thicker than before, as though the trees were feeding greedily on her voice.

'I know you know the area, and I'm sure that wherever you are, you're safe and well, but you don't want to be out in weather like this for too long.'

Liz pushed further into the woods, glancing back occasionally to keep an eye on her bike. Then it was gone, the edge of the woodland cut from view by the trees. For a moment, she felt a little vulnerable, a childhood fear clutching at her from another time, another woodland, where she had wandered too far, too deeply, and become lost. Panic had chased her like a pack of wolves that day, and all the way into the darkest of nights. When her parents had found her, she had been hiding beneath the bows of a tree, a thick, pointed stick clenched in her fists, and shivering with the cold.

'Thomas? Can you hear me? Thomas!'

Still nothing, and then Liz found herself striding out of the other side of the woodland to be greeted not by falling snow, but a cold, hard wind, whipping its way through the trees with ferocious abandon.

Shivering, Liz quickly turned back into the relative shelter and warmth of the trees, making her way back to her bike. Then, as she walked through the heart of the woodland, retracing her own footprints where she could, she spotted something she had missed on her journey through just a few minutes ago.

Between two large trees, a wall of branches and fallen trunks had been dragged and stacked. The construction was for sure not a natural one, so Liz headed over for a closer look. On doing so, she found that the trees had been placed to provide a small shelter; the roof formed from branches plaited together, and then covered in pine needles. The entrance was wide but low enough to cause her to have to stoop.

'Thomas? Are you in there?'

No answer came, so Liz pulled a torch from her belt and pressed on to see what it was she had found.

Inside the shelter, the ground had been swept clear, leaving bare earth. She was amazed by just how dark it was inside, and how warm. In the corner, she saw a large metal box, and on closer inspection found that it was an old battered ammunition box, probably bought from an army surplus store.

Liz knelt down beside the box and pulled open the lid. She wasn't really sure what she had been expecting to find. If this was Thomas's secret hideaway, which she suspected it was, she would've guessed on coming across a few snacks, a magazine or two he probably wouldn't want his parents to know he'd somehow got his hands on, maybe a blanket to help him keep warm. Looking inside, she found a sleeping bag, a camping mat, even an old camping stove and some tins of beans. There were also a few packets of biscuits, some chocolate, and right at the bottom, half a dozen bottles filled with a brown liquid.

Liz lifted one from the box, which like the others, was the size of a bottle of wine and had a screw top. There was no label to tell her what it was inside, so allowing her inquisitive nature to take over, she unscrewed the lid and took a tentative sniff.

'Bloody hell!'

The shock of hard alcohol blasting up her nostrils made Liz cough, and she nearly dropped the bottle. Staring at the bottle, she heard a scuffling sound outside the shelter.

'Thomas? Is that you?'

The scuffling quickly turned into the sound of retreating footsteps.

Liz burst from the shelter, and looked left and right.

'Thomas? Thomas! I'm just here to make sure you're okay, that's all. You don't need to run!'

The wood was silent again.

'Damn it ...' Liz muttered, and set off at a sprint, back towards her bike and Thomas's quad, guessing that right now, that was exactly where he was heading.

Branches slapped and snapped at her, stinging her face, pulling her hair, scratching her skin. Roots seemed to burst from the ground to trip her up, and more than once Liz fell to her knees, only to bounce straight up onto her feet again.

When she arrived at the place where she had found Thomas's

quad bike, the very last thing she had expected to find was it to still be there. And yet, there it was, tucked behind a tree, waiting for its rider.

She called for Thomas again, staring through the trees to see if she could see any movement. She had no doubt that it was him she had heard from inside the shelter, but he was obviously refusing to be persuaded to come any closer.

Realising then that she was still holding the bottle she had taken from the old ammunition box, Liz pulled out her notebook and pen. She then jotted down her name and her number, along with a quick note explaining why she was there and to call her. Then she stuck the note in the gap between the seat and the fuel tank on the quad.

Walking back to the edge of the trees, Liz pulled on her helmet and secured the bottle she had carried over from the hideout in a zip-up bag attached to the fuel tank. She wasn't really sure why she was taking it with her, but then she was also fairly sure a teenager shouldn't be hiding out in the woods with a secret stash of dodgy booze. One less bottle, would be one less he'd have to neck.

With the snow blowing across the fields in ghostly shapes, Liz started the engine and kicked back the stand. With one last glance over at the quad bike, she headed back to the village of Marsett.

Pulling up outside the farm, she found Harry standing in the snow, the bonnet of his precious Rav4 open to the elements. He was gazing at his phone.

'Something wrong?' she asked, pulling off her helmet.

'Won't start,' said Harry. 'And I'm fairly sure staring at the engine isn't going to fix it.'

'You're checking Google, then?'

'Wouldn't know what to check for, even if I was,' said Harry. 'Just got a message from Dave Calvert.'

Liz climbed off her bike and stood at Harry's side.

'You tried WD40?'

'Not something I generally carry around with me,' Harry said.

'And even if I did, I'd have no idea what I was supposed to do with it.'

Liz walked back to her bike, opened the zip-up bag on the fuel tank, and returned carrying a can. She then reached into the engine, fiddled about with something, sprayed oil from the can, and stood back up. She then popped around to the driver's door, jumped in, and a moment later, the engine was purring again.

'And what kind of voodoo was that, then?' Harry asked when she joined him again.

'Bit of damp in the distributor cap,' she said. 'Weather like this, it can happen, particularly with an old vehicle like this.'

Harry dropped the bonnet down with a clunk.

'What did Dave want, then?' Liz asked.

'The usual,' Harry said. 'A pint or two at the Fountain.'

Liz laughed.

'That's your evening sorted, then.'

'I'm going to assume you didn't find Thomas.'

'Yes and no,' Liz said, then explained what she had found; the sleeping bag, the snacks, and the bottles.

'Well, that's the best we can do for now,' Harry said. 'Well done on leaving the note.'

'How were the parents?'

'Interesting enough for me to want to keep an eye on them,' Harry replied. 'Well, the dad, especially so.'

'Any reason?'

Harry led Liz to the back of the Rav and opened the boot.

'A gun,' she said, seeing the case.

'He wasn't best pleased that I confiscated it. Got a bit ... shouty.'

Liz smiled at that, imagining Harry's response.

'There's a dog chained up in the kitchen,' Harry added. 'And his wife seems terrified of him.'

'So, what do you want to do?'

Harry rubbed his chin, scratching at his scars.

'Right now, I don't know,' he said. 'Think on it all for a bit, I reckon. Something's not right in there, I'm sure of it. Can't say what, but it's like I've seen something but missed it, if you know what I mean.'

As Harry stopped speaking, a gust of wind threw itself down the lane and Liz shivered.

'The snow's coming in again,' she said, seeing thick grey clouds gathering. 'Reckon we should get back to the office before we can't.'

Harry slammed the rear door of the Rav, then climbed into the driver's seat.

'Last one there buys the bacon butties,' he said, then headed off, tyres crunching through the snow as more began to fall.

CHAPTER TWELVE

HAVING MADE IT TO THE TOILET JUST IN THE NICK OF TIME, bumped into the chef, and then been given a quick tour of the house by none other than Carl Walsh himself, Peter Jameson had headed to his room only to pass out on the bed just minutes after shutting the door.

He'd had a quick scout around the room, found it to be warm and homely, and with an ensuite bathroom bigger than his own bathroom back home. There was a television on the wall, tea and coffee and a few biscuits, and a view that was, frankly, breathtaking.

Looking out over the car park at the front of the house, the snow had stalled just enough to give Jameson the chance to see down the valley to the lake. The fells to either side were draped in white sheets of snow, and the only sound he heard was the growl of an engine. His eyes had caught sight of a motorbike on the lane he'd himself travelled along about half an hour ago, but it had soon disappeared again, turning off the lane and into a field.

The view, however, was not enough to keep Jameson's attention, as a yawn reminded him of just how early he'd risen that morning to get to the house in the first place. Turning from the window, he'd then sat down on the bed, thinking he would unpack, but the next thing he knew, he was lying back, hands folded across his stomach, staring at the ceiling. The bed had welcomed him keenly, and he'd closed his eyes, thinking that a quick nap would do him the world of good.

Waking up, his face stuck to the pillow with an almost frightening quantity of drool, Jameson checked his watch. To his surprise, the day was now tripping past four PM, and the room was growing dark. Outside, the world was roofed in grey, yet bright still, and he pushed himself to his feet to have another look at the dales.

The first thing Jameson noticed was that the car park was now full, a collection of cars all snuggled up together, each wearing a thin cap of snow. Beyond them, more snow had fallen. Though it had stopped for now, the grey sky looked thick and heavy, as though it was barely holding back the next wave of the storm.

Walking over to his suitcase, Jameson quickly unpacked, then checked the plan he'd received by email as to the diary of events for the weekend ahead. He was a little shocked to see that the first thing on the timetable, an introduction from their host and a chance to meet the other attendees, was only minutes away.

With a quick dash through to the bathroom, Jameson gave his face a quick wash to get rid of the drool, brushed his teeth, ignored his hair seeing as he didn't really have enough left on top of his bonce to be worrying about, then headed out of his room onto the landing. Walking down the large staircase, he heard voices from one of the rooms below and was surprised by a sudden twist of fear in his gut. He hesitated, pausing on the stairs, nervous to move on. What the hell was wrong with him? His hands were clammy and he felt hot like he was about to faint.

'Pull yourself together, Pete ... Come on, sort yourself out ...'

Jameson gripped the bannister tightly, and closed his eyes. He saw Ellen then, standing in front of him, smiling. She was saying something, but he couldn't hear her voice. Then it came to him, and he laughed.

'Just remember that not everyone shares your sense of humour,' she said. 'And by not everyone, I mean no one. And try not to be too rude. Now go!'

Jameson opened his eyes, but kept the memory of Ellen alive in his mind as he continued on his way.

At the bottom of the stairs, he turned immediately left and walked into a large room with a high ceiling, from which hung an impressive and well-lit chandelier. He was immediately hit by the smell of burning wood and saw a fire roaring in an iron grate, the fireplace itself large enough to roast a pig on a spit. The room was well-lit, the windows draped with thick curtains. The fire was contained by three large sofas, each liberally covered with cushions and folded blankets, and a low table on which various drinks were rested.

There were two large windows, one facing out towards the car park, the other in the far wall, overlooking a tall hedge. Other comfy chairs were dotted around and about, and the walls were decorated with paintings hung between bookshelves, a couple of display cabinets, and an incidental table or two. Directly to the right of the door was an old, oak desk, the kind, Jameson imagined, that a century or two ago, someone had sat behind to write letters in the kind of elaborate, cursive script no one bothered with anymore. The front of the desk, which faced out into the room, was a polished panel reaching to the floor, and its surface was inlaid with dark green leather.

The sound of enthusiastic chatter from the occupants of the room caused Jameson's gut to twist once again, and he had the sudden urge to slink back out, hopefully unnoticed.

'Ah, there you are, at last, Peter! Come on in and meet everyone else.'

Carl Walsh, hand outstretched, strode over from a small bar to his left, the one area he had yet to cast his eyes over. It was well stocked, Jameson noticed, taking note of the single malt whiskies on one of the shelves. He recognised the young man serving behind the bar as the chef he'd bumped into earlier. Probably early twenties, though his eyes looked older. Various bowls of nibbles were lined up along the bar as well.

Jameson shook Carl's hand, who then pulled him in for an unexpected hug. He was carrying a glass containing a two-finger measure of something strong and spilled a little of it as he let go of the embrace.

'Oops,' Carl said, brushing himself down.

His eyes didn't look as bloodshot as before, Jameson thought, but there was an odd energy to the man. Nerves, he suspected, which was fair enough.

'I fell asleep, I'm afraid,' said Jameson. 'It's a long journey all the way from Somerset. I'm not used to it.'

'Well, you're here now, and rested, I hope?'

'I am, very much so, actually. The bed was just far too comfortable; nearly didn't make it down here at all. Lovely place, by the way.'

'Isn't it? This is the first weekend I've ever run, so I thought why not have it somewhere special? Drink?'

Jameson glanced at his watch, then over at the bar. The barman was throwing a few moves as he mixed a cocktail, spinning the shaker in the air before cracking it open on the counter in front of him and pouring it out into a glass with his left hand.

'Tempting,' he said. 'A little early, though. My rule's always been to never drink before six.'

'Rules are for breaking,' Carl said, slapping Jameson on the back. 'Come on, what'll it be?'

'I'm not sure they are,' said Jameson.

Carl laughed, a little too loudly, Jameson thought, the sound forced, coming out of the man like air from the neck of a balloon.

'How about starting with a beer? Gin and tonic? A glass of wine? There's a cocktail menu as well, if you prefer. Me, I'm on the good stuff; single malt.'

The closest Jameson ever got to drinking cocktails was a pint of bitter shandy. And he didn't drink bitter shandy.

'No, I'm going to stick to my rule. Not broken it in forty years of marriage, and I'm not about to do so now.'

From the corner of his eye, Jameson noticed the smile on Walsh's face fade. Ellen's voice came to him at the same time.

Try to not be too rude ...

'Thank you, though,' he said, forcing a smile. 'Come six o'clock, I'll be joining you in that whisky myself, that's for sure, so don't drink it all.'

The smile on Walsh's face looked pained now. This really wasn't going well, Jameson thought. He reached past the man and grabbed a handful of peanuts from a bowl. He then held them up to his ear, before lobbing a few into his mouth.

'The peanuts like the place as well,' he said. 'But then they're complimentary, aren't they?'

Jameson watched as Walsh's smile crashed and burned.

'What?'

'The peanuts,' Jameson said, opening his hand to reveal the ones not yet in his mouth. 'They're free, so they're complimentary, aren't they? They're complimentary peanuts. That's why they said they liked ...' His voice faded. 'It's a joke. Sorry. Ellen, my wife, warned me ...'

Walsh gave a nod, and the smile was back, though it reminded Jameson of how a weary therapist might look at a patient.

'And what's she getting up to while you're away, then?' Walsh asked. 'While the cat's away, right?'

Jameson wanted to kick himself. He still had the habit of talking about Ellen as though she was still alive, still the beating heart he would always return to.

'Oh, you know,' he said, in no mood to explain. Not now, anyway. 'Something like that, I guess.'

'You've not met the others yet, have you?' Walsh asked.

Right then, Jameson wasn't sure that he wanted to, either.

'Come on,' Walsh said, and Jameson felt the man's hand on the small of his back as he was guided swiftly from the bar over to the fire.

Sitting on the sofas were an Asian couple who Jameson guessed at being in their early fifties, their clothes, and especially the man's watch, telling him that they weren't exactly lacking in money. Or at least that was the impression they were trying to give, anyway. Opposite them was a younger woman in a smart, navy-blue jacket and trousers. Possibly in her early forties, he thought.

And in the other sofa, which directly faced the fire, sat two men. One with a dark beard who was wearing a thick, black pullover, jeans, and deep brown leather shoes. The other was dressed in light trousers and a shirt, with the sleeves rolled to the elbows, the collar open and flicked up. The one with the beard looked around the same age as the woman on her own, the one in the light trousers the youngest of the lot, probably late twenties, early thirties, he thought. All of this was guesswork, though he was usually within a year or two when it came to ages.

The conversation died as the five faces turned to stare up at Jameson and Carl Walsh.

'Our final attendee has joined us at last,' Walsh said, then added a slightly slurred, 'Hurrah!'

No one moved, no one spoke.

'This is Pete Jameson,' Walsh said. 'He's a retired detective chief inspector, so he might come in handy later on.'

That's an odd comment, thought Jameson.

'He's travelled all the way from Somerset as well, just to be here. Isn't that great? And you know, I'm sure his stories are almost as exciting as mine. Isn't that right, Pete?'

'It's Peter,' Jameson said under his breath, as the occupants of the sofas all waved, though he noticed that the man with the beard, who was now leaning forward with his elbows rested on his knees, simply raised an index finger and gave the slightest of nods.

Jameson lifted his left hand just enough to give a modicum of a wave back. 'Afternoon,' he said. 'So, which one of you is Poirot, then?'

No one laughed.

The man in the light trousers and shirt stood up and extended a hand, which Jameson shook.

'Grab yourself a seat, Pete,' he said. 'We're just getting to know each other a little. I'm Tony Pearson, by the way. You're a detective, then, yes?'

'Retired,' nodded Jameson, taking a seat beside the woman in navy blue, deciding it was probably best for everyone if he just let the over familiar use of his name slide for now. 'Like Carl said.'

'I'm a doctor myself. What are you doing here, then, if you don't mind me asking?'

'I could ask you the same thing.'

Tony gave a shrug.

'Not really sure being a doctor's for me. I read a lot of crime, love solving puzzles, so I thought, you know, why not go and find out about being a PI? So, here I am.'

The woman in blue then asked, 'So, why are you here, then?'

Jameson turned to find her looking up at him with narrow, inquisitive eyes.

'Actually, I've been asking myself that exact same question the whole day,' he said. 'And I still haven't come up with an answer.'

'I'm Kirsty,' the woman said, 'Kirsty Cropper.'

'Nice to meet you,' said Jameson.

'You're not drinking, then.'

This observation was from the man of the couple opposite, his accent London, but with the rough edges smoothed off.

'Not till six,' Jameson explained again, then held up his hand and shook it. 'Just a few peanuts for now. And you are?'

'Hazeem Rasheed,' the man said. 'And this is my wife, Yalina.'

For a few seconds, everyone just sort of glanced at each other, their voices stilled by a sudden awkwardness, broken only by the sipping of drinks.

'So, what happens now, then?' Jameson asked, turning to Walsh. 'Embarrassing icebreaker games and a focus group or two? If I see a flip chart or a parachute, I won't be held responsible for my actions.'

'Actually, I've a little surprise planned,' Walsh said, tapping the side of his nose.

Jameson wanted the ground to open up and swallow him whole.

Walsh shuffled over to stand by the fire and in front of the group.

'First, I wish to thank you all for coming along to this, my first-ever, and depending on how things go, possibly my last weekend for people thinking about becoming a private investigator.'

Carl laughed at his own joke. Walsh had clearly had a couple of drinks, and Jameson had noticed that something was going on with the man when he'd arrived earlier. His behaviour was off, and nerves were one way to explain it. Perhaps he'd have a word with him in a bit, check he's okay, and get him to ease off the booze for a while.

'As you'll have all read in the programme,' Walsh continued, 'it's a very busy weekend. My aim is to pass on as much information as I can about what it's like to be a private investigator, the kind of work you will be expected to do, and so on. As for the evening ahead, once we've had dinner, I've decided to switch things up a bit.'

'Can't say I like the sound of that,' said Jameson, and from the looks he received from some of the others, neither did they.

'Well, I'm in charge, aren't I?' said Walsh. 'This is my weekend, and you're here, so what we're going to do is ...'

He paused, for dramatic effect, Jameson suspected.

'... a little bit of a murder mystery.'

The way Walsh said those last two words, Jameson could tell that the man had expected rather more excitement from the gathering than he had actually received. Instead, all he got was a few strange looks, the rolling of eyes, and a shaking head or two.

'Honestly, it'll be a lot of fun, trust me,' continued Walsh. 'I know what I'm doing; private investigator, remember? I'm going to set up a murder scene and you'll all have the opportunity to examine it and then catch the killer! How exciting is that?'

Jameson caught movement from the corner of his eye and turned to see that Hazeem had his hand raised.

'Yes?' Walsh asked.

'PI's don't really investigate murders, do they?' he said. 'That's the job of the police, isn't it?'

'Well, that all depends, really, doesn't it?' said Walsh, his voice falling almost to a whisper. 'I've handled a few cold cases in my time, you know. I have. Solved them, too. Put the killers behind bars. And murder can happen at any moment, you know, the victim taken by surprise, the perpetrator left with blood on their hands for the rest of their lives.'

Yes, Jameson thought, having a word with Walsh seemed like a very good idea indeed.

Then Walsh seemed to snap out of it, and beamed at the gathering.

'Dinner is at seven,' he said. 'See you then!'

Then he was gone, sweeping out of the lounge a little too quickly, Jameson thought, almost as though something or someone was chasing him.

For a moment, no one said a word.

'Right then,' Jameson said, and never a fan of awkward silences, turned to the rest of the group, 'who's up for a game of Twister?'

CHAPTER THIRTEEN

A COUPLE OF HOURS LATER, JAMESON WAS ABSOLUTELY stuffed, so much so he had to loosen his belt a couple of notches. He was sitting in the dining room with the rest of the group and so far, the chef had really done himself proud.

The starter had been good, but then when were scallops anything else? Jameson thought. Then came the main course, and though he felt sure that he'd had goose before, he couldn't remember when and neither did he care, because there was just no way on God's green earth that it would have been able to compare. The pudding had been something clever with meringue and ice cream, and now he was just leaning back in his chair, wondering if this wasn't a weekend learning about being a private investigator at all, but an excuse to just sit around and eat like a king. Which, if he was honest, he was more than happy to do because that idea sounded a lot more palatable than having to put up with Walsh and his insufferable stories.

Jameson had, in his time, met plenty of coppers who could tell a tale or two. He was one of them himself, after all, and everyone enjoyed talking up their own exploits now and again. Walsh, though ... well, he was something else entirely. And if he was to be believed, thought Jameson, then the man had single-handedly helped solve more crimes and dodgy goings on than every police officer put together. A man who clearly enjoyed the sound of his own voice, he had managed to drone on for most of the meal, bigging himself up further and further with every course. Jameson had no doubt that the man was simply trying to impress, to make sure that everyone would be confident in the skills and experience of the man they had paid to come and learn from. All it made Jameson want to do was leave, because really, there was only so much utter bollocks he could listen to.

With the meal over, and Walsh drawing yet another story to a close, the young chef cleared everything away and was now serving everyone drinks, having taken orders and popped through to the bar over in the lounge. Jameson was sitting next to Kirsty and had discovered that her reason for being there was very personal.

'I'm here because my friend was scammed,' she explained, her voice quiet. 'And it very nearly destroyed her.'

'What happened?' Jameson asked.

'She needed money, couldn't go to the banks, and ended up asking for help from the wrong type of person, if you know what I mean. Even tried to pay them off with jewellery her mum had given her. It was nothing much, just a bit of gold, but it meant the world, you know?'

Jameson did, all too well.

'I'm very sorry to hear that,' he said.

'So was I,' said Kirsty. 'Which was why I had to do something. It took a while, but I found them eventually, the person responsible, I mean.'

'Really?' Jameson said. 'That's risky, going after someone like that; you never know what they'll do.'

He'd dealt with loan sharks in his time. Most of them had been grubby little scrags, but a few had been proper nasty pieces of work. They preyed on the weak and the desperate, offered a way out, but with a catastrophically high interest rate. And some of them weren't shy in using violence and intimidation to get their money.

'I guess,' said Kirsty.

'And how's your friend now?' Jameson asked.

'Better,' said Kirsty, with a smile Jameson could see was genuine. 'Much better, actually, thank you.'

'And now you're here.'

'Yes, I am.'

'Makes more sense than it does for me, I have to say,' Jameson said, realising then that their conversation was being listened in on.

He looked up to see Tony staring at them over a glass of wine. Sitting beside him was the man with the beard whose name Jameson still didn't know.

'Sounds like you're a natural,' Tony said, looking at Kirsty.

'I agree with Pete, though,' said the man with the beard. 'You were lucky. Someone like that? There's no telling what they won't do if they suspect you're on to them.'

'I didn't catch your name,' Jameson said.

'I didn't give it to you,' was the brisk reply, but then the man said, 'I'm Scott Williams.'

'What's your background?' Jameson asked, though he could easily have guessed.

'Military,' Scott said. 'Left a few months ago. Was thinking of heading into the prison service, but not sure I can hack being locked in all the time, you know? Thought I'd find out about this. Matches my skill set, anyway.'

That was an interesting statement, Jameson thought, but decided to not press further.

At the end of the table, Hazeem and Yalina Rasheed were busy talking to Carl Walsh, the man clearly enjoying the chance to tell yet more stories. He had been moving around the group during the meal, but they had somehow managed to corner him for longer than anyone else, not that Jameson was all that bothered. As for the Rasheeds, all he had learned about them so far was that they had run a number of businesses together, made plenty of money, and now fancied doing something that was focused more on helping people than the bottom line.

Jameson tried to catch what they were talking about, but no sooner had he managed to tune in than Walsh was standing up, signalling for everyone's attention.

'Right then,' he said. 'Who's up for a nice little murder mystery, then?'

Inside, Jameson died a little, but on the outside, he managed an almost enthusiastic nod.

'Excellent,' Walsh said. 'So, here's what's going to happen. I'm going to set up a crime scene back in the lounge. Won't take long, I promise. The signal will be the sound of a gun being fired. Once you hear that, wait for one minute, then come on in.'

Jameson was a little shocked to hear this and judging by the murmuring around the table, so was everyone else.

'I'm sorry, what?' said Tony. 'A gun?'

Walsh held up his hands in an attempt to calm everyone down.

'Firstly, I have a gun license. Secondly, it's a starter pistol. Fires blanks. All part of the drama and excitement, you see?'

'And what then?' Scott asked.

Walsh pulled out six envelopes from a jacket pocket and walked around the table, handing them out.

'These are your characters,' he said. 'There's a back story for each one, and for the victim, and you will all be expected to come in and examine me and the crime scene, first as a group, so you can all see what's there, then individually, so that you can have a really good look around. How does that sound?'

'Absolutely ridiculous,' Hazeem said, shaking his head. 'This isn't a joke, you know.'

'I know,' said Walsh, 'and neither is it ridiculous, I promise you. It's simply a fun way to get you all in the mood for being an investigator and looking for clues. You just have to relax a little and join in.'

'Well, I think it sounds great,' said Tony.

'That's what I like to hear,' said Walsh. 'Well done, Tony! Now, like I said, once you hear the gun go off, in you come!'

With a dramatic wave, Walsh left the room, heading out into the hall, and pulling the dining room door shut behind him.

'He's an odd one, that's for sure,' said Jameson. 'Best we just go with it, though; it's not like we're going anywhere, is it?'

For a moment or two, and with the food now finished, no one said a word. In the quiet, Jameson heard a door open and close, and again a few seconds later, and assumed that Walsh was popping in and out of the lounge as he sorted out what he had planned.

The group opened their envelopes to read the character sheets Walsh had given them, and once again started to chat and get to know each other. Jameson found himself almost daring to relax, something he'd never really been all that good at. Well, not unless Ellen was with him. And he supposed that she still was in some way, the memory of her a permanent resident in his mind and heart.

The sound of a gun going off made everyone in the dining room, bar Scott, jump.

'He wasn't kidding, was he?' said Tony. 'One minute then ...'

Jameson checked his watch, counted down sixty seconds, then stood up.

'Well, let's get on with this then, shall we?' he said.

The chef, who was still in the room, said, 'I'll just stay here. When you come back, I can take another drinks order if you want.'

Leading the way out of the dining room and across the hall, Jameson pushed open the lounge door. Inside, the first thing he saw was Walsh on the floor by the fire, his head and face covered by a large hat. He had changed, too, and was dressed in scruffy jeans and a black, baggy jumper, leather gloves on his hands.

The coffee table was now under the far window, which was wide open, snow slipping in as though the world outside was breathing through the gap. The desk looked like it had shifted a little as well, though he wasn't entirely sure about that.

There was something else, too, he thought, staring at the desk, but what, he wasn't really sure. He scanned the room, the walls, the floor, but whatever it was, it was staying just out of reach for his weary mind to grasp. Then, just as he thought he had something, a voice interrupted his thoughts.

'So, what are we looking for, then?' Kirsty asked. 'I've not actually been to many murder scenes. By which I mean none.'

'Well, I have,' Jameson said. 'And that's not a brag, I promise you.'

'Then maybe we should defer to you for now,' suggested Yalina. 'That way we might all learn something.'

'Great idea!' said Walsh from his position on the floor.

Jameson couldn't help but laugh.

'Corpses don't usually talk,' he said. 'Though they can make odd noises and move a bit,' he added.

'Really?' said Tony.

Jameson frowned, staring at the young doctor for a moment.

'As a body decomposes, gas escapes from inside the body,' he explained. 'Depends how long a body has been left, obviously. I'm not saying that they get up and dance, but like I said, they do move. And when you hear air and gas escaping from the mouth of a corpse, you have some understanding of why centuries ago, people worried that the dead might walk.'

'Well, thanks for that,' said Kirsty. 'Not disturbing at all.'

'What next, then?' Hazeem asked.

'For this, we're going to assume he's dead,' Jameson said. 'In real life, you'd want to make sure. And, if he was, then we would still need the district surgeon to come out and confirm it. We'd have the photographer, and the scene of crime team and pathologist, come out to collect evidence.'

'You mean CSI?' asked Tony.

'The terms are interchangeable,' said Jameson. 'Both are used. Anyway, if we assume as well that we are first on the scene and are the ones who've found the body—'

'Which we are,' said Yalina.

'—then I'd do my best to examine the crime scene without disturbing it.'

'And what would you be looking for, exactly?' Kirsty asked.

Jameson shoved his hands into his pockets, slipping easily into the role of tutor, which rather surprised him.

'There's lots of fancy stuff you can read up on,' he said, 'and obviously there's always the forensics stuff, the crime scene photographs, that kind of thing. But I have a very simple rule, one that I've always lived by.'

'Well, what is it?' asked Hazeem.

'You're looking for two things,' Jameson said, then pulled his left hand out of his pocket and held up a finger. 'One, you're trying to find things that should be there, but aren't. And second,' —He held up another finger— 'you're trying to find things that shouldn't be there, but are.'

The group fell silent.

'Should be there but isn't and shouldn't be there but is, right?' said Scott. 'I like that. Simple.'

'And effective,' Jameson added. 'Look ...' He pointed over at the coffee table. 'That's been moved, right? And the window's open. Certainly, it wasn't like that when we were in here earlier, was it? And I might be imagining it, but the desk looks like it's shifted a little as well. So, you have to ask why, don't you? Worth keeping an eye out for other things, too,' he continued. 'Cigarette butts, chewing gum wrappers, receipts; the kinds of things that fall out of pockets without people noticing.'

Jameson was on a roll now, slipping into his old job far too easily, like he had pulled on a favourite jumper.

'There's one question we should all be asking, isn't there?' he said, standing up to cast a look around the group, looking for an answer.

After a moment or two of silence, Scott spoke up, and judging by the tone of his voice, he was as surprised as Jameson that no one else had got it.

'The gun,' he said. 'We heard it. So where is it?'

'Exactly,' said Jameson. 'And as our victim is currently lying on his front, and we can see no exit wound, we can't be sure that he was shot.'

'But we heard the gun,' said Kirsty.

'We did, but that's all,' said Jameson. 'For all we know, the killer fired the gun as a distraction. Maybe it's outside the window. Maybe it's under the body. Maybe he wasn't shot at all. Also, why is he wearing gloves? And what's with the hat? You see, that's how your mind has to work; ask questions and keep asking them until you start getting some answers.'

'I'm impressed,' said Scott. 'You really know your stuff.'

'I was a DCI,' said Jameson. 'Detective chief inspector, I mean, like Walsh said earlier. Did the job for so long it becomes second nature.'

Deciding he'd said enough, Jameson then stepped back and allowed everyone else to have a look at the body, and to examine the room. Yalina, he noticed, immediately stepped away from her husband to examine the crime scene herself, while Hazeem stood back, observing. Tony seemed to be more interested in the bar, and poured himself a drink. Kirsty took photos of the crime scene, and Scott headed over to the window. Soon, though, everyone was standing together again. And Jameson, realising he had somehow managed to put himself up as the leader of the group, at least for now, led them all back over to the dining room, where they found the chef sitting on a chair in the corner staring at his phone.

'So, who wants to go first, then?' Jameson asked. 'You'll probably all be thinking there's nothing else to see or find, but it's not just about that. Sometimes, just looking at a crime scene again, even when it's very, very cold, can get you thinking in a new way about something.'

Scott raised a hand. 'I'll go,' he said. 'There's footprints outside the window in the snow, so I'm going to have a closer look at those for a start.'

He left the room and was out for a good ten minutes. When he came back into the dining room, Kirsty took his place. She was a little quicker, and Jameson watched Hazeem and Yalina hesitate just enough to have Tony try and get in front of them.

'Won't be long,' he said, and made to head out of the room, only to be cut off at the pass by the Rasheeds. Ignoring Walsh's request, they headed off together. When they returned, they moved quickly to a corner of the room to discuss in hushed tones what they had seen.

Jameson glanced over to Tony, who said, 'You go. I don't mind waiting.'

Jameson headed over, staying long enough to make it look like he was interested. When he came back, Tony walked off to take his turn alone.

When, barely two minutes later, he came back, however, the young doctor crashed through the door, fear scrawled across his face.

'He's ... he's dead!' he said.

'What?' said Jameson, staring across the room, wondering if the man had decided to go a little am-dram on them all for no reason.

'Walsh; he's actually dead! Like dead-dead. He's dead!'

'He's the victim,' laughed Kirsty. 'Of course he is.'

'No, you don't understand,' said Tony. 'He's dead He's really properly dead.'

A chill fell across Jameson like he'd just stepped into a cold shower. He walked over to Tony.

'You're sure of this?'

'We need to call the police,' Tony said. 'He's dead. Walsh is dead!'

Jameson turned to the rest of the group, who were now more than a little agitated.

Jack, the chef, was, for the first time, front and centre, and walked up to Jameson.

'He can't be dead,' he said, shock in his voice. 'It's impossible. He just can't be.'

'Probably best I go and have a look,' Jameson said. 'Retired I may be, but I'm still the most qualified here to deal with this and see what's actually happened.'

Jack tried to push past Jameson.

'I'm going to have a look,' Jack said. 'There's just no way ...'

Jameson held up a hand to stop the chef from going any further, resting a firm hand against his chest.

'Stay here,' he said.

Jack pushed, but Jameson held fast.

For a moment, he wasn't sure that Jack was going to take any notice. Then he relented.

'He can't be dead, though,' he said. 'He just can't. You don't understand ...'

'Stay here,' Jameson said. 'All of you.'

He then turned to Tony and gestured for the doctor to lead the way.

In the lounge, Jameson saw that Walsh was still on the floor. He noticed that he wasn't in quite the same place as before, as though he'd shuffled around a bit.

'Tell me everything,' Jameson said, checking his watch to see that the time was six-thirty, if only to give him a rough idea of the time of death.

'There's nothing to tell,' said Tony. 'I thought I'd check the crime scene first, so I went over, knelt down, and then I noticed that Walsh wasn't breathing. So, I checked his pulse, because I'm a doctor, right, like I've told you? And it's what we do, isn't it, check stuff like that? But then I saw it. That's when I came in and told you.'

'Saw what exactly?' Jameson asked, glancing around the room, a little confused.

Tony pointed over at the body.

Jameson stared, edged a little closer.

'That,' said Tony.

Sticking out of Walsh's back, and barely visible in the folds of the baggy jumper Walsh was wearing, was the slim, black handle of a knife.

CHAPTER FOURTEEN

'WELL, THIS IS LOVELY AND COSY, ISN'T IT?' SAID MARINA, AS she snuggled up on the sofa, a thick, fleece blanket pulled up over her knees, her legs tucked underneath her. She was already warm thanks to the hot bath she'd just climbed out of, but also because of the thick dressing gown she was now wearing. In front of her, the wood burning stove burned brightly, tongues of yellow and orange licked at the glass window in the door. Outside, wind hammered at the window. She'd left the curtains open so that she could see the snow, and it was banking up against the glass.

In Marina's hand was a generous glass of red wine. She took a sip, then another, and sunk deeper into the soft cushions around her, soaking in every glorious moment.

She picked up her phone, flicked through a few photos, placed it back down.

'Come on, darling,' she called. 'You're needed.'

'Just sorting us a little cheese board,' Harvey called back from the kitchen, his voice echoing across the hall. 'You warm enough?'

'I'm melting and it's lovely.'

'I'll take that as a yes, then.'

When Harvey walked into the room, closing the curtain across the window on the way, Marina leaned back to look at him over her shoulder. Like her, he was wearing his dressing gown, the thick, fleecy material as white as the snow falling heavily beyond the walls. He was carrying a thin wooden tray and came over to place it down on the coffee table, which rested on the dark brown sheepskin rug. Marina loved the way the rug felt on her toes and had been tempted to snuggle up there instead, but the sofa had won out. Just.

'Thought we could do with a few nibbles,' Harvey said.

'I think you've had enough nibbles for now, don't you?' she giggled.

Harvey feigned a look of shock.

'You saucy minx,' he said.

'You love it.'

They'd had a lovely first couple of days together and had certainly had a good go at making up for lost time. Not that they could squeeze in eight years of missed slap and tickle, as Harvey called it, and they weren't exactly in their twenties, but they'd certainly enjoyed being close enough again to have a good try.

Marina knew all about Harvey's life, everything he'd been mixed up in and done. But she loved him, always had, always would. And now here they were, just the two of them. She couldn't help feeling rather a bit giddy with it all.

Harvey came over and sat down beside Marina, holding his own glass, which he raised to his wife.

'Here's to us,' he said, 'and to new beginnings.'

'You do mean that, don't you?' Marina said, unable to disguise the concern in her voice.

'Of course I do,' said Harvey. 'With every part of my soul.'

'You won't go back, then? Back to your old life?'

Harvey shook his head.

'God, no. I'm done with all of that,' he said. 'Far too dangerous, and I'm much too old. The world's changed, Marina. No room in it for someone like me. Which is why I did what I did, so that we could leave it all behind and be here together now.'

'And we're safe?'

'The safest we've ever been,' said Harvey. 'New names, new identities. No one knows where we are, who we are, anything at all. For the rest of our lives, it's just you and me.'

'And this very delicious wine,' Marina said.

They chinked glasses, took a drink.

Harvey leaned back and Marina shuffled in close.

'I could get used to this,' she said with a sigh, and leaned in for a kiss, as a shotgun blast crashed through the house from the front door.

Marina, her ears ringing, screamed. Then came another blast, followed by the sound of splintering wood, voices ...

Harvey leapt up, spilling his wine, and knocking Marina's all over the sofa.

'Harvey? What's going on? What's happening?'

Harvey didn't answer. He raced over to the lounge door, grabbing a poker from the side of the stove as he went.

The lounge door burst open.

'Harvey!' Marina cried.

She saw shadows gathered on the other side of the door. Then Harvey was swinging the poker. He crashed it down onto the skull of a man barging into the room, the sickening thud like a coconut being hit by a hammer. The man dropped to the floor like a puppet with its strings cut.

Harvey yanked the poker out of the skull of the man on the floor, pushing against the body with his foot as he heaved it up to use it again. Someone else appeared in the door. A woman this time, Marina noticed. Harvey roared, thrusting the poker out like a spear, impaling her with it, the spiked end piercing a T-shirt and sinking into the body it covered. The woman roared in pain as Harvey pushed forward, driving the poker in deeper, forcing her out of the door.

'Get the hell out of here, Marina!' Harvey called back. 'Run!'

Marina wanted to do exactly that, but she couldn't move, couldn't speak.

Harvey was out in the hallway now and Marina had lost sight

of him completely. Then she saw him, fighting and tussling with shadows throwing themselves at him, Harvey pushing them back, the poker swinging and rising and falling, rising and falling. She heard screams, cries of pain, swearing. Then the house shuddered to the sound of another blast from a shotgun.

Silence.

Marina stared at the open door. Beyond it, the shadows had stopped moving.

'Harvey?'

No answer.

One of the shadows broke away from the others. Marina watched as it reached down to grab something heavy off the floor, then drag it through the door into the lounge.

'Hello, Marina.'

Marina recognised the man immediately.

'It's you,' she said. 'You were at the door yesterday. With a parcel. You're a delivery man! You can't be here, you can't be in our house! You can't! You—'

Marina's voice snapped in two when she realised what, or who, it was that the man had dragged into the lounge. In his other hand she saw the poker, blood dripping from it and onto the floor.

'He's still alive,' the man said, and Marina heard Harvey moan, as the man moved around to stand in front of the stove and dump Harvey's blood-soaked body onto the tray of cheese he had, just a few moments ago, carried through.

Marina realised then that she was holding the bottle of wine in her hand, her fingers clasped around the neck. She stared up at the man, tears clouding her vision, terror crushing her so hard she could barely breathe.

'Why?' was all she could manage, her voice a thing ripped to pieces like the shredded and bloody dressing gown Harvey was wearing.

'Your husband should've known better,' the man said. 'Grassing people up, giving names, thinking he could protect himself, protect you.'

Marina wasn't listening; instead, she was staring at Harvey, at his barely moving chest, at the blood.

The man stepped over Harvey's body and towards Marina.

'Because of what he's done, a message needs to be sent, you see? That's why we're here. What we're doing, it's a service, a way of telling others that the choices Harvey made? They were bad, Marina, real bad.'

He lifted the poker above his head.

'You might want to close your eyes for this bit,' he said.

Marina leapt from the sofa, bottle of wine swinging around in an arc, wine spraying from the open neck to cover her in claret. It connected with the side of the man's skull with a dull thud, the glass bursting around his head in a shower of green shards. He toppled, fell to his knees. The next thing Marina knew, she was on top of him, her hand still clutching the neck of the wine bottle, only now the ragged, jagged end of it was rammed deep into the man's throat. Blood foamed from the wound, bubbling out over his neck, its warmth creeping stickily across her hand.

Marina stared into the man's eyes, saw death in them.

She shuffled over to her husband, rolled him over, saw blood blooming on his chest.

'Harvey?'

A thin, hot breath escaped Harvey's lips.

Marina held him, hugged him, squeezed him, her face hot with rage and tears. She looked around for her phone, only to realise that the room was now busy with bodies. She counted four people standing in front of her now, three men, and the woman she had seen Harvey impale with the poker. She was holding her left hand against the wound and groaning through gritted teeth. One of the men stepped forward, and Marina saw, dangling from his left hand, a bike chain.

'Now then,' he said. 'Where were we?'

CHAPTER FIFTEEN

HARRY WAS BACK AT THE OFFICE IN HAWES AND COMING TO the end of his day. The snow had continued to fall and gradually the team had returned from their various outings, though Jadyn was the only one who had not returned alone. Detective Superintendent Walker, his acting D-Sup and replacement for Swift, had called for a quick chat. Harry wasn't entirely sure he would miss Swift, but he had certainly grown to respect the man more as they had got to know each other. The conversation with Walker had been little more than a catch-up and an update on various police matters, and Harry had chatted through how things were in the Dales. Now, however, he was staring at the clock on the wall, counting down to seven, and not because he would be heading home and then out for a pint or two with Dave Calvert; he was also expecting another call.

Having spent a while jotting down a few notes on the board about what had happened over at the Cowper's farm, Harry was rereading it all, wondering if he had missed anything. He had covered not only what he and Liz had been told, but what they'd observed, such as the dog, the gun, and the unlabelled bottle of booze Liz had found out in the woods, even all the stuff he had spotted in the hallway: the urns, the copper pipes.

Drawing his eyes away from the board with a yawn and a stretch, Harry looked over at Jadyn, who was sitting on the floor.

'Just what we need,' he said with a laugh. 'Another dog ...'

'I'm not keeping it,' said Jadyn, the grey dog—a Whippet according to the call Harry had received from Grace after Jadyn's visit—curled up on his lap.

'That's what I thought about Smudge,' said Harry. 'And yet, here we are.'

Hearing her name, Harry's black Labrador, who had spent most of the day curled up in the corner keeping warm by a radiator, wagged her tail. For a moment, she looked like she was going to stand up and come over for some fuss, but in the end, she just flopped down and curled up again with a contented huff.

Matt was no longer around; a call had come in from the mountain rescue team, and he'd rushed off. Something about a farmer in trouble out on the moors. Jadyn had stayed behind, the call not requiring the full complement of the rescue team. Matt had sent Harry a message a while later to tell him the farmer had been found, having half disappeared down an old foxhole, and breaking his ankle. He'd then headed home to Joan and their daughter.

'Anyone for another brew?' asked Jim, who was standing over at the urn and making himself a mug of tea.

Jen, who was on the computer with Liz, raised a hand.

'The Land Rover fared well enough, then?' Harry asked, as Jim walked over with Jen's drink.

'More than,' Jen said. 'Looks rough but drives like a dream. Took a while to clear the accident. The two drivers were very lucky; could've been a lot worse.'

Knowing the Buttertubs Pass, Harry could guess just how terrifying a crash up there must have been for those involved.

'Wasn't exactly anyone's fault,' said Jim. 'Bad weather, a difficult road, these things happen. No one was injured, which is the main thing.' He smiled. 'There was actually a fair bit more snow when we came back down. And it was great fun driving through it.'

'Have to feel sorry for the older bloke, though,' said Jen. 'He's not had the best of days, what with a trip to the vets with his dog, and now this.'

'His dog not doing too well, then?' Harry asked.

'He didn't really say much about it,' said Jen. 'Just that he'd had to leave her there and now, because of the accident, wouldn't be able to get over to see her when the vet called.'

'What about the other driver?'

'Young lad, bit shaken up,' said Jim. 'Both vehicles are now over at Mike's place, waiting for the insurance companies to pop by and have a look.'

Harry glanced over at the office window and darkness on the other side. 'The snow's really coming in though, isn't it? Which is making me a little worried.'

'About that farmer's lad, you mean?' said Jen.

Harry gave a nod.

'We've not heard anything, then?'

'No,' said Harry. 'I called earlier, but Mr Cowper seemed to be under the impression that what I really wanted wasn't news about his son at all, but my ear burning off as he yelled at me for ... Actually, I don't know what for; I couldn't make much of it out beyond the swearing.'

'Jane called you, though,' said Liz.

'I think she waited until her absolute delight of a husband was out,' Harry said. 'She's giving me another call in a couple of minutes.'

'What did she say?' Jim asked.

'That she was heading off up to the woods herself,' answered Harry. 'They've another quad bike and her husband hadn't taken it, so she was going to ride over on that, see if she could find her son herself and that little hideaway Liz stumbled on. Hopefully, Thomas is there, and she'll have him home. A mother's love, right?'

'And what if he isn't?' asked Jim.

'That's what concerns me,' Harry answered, his eyes on the clock again, as the hands moved forward and hit seven dead.

Harry continued to stare. Only his attention was now on the phone rather than the clock.

It didn't ring.

'She might still be on her way back,' said Liz.

'She said seven,' Harry said, pointing at the clock, then the phone. 'And it's seven. So, that phone should be ringing.'

A minute ticked by, then another.

'Right, that's it, I'm calling,' said Harry, and reached for the phone, but as he did so, it burst into life with a sharp trill. He snatched up the handset.

'DCI Grimm.'

'It's Jane,' said a quiet voice. 'Jane Cowper.'

'Did you find him?' Harry asked. 'Is Thomas okay?'

Harry heard Jane try and speak, but her voice choked on her words, strangled by a cry.

'Jane? What's wrong?'

All Harry could hear was sobbing.

'Jane, you need to tell me what's happened. Just take your time, okay?'

Harry saw that the rest of the team had hushed and were now all staring at him expectantly.

'I'm out at the woods right now,' Jane said. 'I've been shouting for him for the past half hour at least, but there's no answer. I found that little den of his, but there was no sign of him. So, I went back to where I'd parked up, next to the other quad bike, the one he'd taken? Only it wasn't there. Just these tracks, heading off.'

'Tracks?' Harry said. 'What tracks?'

'I think he's gone round the woodland and headed up into the fells,' Jane said. 'But that's all I know. I've no idea where he thinks he's going because there's nowt out there for a good long while, not until you hit the track taking you over to Kidstones. It's so bleak and the moors are treacherous at the best of times, but with the weather like this? I just don't know what he's thinking. I've had a look at the map, like, and the direction he's heading, he could end up at Kidstones, like I said, but the weather … I mean …'

Jane started to cry again.

'Jane, you're sure he's gone, yes?'

'I've even checked all the barns,' she said. 'There's a couple out that way, and it was a bugger getting to them, but they're empty. He's gone. He's just gone!'

Harry glanced over at Jadyn, clicking his fingers to get the constable's attention.

'I'm calling mountain rescue,' Harry said. 'Jane, you need to get back home, out of the snow. Tell Brian what's happening. The next person you hear from will be one of my team to tell you they're on their way.'

'Thank you,' Jane said, and disconnected the call.

Jadyn was on his feet, the Whippet in his arms.

'You may as well call this in yourself,' Harry said, looking over at the constable. 'You know the details, but just to be clear: we have a missing teenage boy, Thomas Cowper, last seen early afternoon heading out of Marsett on a quad bike. An initial search was carried out, and though he wasn't found, on the discovery of a shelter in the woods, we had good reason to believe he was safe. Also, Liz was pretty sure Thomas was in the wood when she was there. We now believe that Thomas has moved on from the wood, but we don't know where exactly. He is on a quad bike. We have no idea what he has with him, whether he is appropriately dressed or not, or if he has a destination in mind. No doubt the rescue team will want to speak with Mr and Mrs Cowper both on the phone and in person; Liz will provide you with their number and address.'

'One problem,' said Jadyn.

'And what's that?' Harry asked.

'This,' said Jadyn, gesturing to the small dog still curled up in his arms. 'I can't take him with me, can I?'

'No, I suppose not,' said Harry.

Jen said, 'I'll take him.'

'What about Steve?' asked Jadyn.

'Oh, Steve can look after himself,' said Jen. 'He's used to dogs anyway, so there's no problem if I have to take that one home with me.'

Jadyn knelt to let the Whippet go, but the dog made no move at all to climb out of his embrace.

'I need you to move,' Jadyn said, talking to the dog. 'I've got a job to do, and you can't come, you see ...'

Jen lifted herself out of her chair and met Jadyn halfway across the office floor. She knelt down and gently lifted the Whippet into her own arms. The dog lifted its head to stare at her for a moment, before gently licking the tip of her nose.

'Well, that's you won over, isn't it?' said Harry.

As Jadyn moved away to call the mountain rescue team, the phone rang once again.

Liz answered it.

'Is that Jane again?' Harry asked. 'You can tell her then that we're contacting the rescue team right n—'

When Liz turned to look at Harry, her eyes were wide, her face pale.

'What is it? What's happened?'

Liz said nothing, wrote down a few notes, then finished the call.

'We've had another call in from up beyond Marsett, would you believe it?' she said.

'They've found Thomas?' asked Jen.

'No,' said Liz. 'It's not Thomas, it's something else.'

'What's happened?' Harry asked.

'They've found a body,' said Liz.

Harry couldn't quite believe what he was hearing.

'Who has? What body? Where?'

'Out the back of Marsett,' she said.

'But we were up there only a few hours ago,' said Harry. 'Where exactly? And what do you mean by a body? Is it an accident?'

'There's a house at the end of the lane,' Liz explained, and handed Harry the notes she had written. 'Some private investigator weekend or something being held there. The person running it has been found dead.'

Harry read the note, looked back up at Liz.

'You sure this is the name you were given?' he said.

Liz nodded.

'I am,' she said. 'He called it in just a few minutes ago. The body is in the lounge, with a stab wound to the back.'

'What's wrong?' Jen asked. 'Beyond the stab wound, I mean.'

'Remember at my housewarming party,' Harry said. 'Grace had invited an old friend of mine from down south?'

Jen frowned, thinking. 'That old DCI,' she said. 'The one who had all those stories about you. What about him?'

Harry showed Jen Liz's notes.

'He's the one who put in the call.'

CHAPTER SIXTEEN

AFTER THE TROUBLE HE'D HAD WITH TRYING TO GET THE Rav4 started just a few hours ago, Harry decided it was best to leave the vehicle in Hawes and take the new Land Rover. The snow had been on the way to getting bad when he and Liz had last been up in Marsett. Since then, more had fallen, and for the past couple of hours, it had turned from a shower to a storm. The Land Rover, then, was a much safer bet.

With Jadyn being picked up by Helen Dinsdale, another member of the mountain rescue team who, despite the name, was no relation of Matt's, and who lived just a five-minute walk out of Hawes on the road to Appersett, Harry decided to leave Jen, with her new pal the unnamed Whippet, manning the office while he and Liz headed back up to Marsett.

In the time it had taken him to pull on his jacket, Jim had been called by his dad asking for urgent help. Not with his own flock, because he'd managed to get them all in before the weather had worsened. However, another farmer in Burtersett hadn't been quite so lucky thanks to a run-in with a patch of ice that had flipped him off his bike. He'd been checked over and there were no broken bones, but because of the accident, he'd been unable to get the rest of his sheep in. So, Jim, his dad, and Fly were heading out into the snow to gather them in for him.

With Liz next to him, and Smudge clipped in the back, Harry eased the Land Rover out of the marketplace and on towards their destination. The road was white, and the few vehicles foolish enough to be out on it soon had their tracks erased by the squalls chasing them onward. The snow was so heavy now that it was like driving through fog. Harry did his best to not stare at it, the snow flying at them like a swarm of bees exploding dramatically on the windshield.

Hawes looked beautiful in the snow, Harry thought; there was just no getting away from the fact. Golden light shone out through cracks between curtains, thin swords cutting through the snow. Roofs wore thick, fluffy caps of white, and gardens were lunar land-scapes now, lumpy with bushes and sleeping perennials hunkered down under the ever-thickening blanket. The fells were hidden from view, the snow an impenetrable wall behind which the night was coal dark and fathomless.

Climbing up the hill from the main road to Burtersett, Harry couldn't deny that the look of the Land Rover was no measure of its capability. Slopes were managed with ease, the vehicle crunching through the freezing crust, pulling them effortlessly through the village and onward.

Harry tried to spot Jim and his father out in the hills, but he could see nothing beyond the dipped beam of the headlights, and it seemed for a while as though they were adrift in a sea without end, white waves crashing against them as they motored on.

Marsett came out of the snow with eerie force, the houses dark, the lights from the windows little more than the glow of candles in an endless cavern of night. Driving past the Cowpers', Harry was tempted to stop, but continued on; the mountain rescue team were on their way, and wherever Thomas had taken himself, they would soon be out to find him.

'The house is just ahead,' Liz said, pointing through the wind-shield. 'You can't miss it.'

Harry leaned forward, slowed down, strained his eyes to see, but there was nothing in front of them but snow. Then the house was there, rising up out of the ground as though it had just dropped out of the endless sky.

'Nice place, isn't it?' said Liz, as Harry crept into the car park in front of the house, pulling up next to a Porsche thick with snow.

'Imagine the upkeep though,' said Harry. 'Own a place like this and you end up spending half your time trying to stop it falling down and the other half finding the money to do it.'

Liz laughed.

'Says the man who's just moved into an old cottage,' she said.

Leaving Smudge in the back, Harry went to open his door, only to find that it required a hefty shove with his shoulder to get it to move. Then he was out in the snow, surprised to find that it was at least a foot deep.

He turned to look along the way they had just come, down the lane and back to Marsett. The tracks left by the Land Rover were deep tramlines. He saw drifts forming against the walls, their tails stretching across the road, while spindrift danced between them. He caught a faint howl on the wind, an ethereal call out of time and the distant stars.

'Let's get inside quick,' he said, checking his watch to see that the time was now rolling on towards a quarter to eight. 'And pray that when we come back out again, we won't be completely snowed in.'

That said, Harry dashed across to the large front door, Liz in step beside him, and knocked.

A heartbeat later, the door opened, the light from the small window casting itself across the parking area like a searchlight.

'Well, then,' said the man now standing in front of Harry, bathed in the warm glow of the house behind him.

'Indeed,' said Harry.

'You'll be wanting to come in, then, I suppose?'

'That's usually how this works,' Harry said. 'As you well know.'

The man held out a hand.

'I'd like to say it's good to see you, Harry,' he said. 'But all things considered, it isn't really, is it?'

'No, it isn't,' Harry replied, shaking the outstretched hand, and stepping out of the snow and into the house. 'Not like this, anyway.'

Liz followed him inside and the man shut the door behind them.

Harry, for once, was momentarily lost for words. He'd not seen his old mentor and friend in a good few years, and now, here the man was, standing in front of him for the second time in barely three months.

'Pete,' Harry said, 'this is PCSO Liz Coates. Liz, you remember Pete, I'm sure? He was at that little housewarming Grace organised before Christmas.'

'DCI Jameson,' Liz said, and held out a hand. 'If you don't mind me saying so, you've confused the hell out of the Boss by being here.'

'I was going to give you a call, on my way up yesterday,' Jameson said looking at Harry, 'but to be honest, I thought you'd just laugh.'

'And why would I do that?' Harry asked. 'A detective chief inspector, retired and taking it easy, suddenly turning up at a weekend for wannabe private investigators? Nothing to laugh at there, now, is there?' He shook his head then, emphasising the point. 'Nope, not a thing here that is in any way amusing. Not least because of the reason my colleague and I have been called out here. Where is it, then?'

'The body? It's in the lounge, through there,' Jameson said, pointing to a door on his left at the bottom of the stairs. 'The doctor's the only one who's touched it or been close enough to. I've kept everyone out, preserved the crime scene.'

'Where are they?'

Jameson pointed at another door, this one on their right.

'In there,' he said. 'That's the dining room. All in a bit of shock, too, as you can well imagine. The chef's trying to keep their mind off it with some food and a drink or two.'

Harry shook his head in disbelief.

'There's a chef? What kind of Let's Play PI weekend has a chef?'

Jameson gave a shrug.

'The food's good,' he said. 'And it was a good job he was here, really. Phone signal's terrible, so I had to use the shortwave radio the house has to call this in; once he'd calmed down after the news of what had happened to Walsh, he was able to show me where it was. He's in the kitchen sorting sandwiches for everyone at the moment.'

'The house has a shortwave radio?' Harry said. 'Really? Why?'

Liz said, 'Some farms still do, though it's not as common now. In the days before mobile phones, if the lines went down, they'd have a way to communicate with the outside world and with each other. A lot of vehicles used to have CB radios.'

'Well, you learn something every day, don't you?' said Jameson. 'So, where do you want to start?'

Harry rubbed his chin, gave a scar a scratch.

'Well, where I want to start and where I have to are two different things right now, aren't they?' he said. 'And my guess is that whatever brought you here is what a certain friend of mine would call a four-pint problem.'

'Dave Calvert, right?' said Liz.

Harry smiled.

'The body, then?' said Jameson.

'The body,' nodded Harry, quickly pulling from a pocket a pair of thin, rubber gloves, and some shoe protectors. Liz did the same and handed some spares she had with her to Jameson. Then they all headed through the lounge door.

The room was cold, Harry noticed, his eyes immediately sweeping the space in front of him and taking in the dying fire in the grate and the open window in the wall opposite. The body was clear to see, lying facedown in front of the fire, surrounded by sofas which stared down at it with silent disregard. The face and most of the head were covered by a large hat. The victim was wearing gloves, the right hand visible, though the left hand was tucked under the body.

'You're going to have to run me through everything,' Harry said. 'Though, right now my worry is the scene of crime team.'

'There's no way they'll be able to get those vans of theirs up here,' agreed Liz. 'It was easy for us, but it's only going to get worse.'

'And I'm not having Margaret drive up here either,' said Harry. 'Though I'm fairly sure she'd give it a good try.'

'Margaret?' asked Jameson.

'District surgeon,' Harry explained. 'She's both terrifying and delightful all at once. You'd love her. And her daughter's the pathologist.'

Jameson laughed.

'That's keeping it in the family, isn't it?' he said.

'We'll just have to do the best we can,' said Harry. 'Preserve everything, let them know what we've got, and just wait it out. Liz?'

'Yes, boss?'

'You mind taking photos of the crime scene on your phone? It's the best we can do at the moment, but at least we'll have a record of everything as it is right now.'

Liz pulled out her phone and started taking photos.

Harry looked at Jameson.

'Anyway, where were we?' he asked.

'You were asking me to run through everything,' Jameson replied. 'Trouble is, I'm not really sure where to begin. I've been trying to get my head round it, but nothing makes sense.'

'On that, we are very much agreed,' said Harry, and with Liz having finished taking photos of the body, walked over for a closer look.

He could see a small knife jutting out of its back. He hadn't noticed it when he'd first entered the room, even though he'd known it was there. The black of the handle was close to invisible, hidden by both the colour of the jumper the victim was wearing, and the folds of the material rucked up around it.

'Who found him?' he asked.

'Tony Pearson,' Jameson said. 'He's the doctor, like I said. He saw that Walsh wasn't breathing, checked for a pulse, then saw the knife. And now, here we are.'

'You said no one else other than you and this doctor has been in the room?'

'We were all in here to begin with as a group,' Jameson explained. 'That was part of the murder mystery thing, before Walsh was found dead. Then we all headed back into the lounge before being given the opportunity to look at the crime scene again, this time on our own.'

'And you're sure the room looks the same as when you were last in here?'

'Yes,' said Jameson. 'That was, what, just over an hour ago, perhaps?'

'The window was open as well?'

'It was.'

'And you're sure he was alive when you were all in here?'

'Very much so.'

'Any reason?' Harry asked. 'If he's playing dead, then ...'

'He was talking to us,' said Jameson. 'And one thing I've learned over the years is that dead bodies don't talk.'

'They do move and make a noise now and again though,' said Harry.

'You know, I told everyone that earlier. Not sure that they believed me. Even Tony seemed surprised.'

'He's the doctor.'

'I've only known him a few hours, I know,' said Jameson, 'and I'm not one for casting dispersions, but he doesn't strike me as the kind of person I'd want on the other end of a scalpel or a needle, if you know what I mean.'

Harry fell quiet for a moment.

'Fetch him,' he said. 'Best I have a quick word with him first, I think, before I speak to the group as a whole.'

Jameson returned with a young man who had fear in his eyes.

'Tony Pearson?' Harry said, walking over to meet him on the other side of the lounge door, out in the hall.

'Yes?'

'I'm DCI Grimm. I understand it was you who found the body.'

'Not exactly,' Tony replied. 'I didn't find it; we all knew it was there because we'd seen him when we were in the room as a group. It was only when I came in on my own afterwards. That's when I noticed.'

'The knife?'

Tony shook his head.

'No, not that, not at first anyway. I didn't notice it at all. It was the fact that he wasn't breathing, Walsh I mean. That's what I noticed. So, I checked his pulse, couldn't find one. Then I saw the knife.'

'Did you move the body at all?' Harry asked.

Tony shook his head.

'I checked his pulse, that's all. I didn't dare touch anything.'

Harry looked at Jameson and said, 'So, no one's touched the body?'

'Not since Tony here came bursting in through the dining room door to tell us Walsh was dead, no,' Jameson replied. 'Before that, everyone took their turn in here to have a look around, even me. Tony was last.'

'I was,' Tony confirmed.

Harry asked Tony to return to the dining room.

Alone again with Liz and Jameson, Harry said, 'You know what this means, don't you? Everyone had an opportunity to use the knife.'

'Even me,' Jameson said.

Harry heard a murmur from Liz and looked over at the PCSO.

'Penny for your thoughts,' he said.

'It doesn't make any sense,' answered Liz. 'Why would anyone risk stabbing him? I know the knife's difficult to see, but even so. And stabbing someone isn't easy, is it? The knife is in his back, and that takes some force to bury it that deep.'

'How do you mean?' Harry asked.

'I'm just saying,' continued Liz, 'that stabbing him like that, when everyone is taking their turn to come into the room, you're risking being found out straight away, aren't you? You come in, stab him, the next person in the room is going to see the knife. And killing someone with a knife, it's usually multiple wounds, isn't it?'

'Thought you said you were a PCSO?' Jameson.

Liz gave a smile.

'I am, but I'm always learning,' she said. 'And roles are kind of blurred with this team.' She looked up at Harry and asked, 'Shall I call the SOC team, then?'

'You'll need to use the radio rather than your phone,' said Jameson, moving to head off down the hall. 'I'll show you where it is.'

Harry said, 'Tell Sowerby we won't be expecting her, or anyone else, here any time soon, not with the weather like this.'

When Jameson returned from taking Liz to the radio, Harry asked, 'Who was the last person in here before the doctor?'

'You're not going to like the answer,' Jameson said.

Harry hung his head and rubbed his eyes, then looked over at his old friend.

'It was you, wasn't it?'

'It was,' said Jameson. 'Which makes me—'

'Prime suspect,' Harry said. 'Bollocks ...'

CHAPTER SEVENTEEN

'WELL, I DIDN'T KILL HIM, IF THAT'S WHAT YOU'RE THINKING,' Jameson said.

'Of course you bloody well didn't!' Harry said, unable to disguise the contempt for the idea in his voice. 'What would be the motive? That the food was a bit off?'

'No, not that,' said Jameson. 'But I can tell you this; the man was an insufferable pratt. Needed a proper slap. Not with a hand either, something bigger. Like a whale.'

'Don't hold back, now,' said Harry.

Jameson shook his head.

'Sorry, but he was so full of himself. Endless stories about his exploits. You'd think he wasn't just a PI, but Magnum, Poirot, John McClane, and Dirty Harry all rolled into one.'

'You're not a fan, then?' said Liz, having rejoined them after calling in the cavalry.

'Which begs the question of why you were here at all,' said Harry. 'But like I said, that's a four-pinter and we can talk about that later.'

'There was definitely something about him that stank a bit, though,' said Jameson. 'Not just the bragging, but the ... I don't know ... something.'

'Well, that's mysterious,' said Harry. 'What do you mean, exactly?'

'Not entirely sure,' Jameson said with a shrug and shake of his head. 'He was behaving a bit strangely, but then maybe that was just his way; rather over the top and dramatic. Then there's that car of his, isn't there?'

'Which car?' Liz asked.

'You passed it,' said Jameson. 'It's the clearly very new Porsche. How does a private investigator make enough money to own something like that?'

'Good question,' said Harry.

'Is it?' asked Liz. 'Why?'

'The pay is more second-hand Ford Mondeo than shiny new Porsche, that's why,' said Jameson.

'A PI usually earns around thirty grand, I think,' Harry explained. 'A few years in the job, a good CV, and you can earn double that. But it's still not enough to cover wheels like those out there in the car park, that's for sure.'

'Maybe he came into a bit of inheritance,' suggested Liz. 'Happens, doesn't it? Someone dies, leaves a bit of money; why not splash it on new wheels?'

'That's possible,' said Jameson, but then he turned his attention once again to the body on the floor. 'But my gut tells me there's something else at play. And whatever that maybe, it's led to this.'

'You may well be right,' Harry said. 'But if we're going to unravel any of this and find out what that could be, we need to start from the beginning.'

'Agreed,' said Jameson as Liz gave her nod of approval.

'First, I'll need the details of everyone on-site,' Harry explained. 'Then I'll need to interview them so we can try and establish where they were, what they were doing, the usual.'

'I've already collected names and whatnot,' said Jameson, and handed Harry a notebook. 'Yeah, I still carry one. Old habits, and all that.'

Harry took the notebook.

'Six suspects,' he said.

'Seven, actually,' said Jameson. 'I didn't put my own name down seeing as you know it well enough yourself.'

Harry turned to Liz.

'There's no way Sowerby or anyone else is going to be getting to us for a good while yet, but I'll still need you to guard the crime scene while I conduct the voluntary interviews.'

Liz nodded in agreement.

Jameson glanced over at Liz and said, 'You'll find a chair in the dining room. Just post yourself outside the door. No one comes in here other than Harry.'

Harry tapped Jameson on the shoulder, who turned around to find the gruff DCI staring at him.

'What?' said Jameson.

'You're retired, remember?' Harry said. 'And a suspect.'

'Ah, yes, right, sorry about that.'

Harry led Jameson and Liz out into the hall.

'Tell you what, I'll grab that chair from the dining room,' said Jameson, and led Harry over to the door opposite, pushing it open and leading him through into the room beyond.

Inside, Harry found six pairs of eyes all sweep around on him like searchlights. Jameson walked over to the table, picked up a chair, and took it outside to Liz, returning a few seconds later to stand beside Harry.

There were two women and four men in the room, of whom five were sitting around a large dining table. Two of the group were darker skinned than the others and clearly a couple, Harry noticed, as they sat at the table holding hands. The other woman was sitting on her own, her hands in her lap as she stared at her phone. Of the others, one had a hardened edge to him, and he looked fit, too, like what he did as a day job was physical. Next to him, Tony Pearson, the doctor they'd already met, seemed to be doing his best to disappear into his chair.

The last member of the group was a slim man leaning against the wall. He was wearing an immaculate white chef's top, over black trousers pinned in place with a brightly buckled belt. He too was staring at his mobile phone, clasped in his left hand, a deep frown on his face, as his thumb tapped furiously at the screen.

'How do,' he said, holding up his ID. Then quickly added, 'I mean, hello. I'm Detective Chief Inspector Grimm.'

Wensleydale, it seemed, was really getting under his skin, so much so that he was starting to talk like the locals.

'Obviously, you are all aware of the situation.'

'He's actually dead, then?' the chef asked, looking up from the screen of his phone.

Harry said, 'I, along with my colleague, PCSO Coates, are here to start the investigation. I've posted her outside the lounge, and no one is to enter that room, is that clear?'

Everyone nodded. The chef, Harry noticed, wasn't the only one shaking his head in disbelief.

'Good,' he said, and waved Jameson's notebook in front of him. 'I've everyone's details here, names anyway, but what I'll be needing now is a little chat with each of you in private.'

'We're suspects, you mean?' asked the woman sitting alone.

'Right now, what I need to do is to find out exactly what's been going on. And, just so you all know, these are voluntary interviews. No one here is being placed under arrest.'

'What do you mean by voluntary?' asked the other woman.

'Exactly that,' Harry replied. 'You don't have to attend and are free to leave at any point.' Harry paused, giving that a moment to sink in, then added, 'However, I do need to state that not attending can have serious consequences.'

'Not sure I like the sound of that,' said the man who was still holding her hand.

'Everyone has the right to silence,' Harry said, trying to explain things simply and in a way that would not cause concern. 'It is my duty, however, to make it clear that if a person is taken to court for an offence, providing explanations at that time that they did not offer when interviewed, can cast doubt on the truthfulness and validity of what is being said.'

Harry waited to see if there were any further questions. He was about to invite the first person over for a chat when he realised he didn't have an interview room. He called Jameson over and explained, and Jameson gave a nod to the chef, who walked over.

On hearing Harry's problem, the chef said, 'There's a room just down the hall. I can show you if you want?'

'That would be very useful,' Harry said, as the woman who had first spoken raised her hand.

'He was murdered, then, yes?' she said. 'That's what this is. That's what's happened. Walsh was murdered?'

'And you are ...?' asked Harry, not answering the question.

'Kirsty,' she replied, then added, 'Ms Kirsty Cropper.'

Harry cast his eyes across the group. It was hard to believe that any of them could be the killer, but then, wasn't that always the case? Murderers didn't have a look. Most times, they were no different than anyone else, just a normal person living a supposedly normal life, only with blood on their hands.

'Well then, Ms Cropper,' Harry said, 'how about you and I have the first chat, if you're okay with that?'

'Of course, yes, not a problem,' Kirsty replied, and walked over to stand with Harry.

Harry caught the eye of the chef.

'That room, then?' he said.

The chef stood up and walked to the door, stuffing his phone into his back pocket.

'This way,' he said, and led them out into the hall.

As they left the room, Jameson pulled him to one side.

'People are going to be needing toilet breaks at some point,' he said.

On the other side of the front door, Harry heard the wind howl and crash into the house like it was trying to get in.

'The storm's getting worse,' he said. 'Right now, I'm not exactly worried about anyone trying to make a run for it. Also, if I'm interviewing, then it's probably best I'm not on my own.'

'You want me to join in?' Jameson asked.

Harry almost laughed.

'Not entirely appropriate for numerous reasons,' he said. 'Liz?'

Liz Coates, who was now sitting on a chair outside the door to the lounge, looked over.

'You need something?'

'Yes,' said Harry. 'You, in the interviews, with me.' He looked at the chef who was standing with them. 'Don't suppose there's a key for that door now, is there?'

'I'll go check,' the chef said. 'There's a load of keys on hooks in the kitchen.'

The chef ran off and returned shortly after.

'They're all labelled,' he said, and handed Harry a large key.

Harry saw a plastic tag attached to a key with the word *Lounge* on it. Trying it in the door, he was pleased to feel it turn smoothly in the mechanism.

'Perfect,' he said. 'Liz, you're with me, then. Pete, my guess is, retired or not, that old police brain of yours is already nicely warmed up to keep an eye on things for me, just in case anyone starts looking a bit shifty, if you know what I mean. And you can monitor those toilet breaks as well, can't you?'

'Of course.'

'Don't forget though,' said Harry, 'you're still a suspect.'

'Understood.'

Ducking back into the dining room, Harry quickly explained that the lounge was out of bounds and locked. Then, leaving Jameson in the room with the others, he led Liz and Kirsty in following the chef. Soon they were in a small room beyond which Harry could see the kitchen.

Inside, the room was lined with bookshelves and furnished with a couple of comfy chairs, a cosy two-seater sofa, and a small table.

'Reading room or library or something, I think,' the chef said.

'Could you grab us some water, please?' Harry asked. 'Oh, and I didn't get your name,' he added. 'You are?'

'Jack,' said the chef. 'Jack Miller. I'll get that water for you now.'

Jack then dashed out of the room, returning a moment later with a jug and a stack of glasses.

'Shall I make some sandwiches?' he asked.

'That's not a bad idea,' Harry agreed.

'I know everyone's had dinner,' continued Jack, 'but a few nibbles might keep their mind off of things, don't you think? Help them relax.'

'I'm a bit peckish myself,' said Harry, checking his watch to see that the time was now close to eight-thirty.

'I'll bring something in for you as well, then,' Jack said, and left the room, pulling the door closed behind him.

Harry gestured to the sofa, inviting Kirsty to sit down as he took a seat himself. Liz took the remaining chair.

'So, then, Ms Cropper,' he said. 'No doubt this is all somewhat of a shock.'

'It is, and please, call me Kirsty.'

Harry gave Kirsty a moment to get used to where they now were, her eyes darting around the room, her hands clamped together on her lap.

'Water?' Harry asked, pouring out two glasses.

'Yes, please,' Kirsty replied, taking a glass.

Harry allowed a minute or so of quiet, just to help Kirsty relax, which was never easy under such circumstances. Then, as he went to speak, there came a knock at the door.

'Come in,' Liz said.

Jack pushed into the room with a small plate of sandwiches for Harry and Liz, and one for Kirsty as well.

'That didn't take long,' Harry said.

'Did yours first,' said Jack. 'I'll get on with something for everyone else now.'

'I'm not really very hungry,' said Kirsty, but took the plate anyway.

'I hope cheese and pickle is okay,' Jack asked.

Harry took the plates and placed them on the table.

'More than,' he said. 'Thank you.'

'Not a problem.'

Jack left the room.

As soon as he was gone, Kirsty asked, 'Can I ask, am I a suspect? I mean, is that why I'm here? Do you think I did it? Because I didn't. I'd never kill anyone.'

'As I explained earlier, this is a voluntary interview,' Harry explained, wondering how many times he'd heard someone say that, only to find out that the opposite was very much the case. 'You have a right to silence and can leave at any time. PCSO Coates, here, will be taking notes, and you'll be able to read through them when we're done.'

'But I didn't kill him,' Kirsty repeated, and Harry heard the shock in the words. 'I don't know who did. I mean, why would anyone do that?'

Harry gave Kirsty a moment to settle, then said, 'The first thing I have to do is caution you.'

Kirsty's already shocked expression quickly turned to white terror.

'But I didn't kill him! You can't arrest me! You can't!'

'I'm not arresting you,' Harry said. 'Legally, as a police officer, I have to caution everyone I interview. That way, your rights are protected, as are ours. Does that make sense?'

Kirsty gave a quick, nervous nod.

'Okay, then,' Harry said. 'Kirsty Cropper, you do not have to say anything. But it may harm your defence if you do not mention when questioned something which you later rely on in court. Anything you do say may be given in evidence.'

Kirsty had a quick sip of water.

'Why don't you tell me a little bit about yourself, first of all?' Harry said. 'Why you're here, how you know Mr Carl Walsh, that kind of thing.'

'I don't,' Kirsty said. 'Know him, I mean. I know of him, but that's all.'

'Can you tell me a little about that?' Harry asked.

Kirsty took a deep breath before exhaling and reaching for her glass and taking another sip. She then picked up a sandwich, but rather than eating it, just held it instead, staring into the middle distance as it opened a little in her hands, spilling cheese back onto the plate.

'Ms Cropper?' Harry said. 'Kirsty?'

Kirsty snapped around at Harry, her eyes wide.

'Yes?'

'You were going to tell me a little about yourself, why you're here, what you know about Carl Walsh.'

Kirsty nibbled at the sandwich.

'Walsh, he's quite a big name in crime circles,' she said. 'He's interviewed a lot on podcasts, in magazines, that kind of thing. I'm sure you've heard of him?'

Harry shook his head.

'I'm afraid not, no.'

'Well, I've heard him speak before, but this is the first weekend he's ever done for people who are thinking of becoming a private investigator.'

'So, that's why you're here, then?' Harry asked. 'You want to become a PI, yes?'

'I ... I helped a friend,' Kirsty said. 'She'd been scammed; I think that's what you call it. Nearly ruined her. Single parent, too, you see; twins. So, I tracked down the person responsible.'

Harry was impressed.

'What is it that you do when you're not tracking down scammers, then?' he asked.

'I'm just an office manager,' Kirsty replied. 'It's not very exciting. But doing that was, you see. Helping my friend, I mean, and her boys. So, when I heard about this weekend, I just had to come.'

'There are plenty of courses, though,' Harry said. 'Why this one?'

He'd had dealings with private investigators on various cases over the years. Some were absolute charlatans, others were proud of the bits of paper stuck in frames on their walls, and not one of them had managed to get on his good side. But then, his good side wasn't exactly an easy place to get to.

Kirsty gave a shrug.

'Seemed like a good opportunity to learn from one of the best in the business, I suppose,' she said.

'And that's what he is, yes?'

'He certainly thinks so,' said Kirsty. Then added, 'No, what I mean is he's well known, isn't he? And that's a good thing, I'm sure. Means you can trust him. And being a PI, there has to be trust, doesn't there?'

Harry wasn't so sure those things were connected, but kept that to himself.

'He's a bit of a celebrity, then?' Liz asked.

'I suppose you could say that, yes,' said Kirsty.

'You mentioned that you've heard him speak before. So, had you met him before this weekend?'

'Carl Walsh?' Kirsty said, shaking her head. 'No.'

Harry was already having quite a job imagining the woman sitting with him ramming a knife into the back of the PI.

'Can you tell me what happened this evening?'

'I've told you,' Kirsty said, 'I didn't kill him. Why would I?'

Liz said, 'We're just trying to establish a few facts, that's all. Any details you can give us will be hugely helpful, as I'm sure you can understand.'

'Yes ... Yes, of course,' Kirsty said, then explained about how everyone had arrived, the drinks, then the meal. 'Then we did this murder mystery thing,' she said. 'It was just a bit of fun, really. Seemed a bit silly, if I'm honest, but I didn't mind. It was a good way for everyone to get to know each other a bit better. And we had that retired DCI as well; he was very good. Can't really see why he's here at all, to be honest; seems to know more than enough to just get on with doing the job.'

Harry skipped Kirsty's mention of Jameson and asked, 'I

understand that after everyone had been in the room together, with Carl Walsh as the victim, you then took it in turns?'

'I was second to go in,' Kirsty said. 'Scott was first. He's ex-military. Then it was Hazeem, Yalina, Peter—he's the retired police officer—and Tony was last. He's the one who found ...'

Kirsty's voice died.

'What did you see while you were in there?' Harry asked.

Kirsty nibbled at her sandwich, her eyes darting around the room like a mouse half expecting to be snatched away by an owl.

'Only what I'd seen before,' she said. 'I took photos when we were all in there together, and also just before I left the room when I was on my own. I thought that would be a good idea.'

'Do you have them with you? The photos, I mean?' Harry asked.

Liz then asked, 'Did you take any notes at all of what you saw?'

Kirsty pulled out her phone and a small notebook.

'Here,' she said, and pulled up a photo file before handing it over to Harry. 'There's not much in the book, really.'

Harry flicked through the photos, found one of Walsh, and used his fingers on the screen to zoom in a little.

'Hmm,' he said, then handed the phone back to Kirsty. 'Can you share these with PCSO Coates, even though there's no signal here?'

'By Bluetooth, yes,' Kirsty said.

'Then do that,' said Harry.

While Kirsty did as he had asked, Harry flicked through the first few pages of the notebook and Kirsty was right, there wasn't much written there at all; just the names of everyone at the weekend, and a few details about them all.

Liz said, 'If you want, I can just take photos of those pages?'

Harry handed the notebook to Liz, who did just that before handing it back to Kirsty.

.   .   .

HAVING LOOKED through Kirsty's photos, Harry wanted to have a quick chat with Liz and Jameson. It wasn't exactly protocol to include the retired detective, but all things considered, Harry wasn't too bothered right then.

'Well,' Harry said, 'thanks for your time, Kirsty. We'll walk you back to the dining room now, if that's okay?'

'Is that it?'

'For now, yes.'

Harry, with Liz behind him, led Kirsty out of the room and back into the dining room. Jameson came over and they stepped into the hall.

'How are you doing?' he asked.

Harry asked Liz to pull Kirsty's photos up on her phone.

'Look,' he said, zooming in on the same photo he'd looked at earlier. 'There ...'

Liz and Jameson stared at the image on her phone.

'What are we looking at?' Liz asked. 'I don't see anything.'

'Exactly,' said Harry.

'Exactly, what?'

'You don't see anything, because it isn't there, is it?'

'What isn't?'

'The knife,' said Harry. 'When Kirsty took these photos there was no knife. So, Walsh was still alive.'

'She could've taken the photos before she stabbed him,' Liz suggested.

'She could,' said Harry. 'But what's the motive? She's here because she wants to be a PI after helping her friend with a scammer. All she knows about Walsh is that he's a bit of a celebrity in the world of crime podcasts or something. Obviously, her story will need to be checked, but right now, it's not enough, not by a long shot.'

'Best you get on with interviewing the others, then,' said Jameson. 'And me.'

CHAPTER EIGHTEEN

POPPING HIS HEAD AROUND INTO THE DINING ROOM, HARRY called Scott Williams over next. As he did so, Jack came up from behind carrying a large tray of food and Harry allowed him through. Harry then took Scott to the reading room with Liz.

The man was certainly reserved, thought Harry, and getting any information out of him at all was frustrating from the off.

Having cautioned him, Harry said, 'So, you're ex-military, then.'

'I am.'

'What were you in?'

'This and that.'

'Rank?'

'Corporal.'

'In for long?'

'Long enough.'

'Tough decision to leave, as I know myself.'

'It was and it wasn't.'

'Married? Single?'

'Divorced. Two kids.'

Harry then asked how Scott had found out about the weekend and what he knew about Carl Walsh.

'I'm afraid I'm not at liberty to say,' said Scott.

The answer confused Harry.

'And why would that be?'

'Client confidentiality.'

Harry narrowed his eyes at the man in front of him and hid a smile. Regardless of how they were trained to be the grey man—someone who would just blend into the crowd—the SAS, were always easy to spot. And he had dealt with, and worked alongside, plenty of them during his own days in the Paras. Scott looked fit, but not just gym fit. This was a man who Harry guessed had done the Fan Dance, the notorious SAS twenty-four kilometre test march over Pen y Fan, the highest mountain in the Brecon Beacons, enough times to know the route backwards.

Harry sat back and folded his arms.

'When's the last time you were over in Hereford?' he asked, referring to the home of the SAS.

At this, a faint smile slipped across Scott's otherwise impassive face.

'Well spotted,' he said.

'Detective, remember?' said Harry, unable to hide the smile. 'And I've worked with some of your colleagues before. A good few years ago now, mind, but the memory's fresh enough. Do you miss the Regiment?'

'I've always thought that you can leave the SAS, but it never really leaves you, if you know what I mean,' Scott answered.

'I do,' Harry said.

'Thought you might,' said Scott. 'Those scars—IED?'

'Paras, Afghanistan,' said Harry. 'Trust me, I looked worse before.' He saw Scott's eyebrow raise with renewed interest. 'Sergeant,' he said, answering the silent question in the man's eyes. 'Life was certainly exciting.'

'You miss it?'

'I'm the one asking the questions, remember?' said Harry. 'So, you're working for someone, then, is that it?'

'I am. Needs must.'

'As the devil drives?' finished Harry. 'And this particular devil would be what, exactly? Boredom? Curiosity? Money? A bit of all three?'

There was enough of a twitch in Scott's body language to tell Harry he'd hit it right with that last guess.

'I'm going to need a little more,' he said.

'Client confidentiality,' Scott repeated.

'Doesn't mean a thing right now,' Harry said, adding a harder edge to his voice and jabbing a finger at the hall on the other side of the door. 'I have a dead man in a room just down that hall. There's only a handful of people who were here when it happened. You're one of them. Your reason for being here is very important to this investigation.'

Scott said nothing.

'Unless, of course, you're happy for me to look into having you arrested for obstruction. Your choice.'

Harry waited.

'My client,' Scott eventually said, 'believes Mr Walsh isn't all he says he is.'

'How do you mean?' Liz asked. 'He's a private investigator.'

'He is,' Scott said. 'He's also a blackmailing bastard.'

'That's quite a strong statement,' said Harry. 'Perhaps you can elaborate a bit?'

Scott poured himself a glass of water, took a sip.

'My client is a building contractor. He employed the services of Mr Walsh about eighteen months ago. He'd had a number of vehicles and other pieces of equipment stolen from a few sites he was working and suspected that some of his employees were involved.'

'And were they?'

'Of course they were,' Scott said. 'The police had found nothing, though, so my client paid for Walsh's expertise. However, in the process of carrying out the investigation, which he concluded successfully, by the way, Walsh went, well, a little off-piste, shall we say?'

'How do you mean?'

'Walsh found out that my client was having an affair. He took photos, videos, then gave him a choice; pay up or ... Well, you can guess.'

Harry glanced over at Liz, and he saw his own shock and not inconsiderable confusion reflected right back at him.

'So, what are you here to do, then?' Harry asked. 'You're not a PI.'

'True,' Scott said. 'But I can be very, very persuasive.'

Harry laughed at that, couldn't help himself.

'You SAS lads really do think you're the bollocks, don't you?'

Scott gave a couldn't-care-less shrug.

'I'm not denying that you are,' Harry continued, 'but sometimes, those egos? They're just a little too inflated for my liking.'

'I don't have an ego.'

'Saying that pretty much says that you do,' said Harry. 'As for your *being very persuasive* comment, that doesn't paint you in a very good light, does it?'

'I didn't kill him, if that's what you're suggesting, and neither did I come here to,' said Scott. 'But like I said, I can be very, very persuasive.'

Harry had to admit that he was impressed with the man's self-confidence; Scott was openly suggesting that he was here to threaten Walsh, but was steering clear of saying exactly how. Harry was also now aware of the fact that the knife in the PI's back had appeared after Kirsty had been in the room alone. Scott had been in there before her, so he hadn't wielded it either, which meant he was in the clear.

'Between you and I,' Harry said, 'throwing someone in the boot of a car, waterboarding them, effective as it may be, it's rather frowned upon by the likes of me.'

'Never said I was going to do anything like that, now, did I?' said Scott.

'No, you didn't,' Harry replied, but with just enough steel in his voice to tell Scott they both knew that something along those lines had been planned. He asked, 'Are you someone I need to keep an eye on, then, Mr Williams?'

'Can't see why. Are we done?'

'We are,' Harry said. 'For now.'

Harry took Scott back to the dining room, but just before he allowed him back into the room, he placed a firm hand on the man's forearm and pulled him to one side.

'Soldier to soldier,' he said, 'make better use of who and what you are.'

'You have no idea who or what I am, Detective,' Scott replied.

He tried to pull away, but Harry's grip was made of iron.

'Maybe not,' Harry said. 'But you're better than this, and you know it.'

'Am I, now?' Scott said. 'Aren't you stepping over the line here, Detective? I didn't ask you for advice and nor do I want it, if it's all the same with you.'

'Joining civvy street is hard,' continued Harry, ignoring what Scott had just said. 'Trust me, I know what I'm talking about. So, don't take the path of least resistance as you do, you hear?'

'I've bills to pay, mouths to feed,' Scott said. 'Divorced, remember?'

'And if those mouths mean anything to you at all,' said Harry, 'then you'll give yourself a damned good kick up the arse for being here at all. Is that understood?'

Scott went to speak, but Harry hushed him with nothing more than a look.

'Money can be earned, and those bills will get paid. But the most valuable thing you can give them is you. Don't bugger that up. And that's an order.'

At that, Scott laughed.

'You pulling rank now?'

'I'd rather do that than pull you in and have you arrested because something you've done has gone seriously south. And it will, Scott, I promise you that.'

With nothing more to say, Harry showed Scott back into the

dining room and called out the next name on his list: Hazeem Rasheed. He waited as the man walked over, a woman with him.

'Mr Rasheed,' Harry said.

'And this is my wife, Yalina,' Hazeem said. 'We examined the room together, rather than alone.'

'We always work together,' Yalina said.

Harry led them through to the other room, and sat them down on the small sofa. With the caution given, he asked if they could go through why they were there and how they knew of Walsh.

Before either of them answered, Harry saw a conspiratorial glance flicker between them.

'Can I ask,' Hazeem said, 'this is confidential, isn't it?'

'We're the police, remember?' Harry said. 'Confidentiality is kind of what we do.'

'So, you won't be going in there and telling everyone what we're about to tell you, right?'

'As I've just said in the caution,' explained Harry, 'anything you say—'

'No, we understand that,' said Yalina. 'But it does make things a little ... complicated. '

Harry was confused.

'Conplicated? Why's that, then?'

'Walsh, you see,' Yalina continued. 'He's the reason we're here.'

'Well of course he is,' said Harry. 'It's his weekend, isn't it? And you're here to learn all about being a private investigator.'

'No, that's not what she means,' Hazeem said. 'We're not here to learn from him; we're here to learn about him. And to confront him.'

'That's more than a little mysterious,' said Liz.

Harry had to agree. He was also having déjà vu, having just heard what Scott had told them only a few minutes ago.

'I think you need to get to the point,' he said.

Like an electric pulse, another glance zipped between Hazeem and Yalina.

'Look,' Hazeem said. 'We're not who we say we are.'

'Then who the hell are you, exactly?' Harry asked. 'And just so you both know, I'm not a massive fan of being led up the garden path, if you know what I mean. So don't.'

'We're here because of my sister,' Yalina said. 'We're here because of what happened to Aamina.'

'Another bloody ulterior motive,' Harry muttered, remembering his chat with Kirsty.

The Rasheeds looked at him, confusion in their eyes.

'Sorry,' he said, encouraging them to continue with a wave of his hand. 'You were saying?'

'She ... she took her own life,' Yalina said. 'Nine months months ago.'

Harry thought on that for a moment then said, 'I'm very sorry to hear that, truly I am. But I'm not sure what that's got to do with Walsh.'

The thing was, though, after what he'd heard from Kirsty, and then from Scott, he was going to guess that it had an awful lot to do with him, but he kept that to himself for now.

Hazeem removed something from a pocket.

'Here,' he said, handing it over. 'This is what he had to do with it.'

Harry looked down to see a small notebook resting in the palm of Hazeem's hand.

'And what's this, then?' he said, taking it and holding it up to flick through the pages.

'It's everything that you need to know,' Hazeem said. 'About Walsh and about Aamina; what he was doing ... to her ... the cost of it ...'

'She sent that to me, after she had ... gone,' Yalina said. 'It arrived in the post a couple of days after ... Anyway, we knew nothing about any of it.'

'Any of what?' Liz asked.

Harry saw tears building in the corner of Yalina's eyes.

Hazeem reached out and rested a hand on Yalina's knee.

'There are photographs, as well,' Yalina said, reaching out to give her husband's hand a squeeze for reassurance, Harry guessed. 'We have those, too, but, well, they're just too explicit.'

Harry was starting to feel the thin needles of a headache poking its mean way through his skull.

'Please,' he said, 'you really do need to get to the point here, instead of circling around whatever it is that you're trying to tell us.'

'Aamina was a wealthy woman,' Hazeem said. 'She was also single, after a not entirely pleasant divorce from a man she was very much better off without.'

Yalina said, 'We knew nothing about Walsh until that notebook arrived in the post for me. Aamina had sent it, but by then, it was too late.'

Harry could see that what the couple were telling him was hurting them both, so he stayed quiet and allowed them the space to speak. Next to him, Liz continued to take notes.

'What we know is that she met Walsh through a dating site,' Yalina said. 'He was going by another name, John Setton. She kept it all secret, worried, we think, of what people would say. Then ... then something happened.'

'We noticed a change,' Hazeem said. 'Aamina suddenly seemed so quiet, reserved. She refused to go out, took to just staying at home. All because of him.'

'You mentioned photographs,' Liz said, and Harry was impressed with the gentle prompt from the PCSO to get to the real point of what had happened.

'Everything was sent from an anonymous email,' said Yalina. 'The photos of Aamina, what he made her do.'

Harry had a sinking feeling in his stomach as to where this was going.

'Look,' he said, 'if this is too difficult ...'

'No, we need to tell you,' Hazeem said. 'We have to tell you. We thought we could help, you see? It's what Aamina wanted, why she sent us the notebook. And it is why we are here now.'

Yalina said, 'As I said, the photographs are explicit. But in the notebook, Aamina says she remembered nothing about what happened, and that she was just too afraid to go to the police. We know it was Walsh, and we know that he was using the photographs to extort a large sum of money from her, all of it in cash.'

Harry flicked through the notebook. The handwriting was spidery, as though written in a state of panic.

'We were going to confront him with the evidence,' Hazeem said. 'Expose him. For Aamina. It's too late to bring her back, but it's not too late to bring him down, to stop him doing this to someone else. You can understand that, can't you?'

Harry said, 'Whether I understand it or not doesn't actually matter. The least you could have done was to go straight to the police. That's what you should've done. If you have evidence that the man drugged her and whatever else, then it's a police matter. You both know that, I'm sure.'

'We don't trust the police,' Yalina said. 'I'm afraid that we have had our own problems with them.'

'What problems?' Liz asked.

Harry saw a flicker of rage burn in Hazeem's eyes at the question, which he quickly quenched by taking a deep, calming breath. When he spoke again, his voice was shaking.

'Let's just say that I've met police officers who become deaf when dealing with ... with people like us,' Hazeem said. 'If you know what I mean.'

Harry frowned.

'I think that I do,' he said. 'Unfortunately.'

'Then you can understand why we were unable to do as you suggest.'

'I understand it,' said Harry, 'but that doesn't make it right. We both know that.'

'Well, we're making it right now,' said Yalina. 'By telling you.'

'What you're telling me,' Harry said, 'is that you're here because you believe Walsh is responsible for blackmailing, and thus ultimately causing your sister to take her own life.'

'Exactly that,' said Hazeem.

'Then you can see how that looks from where I'm sitting, can't you?' Harry said.

'We didn't kill him,' Yalina said. 'We were in the room with everyone else when that doctor came in and told everyone what had happened.'

Hazeem, Harry noticed, was staring at him, so he met his gaze.

'You have something to add?' he asked.

'I do,' Hazeem said. 'I'm not ashamed to say that I wanted to see that man dead. Of course I did! He doesn't deserve to live. But I also believe that death would have been an escape. He should suffer. The world should know what he did and he should live with that, the guilt of it.'

'What if he didn't feel any guilt at all?' Harry asked.

'That doesn't matter,' said Hazeem, his voice rising as he spoke, anger fuelling it. 'He can answer for that when his time comes. But until then, the right thing is that he lives, but that whatever life he has is an empty one, emptier even than death. He should spend behind bars, with all that he has built, all the riches he has made, everything taken from him, and burned!'

'That's a strong viewpoint,' Harry said, as Hazeem calmed himself again.

'It is,' said Yalina, now holding her husband's hand. 'But we did not kill him.'

Harry allowed everyone a minute to think about all that had been said. He then thanked the Rasheeds and asked Liz to return them to the dining room with the others.

Next, was Jameson.

CHAPTER NINETEEN

'WELL, THIS SHOULD BE GOOD,' HARRY SAID WHEN LIZ returned, and his old friend sat down in front of him.

'Where do you want me to start?' he asked.

'You tell me,' Harry said. 'Right now, I'm rather at a loss, which I doubt surprises you.'

'It doesn't,' Jameson said. 'But it's because of Ellen, really. I don't mean it's her fault I'm here, just that ...' He stopped talking for a moment, deep in thought, then said, 'Just that I've been kicking my heels ever since I lost her, and I'm pretty sure that's not what she would've wanted.'

Harry remembered Ellen well. All those years ago, Jameson had been the one, right at the beginning of it all, who had stopped him from taking the wrong path. After deciding to leave the Paras and join the police, it was Jameson who had been there to advise and guide him. They'd become good friends, though as Harry's career had moved on, they'd kept in touch less and less. Ellen had never tried to be like his mum, or to take her place, but sometimes, even though Harry doubted she ever realised it, she had been close enough. And her full English breakfasts had been epic.

'And becoming a private investigator is, is that it?' Harry asked.

'It's something to do, isn't it?'

'So's fishing.'

'Tried it. Hated it. Never realised it was possible to get so angry at water.'

'Can't say I'm surprised,' said Harry. 'But why a PI? And why this weekend?'

'Walsh has made a name for himself,' Jameson said. 'Ellen used to read that true crime stuff, you see? Found some of her old magazines when I was doing a bit of a tidy, and one thing lead to another. Plus, it was a good excuse to get away. And it was in the back of my mind that I'd maybe pop over to see you again, too. Talk it through, that kind of thing.'

Harry laughed.

'What, you come to me for advice?'

'You owe me, I think.'

Harry nodded at that; Jameson was probably right.

'What do you know about Walsh, then?' he asked.

Harry was thinking then about what he had learned from Scott. Obviously, there was a lot there to check up on, but that was the case with everyone in the house, and it wouldn't be done until they were able to conduct the investigation under normal circumstances. Until then, he'd just collect all the information that he could. It wasn't like there was anything else he could do.

'Not a damned thing,' Jameson said with a shrug. 'Honestly, it was a random decision. There I was, tidying up, by which I mean sorting through Ellen's stuff, which is something I'm not doing very well at, as you can imagine. But anyway, I find her crime magazines, don't I? And flicking through one of them, I see this advert to come here. Walsh had an article in the magazine as well, so it seemed legit, and that was it, really.'

'How's it all going for you so far?' Harry asked.

'It's certainly more exciting than I expected,' Jameson said. 'Makes you realise how much you can miss the old life, if you know what I mean.'

'Not enough to want it back, though?'

'I'm too old.'

'Not necessarily,' said Harry.

Jameson shook his head, laughed.

'You mean be a rejoiner? Didn't take you for the comedian, Harry.'

'Not sure what's so funny,' Harry said. 'With a record like yours, and it's not yet five years since you left, is it?'

Jameson was quiet, then said, 'Can you imagine what Ellen would say, though?'

'Look, I know I don't really know you,' Liz said, joining in, 'and I don't know what happened to Ellen, but my guess is that she'd want you to be happy.'

Jameson looked at Liz.

'Cancer,' he said. 'After the diagnosis, knowing we only had a few months left together, we did something we always said we would but never had; went off travelling. Didn't really have a plan, just kind of set off. No end date either, well, not except for the clock ticking down in Ellen's body.'

'I'm so sorry,' Liz said. 'That's awful.'

'It's coming up to a year soon enough,' Jameson said. 'She died in my arms watching the sun rise over a beach in New Zealand. We'd hired a campervan, just went touring. It was glorious. She was so happy. We both were.'

For a moment or two, no one said a word. Harry watched as Jameson wiped his eyes of tears, though he was smiling sadly as he did so.

'I've no idea who did this, Harry,' he then said. 'None of it makes any sense. We were all in the room together, saw him on the floor. We then all took turns to go in on our own, except for the Rasheeds who went in together, and it was only when the doctor went in that we all found out what had happened and I made the call.'

'I'm going to speak with the doctor next,' Harry said. 'Unless there's anything else to discuss, my thinking is I get on with that now.'

'What else is there to say?' asked Jameson.

'Just this,' said Harry. 'Ellen would want you to be happy. That you're here suggests that you're looking for the right thing, just in the wrong place.'

'Perhaps you're right.'

'I am.'

Jameson smiled, stood up.

'I'll follow you out,' Harry said. 'Smudge needs to be let out anyway.'

'Ah, so she's your dog,' Jameson smiled. 'A new house, a serious relationship, *and* a dog? You've changed, Harry.'

'We both have,' Harry replied. 'And that's no bad thing either, don't you think?'

Leaving Liz to see Jameson back into the dining room, Harry opened the front door to find himself staring at a wall of snow. He pushed out into it and over to the Land Rover. Inside, Smudge was still curled up to keep herself warm. She sensed him before he opened the door, looking up through the ice-encrusted window, tail wagging.

'Come on,' Harry said, 'let's have you inside, then.'

Smudge stood up and jumped out into the snow. Then, instead of following Harry over to the house, she suddenly decided to run around in circles, her nose stuck into the ever-deepening snow, tail going like a propeller.

Ignoring the wind, and the fact he was getting drenched, Harry ducked down, crunched a snowball in his hands, then lobbed it at the dog. Smudge raced after it, diving on it, biting it, and bringing just enough of it back for him to throw it again.

A few minutes later, when the cold and wind finally became too much, and Smudge had relieved herself behind the campervan, Harry clipped her to a lead and headed back inside. Liz met them in the hall and immediately made a fuss of Smudge, who rolled onto her back for a tummy rub.

'You mind holding her for a minute?' Harry asked.

Liz took the lead, and Harry pulled a key out of his pocket and headed back into the lounge.

CHAPTER TWENTY

THE FIRST THING HARRY NOTICED WAS THE CHILL IN THE room from the open window. Small flurries of snow were bursting in on the whip tips of the wind. The coffee table in front of the window was wet with the stuff, and small drifts had started to form on the windowsill.

Taking a careful walk around the room, Harry noticed some faint, parallel scratches on the wooden floor, as though something heavy had been dragged across it, but from where and to where, he couldn't work out, the scratches a mix of straight and curved lines in the varnished timber. Other than that, everything looked as it had when he'd first arrived. He saw no sign of disturbance, nothing that gave him the impression there had been a struggle. Whoever had killed Walsh had crept up on him and sunk the blade into his back quick enough to ensure he could do nothing about it.

Turning back towards the door, Harry reached for the handle, but found himself hesitating. He turned back to the room, a deep frown creasing his brow. Something was bothering him suddenly, but what? The room was the same, the body was the same, the window was the same. The scratches, yes, he'd not noticed those before, but other than that, what was it that was now scraping at the inside of his skull?

Harry opened the door.

'Liz, can I have those photos on your phone for a minute, please?'

'Here you go,' said Liz, and opened the photos and handed her phone to Harry, who then headed back into the room.

'Something wrong?' Liz asked, calling to him from the hall, where Smudge was now lying up against a radiator.

'I don't know,' Harry said, swiping through the photos, each time glancing back up at the room before them. 'Something ...'

Harry stopped swiping.

The photo in front of him was a close-up of Walsh's body, one taken by Kirsty before Walsh had been killed. There was no knife in his back. He was just lying on the floor on his front, face hidden by that large hat.

'He's moved,' Harry said.

'What?' said Liz.

Harry stepped out of the room, leaving the door open, and handed her back her phone.

'He's moved,' Harry said again. 'Not much, but enough. Look ...'

He dropped a finger onto Liz's screen. The photo responded by disappearing.

'Bollocks,' said Harry.

'Just a sec,' said Liz, and pulled the photo back up onto the screen. 'There we go.'

Harry looked from the photo to the body and back again.

'He's definitely moved,' he said. 'I'm sure of it.'

Liz was quiet for a moment as she compared the photo with the crime scene.

'I guess,' she said. 'But I'm not sure what you're getting at. Surely anyone would move if they were stabbed in the back?'

'That's my point,' said Harry, walking back over to the body and speaking to Liz from in front of the now barely smouldering fire. 'They'd move, wouldn't they? The shock of it alone would be enough to have the victim spasm in some way. The body would respond, react, they'd try to get away, even if someone did it quickly enough that you'd be dead before you could do much at all.'

'And he has moved,' said Liz. 'You've just said that yourself.'

'But not enough, though,' Harry said. 'I don't know why, but something's wrong here. I just can't put my finger on it. And this hat and those gloves, they're bothering me, too.'

'I think they're just props from the murder mystery thing he was trying to do when he was stabbed,' said Liz.

'No, there's something else about them,' said Harry. 'I just don't know what.'

His mind busy with unspoken questions, Harry left the lounge once again. He headed across the hall and into the dining room. Everyone turned to stare at him. He had two more suspects to chat with: the chef and the young doctor. He thought about flipping a coin, but then decided that it was fairly obvious who he should talk to next.

'Mr Tony Pearson,' he said, looking over at the doctor.

He was leaning back on a dining chair, arms folded, and seemingly staring very hard at an empty wine glass. Hearing his name, he looked up, sighed, then walked over to Harry, who then led him through to the reading room. Liz followed, as did Smudge.

When they were all sitting down, Harry poured a fresh glass of water and handed it over.

'Thanks,' Tony said, taking the glass.

'Don't mind the dog,' Harry said, as Smudge curled up under the window at the end of the room, next to another radiator. 'So, how are you doing?'

'I've been better,' Tony replied, then added, 'Walsh never said it would be like this.'

'No,' said Harry, 'I can't imagine he thought to include his own murder in the marketing material for the weekend.'

Tony sipped his water, but it didn't disguise the faint laugh he let out in response to Harry's reply.

Harry cautioned the doctor, then explained why they were having their chat and that Liz would be taking notes.

'Perhaps you could give me a little bit of background,' he said. 'Why you're here, that kind of thing?'

'I suppose so,' said Tony.

'You're a doctor. Where did you train, then?'

'What?'

'Your degree,' Harry said. 'Where did you get it?'

'London,' said Tony.

'And now you're thinking of becoming a private investigator.'

Tony gave a nod.

'Mind if I ask why?'

'Why what?'

'Why you want to become a PI,' Harry said. 'You've spent an awful lot of time and effort to qualify as a doctor, and probably collected a hefty amount of student debt, too, I should think.'

'I guess.'

'So, why the possible career move? It's not like the salaries are comparable, so something must have attracted you to what Walsh was selling.'

Tony said, 'I just fancy a change, you know? That's all.'

'Plenty of other careers to choose from,' said Harry. 'Why this one?'

'It's interesting, isn't it?' Tony said. 'Investigating things, helping people.'

'You'd be helping people as a doctor, though,' offered Liz.

Tony said nothing, sipped his water.

'So, Carl Walsh,' said Harry. 'How is it that you know about him, then?'

'Google,' said Tony, like it was the most obvious thing in the world.

'And that's it? You just googled *how to become a private investigator*, his name came up, and the next thing you know, you're signed up for a weekend in the Dales?'

'Pretty much.'

Tony wasn't exactly tripping over himself to be helpful, so

Harry decided to take him back to when he'd realised Walsh was dead.

'Run me through it again,' he said. 'Everything that happened, just so we're all clear on the details. You'd be amazed how you forget things and then, when you run through it all again, a little detail that you'd forgotten pops into your head.'

So, as requested, Tony ran through everything that had happened, telling Harry about arriving at the house, the meal, the murder mystery, supporting what he'd heard from the rest of the guests.

'Then, like I said earlier, I realised that he wasn't breathing,' he said. 'So, I checked his pulse, and then I saw the knife.'

As Tony spoke, something that had niggled Harry earlier, when he'd headed back into the lounge to have another look at the crime scene, did so again. At the time, he hadn't been entirely sure what it was, exactly, but now he knew.

'Now, about his pulse,' said Harry. 'You mentioned that you saw how Walsh wasn't breathing, so you checked to make sure. Seems a sensible thing to do. And, being a doctor, I'm going to assume you know what you're doing.'

Tony shrugged, gave a nod.

'Could you just tell me, then, what it was that you did, exactly?'

'How do you mean?'

'How you checked Walsh's pulse, that's all. Nothing too taxing, I'm sure. Details, you see; important.'

Harry watched Tony drain his glass, fill it up again, then take another gulp. The man was nervous and he could tell that Liz had noticed, too.

'Well,' he began, 'like I said, I saw that he wasn't breathing. What I mean is, he wasn't moving at all, you see? And people move when they breathe, don't they? So, I checked his wrist and—'

'Which one?'

'What?'

'Which wrist?'

Tony paused, his eyes darting about the room.

'He has two wrists,' said Harry. 'Which one did you use to check his pulse?'

'The ... er ... this one,' Tony said, and lifted his right hand. 'Yes, that's the one I checked, his right wrist.'

'How?'

'How what?'

'How did you check it?'

Tony, wearing a confused frown, touched the wrist of his right hand with his left.

'Like this,' he said.

'So, you were able to do that with the glove still on,' Harry stated.

'I wasn't wearing gloves.'

'The victim is the one wearing gloves,' said Liz.

'If you remember, and I'm sure you do,' Harry then explained, 'just like my colleague here has said, Walsh is wearing gloves. So, did the one on his right hand get in the way?'

'No,' Tony spluttered, then said, 'I mean, yes ... Yes, it got in the way, and I couldn't find the pulse, so ... so, I checked his neck.'

'You moved the hat, then.'

'I must've done.'

Now that is a strange response, Harry thought. Keeping that to himself, however, he said, 'And you put it back in exactly the same position it had been in before?'

'Probably. I mean, yes, I suppose I must've done. But what does it matter? When I saw the knife, I knew there was nothing I could do. That's when I came through and told everyone.'

'When you saw the knife,' Harry said, repeating Tony's words slowly and deliberately. 'Did you kill him, Tony?'

Harry saw shock flash in the doctor's eyes.

'What?'

'With the knife,' Harry said. 'Did you kill him? And if so, why?'

Harry wasn't usually this direct, but he could tell that something was up, so he was trying to get a rise from Tony, just enough for him to let slip whatever it was that was clearly bothering him.

'Of course I didn't kill him! Are you mad? That's not what any of this is about, it really isn't!'

'How do you mean?' Liz asked.

'You were the first person to see the knife,' said Harry, before Tony could answer. 'In fact, I don't think it was there at all until you entered the room. Which is a little odd, don't you think?'

Tony was twitching now, Harry noticed, his hands shaking.

'This isn't right,' said Tony, shaking his head. 'None of this is right. It needs to stop.'

'What needs to stop, Tony?' Harry asked. 'Maybe there's something you're not telling us, is that it? How do you know Walsh? Why are you really here?'

'It's not supposed to be like this,' Tony said, almost to himself. 'It's not. You know that, don't you? You can see that it's not supposed to be like this; you must be able to see it. What you're saying, what you're asking, what's in that room, it's not what you think.'

'We think there's a body in that room,' Liz said. 'The body of Carl Walsh. And that someone in this house is responsible for his death.'

Having pressed Tony on how he'd managed to take the victim's pulse without disturbing the glove and the hat, Harry was confused by how Tony was reacting. He wasn't confessing, he wasn't giving away any motive at all for the murder. Instead, it was like he was trying to tell him something, but whatever it was, it clearly wasn't making any sense, not even to himself.

'What's not supposed to be like what, exactly?' Harry asked. 'What do you mean, Tony?'

'This!' Tony said, jumping out of his seat. 'All of it! The whole bloody charade! Because that's what this is, everything single bit of it.'

'I need you to sit down and calm yourself,' Harry said, remaining seated, his voice firm. 'And what do you mean by charade?'

Tony stayed on his feet.

'He forced me, you know? That bastard Walsh forced me to do this. I didn't have any choice. If I'd said no, he'd have ruined me. You know that, don't you? That's what he does, that's all he's ever done. It's all blackmail and lies, all of it.'

'Tony,' Harry said, and pointed at the other chair. 'Sit. Right now.'

Tony hesitated for a moment, then slumped down into it, his head in his hands.

Harry, however, was thinking back to everything Scott had said earlier.

'Anyway, it doesn't matter now, does it?' Tony said, his voice quieter now. 'He's gone, isn't he?'

'Gone?' Harry said. 'He's dead, Tony. You checked that yourself.'

At this, Tony sat up and leaned back in his chair. His head fell back and he laughed, but the sound was humourless and desperate.

'Detective,' he said, rolling his head forward to stare at Harry, 'I didn't check shit. You know, I wouldn't even know where to start.'

'But you're a doctor,' Harry said.

Tony shook his head, a dead, emotionless smirk on his face.

'I'm an addict,' he said. 'That's what I am.'

Harry narrowed his eyes.

'Tony ...'

'Gambling,' Tony said, clearly not listening to Harry now. 'Very good at keeping it hidden, too, I might add. Then this one day, I'm having a coffee out, and he just comes and sits opposite me, doesn't he? Walsh, I mean. He just sits down, says not a word, but he's got this envelope and he hands it to me.'

'Not sure I understand where this is going,' said Harry.

'You will.'

Harry didn't reply, just let Tony keep talking.

'The envelope, it's stuffed with photos. And they're not just of me at the bookies either, are they? No. There's ones in there of me at high stakes poker games, the kind no one knows about, if you know what I mean. I've no idea how he got hold of them, but he's got me, hasn't he? Right in that moment, he's got me. And there's fuck all I can do about it.'

'You're saying Walsh was investigating you, is that it?' Harry said. 'That's why you killed him?'

Tony laughed, the sound short and sharp and empty as hell. 'I didn't kill him,' he said. 'But I'd like to, that's for sure.'

'You need to get to the point, Tony,' said Harry. 'And quickly. Because right now, I'm close to reading you your rights and arresting you for—'

'Murder, is that it?' said Tony, his voice loud now, and broken. 'I just told you; I didn't kill him. You're not listening, Detective, or maybe you are, but you're not hearing me, and that's the problem.'

'That's because so far, what you're saying isn't exactly making any sense,' Harry said.

'He threatened to tell my wife,' Tony said, 'my parents, my friends, everyone; tell them about my gambling, the money I owed loan sharks. He threatened to destroy my life, unless ... unless I did something for him.'

'What?' Harry asked. 'What did Walsh ask you to do?'

Tony sucked in a slow, deep breath, then exhaled, as though attempting to calm himself down.

'I'm here,' he said, his eyes now on Harry, 'because Walsh asked me to be. I'm here because he asked me to do something in exchange for that file. And if I didn't do as he asked, he was going to ruin me, and not just me, my whole family.'

'What are you saying?' Harry asked.

'I'm saying, Detective,' Tony replied, 'that I'm no doctor. And my guess is, that right now, that's probably enough.'

Harry was out of his chair and, having grown very tired, very quickly, of Pearson flatly refusing to get to the point, was about to say something not entirely polite, when a sound caused him to pause.

'What was that?' said Liz.

Harry held up a finger as they all listened. He then pointed at the door and out into the hallway.

The sound was faint, but it was definitely there; the chatter of voices caught on the wind.

Harry stood up and stared down at Tony.

'You, stay here,' he said, then he looked at Liz. 'If he so much as crosses his legs ...'

'He's not going anywhere,' Liz said.

'Don't worry,' Tony said, raising his hands in submission. 'It's not like there's anywhere for me to go, anyway, is there? I don't want to freeze to death.'

Harry left Liz with Tony in the reading room and headed out into the hall. He made his way over to stand between the lounge and the dining room and stared at the front door, straining his ears to try and hear the sounds better.

Here, the voices were much clearer. And they were definitely coming from outside, Harry realised, and judging by the fact that they were growing louder, whoever it was who owned them, were making their way towards the house.

Jameson came over and stood with him.

'What the hell is anyone doing out in this?' he said.

'Could be walkers caught out by the storm,' Jameson suggested.

Harry gave a nod in agreement, though he couldn't imagine why anyone would have stayed out in the snow this long. Surely they would have come down off the hills earlier in the day, at the very least before darkness fell?

'Well, whoever they are, they're outside,' said Harry. 'And it can't be the scene of crime team, can it?' he added. 'For a start, we've been here for what, an hour? That's not even long enough for them to have packed their kit, never mind actually get here as well.'

'Seems like we've got ourselves some visitors, then, doesn't it?' said Jameson.

Harry heard footsteps crunching through the snow.

He turned to look at Jameson as a barrage of knocks rattled the door, hard and urgent.

The thuds came again, louder this time; a rapid volley hammering at the door, and there were voices behind it.

'Who the hell is it, though?' Harry said, not looking for an answer.

'Only one way to find out,' Jameson said, gazing pointedly at the door.

Harry walked over to open it.

CHAPTER TWENTY-ONE

WITH THE CALL MADE TO THE MOUNTAIN RESCUE TEAM about the missing Thomas Cowper, and the understandable concern about his safety, Police Constable Jadyn Okri had soon found himself in the passenger seat of a small Suzuki 4x4 that had clearly seen better days, and those days had been a very long time ago indeed. The fading red paint was scuffed, the waterproof covers on the seats were ripped and torn, and Jadyn could see the snow-covered road beneath them through a number of disconcertingly large holes.

They had headed out of Hawes and through Gayle and were now chewing their way up Beggarman's Road. The snow was deep, but Helen Dinsdale, the driver who had picked him up, navigated it all with calm confidence. Where the snow was drifting, she picked her line perfectly, steering them up the hill like a sailor tacking through a storm.

'Sorry about noise from the heater,' Helen said, shouting above the rattling din the thing was making. 'I keep meaning to get it fixed, but just haven't got round to it yet.'

Much like with the rest of the vehicle, Jadyn thought, though it hadn't escaped his notice that money had clearly been spent on it, just not in a way that made it either pleasant to look at or comfortable to be in.

The vehicle had been lifted, with the suspension seriously upgraded from what it must have been fitted with when it left the factory. The wheels were huge, with tyres that looked mean enough to drag it up a cliff. A snorkel had been fitted, pinned to the edge of the windscreen on the driver's side, enabling it to wade through deep water with ease without the risk of the engine being flooded and locking up.

Jadyn had also spotted a winch on the front. The roof was hidden beneath a rack covered in everything from a spare wheel, a toolbox, and rescue boards, to a couple of large, well-stuffed waterproof bags, rope, and a battered army surplus ammo box.

Having climbed into the vehicle, Jadyn had introduced himself to Helen, a face he'd recognised only from the small number of meetings he'd attended with members of the team. It was mostly hidden inside the fur-lined hood of a very warm jacket. Jadyn guessed she was around the same age as Harry, but it was hard to tell, seeing as he could see so little of her at that moment.

'Nice jacket,' Helen said. Then added, 'Shiny.'

Now that he was on probation with the mountain rescue team, Jadyn had bought himself a good amount of new kit, which he always carried with him. In the few minutes before Helen had arrived to pick him up, he'd changed into his winter clothing and was thankful for it. The heater was warm, yes, but the air it was blasting out was doing little more than warming his feet and keeping the windscreen clear.

'Thanks,' Jadyn said.

'That shop in the marketplace sort you out, then?'

'They did,' said Jadyn, thinking back to the hour or so, and the considerable amount of money, he'd spent in the outdoor shop in the Hawes marketplace. 'How did you ...?'

Helen reached over and grabbed something hanging off the jacket's zipper.

'You've left the label on,' Helen said.

Jadyn quickly pulled it off, seeing the warm smile on Helen's face.

'Where are we heading, then?' he asked.

'Well, there's one team already over with the lad's parents. They've been briefed and we'll be coordinating the search with them. We have a fair idea of where he's heading, from what we've been told. The rendezvous point for us is the pub at eight PM, over in Hubberholme. You know it?'

Jadyn shook his head.

'Can't say that I do.'

'Well, the area we're going to search is fairly large, so we've got a couple of other teams heading over to meet us there to join in the fun, and we'll have search and rescue dogs as well. Unfortunately, we won't be able to use drones, not in weather like this, not until it eases, anyway. And hopefully, we won't have to.'

'Helicopter?'

'Only if there's a casualty and we need to lift them off the hill.'

'This is my first call out,' Jadyn said.

'Nervous?'

'A little,' Jadyn admitted. He was excited, too, but didn't want to give the impression he was only in it for the thrill, though there was no getting away from it.

'You're the lad Matt Dinsdale brought in, aren't you?'

'I am,' Jadyn said.

'What made you want to join?'

'Thought it would be a good way to get to know the area and the community better,' he explained.

'Makes sense,' Helen said.

Cresting the top of Beggarman's Road, past the top end of the Roman road, Helen drove on, adjusting her speed and keeping good control of the little 4x4. The vehicle seemed utterly unphased by the terrible conditions and, at last, the heater had started to make a welcome dent into the chilly temperature in the cabin, so Jadyn had not so much as started to warm up, as overheat, thanks to all the clothes he was wearing.

As they headed down into Wharfedale, he thought how the view would have been fantastic if it hadn't been for the thick black night, and the blinding snow sweeping before them. Helen had the headlights dipped to stop the snow from blinding them, but visibility was still only a few metres.

Having safely threaded their way down, Helen followed the road until snow-bedecked trees welcomed them. She parked on the right, behind a large, white, slate-roofed building, pulling up alongside an ageing Toyota Land Cruiser that, to Jadyn, looked like it had been decked out for the zombie apocalypse.

Climbing out into the snow, Jadyn heard his name called out over the howling gale, and saw Detective Sergeant Matt Dinsdale jogging over from the pub to meet him.

'First time I've been here and not had a pint,' the DS said. 'How are you doing, then?'

'I'm good,' said Jadyn. 'Looking forward to it.'

'Don't worry if you don't quite know what's going on. You'll be sticking with me anyway. Come on.'

Matt led Jadyn back inside the pub, Helen just a few steps ahead of them.

'So, what happens now?' Jadyn asked.

'The team leader will brief everyone on what we're doing, where we're heading, what we're looking for,' Matt answered, as they headed through into a room packed with people all decked out in winter gear, coming to stand alongside Helen.

'Where is it we're heading?'

'There's a lane heading up onto the pastures just before Kidstone Bank,' Matt explained. 'We'll be using that for access, spreading out across the fells in a wide enough sweep to cover the area as best we can. And we'll be in touch via shortwave radio with the other team; they're walking over from Marsett.'

'Try and find him from both sides, you mean?'

'Sort of a pincer movement,' said Matt.

'Then what?' Jadyn asked, trying to not be that one person who asks all the questions, but at the same time, being exactly that person.

'Then we'll all be back in the vehicles to spread us out in a wide enough line to then walk up and hopefully meet young Thomas coming the other way. The team leader really knows what he's doing, so this should all run very smoothly.'

Jadyn heard Helen laugh.

'You would say that, wouldn't you?'

'Why's that?' Jadyn asked.

Matt looked at Jadyn and winked.

'Because it's me,' he said, and walked to the front of the room.

For the next few minutes, Jadyn stood and listened. Not only to his DS, either, who explained the search again, and in considerably more detail, including his briefing with the search party heading out from over in Marsett. Various other individuals in the room joined in with questions, important points, and reminders, as teams were allocated to team leaders, and people checked and clarified details, and made sure they all knew exactly what they were doing.

'I've already sent two vehicles out to call in at various houses in the area,' Matt said. 'I know it's late, and will soon be getting on for early, if you know what I mean, but a lad's life is more important than worrying about waking folk up.'

Helen raised a hand and asked why Thomas had gone, if only to give them all a little bit of extra background on what they were dealing with.

'We've spoken with the parents, Mr and Mrs Cowper,' Matt said, 'and we have no reason to believe that Thomas knows anyone over this way, or that this was all planned in advance. This has all the signs of a spur-of-the-moment decision. Which means we've a scared kid, out in the wilds, in this bloody awful weather, too, so we need him home. And part of that, in addition to the search from both sides, is doing our best to make sure that as many people are keeping an eye out for him as possible.'

Jadyn raised his hand.

'Do you know long will we'll be out?' he asked.

'Until we find him,' Matt said, 'simple as that. However, on a good day, it's about a three-hour trek from here to where Thomas set off,' said Matt. 'And as we can all see, this is not a good day. Hopefully, we'll find him quickly, and have him off the hill, warmed up and back home, but this could be a long one.'

With no other questions offered, and having thanked the other teams who had joined them, and in such atrocious conditions, Matt then concluded the meeting.

'We've enough local knowledge and expertise in this room to go out into those hills, and regardless of the weather, find a tic on a sheep's arse,' he said. 'We've also got night vision, thermal imaging, and GPS. Not enough, true, but more than we had a few years ago, when had nothing at all. So, let's get out there, find Thomas, and get the lad back home.'

'If he's run away, then he might not want to go back home,' Jadyn said.

'And we'll cross that bridge as and when,' said Matt. Then he clapped his hands and added, 'Right then everyone, let's get shifting and bring Thomas home.'

No sooner had Matt stopped speaking than the gathering burst into activity, as everyone headed off, the air rich with excited chatter.

'Jadyn, you're with me,' Matt called over.

Jadyn joined the DS.

'What do you want me to do?'

Matt rested a hefty arm across Jadyn's shoulders.

'You're here to learn,' he said. 'Just stay with me, keep your eyes and ears open, and do as you're told.'

'Yes, Boss,' Jadyn said.

Matt smiled then.

'It's good to have you here,' he said. 'You'll be fine, I promise.'

And with that said, Matt led Jadyn back out into the snow.

CHAPTER TWENTY-TWO

HARRY OPENED THE FRONT DOOR ONLY TO FIND HIMSELF thrust backwards as the storm crashed into it and tried to rip it off its hinges. Snow swelled in the darkness, a murmuration of winter's brood casting itself against the wood.

In the bare hallway light, he saw four figures standing in front of him. He also caught sight of a large vehicle parked at an angle some way behind them, partly blocking the driveway, up by the lane. Then, before he had a chance to ask who they were, and what it was they wanted, they barged into the house, half falling as they stumbled in out of the cold.

Harry fell back as the four figures crashed into the house, two of them carrying a third, the fourth of their group walking into the house behind them to grab the door and swing it shut with a deafening slam.

The one being carried was a woman, her face the colour of fresh dough, her brow wet with sweat as well as melting snow. The two carrying her lowered her to the floor and she cried out in pain.

'Who are you?' Harry asked. 'What's happened?'

The man who had just shut the door turned to look at Harry. Harry watched his eyes widen as he took in Harry's scarred face.

'There's been an accident,' the man said, staring still, his words hesitant. 'We ... we came off the road in the snow. Managed to get ourselves here.' He gestured towards the woman. 'She's injured. Needs to rest.'

Jameson was over to the woman in an instant.

Harry called for Liz, who appeared a few seconds later from the reading room.

The door to the dining room opened and the occupants spilled out.

'Back inside,' Harry said, pointing at the room behind them. 'Now.'

Liz dropped to Jameson's side to help him with the injured woman.

'That woman's injured,' said Kirsty, ignoring Harry's command. 'What about Tony? Where is he? He's a doctor, he can help.'

'No arguing,' Harry growled, then softening his voice, added, 'All of you, back inside.' When no one moved, he said, 'Please? I'll be through in a minute and will be able to explain everything then, I'm sure.'

The door to the dining room closed, though the sound of agitated muttering behind it was more than apparent.

'There must be a first aid kit in the house,' Liz said, checking over the woman's injury. She then looked up at Harry. 'There's not much we can do here, but if we can find a few bandages, some dressings, we can stem the blood, keep her stable, get some painkillers inside her; it'll make it easier for her between now and when we can get her to the hospital.'

'Get the chef, he'll know where the first aid kit is,' Harry said, then he turned to the new visitors and took in everything before him in an instant.

The group consisted of three men and the injured woman, and they all looked like they'd been through the wars. Harry saw cuts and grazes, ripped clothing, blood. On the one hand, he knew that this had all the markings of a car accident, people being thrown around, knocking into each other. But on the other hand? Something wasn't quite right. Maybe, though, he was just on edge from what had already happened that evening.

'The rest of you don't look so great either,' he said, as Liz popped through into the dining room, returning a few seconds later with the chef.

'You were right, Jack here says there's a first aid kit in the kitchen,' she said. 'Won't be long.'

'It's not that good though,' Jack said, looking at the injured woman, then at Harry. 'Just plasters and paracetamol really. There's a better one in my van.'

'Get it,' said Harry.

The man from the group who had so far done all the speaking stepped forward. He then put himself between Harry and the others.

'We had a job of it getting the Jeep out of what we'd ploughed into. Not easy.'

He held up his hands. They were cut and bleeding.

'That looks sore,' Harry said.

The man lowered his hands again, though the markings on one of them caught Harry's eye; something about them didn't sit right. To him, they looked like something had been wrapped around the fingers, the hand, tight enough to leave bruises. What, though? He'd seen markings like that before, just couldn't place them, not yet, anyway.

'It's nothing,' the man said.

Harry nodded towards the door.

'How's your vehicle, then?' he asked.

The man ignored Harry's question.

'She needs to lie down,' he said, then pointed at the door to his right. 'That the lounge through there? We'll use that.'

'I'm afraid you can't go in there,' said Harry, offering no further information as to why.

The man ignored him and walked over to it with his hand raised to push it fully open.

Harry got in front of him, shutting the door before he had a chance to head on through.

'Like I said, you can't go in there,' Harry repeated, a little firmer this time.

The man stared up at Harry for a moment, eyes narrow, chest heaving.

Harry stood with his back to the door, barring the way.

'Hey, no problem,' the man said with a nod. He held up his hands, palms facing Harry. 'Look, we're sorry to barge in on you like this, we really are.' He stepped away from Harry and walked around the hall, looking up the stairs, then at one or two of the paintings on the wall. 'Nice place you have here, by the way. Anyway, we took a wrong turn, you see, otherwise we wouldn't be here at all.'

'More than one I should think, to end up where you are now, and looking like you do,' said Harry.

That comment, he noticed, caused one of the men on the floor to glance up at the man in front of him, concern blooming in his eyes for a moment.

'We saw the lights, didn't know what else to do,' the man said. 'We just need to wait the storm out, that's all. You won't even notice us, I promise.'

'Well, we've already noticed, haven't we?' Harry said. 'Kind of hard not to. And as far as waiting the storm out goes, you've not really got much choice; no way an ambulance is getting through to us any time soon. Though we'll put a call through once your friend there is comfortable.'

'That's okay,' the man said. 'She doesn't need an ambulance, I'm sure. Just rest.'

'Oh, you're sure, are you?' Jameson said from down on the floor. 'She has a serious puncture wound, from what I have no idea, but she's bleeding heavily. And the rest of you are all injured as well.'

'When it calms down outside, we'll be on our way,' said the man, ignoring Jameson. 'That's all you need to worry about.'

'And why would we be worried?'

The question was from Jack, the one person Harry had yet to question about what had happened with Walsh. He had returned from his van with the promised first aid kit, and handed it to Liz, who was kneeling beside Pete, and working together to do what they could to help the injured woman.

Jack was standing outside the dining room and staring at the new arrivals, phone hanging from his right hand, the hems of his trouser legs damp. Harry thought he noticed something else about the trousers, but was interrupted by the man who had just answered Jameson.

'I'm just saying you don't need to be concerned,' he said. 'We'll make our own way to the hospital once the storm has died down. We'll probably get there quicker than an ambulance anyway. As for whatever it is that you've got going on here, we'll make sure we keep out of your way, I promise.' He held up a hand. 'Scout's honour.'

Harry looked down at the injured woman, quietly considering his options, not that there were any. This complicated things a little, that was for sure. Investigating a murder would be difficult enough under normal circumstances, the storm made things infinitely more so. And on top of all that, he now had to deal with these new arrivals. Sometimes, he almost missed being in a war zone with the bullets flying. Almost.

'What about a bedroom?' Jameson suggested.

'They're all full,' said Jack, jumping in before Harry had a chance to reply. 'We can't put them up there, can we?'

Harry heard concern in the chef's voice. Probably professional more than anything, he thought, worried about those who had paid money to be there in the first place having to go without.

Liz said, 'Getting her up the stairs isn't going to be easy, not with the pain she's in.' She then looked up at Harry. 'Why don't I just put Pearson upstairs, seeing as he's already got an allocated room, then we can use the reading room?'

'Agreed,' Harry said. 'Great idea.'

'Makes more sense,' said Jack, relief clear in his voice.

Liz dashed off and Harry watched as she led the doctor out of the reading room, Smudge at her heels, then up the stairs to the first floor. She returned soon after, minus the doctor and the dog.

'Smudge is keeping an eye on him,' she said.

'There's a small room just down there on the left,' Harry said, gesturing towards the now empty reading room. 'Take your friend through there. I'll have something brought in for her to lie on so that she's comfortable. How does that sound?'

'You know, I didn't catch your name,' the man said, as behind him Liz and Jameson helped the two men lift the woman off the floor to carry her through to the reading room.

'Generally, when a stranger turns up at my door, I expect them to do the introducing,' replied Harry.

The man said nothing, his eyes dancing around the hall and across the paintings once again, before coming to rest on Harry for a moment, the slightest of grins on his face.

'Nicholls,' he said at last. 'The name is Patrick Nicholls.'

'Well, let's get you all settled, then,' Harry said, and directed him to where Liz and Jameson had taken the others.

Walking into the reading room, Harry found the woman sitting on the two-seater sofa, her face ghostly white. Liz was next to her, while Jameson worked on securing her arm and shoulder. The two men who had carried her through were munching their way through the sandwiches Harry hadn't eaten.

'Hungry?' he asked.

'Too bloody right we are,' said one of the men. 'Worked up a bit of an appetite earlier, you see.'

At that, the other three laughed, though the sound the woman made was strangled by the pain she was in.

'I'll have some food and drink brought in,' Harry said, then looked at the injured woman. 'And as I promised, we'll get something in here for you to rest on, help you get comfortable. But that's all we can do for now.'

'Thanks,' the woman said, the word barely a strained whisper.

Harry closed the door.

'One more thing,' he said, popping his head back around the door. 'I'm afraid you've not exactly arrived at the best of times. We've a situation here, which we're currently trying to resolve, so it would be greatly appreciated if you stayed in here for the duration, if that's okay? Toilet is just across the hall, so you should be comfortable. This room is warm, and if you get bored, well, there's plenty of reading material, as you can see.'

'Much appreciated,' said Nicholls, 'Mr ...?'

'Grimm,' Harry said. 'Detective Chief Inspector Grimm.' He gestured over to Liz and Jameson. 'And over there we have DCI Jameson and Police Constable Coates.'

Harry watched the group look at each other as they digested this information.

'Now, is there anything else you need?' he asked. 'Or can I leave you alone now, and get on with a few things?'

'Detectives?' Nicholls said. 'You're with the police, then?'

'We are,' Harry said, noticing Liz looking at him out of the corner of her eye now.

'Interesting,' Nicholls said.

'Is it?' Harry replied.

Jameson stood up. Liz joined him.

'I'm done,' he said.

'We'll be leaving you then, for now,' said Harry. 'We'll get those things to you as soon as we can. If you need anything, just shout.'

'Thanks, we will,' Nicholls said.

Out in the hall, Harry walked back over to the lounge and stood for a moment, staring back down the way he had just come.

Liz and Jameson joined him.

'Not sure you can just promote me like that,' Liz said.

'Yeah, what's going on, Harry?' Jameson asked. 'You didn't mention that I'm retired, either.'

Harry wasn't sure what to say.

'Right now, I really don't know,' he said, then he turned to the front door and pulled it open far enough for them to all see out into the parking area. 'Just thought it was a good idea to let them know we're police.'

In the thin bar of light laid out across the snow from the open door, Harry looked at the vehicle which he could now see was a large and imposing Jeep. It was so different from the vehicle he and Liz had driven over in from Hawes that it may as well have been from another planet. It was a monster, he thought, all knobbly wheels and meanness and shiny black paint, like it was designed with no other aim than to drive to Hell and back.

'That what they came in, then?' Liz asked.

'It is,' said Harry.

Jameson leaned over to have a look.

'Might just be the snow,' he said, 'but I'm struggling to see where it's been in an accident bad enough to cause someone to break bones.'

'So am I,' said Harry, scratching a deep scar on his chin. 'Anyone have a torch handy?'

CHAPTER TWENTY-THREE

'A torch?' said Jameson. 'Actually, yes, I do. If you give me a second, I'll—'

'It was a rhetorical question,' Harry said. 'Liz has one anyway.'

'Well, as you once told me, one is none, two is one,' Jameson said.

Harry laughed.

'You still remember that, then?' he asked.

'I do,' Jameson said. 'Wise words.'

'One is what?' asked Liz, handing her torch to Harry.

'It's just something from my army days,' said Harry. 'It's about redundancy really, always making sure you have reserve kit.'

'How is one none, then?' said Liz. 'That doesn't make any sense. One is one, isn't it? And two is two.'

Harry held up her torch.

'What happens if the battery's dead in this, then?' he asked.

'Then we haven't got a torch,' Liz answered.

'Exactly,' said Harry. 'One is none, see? So, you always try and make sure you have a backup. That way, two is one. It's all about redundancy.'

'Oh right, I see,' said Liz.

'You don't, do you?'

'No,' said Liz. 'But I'll survive, I think.'

Jameson left Harry to talk to Liz and jogged over to where he remembered knocking a torch off a shelf under the stairs earlier that day. Yanking open the door to the cupboard, he saw the torch, grabbed it, checked it was working, then headed back to Harry.

'Here you go,' he said, but as he went to place the torch into Harry's outstretched hand, he paused.

'Something up?' Harry said, taking hold of the torch.

Jameson didn't let go.

'I don't know,' he said. 'That cupboard.'

'What about it?' Liz asked.

Jameson frowned.

'Seemed bigger,' he said. 'Though that doesn't make any sense, does it?'

Harry clicked on both torches, handing Liz's back to her.

'Liz, you stay inside and keep an eye on the others. Pete and I will have a look outside.'

Outside, Harry led Jameson over to the Jeep. Jameson followed as best as he could, though the wind and the snow did its best to throw him onto his arse a couple of times. The light spilling from the house behind him made the shadows in the parking area seem all the darker.

As he trailed behind Harry, Jameson couldn't shake the feeling that something was off, but what? How could a cupboard seem bigger? That just didn't make any sense.

'Well, there we are, then,' Harry said, having completed a full circuit of the vehicle.

'And where's that, exactly?' asked Jameson, his mind still back in the cupboard, his body starting to freeze in the thick snow.

Harry cast the beam from his torch inside the Jeep, then along the side of the vehicle.

'Not a scratch,' he said. 'And the keys are still in it.'

'Looks like a tough machine though,' Jameson said. 'A bit too fancy for my liking, but you could probably drive this into a brick wall, and it wouldn't notice.'

'Might make it look a little less ugly,' Harry said.

'It's got a bulbar up front, full external roll cage,' Jameson added.

Harry said nothing, just kept staring at the vehicle.

'Is that it, then?' Jameson asked, a shiver juddering his words like he was biting a drill. 'Because if it's all the same with you, I wouldn't mind being back in the warmth.'

He didn't wait for an answer, and headed back inside, going as fast as he could without slipping in the snow.

Back inside the house, Jameson waited for Harry to join him, then heaved the door shut behind them once they were in.

They stood there staring at each other, covered in snow. Liz popped back out of the dining room and came over to join them.

'We've only been out there for a few minutes and look at us,' Jameson said, wiping his face. 'Like extras from The Snowman.'

'Never seen it,' said Harry.

'You must've done,' said Liz.

Harry shook his head.

'Anyway,' he said. 'Moving on with slightly more important matters ...'

Jameson, however, wasn't listening. His mind was back in that cupboard again.

'Harry?' he said.

'What?'

'You mind unlocking the lounge for a moment?'

Pulling the key out of his pocket, Harry hesitated before handing it over to Jameson.

'I wouldn't normally let a someone who is still, theoretically at least, a suspect roam freely around my crime scene. But seeing as it's you and under the circumstances...'

Jameson said nothing, just raised a questioning eyebrow.

'Liz,' continued Harry, 'stay in the room with him for proce-dure's sake. I'm going to go and have another word with our new guests.'

As Harry headed off, Jameson turned to the lounge door,

unlocked it, and stepped inside. The room was even colder now, if that was at all possible, the fire close to death. In front of it lay Walsh's body, a dusting of snow from the window having danced in on the breeze to settle on his back.

With Liz staying at the door, Jameson stepped deeper into the room, damp shoe prints tracing his path. Something in here was bothering him, he thought, something linked to the cupboard, but what on earth was it?

He looked around once again, his eyes scanning the walls, the ceiling, the floor, and that was when he saw them, the scratches etched into the polished, worn planks beneath his feet.

Jameson turned back to Liz at the door.

'Coming through,' he said.

Liz stepped out of the way as Jameson dashed past and ran down the hall to the cupboard under the stairs.

He tugged open the door. In front of him, a small well of darkness sent out a waft of dust, the smell of old things long forgotten.

'What's going on?' Liz asked, having followed him.

'The suitcase,' Jameson said. 'It's gone.'

'What suitcase?'

Jameson was too deep in thought to reply. He remembered how the cupboard had seemed so empty when he had fetched the torch earlier. He realised now that was because the last time he'd been in there, he'd thumped into the suitcase. So, where was it now, then? And what had it been doing in there in the first place to warrant it having been moved? And more to the point, why the hell did he even care?

'Pete?'

Harry's voice came to him from out in the hallway, behind Liz.

'Just a minute, Harry, I'm thinking,' Jameson replied. 'No, wait; you got that torch with you still?'

Harry handed it over.

Jameson switched it on.

'What are you looking for?' Harry asked.

'Not sure ...' Jameson said, sweeping the gloomy space with the small searchlight. 'It was in here, you see, but now it isn't, and I want to know why.'

The shelf was the same, the walls, it was just a storage space; there was nothing special about it at all. The owners hadn't even bothered to carpet it.

Jameson stared at the floor, the torch burning a bright white circle on the wooden planks at his feet.

'Pete ...'

Jameson knelt down, touched some marks on the boards.

'When I arrived, I came in here, thinking this is where the toilet was,' he said. 'There was a large suitcase in here.'

'And now it's not,' Liz said.

'Exactly,' said Jameson, his fingers still tracing the marks on the floor.

He stood up, pushed past Harry and Liz, and headed back to the lounge.

At the door, Liz reached out with the keys and unlocked it again.

'What is it?' Harry asked, following him into the room, Liz staying at the door.

Jameson pointed at the lounge floor.

'There,' he said. 'Those scratch marks; they look the same to you? Like the ones in that cupboard?'

Harry peered over Jameson's shoulder.

'Could be,' he said. 'They're just scratches though, aren't they?'

'Yes and no,' said Jameson, and traced the path of the marks, faint as they were, with the milky beam of the torch. He then followed the marks around to behind the back of the desk to the right of the door.

At the same time, Harry spotted something on the floor over by the body. Dropping to his knees, he pulled out an evidence bag. From the carpet, he picked up a cigarette butt, stowed it in the bag, then slipped the bag into his pocket.

Harry was back on his feet as Jameson said, 'Well, then, would you look at that.'

'Well then, would I look at what?' Harry said, heading over to see what Jameson was talking about.

Jameson clicked the torch off and handed it to Harry, then reached behind the desk. Hidden from the rest of the room by the panel at the front of the desk was a large suitcase. He dragged it round to Harry.

'Two things,' Jameson said. 'First, it seems that I'm still a decent detective.'

'Debatable,' Harry said, though Jameson noticed the smile. 'And second?'

Jameson lowered the suitcase to the floor and then unzipped it, flapping it open on the floor like a huge clam.

'Second?' he said. 'If this was heavy enough to scratch the floor in the cupboard and here in the lounge, then what was in it? More importantly, though, why is it in here now?'

'And, for that matter, empty,' Harry said.

'Exactly.'

Jameson stared up at Harry as he glared down at the suitcase then turned his head to allow his gaze to fall on Walsh's body by the fire.

'You have got to be kidding me,' Harry said, then before Jameson could reply, he was past Liz and out the door, and running up the stairs two at a time. 'And lock that bloody door!' he called back, his voice a bellowing roar.

CHAPTER TWENTY-FOUR

Harry stood for a moment, trying to get his ducks in a row, as he stared at the man who was sitting in front of him on the edge of a comfortable-looking double bed. Trouble was, after what Jameson had just shown him, the ducks made no sense at all, no matter what order they were in.

Smudge was on the other side of the room, having managed to find another radiator to curl up beneath. She was snoring, too, Harry noticed.

He had been called out to this house in a snowstorm to investigate a murder. And up until now, he'd still been sure that's exactly what it was. But now? Just what the hell was any of this? What was Tony actually saying? What had Walsh blackmailed Tony to do? Certainly not kill him, that was for sure. And something about what Tony was, and wasn't, saying was telling him that the man was definitely no killer. Not only that, and by his own admission, he wasn't a doctor either. Then there was what he'd learned from Scott and now that suitcase ...

Harry pulled a chair out from under a vanity cabinet, thumping it down on the floor hard enough to make the doctor flinch.

'So, you didn't check his pulse,' said, sitting down.

'Of course I didn't,' replied Tony. 'Not a doctor, remember?'

'If you're not a doctor, then what are you exactly?' Harry asked.

'I'm a teacher, actually,' Tony said. 'A-level Mathematics. Probability always fascinated me. A little too much, it seems, otherwise I wouldn't be here now, would I?'

A few things clicked into place in Harry's mind, but together they were all so completely ridiculous that the thought alone was enough to have him out of his chair again, even though he had just sat down.

'Walsh blackmailed you to be here,' he said, Scott's own story now echoing in his mind.

'That's what I'm telling you.'

'You mean, that he blackmailed you to force you to come here and pretend to be a doctor?'

'Yes.'

'Why?'

The doctor shook his head, rolled his eyes, and Harry had an urge to slap the man hard enough to knock those eyes out of his skull. But he resisted, just.

'You really can't guess?'

'Probably best you tell me yourself,' Harry said.

Tony leaned forward, his elbows on his knees.

'If you want people to think you're dead, you need a doctor, don't you?'

'Go on,' encouraged Harry.

'My job was to be convincing enough so that everyone would believe me when I told them Walsh was dead, so much so that the police would be sent out.'

'And here I am.'

'Exactly.'

'There's no "exactly" about any of this,' said Harry, his voice raw and angry now, refusing to believe what was now forcing its way to the front of his mind. 'Walsh is in that room. We've all seen him. *I* have seen him. Just a few minutes ago, as it happens. We've all seen the knife. Whether you're a doctor or not, that doesn't get us away from the fact we have a dead—'

Harry stopped talking, then stared at Tony.

'There it is,' said Tony. 'Now he sees it.'

'The suitcase,' said Harry.

'Wondered when you'd get around to finding that,' Tony said, and did the slowest of claps. 'Well done, Officer. Sounds like you've got there at last. Quicker than Walsh wanted, but long enough I should think.'

Harry was fairly sure the sensation inside his head right then was that of his brain melting, unable as it was to deal with the revelation forcing itself to the front.

'You can't be serious ... You just can't be. This is ... well, it's ridiculous!'

Harry waited a moment, waited for Tony to tell him something —*anything*—that would prove these clearly mad thoughts in his head to be not just wrong, but impossible.

Tony shrugged, folded his arms, and said nothing.

Harry was at the door.

'You bloody well stay here,' he said, jabbing a finger at Pearson. Then he yanked the door open and raced back down the stairs.

Jameson and Liz were waiting for him outside the lounge door.

'Key!' Harry demanded.

Liz pulled the key from her pocket, but it got caught up and twisted in the material. She tugged the key harder. Harry heard the material rip, and the key was free. Then the door was open.

The room, Harry thought, looked the same; the window was open, the scratches on the floor were still there, Walsh's body was on the floor in front of the fire, knife in his back. And there was that suitcase, just lying there exactly where Jameson had laid it, staring up at him, open-mouthed, like it was laughing. And who could blame it? he thought. Because if what he was about to reveal was true, then he would be a laughingstock.

Harry heard Liz behind him.

'What is it? What's wrong?' she asked.

Harry looked behind him to see that Jameson was now standing next to Liz.

'Harry?' Jameson said.

Harry held up a finger to have them both wait at the door.

He walked over to Walsh, dropped to the floor, then reached out for the hat, pulling it off the dead man's head.

'Oh, Walsh, you absolute bastard ...'

Harry jumped to his feet and slammed the hat down in a crumpled ball onto the floor. Then he kicked it, and the hat landed in the embers of the fire, and a second or two later started to burn.

'What is it?' Liz asked, from over by the door. 'What the hell's going on, Boss?'

Harry didn't answer, and stormed out of the room, tripping over the suitcase on the way, then pushing through Liz and Jameson to march back up the stairs again to where Tony was still sitting in the bedroom.

'So, where the hell is he, then?' Harry demanded, his voice the roar of a lion. 'And you'd better tell me right now, or I'm going to make absolutely bloody sure that you both end up locked away for so long that when you finally get out the only way anyone will know it's you will be to dig up your bones and do a DNA check!'

'Harry?'

Jameson was at the door, Liz beside him.

'I'm busy!'

'You're shouting is what you are,' Jameson said. 'What's going on?'

'Right now, I don't exactly know, but I'm going to find out, aren't I, Tony?'

Harry moved closer to where Tony was sitting on the bed, towering over him, his fists clenched.

Against the wall, Smudge thumped her tail on the floor, oblivious to everything that was going on, just happy to be warm.

'I've told you everything I know!' Tony said, desperation in his voice. 'Honestly, I have!'

Harry laughed at that.

"'Honestly?' Not a word I'd choose, that's for sure. You're not even a bloody doctor. This whole damned thing has been one big lie, so you need to stop pissing me about and tell me where he is! Now!'

'Who?' Jameson asked. 'Where who is?'

'Walsh!' Harry said, snapping around to face him and Liz. 'That's who. Isn't it, Tony?'

'But he's in the lounge,' Liz said.

Harry stared hard at Tony, leaning down just enough to cause him to push himself a little further back on the bed, so much so that his feet lifted off the floor.

'Move even an inch from where you are now, and the dog will have you,' he said.

Smudge thumped her tail on the floor again.

'And as you can see, she's already looking forward to it.'

Harry headed back out of the room.

'I think you need to see this for yourself,' he said, and Liz and Jameson followed.

Again, Jameson unlocked the door, and Harry took them both over to Walsh's body on the floor. The hat in the fireplace was now little more than a blackened pile of ash. Then he kicked Walsh hard, flipping the body over onto its back.

'Bloody hell, Harry!' Jameson said. 'What the—'

Jameson stopped speaking as he stared opened mouthed at the body at his feet.

'Yeah, it's hard to know quite what to say, isn't it?' Harry said.

'It's ... it's a dummy?' Liz said, disbelief dripping from her words.

'The technical term is, I think, medical manikin,' said Harry. 'Not exactly cheap, but then, I'm guessing money isn't actually a problem for our Mr Walsh, now, is it?'

Jameson dropped to the floor and held something up. 'Wondered where this was,' he said.

'That's a starting pistol,' Harry said.

'It was all part of the murder mystery,' said Jameson. 'How the hell didn't we notice?'

'Why would you?' said Harry. 'Why would anyone? I mean, isn't that the whole point of this?'

Jameson stared back at Harry, clearly confused.

'You've got someone with you who you think is a doctor, right?' Harry explained. 'They come out of this room and tell you what's happened, so you believe them, don't you? You go in and check, and there it is, a body with a knife in its back, just like the doctor said. Everything confirmed. No need for anyone else to go have a nosy.'

'Except, it's a dummy,' said Liz.

'You've already seen Walsh here, in this room, in these clothes, so you're not going to suspect anything, are you?' Harry said, his eyes on Jameson. 'Then you follow procedure and close the place off from everyone else.'

'But what if I hadn't been here?' Jameson asked. 'I only did that because I'm police.'

'Doubt it would have made any difference to what was planned,' said Harry. 'In fact, I doubt very much that anyone would've gone back in there once Mr Pearson had passed on the news and called the police. Most people aren't too keen on being in the same room as the dead, especially when they're nice and fresh.'

Having kicked the manikin onto its back, Harry, Liz, and Jameson could now see it in all its glory. The skin, the proportions of the body, everything about it was frighteningly real.

'The whole damned thing is a decoy,' Harry said. '*We* are part of the decoy; this whole weekend, the dummy, calling the police, everything. All so that Walsh could bugger off.'

'Disappear, you mean?' Jameson said. 'Why the hell would he do that?'

'That's exactly what I want to find out,' said Harry. 'He blackmailed our friend Mr Pearson to play a doctor. Now that you've seen this, it'll come as no surprise to hear that checking its pulse is a little difficult.'

'He lied, then?'

'Pearson is no doctor,' Harry said. 'Walsh had him over a barrel, blackmailing him with a file on his secret life as a gambling addict. Threatened to tell everyone, destroy his life, his family, unless he came here and played the part.'

'And you believe him?' Liz asked.

'We were called out to investigate a murder,' Harry said. 'By having everyone here think Pearson is a doctor, it was easy to get them to believe him, to stay out of the room, and to have the police called in. My guess is that up to the moment the doctor came into the room, it was still Walsh on the floor. However, when Pearson came in, they did a switcheroo with this dummy here, and the knife. The dummy was in the suitcase and Pearson brought it in from that cupboard in the hall, before hiding it behind the desk. Walsh then buggers off out of that open window over there, and Pearson carries on with his clever little deception. Pearson admitted he was supposed to drag it out a little longer than he's managed to, at least until the forensics team turned up, but like he said, it's probably been long enough.'

'That all sounds very convoluted,' said Jameson.

'Or maybe it's just very well planned,' said Harry. 'Think how much time's been wasted by Tony, by us, by everything that's happened up to this point.'

'What about the weather, though?' Liz asked. 'No one in their right mind would try and disappear in this.'

Harry wasn't so sure.

'No one can control the weather,' he said, 'no matter what the conspiracy theorists say about chemtrails and global elites. This was a plan long in the making. And if you think about it, the weather may even play to Walsh's advantage. My guess is that he has a route out of here, a vehicle somewhere in a barn, something like that, and he's probably already made his way to it by now.'

Harry looked at Liz and Jameson and their pained expressions as they tried to get their heads around the revelation.

'Walsh has money, the Porsche is evidence of that. And,

judging by what Pearson told me, and what Liz and I heard from three of our other witnesses, I'm going to make an educated guess that he's not earned it simply by being a private investigator.'

'Or maybe he has,' said Jameson. 'You said yourself that he was blackmailing Pearson, right? So, he carried out surveillance on him, presented him with the evidence, and gave him an ultimatum. Who's to say he hasn't done it before? Actually, don't even bother answering; he's absolutely done this before, hasn't he? Probably has dirt on dozens of poor bastards who've paid him to keep quiet.'

'Now that's clever,' said Liz. 'Evil, yes, but clever.'

'It's also true,' Harry said.

He told them what he'd learned from Scott, and also from the Rasheeds. The only one who seemed to have a legitimate reason to be there at all, not counting Jameson, was Kirsty Cropper. And that in itself was odd, Harry thought.

'So, they were all here investigating Walsh?' said Jameson. 'What the hell's going on, Harry?'

'Far too much, that's what,' Harry replied. 'And with the weather like it is, there's not much we can do with regards to forensics or anything else, not until the storm abates and they can actually get through.'

'Makes you think though, doesn't it?' said Jameson.

'It does,' said Harry, seeing his own thought process reflected in the eyes of his old friend. 'You're thinking the same, then?'

Jameson gave a shrug.

'Maybe he knew they were after him,' he said.

'Then why have them here this weekend?' Liz asked.

'Ego,' said Harry. 'It's probably like a game to him, and he likes to win. So, he has them think that he hasn't a clue, and they turn up, ready to do whatever it is they plan to do, but before they get the chance, he's already buggered off.'

'Well, at least we're not trapped in this house with a killer,' said Jameson. 'So, every cloud, right?'

Harry said, 'While we're here on our own, I want to find out everything we can about Walsh and where he's gone. I need to speak with Pearson again, and I also need to tell everyone else what's happened.'

'We need to put a call in about Walsh,' Jameson said.

'I agree,' said Harry. 'He's not going to be easy to find, but the sooner word is out, the better. Liz, you can sort that out. You've got the notes from the interviews, so see if you can get anything on that other name at least.'

'John Setton, you mean?'

'Yes,' said Harry. 'Right now, we don't know what his real name actually is. For all we know, Walsh and Setton are both aliases.'

'No problem,' nodded Liz.

'I need to check his room,' Harry continued. 'See if he left anything behind, and have a good look outside to see if we can find out where he's buggered off to. There may be tracks, something that shows us where he's gone, what he planned, anything.'

'Lovely day for it,' said Jameson.

'Isn't it just?'

CHAPTER TWENTY-FIVE

MARINA KNEW SHE WAS DYING; SHE KNEW IT AS WELL AS SHE knew anything. Her body was ruined, and every move she made, even breathing, ripped her in two. But she also knew that she was going to make damn good use of the life left within her.

Opening her eyes, and finding herself lying on her side, the first thing Marina saw was the dead stare of a man on the floor beside her. His neck was a mess of blood and ripped flesh. She could see his windpipe, she realised, remembering then the weight of the bottle in her hand as she had swung it against his head, then jumped on him to ram the jagged edge of it into his throat.

Marina felt nothing. No remorse, no regret. The man had broken into their home, attacked them, and now he was dead, and that seemed all well and good. He probably hadn't expected it, she thought, but that had been his error.

Rolling onto her back, sharp pains like knives drove through her, and she screamed. The sound of it bounced around the empty house, coming back to her lonely and desperate.

The room was cold, but there was a faint glow of orange to the place, and she noticed that there was still life in the fire, enough warmth to keep the wintery chill outside a while longer.

Staring up at the ceiling, Marina's mind spun. Memory upon

memory drove into it, smashing it apart, hammering down into her and forcing out a wild, ragged cry. Harvey was gone. Her whole life was gone. Everything ripped to shreds by a gang who had left them both for dead. And Harvey was, that was for sure. But she wasn't, was she? And those murderous bastards had left, not knowing, driving off congratulating themselves on the fun they'd had, patting themselves on the back for a job well done. All for revenge, all to pay Harvey back for what he'd done.

Marina was about to ruin it for them, and that thought was enough to cause her to smile.

She tried to sit up, but her left arm gave way, hot pain rushing through it, setting her nervous system on fire. She lifted her arm, saw bones sticking out between her elbow and wrist. She tried again, this time using her right arm. The pain was bad, but her arm was strong enough to have her eventually sitting upright, though the effort made her head spin. Nausea swept in then, wave after wave of it, and Marina fell to the side onto the edge of the sofa. She squeezed her eyes shut, forced the queasiness away, and ordered herself to stay conscious.

Opening her eyes again, Marina saw Harvey, the love of her life, the beginning and the end of everything she had ever been or ever wanted to be, lying cold and dead. He was a few steps away on his back on the floor. His chest was a mess, and she remembered the explosion of a gun being fired. She saw a boot print on his face and noticed how his head was an odd shape. She would never again hear his voice, feel him hold her, enjoy his laugh.

Marina wanted to cry. She wanted to wail and scream and weep. And she would, she knew that. She would leave this world drenched in the sorrow of the loss of her one true love. But right now, that would have to wait.

A phone, that's what she needed. She remembered having hers close by, looking through photos, but where was it now?

Forcing herself to look away from her dead husband, Marina scanned the room, which wasn't easy, with her eyes so swollen, her vision blurred. Everything was a mess. She had vague recollections of being thrown and kicked around the place, the sound of laughter following her as her body broke with every impact.

There it was, on the far side of the room, up against the wall. It was so far away ...

Marina closed her eyes, took a deep breath, exhaled.

The first movement she made wasn't the worst, not by a long way. Every inch of ground she gained as she dragged herself towards it cost her; blood oozed from wounds, she heard bone scrape against bone. The worst of it, though, had been pulling herself over Harvey's body, forcing herself to ignore how cold he felt, how still.

Her hand fell on the phone and Marina paused, unsure as to whether she had enough energy, enough time left, to call the emergency services. Maybe it's better to just lie here and die, she thought. To claw her way back to Harvey, wrap herself around him, and fade into the night, perhaps to even meet him again somewhere in the dark beyond.

No. Not yet.

Marina lifted the phone, saw how much time had passed since she had seen Harvey alive, and with her eyes on her beloved, called 999.

JEN WAS SITTING in the office over in Hawes enjoying the sound of the storm, mainly because it was outside, and she was not, which was definitely the best way around. She was supposed to be home by now, but that was just the way things were with this job, and she didn't mind, really. The time had already slipped past nine-thirty, but at least she had some company, thanks to the dog Jadyn and Grace had found earlier that day.

The wind was refusing to relent, buffeting against the window like it wanted to break in. Jen had ventured beyond the front door of the community centre a couple of times since everyone else had left, just enough to allow the dog to go and do its business. Not that the poor animal had been entirely keen, and had done what it need to do barely a metre from the main doors, before dashing back inside.

The day was certainly turning out to be eventful, and her trip with Jim over the Buttertubs Pass to deal with a traffic incident had been the least of it. Jim was now out with his dad, bringing sheep in off the fell. Probably enjoying it, too. She smiled. Jadyn was on with his first rescue, and under the watchful eye of Matt, scouring the fells for the lad who had gone missing from the farm in Marsett. And not too far away from there, Harry and Liz were now investigating a suspicious death.

A large part of Jen wanted to be out and in the thick of it, but she knew that her role back at the office was just as vital. Trouble was, she had never been all that good at sitting still. It was why she was such a keen runner after all.

Reaching down to scratch the dog under its chin, Jen jumped a little when a call came through on her radio. It was Liz.

'Everything okay?' Jen asked.

'Not really, no,' said Liz from the other end of the call. 'That supposed murder we came out here to look into? Nothing of the sort.'

'What? How do you mean?'

'Long story,' Liz said.

Jen then listened as Liz quickly explained everything that had happened, and how a private investigator called Carl Walsh had now disappeared.

'That's incredible,' she said.

'Isn't it, just?' Liz replied.

Jen took down all the information that she could.

'How's the dog?' Liz asked.

'A proper softy,' said Jen, looking down at the Whippet. 'Nice company, though, while everyone else is out and about.'

Liz and Jen said their goodbyes and Jen reached over to pick up the office phone, only to have it ring just before she touched it. She was surprised to find herself talking to an emergency call handler.

'Actually, I was just about to call you,' Jen said. 'Obviously not you specifically, but you know what I mean.'

When the call was over, Jen sat for a moment, staring at the dog. The conversation had lasted little more than five minutes, just long enough for both her and the call handler to give each other the information they needed to share. Word would be put out about the now missing and very much not dead Walsh. Jen, though, had something more urgent to deal with.

Standing up, she grabbed her jacket, the dog, locked up, and dashed outside. Pushing through the snow, the dog huddled in tightly to her chest, she found the last remaining incident response vehicle to be little more than a giant blob of meringue in the marketplace. Jen wiped enough snow away to allow her to put the dog on the back seat, then set to with clearing the rest of the car. With that done, she opened the boot, pulled out four sets of snow chains, and quickly fitted them around the wheels. Then she jumped behind the steering wheel and started the engine. She then made a quick call to Liz.

'Doubt you're calling to tell me he's been found,' Liz said.

'I've passed on everything you told me,' Jen said, 'but I'm calling to let Harry know that I'm no longer going to be in the office.'

'Something up?'

'There's been a break-in at a house up Blean Lane, above Bainbridge, other side of the valley from Countersett.'

'You sure you'll make it?' Liz said 'The roads are really bad now, and they're only getting worse.'

'I'll be fine,' said Jen. 'Snow chains are on, and it's not like I've much choice. Anyway, the ambulance is on its way as well; they've sent the four-by-four one out.'

'Ambulance? Why? What's happened?'

'Not sure,' said Jen. 'Didn't get much from the call handler; two casualties anyway, not sure of the injuries, but it doesn't sound good.'

'Be careful.'

'I'm never anything else.'

Jen hung up and stared out through the windscreen. All she could see was snow. The road was covered, and the air was thick with the blizzard. Right now, though, she had no option but to head out into it.

Jen slipped the gear stick into reverse, eased the car gently out of where it was parked, then pointed the vehicle down dale.

CHAPTER TWENTY-SIX

WALSH HADN'T GOT TO WHERE HE WAS IN LIFE ON LUCK AND making it up as he went along. Well, maybe he had at the beginning, back when he was stupid, ignorant of risk, and strutted around with the invincibility of being young. But then he had been making good money as a loan shark, keeping under the radar just enough to grow his empire. Perhaps he'd grown cocky?

Regardless, that life had imploded quite dramatically, and he'd made a quick and desperate exit. Now, here he was, so many years later, doing exactly the same. Except now, he had resources, he had money, he knew what he was doing, and he was a survivor.

Walsh had planned everything that he could and in the minutest of detail, running through it all again and again to ensure nothing was missed. The weekend had been advertised for well over a year now; he'd kept the ad live, even after the small number of spaces had been filled, just to make sure everyone knew where he'd be and what he'd be doing; all part of that smokescreen. He'd even vetted the attendees—without their knowledge, obviously—and having that retired DCI along for the ride had been an absolute ace in the hole. The new chef had bothered him a little, but there had been no problems there, either.

He'd walked the route from the house at least a dozen times

over the last few months, travelling up in various hired cars, and different outfits, to walk it in all weathers—though the snow was a first—to make absolutely sure he knew where he was going, how long it would take, and what the terrain was like.

He'd also had a damned good try at planning for various other scenarios to make sure that he didn't get caught out. Which was why the weather was no surprise, despite what he'd told the chef back at the house.

Of course he had planned for the weather! He'd arranged the weekend in February because of it. Not that he'd necessarily expected as much snow as this, but at the very least he had hoped for the weather to be on the awful side of things rather than a weekend of sunshine. And he had lucked out, big time.

His escape from the house, and from his old life into something new had, in the end, been made all the easier with the snow, and Walsh had taken full advantage of it. There had been a few last-minute changes for sure, but not enough to have him worried. The opposite actually; it was already working in his favour.

The arrival of Tony Pearson in the lounge a few hours ago had set this final stage in motion. Walsh had jumped up from where he'd been lying on the floor, then pulled the dummy out from where he had stashed it, along with all the gear he needed to put on for what was next.

With the dummy dressed and set, he had then had a little chat with Pearson, just to make sure he knew exactly what he was to do, and what the repercussions would be if he didn't.

'I know,' Pearson said. 'We've been through this.'

'And you're clear on it all? You're sure of it.'

'Of course I am. Just go. Please.'

Walsh had heard anger in the man's voice, not just at the situation he was now in, but clearly also at how hopeless it was; there was not a damned thing he could do.

Just to remind him, Walsh had pulled something from his pocket.

'You know what this is, don't you?'

Pearson said nothing, just stared, jaw flexing with frustration and rage.

'I call it my vault,' Walsh explained, holding the solid-state hard drive in his hand. 'Everything I know about everyone I've dealt with is on this. I keep it with me at all times.'

'Bit risky, isn't it?' Pearson said.

Walsh saw enough movement in the man's arms to know what he was thinking.

'I wouldn't try anything,' he said, shaking his head. 'You can't take it.'

'What's stopping me?'

Walsh smiled.

'Each and every day, this needs to be synced with an online account I've set up,' he explained, holding the drive tantalisingly close to Pearson's face. 'You can guess what happens if it doesn't, can't you?'

Pearson said nothing, but the flex in his arms paused.

'It's a failsafe,' Walsh said. 'Anything happens to this? All the secrets it contains end up in the wrong hands. Something for you to think about over the next few hours, isn't it?'

Conversation over, he had made his exit, confident that Pearson would play his part long enough to give him the time he needed to disappear. And by the time his subterfuge was uncovered, would anyone really be bothered enough to put out a nationwide search? He doubted it. No murder had been committed; the whole thing was just some elaborate plan by a man who wanted to disappear. The why would be irrelevant and unknown because who would come forward to tell anyone anything about how he had really made his fortune? And as for those he was really running from, the ones who had forced him to stage this elaborate charade, who had been threatening him, sending him notes, handing him that final notice at the house? They wouldn't even know where to begin.

Having left the house, the snow and wind had caught him sharply, throwing him hard enough against the house to wind him. Leaving the warmth of the place behind him, his destination so clear in his mind he was fairly sure he could get there blindfolded, he had pushed on, taking just a few seconds to grab a small bag from his car. Which was when his plan had gone a little awry.

Disorientated, Walsh had ended up walking in the opposite direction to where he was supposed to go, and it had taken him far too long to realise. When he eventually did, he was astonished to discover that he had been walking for over an hour and a half. The time had flown by, almost as though he had been walking in some kind of trance, hypnotised by the snow and the sound of the wind. Turning around to head back in the right direction, it was nearly another two hours before he arrived where he was supposed to have been three and a half hours ago. Doing his best to think positively, Walsh convinced himself that, at the very least, he would have led anyone mad enough to try and follow him on a wild goose chase.

Thankfully, he found everything just as he had left it; a very new and very powerful quad bike in black livery, sitting on the small trailer he had towed behind the Porsche, all nicely hidden away and out of sight, and completely undisturbed. This had perhaps been the only real risk of the whole venture, but after a little bit of research, he'd found the farmer who owned the land, and offered enough cash to make the man more than happy to allow him to use it.

Now all that was left for him to do was to enjoy an exciting night-time jaunt across the snow-covered fells, following the line of an old track used by walkers to where there sat a dry barn at the edge of a field he had bought under the name of a company set up just for this purpose. And inside that barn, his new life waited; a car registered under a new identity, a travel bag, various documents, and a one-way ticket off this island to somewhere with more sun, and very little else to do other than enjoy it.

Climbing onto the bike and slipping in the ignition key attached to the keyring for his car, Walsh quickly had the bike's engine purring beneath him. Racing off into the snow, he couldn't help but grin. Not only had everything gone according to plan, but the snow was actually adding a strange sense of magic to the whole affair. This was an adventure, he thought, so why not enjoy it? The lane was easy enough to follow, if only because of the walls on either side of it tracing a path through the storm. So, knowing that the track beneath him was solid, he let out the throttle a bit, and raced on.

The sound of the storm was deafening; all Walsh could hear was the wind, and the snow it carried with it, ripping at his clothes and howling all around. Even the sound of the engine beneath him was drowned out. Riding down the lane was like surfing on a storm at sea, he thought, as tails of white horses galloped before him.

About fifteen minutes later, and now fully confident in his escape, Walsh was more than a little surprised to be suddenly blinded by the brightest of lights, then kicked off the bike and into the snow by a violent thud of something slamming into the back of his quad bike. He tumbled and rolled, the fall pulling back his hood, and the snow found his neck, freezing him in an instant. He tried to cry out, but snow was in his mouth, too, an ice-cold gag that set his teeth on edge.

Dazed, Walsh lay there for a moment, wondering what on earth had crashed into him. At first, he thought he was uninjured, but then a dull ache started to spread. It soon grew barbs as the pain spread out with an odd sensation of wet warmth. He lifted his head just enough to see his quad bike buried nose-first into a wall. The engine was still running.

Walsh tried to roll over and push himself up onto all fours, his mind absolutely focused on just getting on with the plan. He needed to be back on his bike and on his way, but the movement sent such a sharp pain through his body and his back spasmed. With a scream of agony, he started to panic. Something bad had happened to him, but he still didn't know what. All he knew was that his body was on fire, that every nerve was telling him he was in serious trouble, that if he didn't get moving right now, everything he had planned would be for nothing.

Walsh tried again, forcing himself to ignore the pain, to focus on the cold and to use that to help get to his feet. But his feet weren't interested, and his legs gave out and he crashed forward with a scream.

Movement in the snow caught Walsh's eye, a silhouette drifting towards him in the painfully bright light flooding where he lay, the falling snow hypnotising him almost as he stared at it, trying to work out just what the hell it was. A sheep? A deer? No, it was …

Walsh saw an arm raise to point at him as the shape drew closer, at last revealing itself to him.

'You?' he said, as the wind swept the snow away to reveal cold eyes in a face he recognised. 'But …'

Then the person was on him, ripping at his clothes, and darkness, at last, fell.

CHAPTER TWENTY-SEVEN

HARRY WANTED THE DAY TO BE OVER AND TO BE BACK HOME, sitting in front of the fire with Grace and Smudge, and happily falling asleep. No such luck though, he thought, because right now, he was barely able to keep up with the chain of events he had somehow found himself caught up in, never mind have time to think about what to do when it was all over. Though when that might be, was anyone's guess.

Liz had put a call in about the now very much not dead at all, Carl Walsh or John Setton or whatever the hell he was actually called. Harry had little expectation that the man would be found; someone who went to this amount of trouble to disappear wasn't going to be making the kind of errors that would make him easy to find. But that wasn't going to stop him from trying; his brain just wasn't wired that way.

With Liz on with doing that, Jameson was keeping a beady eye on the new arrivals, providing the injured member of their party with enough pillows and blankets to make a comfortable bed on the floor.

Harry was now in the lounge doing his best to explain to everyone who the new visitors were—not that he knew much about them himself—and also inform them about the now-vanished

Walsh. Originally, he would have been asking for a chat with Jack, the chef, seeing as he had as yet not got around to interviewing him. After that, there would've been further interviews with the others, to see if there were holes or discrepancies in their stories. But now that this was no longer a murder investigation, but a search for a missing person, he could see little point in doing so. Although at least three of the attendees had the motive to cause Walsh harm, none of them gained from helping him disappear, other than Pearson, and he'd already owned up to that. What was important, though, was that everyone was aware of what had happened, and to see if any of them knew anything at all, or had seen or heard anything that might be useful.

'What, so first you're telling us that he's been murdered, and now he's not even dead?' said Jack. 'You can't be serious. What you've just said, it's impossible, isn't it?'

'All I'm doing is relaying the facts as they have been made clear to me,' Harry said.

'Where the hell is he, then?' Jack asked, and Harry heard anger in the young man's voice.

'Right now, we don't know. And obviously, searching for him in weather like this isn't going to be easy.'

'What a bastard ...'

It was the first time Harry had heard Jack properly riled.

'Everything okay?' he asked, looking over at the chef.

Jack stared back.

'What? No, of course it isn't. I mean, he hasn't paid the full amount on this weekend, has he? Which means I'm short, too, doesn't it? So, like I said, what a bastard.'

Yalina said, 'This must be a joke. It has to be. You know where he is, you are just not telling us.'

'Oh, I wish that were true, believe me,' Harry shrugged. 'And really, there's no reason at all that I would hide the man away and keep it a secret. Not exactly the way the police work.'

Scott asked, 'You really don't know where he is, then?'

'Right now, your guess is as good as mine,' answered Harry,

'which is why I'm speaking to you all now. If anyone knows anything about this, or perhaps saw or heard something that might help, it would be greatly appreciated if you could share it.'

A wall of silence was the only answer Harry received.

'Well, if any of you think of anything, tell me. You might not think it's important right now, but you'd be surprised how often the most seemingly insignificant things can be key to an investigation.'

With nothing else to say, Harry left the room to stand in the hallway for a moment and try to work out what to do next. Really, what he needed most of all was the rest of his team here to help, but right now, that just wasn't possible. So, he would have to make do with one PCSO and a retired detective.

Harry glanced down the hall and along to the reading room. He could hear voices from the group who, despite claiming to have been in an accident bad enough to injure one of their party, had turned up in an undamaged Jeep. With Liz trying to find out what she could about Walsh, he had also asked her to see if she could get someone to run the plates on the vehicle.

Jameson was in the room with them and would keep Harry abreast of anything odd, of that he was sure. And a small part of him couldn't help but notice that the old DCI seemed to be enjoying himself. Harry knew that something was very wrong with the group, but as to what it was, he had no idea. Perhaps something would come to light later, and perhaps it wouldn't.

Right now, his priority had to be the whereabouts of Carl Walsh. So, he headed upstairs, not to talk with Tony, who was still in the bedroom, pondering on what he had done and how he'd managed to get himself into such a dreadful situation, but to have a look at Walsh's bedroom. Harry had only the faintest hope that he might find something inside that would tell him what to do next, but that was enough.

Having checked with Jack which room Walsh had taken, and having slipped on a pair of rubber gloves and shoe covers more out of habit than anything else, Harry pushed through the door. The room was dark and with a bit of fumbling, he quickly found the light switch and flicked it on.

What he expected to find on the other side of the door was a room empty of any evidence that anyone had stayed there at all. He reasoned that, if Walsh had planned his escape so well, then it was doubtful the man would have left anything behind to point to where he had gone. The flash of bright light from above showed the exact opposite.

The first thing Harry noticed was the suitcase of clothes. It was lying on its side on the floor in front of a folding luggage stand, its contents spewed across a rug like vomit. Harry could tell that the case hadn't simply fallen off the stand behind it, either. No, the case had been violently thrown down, its contents sifted through with little care or consideration as to where they ended up.

The bed had been turned over, the pillows and duvet cast off. The door to the en suite bathroom was open and inside Harry saw a dressing gown on the floor. Every drawer in the room was open, the wardrobe doors hanging loose like the gaping chest of a gutted corpse.

Someone had been in here searching for something, Harry thought, that much was obvious. For what, though? And not only that, but who, why, and for that matter, when?

From what he had learned so far, everyone had been together from the moment Walsh's little murder mystery had started, all the way up to when he and Liz had arrived. Since then, everyone had been kept together or very close to hand. Tony had been up here, yes, but Harry doubted the man would have been brave enough to leave the bedroom he was still in and do this. Also, why would he bother? He was already implicated.

Harry moved across the room, careful to avoid accidentally moving any of the items on the floor, most of which was clothing, though he also saw a toiletries bag, its contents as scattered as the clothes, no doubt thrown out of the bathroom by the frustrated visitor.

Standing on the other side of the room, Harry tried to take it all in and make sense of it. There were two reasons he could think of right then for what had happened. One was that Walsh had done this himself, though why, Harry couldn't fathom. The other was that someone in the house had done it. He had a few suspects, with Scott and the Rasheeds having shared with him their reasons for being there. That in itself struck Harry as strange; had Walsh not known anything about the people attending this weekend? Perhaps, perhaps not; only Walsh would be able to answer that.

Harry went to head back across the room to the door when he spotted a flash of pale white under the wardrobe. He knew it was probably nothing, but had a look anyway, and discovered that what he had seen was the corner of an envelope. Pulling it free, he saw Walsh's name above what he hazarded a guess at being the address of the house. Whatever it was, it had been posted first class only a day or so ago. Harry opened the envelope and pulled out a single sheet of paper, neatly folded. The paper was not a note, however, and neither was it a letter. Instead, it was a hand-written sheet torn from a notebook, the paper itself yellowed with age, the ink faded, but still legible.

The sheet had been divided into two columns; the left was a list of numbers, with the one at the top being two thousand. Each subsequent number beneath that decreased by fifty. The other column contained dates, all in line with the list of numbers.

Harry saw that the first dozen or so numbers and dates had all been crossed out. After that, the next figure in the list had then been altered to show a higher figure, though Harry found the number itself difficult to read, the writing spidery and blotchy. In fact, the whole sheet was covered in blotches, he noticed, as though water had been sprayed over it by accident. Most noticeable of all, however, were two words etched in black in the middle of the sheet: WE KNOW.

What do you know, Harry wondered, and more importantly, just who the hell are you? And why did you send Walsh this note? Did it have something to do with the man's disappearance? Perhaps, Harry thought, but with the planning that had gone into it, he doubted that this note in itself had been the trigger to set everything else in motion. It was linked though, he guessed, it had to be.

How, though, was the question, wasn't it? Had Walsh known someone was closing in? Had he known about Scott, about the Rasheeds, like Harry and Jameson had earlier discussed? And there was something else about the note, wasn't there? Had he seen something like it before, perhaps during another case? That was always possible; he'd attended so many that things did get a bit jumbled now and again.

Deep in thought, Harry stuffed the sheet back into the envelope, then walked out into the hallway, looking to call Jameson over to have a chat about what he had found. Only, as he did so, and as he went to turn off the bedroom room light, he spotted faint, damp boot prints on the floor, leading not only into Walsh's bedroom, but out of it, too, and heading away from the stairs.

CHAPTER TWENTY-EIGHT

HARRY PAUSED OUTSIDE THE DOOR, WONDERING HOW HE hadn't noticed the boot prints when he had first entered the room. The thing was, though, he hadn't really been looking for them; his focus had been to get in the room and see what he could find inside. Plus, they were only really visible because of the light spilling out of the bedroom and across the floor. He had found the room to be in darkness, so the prints had been almost invisible.

Dropping down to the floor, Harry pulled out his phone and snapped a few photos. He could see the prints a little clearer now, and his eyes traced their path from down the hall and into the bedroom, then back out again. What was confusing him right then, however, was that the marks were only there because the soles of the intruder's footwear had been wet and a little muddy. How, then, had they got like that, if they had come to the bedroom from further along the hall, instead of from downstairs and beyond the front door?

Standing up, Harry reached over to flick off the light in Walsh's room and pulled the door shut. Then, with his eyes now firmly set on the faint and drying footprints on the floor, he set off along the hall, at the far end of which a large window glared out into the black night.

Halfway along the passageway, and having passed various doors to other bedrooms, another thought struck Harry; whoever it was, they had made a beeline for Walsh's room. There was no pause at all in their path from wherever it was they had come from. And that told him that they knew exactly where Walsh's room was located. Otherwise, he would have seen evidence in the intruder's trail stopping off along the way to check out the other rooms.

Moving on, Harry followed the prints until, at the end of the hall, they stopped. And if Harry had been confused before, he was absolutely baffled now. There was no left or right turn, no sign that whoever it was had come from any other room, the prints starting and stopping at the wall in front of him.

Harry turned around and stared back down the hall. He made his way back along towards Walsh's room, turned on his heel, and again followed the prints, only to come to the same conclusion; whoever this mysterious person was, they hadn't come from any of the bedrooms. And that left Harry with only one other option.

Turning around to put the hallway behind him, Harry faced the large window. Beyond it, he could see thick snow being pushed and pulled by the wind. It was as haunting as it was hypnotising to stare at, the shapes formed by the snow ghostlike and ethereal. He noticed then, faint damp patches on the floor and the walls.

Harry leaned close to the glass to stare out into the night, but could see little. He brought up his torch and shone the beam out through the snow-dotted glass. Which was when he saw something that the darkness of the night had seemingly conspired with the storm to keep hidden.

Though covered in snow, Harry was able to make out the lines of railing and a platform beyond the window. Looking closer still, he saw that steps led down from the platform to the ground below. A fire escape, he realised, though it didn't look like a modern construction; perhaps something built decades ago when the place had been a grand, private dwelling.

Standing back, Harry carefully examined the window. It was a simple sash affair, rather than double glazing. On the bottom of the frame, he saw two metal hooks. Gripping them, Harry gave the window a sharp yank upwards. With a groan, the window opened a few inches and snow swept in. He gave the hooks another heave, more forcefully this time, and the window shot upwards violently enough to have Harry stumble backwards as his hands slipped from the grips.

Snow swirled in through the black hole he had opened in the wall and Harry, pulling his collar up, thrust his head out into the cold. Though covered now by fresh snow, he was sure that he could see the faintest of impressions on the platform and heading down the steps.

Harry climbed out of the window, pulling it closed behind him. Then, holding onto a thin, snow-covered rail, he stomped down the stairs, making sure that every step he took was secure enough to take his weight; he didn't fancy slipping and ending up with a broken leg, or worse.

At the bottom of the steps, Harry cast his gaze around to see if he could see any further evidence of the footprints he had been following. Dropping to a squat to try and get out of the wind and see through the snow, he was able to make out the footprints, so keeping himself low, he followed.

His head cold, his ears filling up with snow, Harry followed the impressions down the side of the house and to the parking area out front. The prints looked to be heading through the vehicles, but to where? He walked over and, on the way, managed to knock into a tow hitch at the back of Walsh's Porsche hard enough to give him a dead leg.

Cursing under his breath, Harry resisted the urge to give the vehicle a kick. He lifted his torch and spun around to try and find any sign of where the owner of the prints had gone, but all he saw were other vehicles, all of them covered in snow. He also wondered where Walsh's keys were because he'd not found them in the bedroom. He must have taken them, Harry thought, wondering why.

A violent shiver cut through Harry, reminding him of just how cold and wet he was getting. With little else to discover, he continued on his way and made for the front door. Before heading into the house, he glanced back along from where he had come, snow stinging his eyes. Someone had entered the house from out here, heading up the old and dilapidated fire escape, to sneak along the hallway and ransack Walsh's bedroom. And the only way Harry could see for them to do that was to exit the house from the front door. It just didn't make any sense.

Harry turned on his heel and opened the door, but something caused him to pause. He looked once again out into the snow, narrowing his eyes against the ice-laden wind; something was off, he was sure of it, but what?

'Harry?'

The voice was Jameson's, but Harry ignored it. Something in front of him was very, very important, but what? The cold and the wet were almost too much, and it was making it difficult for him to think clearly.

Harry stepped back out into the snow, his hand still on the door handle. The fells beyond the house were hidden by darkness and the wind-thrown snow was doing a very good job at making it seem as though the world had vanished for good. The vehicles parked out front were now little more than giant white mounds. He noticed, too, that the snow on the campervan had slewed off along one side, the weight of it no doubt growing too heavy to stay as it was. There was something else though, he was sure of it, and he stared out into the snow, looking for something, sure that it was in front of him, begging him to notice.

'Harry ...'

Harry turned towards Jameson's voice.

'What?'

'We have a problem.'

'That's a gross understatement,' Harry replied, and stepped back into the house, shaking himself free of the snow he had collected on his little trip. He heaved the door shut behind him and turned around to face Jameson, except he found someone else there in his stead, with his old friend and mentor standing behind him and being held by another from the group of uninvited guests. Jameson, Harry noticed, was sporting a swollen eye.

'Hello, Detective,' said Nicholls, and lifted the barrels of the sawn-off shotgun to point them directly at Harry's face. 'Nice of you to join us.'

CHAPTER TWENTY-NINE

'WHERE ARE WE?'

Jadyn had managed to stay fairly quiet since leaving the pub, but his curiosity had finally got the better of him. Having quizzed Helen and Matt on almost every bit of kit he had with him, just to make absolutely sure that it was all okay, he had then moved on to what he could see beyond the windows of Helen's truck. Which, he had to admit, wasn't all that much.

'This is Gilbert's Lane,' Matt said, as Helen drove them on, breaking fresh snow all the way up into the fells above. 'Not sure of the history, but it's an old track. Makes a nice walk, too, when the weather's right.'

'Not like today, then,' said Jadyn.

'Oh, I don't know,' said Helen. 'I've seen it worse.'

'You have?'

'The fact we can drive up here at all is a positive sign,' Helen explained.

'The lane actually goes all the way up and over the top, to the village of Stalling Busk on the other side, looking over to Semerwater,' said Matt. 'And that's as close to Marsett as you can get without actually being there.'

Jadyn understood.

'So, you think he might be heading down here, then, is that it?'

'He's a local lad, knows the area,' Matt said. 'I doubt very much that he's just buggered off without a thought as to where he's heading. Obviously, I don't know exactly where he'll hit the lane, because we've no idea what route he's taken to get here, but it's almost unavoidable.'

'Might we see tracks, then?' Jadyn asked.

'Worth looking out for them,' said Helen, 'though with this weather, the wind and the snow will make short work of making them disappear.'

'We've got the team spread across a huge area,' said Matt, 'but what we're doing is not only a search, but running patrols along the roads as well. Not just here, along the lane, like, but up beyond Oughtershaw as well. We've good enough reason to believe he's not headed the other way, up onto Dodd Fell and then to the Roman Road. Even so, we'll be checking along there as well, just in case.'

'It's a big operation,' said Jadyn.

'It is,' agreed Matt. 'And every single person involved is a volunteer.'

Helen drove on, the old Suzuki rattling as it came under attack from the angry storm, which rocked it left and right as it continued on its way.

Jadyn stared off into the darkness. He was warm in his winter kit, aided by the noisy heater in the front of Helen's small, but surprisingly capable truck. The snow on the other side of the glass swirled and danced in front of him and he found himself having to fight against the urge to just close his eyes and fall asleep. Then, just as his eyes closed again, his phone buzzed. It was a message from Jen explaining that she was heading out to a call from a woman badly injured in a home invasion or break-in; the details weren't all that clear, so Jadyn messaged back.

'Shouldn't you wait for backup?'

He knew it was a stupid question; this was Wensleydale in the middle of the wintery storm from hell; where was this backup going to be coming from, exactly?

A few seconds later, Jen's reply flashed up on his screen.

'Ambulance on its way. All good. No word from Harry. You?'

'Nothing,' Jadyn replied.

'Then I suppose no news is good news.'

'I guess.'

The vehicle slowed to a stop and Jadyn stowed his phone. Matt handed him a shortwave radio.

'You're taking the right flank,' Matt said. 'And I'll be keeping an eye on you, so you don't go wandering off, not that you'll be far enough to anyway.'

'Don't worry, I'll be fine,' said Jadyn, doing his best to disguise the slight twist of fear that he felt, thinking about what lay ahead.

Matt held up his own radio.

'We'll all be staying in touch with these,' he said, then quickly showed Jadyn how to use the device, and which channel they would be on. 'It's a separate system,' he explained, 'by which I mean that we, the mountain rescue, have a number of designated channels; stops us being bothered by anyone else. The range is about fifty kilometres, though obviously that's very dependent on LOS.'

'Line-of-sight?'

'Sorry, yes,' said Matt. 'You ready?'

I am and I'm not, thought Jadyn. But it wasn't like he was about to back out now, or could do, even if he wanted to, which he didn't.

Pushing himself out into the snow, Jadyn spent the next few minutes listening a lot and saying very little. He could make out the thin line of the rest of the team, stretching out to his left, thanks to the bright red LED lights they were all wearing attached to their jackets.

At last, the signal came, and it was time to head off.

Jadyn had been instructed on the line he was to follow as he walked. There was no rush. The whole point of the search was to be thorough, which was impossible if the whole thing was done at speed.

With an eye on the line out to his left, which stretched off into the blasting freeze of ice and snow, and with a torch in his hand, Jadyn started to wade through the white laid out before him.

Back in Bradford, he had experienced snow, but nothing ever like this. The last time he'd ever seen anything like it had been on a school skiing trip. That had been out in Austria, where the snow had been clean and compacted, the sky bright with sunshine. Here, though, he could barely see ten metres in front of his face. It wasn't just the snow falling out of the thick, black sky that was the problem either; wherever Jadyn looked, the surface of the snow moved, with clouds made up of the tiniest of ice crystals rolling and billowing across it like smoke.

After a while, Jadyn lost all sense of time and space. He was alone in a sea of the brightest white, which blanketed the dales beneath a ruinously dark sky. He could see the line of lights of the search party, but little else. He was sweating with the exertion of pushing through, not just deep snow, but having to deal with the ground beneath. In places, long tufts of grass would snatch at his feet or try to trip him up, and in others, hidden dips and pools of soft peat would conspire to pull him down or make him fall.

Scanning the scenery before him, Jadyn was conscious of ice crusting his eyebrows, of snow forcing its way between jacket and skin. And yet, despite the discomfort, he was enjoying himself. What he was doing wasn't just exciting, it was useful, had purpose; out here, a boy was in danger, and it was down to the rescue team to find him and bring him home.

His radio buzzed, and Jadyn heard Matt's voice come through with surprising clarity.

'How you doing, lad?'

'I'm good,' Jadyn answered, only just managing to keep a hold of the radio in his gloved hand. The snow was up to his knees in most places, and the going had been tough.

'Tiring, isn't it?'

THE DARK HOURS 235

'A little. Anyone seen anything?'

'Nowt yet.'

Taking advantage of a pause in the line's progress, Jadyn glanced around. Wherever he looked, he saw snow and darkness. It was as bleak as it was beautiful. It was also very unforgiving, he thought.

Something caught Jadyn's eye and he snatched a look to his right. Had that been a light? Then he saw the faintest of flashes, before a sound like the sharp crack of splintering wood, drifted by.

Jadyn lifted his radio to his lips.

'Sarge?'

'What is it?'

'I think I just saw something.'

'Really? Where?'

'Up to the right of where I am now.'

'What was it?'

Jadyn explained about the light, the flash, the odd sound that had broken the air.

'Best we go have a look, then, hadn't we?' Matt said. 'You wait there.'

'Understood.'

When Matt came alongside, Helen was with him. Jadyn then pointed to where he had seen the flash. Matt instructed him to take the lead, so Jadyn headed off in what he thought was the right direction. It wasn't easy, but he had kept his eyes on where the flash had come from and not looked away since.

A few minutes later, they came to a wall.

'This is the lane again,' Helen said, then pointed just a little way back along the way they had driven up it earlier to her vehicle. 'See?'

'Then maybe you were right,' Jadyn said, looking over to Matt. 'About the lad making his way over from Marsett to make use of it.'

'Let's not jump to conclusions just yet,' said Matt.

Walking along the wall till they found a stile, they climbed through and kept on. Then, just as Jadyn was beginning to think he had maybe been seeing things, he caught sight of something ahead.

'You see that?' he asked, pointing through the snow.

'I do,' said Matt.

'What do you think it is?'

'Well, whatever it is, it isn't a wall, and it isn't grass,' Matt replied. 'And as far as I'm aware, other than Thomas and the search team, no one else is daft enough to be out here in weather like this.'

Jadyn walked on, his pace upping a little as they drew closer to what he had spotted.

'Well, that's definitely a quad bike,' Matt said.

'The engine's still running,' added Helen.

The bike was on its side, the nose crunched into the wall marking the left side of the track.

'Over there,' Jadyn said, seeing another shape in the snow. 'I think there's someone in the snow.'

His legs burning now, Jadyn did his best to run, lifting his legs high out of the snow to help him go as fast as possible.

Jadyn came to a dead stop as Matt and Helen came up alongside.

Spread eagle in front of him in the snow was a man. He was middle-aged, with grey hair poking out from under a woolly hat, and he was kitted out for the worst of weathers. He was staring up at the sky through lifeless eyes already half-covered with snow.

Matt dropped down at the man's side, pulled off his left glove, and rested two fingers on the man's neck.

'Well, then,' he said, pulling his glove back on, and shaking his head, 'just who the bloody hell are you?'

Jadyn was staring at the man in the snow when he heard something far off. He looked up, saw another flash.

'You hear that?' he asked, staring off into the snow.

'Another engine,' Matt said.

'And it's coming from that way,' Jadyn said, pointing up the lane. Then he saw another splash of light in the distance, only this time it was clear enough to reveal the rear lights of a vehicle heading away from them.

'Helen, stay with the team,' Matt said. 'I'm going to need your keys.'

'What's happening?' Jadyn asked.

Matt pointed at the red Suzuki.

'We're going for a drive,' he said.

CHAPTER THIRTY

'HAVEN'T SEEN ONE OF THOSE IN A WHILE,' HARRY SAID, staring at Nicholls down the short barrels of the gun. 'Very old school.'

Nicholls gave a nonchalant shrug.

'Effective, though,' he said. 'You wouldn't believe the damage something like this can do to the human body.'

'Oh, I think I would,' said Harry, then added, 'Probably not the right time to ask if you have a licence for it, am I right?'

Nicholls laughed, the sound humourless and cold.

'For a man with a gun pointing at his face, you're taking this all rather well.'

'Where's my other officer?' Harry asked, ignoring Nicholls.

'With the others,' Nicholls said, and gestured at the door to the lounge. 'Your friend here got a bit nosy and, well, here we are.'

Harry turned his gaze to Jameson.

'You okay?'

'I'm good,' Jameson said. 'Took a bit of a clout, but I've had worse.'

Harry looked back at Nicholls.

'You know, my gut was telling me something wasn't quite right with you.'

'And your friend's, too, it seems,' Nicholls replied. 'After a little chat with that other officer of yours, he started asking all the wrong kinds of questions.'

'That injury we dealt with,' Jameson said. 'It's a stab wound. Not a knife, though. Something blunter, a spike of some kind. Liz came in after she'd just spoken with Jen, and she told me that—'

The man who was holding Jameson delivered a sharp jab to his kidneys. Jameson's voice broke into a yelp of pain as he doubled over.

'Bastard ...' he said, the word hissed out through clenched teeth.

'What do you want?' Harry asked, hard eyes on Nicholls.

'Your radio, your phone, your cooperation,' Nicholls replied. 'Now.'

Harry didn't move.

'You hard of hearing, Detective?'

'Those cuts and grazes you've all got,' Harry said, looking again at the marks on Nicholls' hand holding the shotgun, recognising them now. 'Thought I recognised what they were from when you first arrived, but I couldn't place it. Now though, up close? They look like bike chain marks, right? So, my guess is, that whatever you did to cause them, it didn't go entirely according to plan, am I right? Not if one of your party was injured and you ended up here.'

'We ended up here by accident, that's all,' Nicholls said. 'And the sooner you cooperate, the sooner we can be on our way when the weather drops enough to let us leave. Then you'll have nothing else to worry about, will you?'

'You're very confident,' said Harry, hiding his concern as to what was hidden behind those words. The dead, after all, had the least to worry about of anyone. Then he found his eyes drawn to the paintings on the wall.

'Nicholls isn't your name either, is it?' he said. 'I mean, that's obvious now, but you took that from one of the paintings on the wall, didn't you?'

'You're good,' Nicholls grinned, and Harry saw the glint of a gold tooth sitting amongst the ivory. 'Phone,' he said again. 'Radio.'

Harry cast a quick look over to Jameson, who was still recovering from the punch, then pulled out his phone and radio, and handed them over to Nicholls.

'Do I need to search you?' Nicholls asked.

'No, and I wouldn't advise it, either,' said Harry.

Nicholls' grin turned into a laugh.

'You know, I like you,' he said.

'Can't say the feeling's mutual.'

Nicholls used the shotgun to point Harry over to the door of the lounge.

'Any particular reason you moved everyone out of the dining room?' Harry asked.

'Well, the reading room was starting to feel a little cramped for us,' Nicholls said. 'So, we thought we'd upgrade.'

Walking over, Harry reached for the door, opening it a little, then paused, a cold blast of air hitting him from the other side. He looked back at Nicholls.

'In,' Nicholls said. 'No arguing.'

'Maybe we should have a little chat,' said Harry.

'Not sure what we have to discuss, if I'm honest,' Nicholls replied.

'Whatever this is, my advice is that you stop it right now,' Harry said. 'Hand over that shotgun and whatever other weapons you have. If you don't, this is only going to get worse for you. We both know that.'

Nicholls leaned in, with his mouth close to Harry's ear.

'I wouldn't bet on it,' he said.

Harry stumbled through the door as Nicholls gave him a shove. Jameson followed soon after, bumping into him on the way, then falling to the floor.

Harry looked over at the door to see Nicholls waving at him as he slammed it shut.

For a moment, the room was silent. Harry was very aware of all the eyes staring at him. He reached down to help Jameson back to his feet, catching sight of the medical manikin still lying on its back in front of the now very dead fire. Nicholls had been right; the room was cold, and snow covered the floor. The window, he noticed, was shut.

'Not entirely sure this is the weekend I was expecting, if I'm honest,' Jameson said, rubbing his side.

'What did they do to you?' Harry asked.

Jameson wasn't given time to answer as they were both quickly surrounded by the others in the room. Everyone started to talk at once, so Harry held up a hand to shush them. As he did so, he noticed that Tony Pearson was also with them.

'Right now, I have no idea who they are or what they want,' he said, answering the one question everyone was asking in a dozen different ways. 'However—'

'Actually, Boss ...'

Harry saw that Liz was staring at him.

'What is it?' he asked.

Liz nodded over to a corner of the room, and then walked over towards it. Harry made to follow, only to find everyone else behind him.

He stopped, turned to face them, and held up a hand to hold them back.

'I need you all to just give me a moment to talk with my officer,' he said. 'The sooner that's done, the sooner we can get on with working out what to do next.'

'That man had a gun,' Yalina said. 'A shotgun! Why?'

'I did notice,' said Harry.

'And it's so cold in here,' said Kirsty, hugging herself and shivering as she spoke.

'You need to call for backup,' Rasheed said. 'Armed response or something. That's what we need, isn't it?'

'What about the SAS?' Tony suggested. 'This is their kind of thing, isn't it? They'd take them all out in no time. Like they did with the Embassy in the eighties.'

Harry noticed a faint smile on Scott's face at that.

242 DAVID J. GATWARD

'No one is coming out here in this,' he said. 'Not yet, anyway. So, what we have to do is get through it on our own for now.'

Everyone started speaking again, but Harry pushed on.

'Like I said, I need to speak with my officers here. Once that's done, we will all sit down and try to work out what we do next. My priority is our safety. How does that sound?'

'Like you've no idea what you're doing, that's how it sounds,' said Tony. 'To me, anyway. We need the SAS. Call them. Now. You have to.'

Scott said, 'The SAS aren't on a hotline. You can't just call them like Batman.'

'How do you know?'

'Please,' said Harry, interrupting before Scott was able to answer. 'Just give us a few minutes, then we'll see where we are. Okay?'

'At least we have the bar,' Tony said, gesturing towards it with a tip of his head.

'Probably best we don't all get drunk, though,' said Jameson. 'By which I mean, don't even think about it.'

With nothing else to say, Harry quickly walked away, with Jameson coming along behind.

Checking that they were far enough away from the others for them to not be overheard, he looked at Liz.

'So, what is it, then?' he asked, his voice hushed. 'What is it you have to tell me?'

'You know how you asked me to call Jen?' Liz said. 'Well, I did, and it turns out she had been just about to call me at the same time.'

'Why?'

'She told me to tell you that she was leaving the office to attend to a call. I caught her just as she was about to leave.'

'In this weather?' said Jameson, shaking his head. 'What is it with you people?'

'We're hardy, that's what,' said Liz, and Harry spotted a faint, proud smile on her lips. 'But it's not like she had any choice in the matter.'

'Why's that, then?' Harry asked, his concern growing, for all manner of reasons now. This had been a murder case, then a missing person, and now they were being held hostage by an armed gang. He'd definitely had better days.

Liz said, 'When I came to find you, you were outside, I think. Anyway, I didn't think much of it right then, what Jen had told me, I mean, but then, when I popped in to see how Jameson here was getting on with that injured woman ...'

Liz's voice fell quiet.

'But then what, Liz?' said Harry.

'I might be wrong.'

Jameson shook his head.

'After what you told me, I really don't think you are.'

Harry frowned, growing impatient.

'The call Jen was heading out to, it was a break-in,' Liz explained. 'She didn't say much, because she hadn't been given much information, but she said enough, if you know what I mean. From what the call handler had told her, it sounded like the break-in got really violent.'

'How violent?'

'Three dead,' said Liz. 'There's a fourth casualty as well, but from what Jen said, it sounds like she's very seriously injured. An ambulance is already on its way to meet her there.'

'Three dead and another seriously injured?' Harry said. 'What the hell kind of break in is that? Where did it happen?'

'That's my point,' said Liz. 'The break-in was at a house over on Blean Lane.'

Harry was still no clearer, and asked, 'Where's that, then?'

When Liz told him, Harry's blood turned cold.

CHAPTER THIRTY-ONE

THE JOURNEY OUT OF HAWES AND OVER TO BLEAN LANE WAS a mix of stark, almost fairytale-like beauty, and harsh, near-terrifying driving conditions. Jen was glad to have the snow chains; she couldn't remember the last time she had cause to use them, and the difference was dramatic. Not that the added traction was encouraging her to go any faster, but at least she wasn't sliding all over the place.

With her headlights on dip, to stop herself from being blinded by the reflection against the falling snow, she stared out into the night. The road was all but hidden from view as the harsh wind cast great curtains of snow in front of her. They would open and close at random, offering her the occasional brief view of what lay ahead; a wintery wonderland that reminded her of The Lion, The Witch, and The Wardrobe book she had loved as a child.

Trees hung low and heavy with ice, white blankets weighing them down as new layers were added. Fields were lost to racing waves of snow chasing across them, the walls between them banking up with drifts. She couldn't see the fells beyond, as not only the darkness hid them from her, but the clawing tendrils of a storm few had seen the like of in years. And yet, deep down, a part of her was excited by it.

Jen knew that when the wind died and the day dawned, her soul would be calling for her to walk out into the snowy wastes. The Dales were a glorious sight at the best and the worst of times, but in the snow, the place was cast by a spell so powerful that all was changed, and to walk out in it was to explore a new land entirely.

Pulling herself out of thoughts of the adventures she would have in the days ahead, Jen focused on the road. It was rising gently now, up towards the village of Bainbridge. She saw headlights coming down towards her, and soon a tractor mooched on past, the driver cocooned in the warmth of the cab.

Driving through Bainbridge, the village green was strangely populated by misshapen shadows, figures caught in the snow and frozen to the ground. Jen smiled to herself at the thought of people brave or mad enough to ignore the weather and head out to build snowmen. And most of them wouldn't have been children either, she thought, thinking of just how late it was.

Out of Bainbridge Jen took a right off the main road, just up from the old Roman Fort and, a few minutes later, turned off right once again, along Blean Lane. If she thought the roads had been tough going before, well now they were getting on for impossible. Snow drifts were creeping out through gates and spilling over the tops of walls. The spindrift was so thick in the air that the view ahead was like staring down a tunnel with a very low roof, as the icy blast raced overhead from wall top to wall top.

Jen pushed on, aware that at the end of her journey, someone was in serious need of medical help. She was also concerned that since turning off the main road, she had seen no other tracks in the snow. There was always the chance that the snow had erased them, but something told her that wasn't the case. And that meant that wherever the ambulance was, four-wheel-drive or not, it as yet wasn't there.

Increasingly aware of the perilous situation she was in, Jen managed to take her worry and lock it away, instead using all of her focus to make it to the house. She crawled along through the snow, her windows all but covered, her windscreen wipers fighting hard to keep her view clear. Driving was now little more than the slow act of threading the vehicle along the narrow lane, which only grew narrower with the snow the further she climbed.

Then, as the road took a sharp bend to the right, the wind slammed into the car, snatching the steering wheel from Jen's hands. She grabbed a hold of it again, trying to maintain control, but the car was already slipping increasingly to her right. Then she felt the rear end coming around, not fast enough to risk a crash, but with enough speed to tell her that whatever was about to happen wasn't going to be good.

The car was now more sideways than pointing forwards. Jen fought to get herself moving in the right direction again, but it was no good. Then the right front wheel slipped into a shallow ditch at the side of the road, and the whole car ground to a halt.

Jen sat for a moment, working out what to do next. It felt like the car had bottomed out, so just how the hell was she going to get it out?

She tried to push forwards, but the car was having none of it. So, she hooked it into reverse, felt the wheels grip, and start to move the car. She increased the power a little, the car moved a little more. It was working, she thought; she would be out in a few seconds and on her way again. Then the rear end bumped to the right and took the whole right side of the car down into the ditch.

Jen swore and hammered her fists on the steering wheel. It did no good, but it made her feel better.

Grabbing her phone, she pulled up a map and checked where she was. The house was perhaps half a mile away, no further. Which gave her little choice but to get out into the storm and walk. But what about the dog?

Jen turned around to see the Whippet curled up in a ball. The journey, the storm, the crash, none of it had stirred the little creature. It looked so warm and so at peace. But Jen knew she couldn't leave it in the car; the poor thing would freeze.

'Hey,' she said. 'How you doing, back there?'

The dog's eyes opened, the tip of its tail wagged.

'You're not going to like this, I know,' Jen said, 'but I'm afraid we're going to have to go on a little walk.'

Jen was pleased that the dog hadn't the faintest idea what she was talking about. Even when she reached over to lift the animal into the front and onto her lap, it simply accepted what she was doing and didn't struggle. Then, when she zipped it inside her jacket and pushed out into the snow, grabbing a first aid kit from the back of the car, she was fairly sure that within the first few steps, it was snoring.

Narrowed eyes forward, her face protected from the elements by her hood, Jen leaned into the wind. All she had to do was push on, take it steady, and get to the house. There was always the chance that the ambulance would drive past and pick her up on the way.

Around her, the world was a thing of wind and cold and she was thankful for the dog. She could barely see her feet, not just because of the depth of the snow she was wading through, but the way the surface of it moved and twisted and spun, blurring her legs beneath her knees.

When the house finally came into view, and despite what she knew was waiting for her on the other side of the front door, Jen was relieved to know she would soon be out of the cold. The walk and the dog had kept her warm, but still, the frozen winds had stabbed deep enough to chill her bones.

At the door, Jen raised her gloved hand to give it a knock, but saw that the door was open, its edges splintered where it had been forced.

'Police,' she called out, stepping out of the storm and into the house. 'Mrs Taylor, this is DC Jenny Blades. Can you hear me? Mrs Taylor?'

The house was dark, warm, and there was a strange, sweet smell in the air, an odd mix of dead fireworks and blood.

'Hello?'

Jen heard a groan from deeper inside the house and flicked

on her torch. The sight that met her in the hall was one of violence and gore, two bodies lying on the floor in front of her. Neither of them were moving. Both had heavy blunt force trauma to their skulls. The floor, the walls, were splattered with red.

The groan came again. Jen pulled her eyes away from the awful view before her and followed, stepping over one of the bodies as she made her way into a room lit by the faint orange glow of a fire behind the glass of a stove in the far wall. Here, she saw two more bodies, one with a chest covered in blood, the other their neck a ruined mess of torn flesh.

'Here ...'

The voice was faint and from over by the fire.

Jen shone her torch over, walking towards the voice, until she was shuffling past a large sofa. She saw a tray of cheese and biscuits on the floor, splashes of red wine, and movement.

'Mrs Taylor? Karen?'

That the woman was still alive at all struck Jen as nothing short of a miracle. Kneeling carefully at her side, close to her head, Jen took in her injuries as best as she could, losing count, wondering where to start, lost as to how she could in any way give this woman any aide or comfort.

Jen saw the faintest of smiles on the woman's face, but the relief it expressed was fleeting, as she saw in her eyes the deepest of sorrows.

'My ... husband,' the woman said. 'I know he's ...'

'Please, try to not speak,' Jen said. 'I need to check you over, okay?'

'They ... they killed him. Thought they'd killed me, too.'

Jen wasn't listening; what was in front of her was just too much. This woman needed the ambulance here, and quick.

'I'm cold,' the woman said.

Jen had seen wood in a basket by the stove. Right now, she wasn't about to concern herself with preserving a crime scene, not when there was a life at stake. And anyway, after what she had already seen, she guessed there was more than enough to be going on with.

Quickly, she was up from the floor and over to the stove, opening the door and lobbing in enough logs to give the thing something to feast on. She pulled open the air intake at the bottom of the door and the fire immediately began to suck air. Soon, flames were licking at the glass.

Jen turned back to the woman, only to feel something move inside her jacket; the dog had been so still, she had forgotten about it completely. But she couldn't just let it out. So, she opened her zip and looked inside, shining her torch onto the animal's face.

'You okay in there?'

The dog looked up briefly, then closed its eyes again.

'I'll take that as a yes.'

For the next few minutes, Jen did her best to make the woman comfortable. The injuries, she could do little about, other than try and stem any bleeding, and she brought a blanket through from a bedroom to keep her warm, stepping over the bodies in the house as she went. Then, as she went to check on the fire and add more fuel, her radio buzzed. Jen answered, listened, shook her head in disbelief.

'What do you mean, the ambulance isn't coming?'

'It is, it's just going to be late,' the voice on the end of the call said. 'The road conditions are bad.'

'I know the road conditions are bad!' Jen snapped back. 'How the hell do you think I got to the house in the first place?'

'I'll call you when I know more.'

'How long will they be?'

'I don't know.'

'You don't know?'

'No.'

'But I've a seriously injured woman here,' Jen said. 'As well as four other bodies.'

'Like I said, I'll call you when—'

Jen hung up.

The woman coughed, cried out.

'Karen?' Jen said, hoping that at least the sound of her voice would be some comfort. 'I'm here, okay? Help is on its way. I'm just trying to hurry it along for you.'

'I'm not ... I'm not Karen,' the woman said.

Jen was confused.

'Karen, I'm not sure I understand.'

'I'm ... not ... Karen,' the woman said again. 'My name, it's Marina. My husband is Harvey... Harvey White.'

'Please, don't speak,' Jen said. 'You need to stay as calm and still as you can. Help will be here soon.'

Jen felt a hand grip her arm and saw that the woman was staring at her.

'We thought we were safe,' the woman said. 'But they knew. They found us. Please ... my name ... my husband ... We're Marina and Harvey White.'

Glancing down at the woman, Jen was back on her radio, desperate to at least get some input from the team on what to do. What the woman was saying wasn't making any sense and she was concerned that she was losing her.

With Jim out in the fields with his dad, and having spoken to her earlier, Jen tried Liz first, but there was no answer. She tried again: nothing. Now, that didn't make any sense at all. Why wouldn't Liz answer? It wasn't too long since they had spoken and, if anything, what Liz and Harry had been dealing with had sounded a lot easier than what they had originally headed out for.

'Please,' the woman said, her grip on Jen's arm weakening. 'You have to believe me ... I'm ... Marina ...'

Jen went to try for Liz again when another voice came through. It was Jadyn.

CHAPTER THIRTY-TWO

JADYN WAS STANDING KNEE-DEEP IN SNOW, STARING AT A QUAD bike crunched into a wall and Helen, who was crouching over the body in the snow. The man was alive, but had taken a beating. Not just from the crash either.

'Jen?' he said, hearing the DC's voice on the other end. 'I've been trying to get through to Harry and Liz; you heard anything?'

'Aren't you out with the rescue team?' Jen asked.

'Yes,' said Jadyn.

'But you've got your police radio with you.'

'Took it with me by accident,' Jadyn said. 'Force of habit, I suppose. Look, I need to speak with Harry. It's urgent. We've found someone and—'

'So's this,' Jen said, interrupting.

Jadyn heard the worry in Jen's voice.

'What's happened? Are you okay? How's the dog?'

'I'm at that house, only I'm here with three dead and one badly injured casualty,' Jen explained. 'So no, I am most definitely not okay. The dog, though, is fine and keeping me warm.'

Jadyn wasn't sure he had heard correctly.

'Did you say three dead?'

'Yes.'

'Bloody hell.'

'You have no idea.'

'What's happened?'

'Police call handler told me this was a break-in,' Jen said. 'But this is no break-in; not like I've ever seen, anyway.'

'How do you mean?'

'They broke in, that much is true, but from what I can see, this had nothing to do with a robbery. And the casualty I'm dealing with, what she's saying, I just don't understand it. Keeps telling me that she isn't who she said she is, or something. I was given the name Karen Taylor by the call handler, but she keeps telling me that her name is Marina White. It's not making any sense.'

'No, doesn't sound like it,' said Jadyn, though right now, what he was staring at wasn't making much sense either. 'Maybe she's just confused, which wouldn't be a surprise by the sounds of it.'

'And the ambulance is delayed,' Jen said, 'so I'm on my own doing the best I can with my first aid kit. Not sure what I should do.'

'And you say you've tried Harry as well?' Jadyn asked. 'And he's not answering?'

'No.'

'That's not good.'

'None of this is good,' said Jen.

A call from Matt had Jadyn turn to see him behind the steering wheel of Helen's Suzuki.

'Get in, lad!' Matt shouted. 'Now!'

Jadyn dashed over through the snow and climbed in. As soon as he had his door shut, Matt started to drive, the little Suzuki pulling them through the deep snow with ease.

'Helen's staying put with whoever that bloke is out there in the snow,' Matt said. 'Whoever it is in that vehicle ahead of us, those tracks out there by the quad bike belong to them. They're not from another quad bike either; they're something considerably larger. So, I don't think that it's Thomas, which means he's still out here somewhere. Who's that on the radio?'

'It's Jen,' Jadyn said. 'She hasn't been able to get an answer from Harry either.'

Matt snapped around at that.

'What? Why?' he demanded.

'No idea,' Jadyn said, then quickly explained what Jen was dealing with.

'Bloody hell,' said Matt. 'She doing okay?'

'It's Jen,' said Jadyn, as though that was answer enough.

'Fair point,' said Matt with a nod. 'Well, whatever Harry's reason is for not answering, I'm sure it's a good one. Tell Jen to get back on the radio and speak with a paramedic; they'll be able to help her better than any of us while she's waiting for the ambulance.'

'What about what she was saying about the woman's name?' Jadyn asked. 'Why would she be saying she's called something else?'

'You can check that for her,' said Matt. 'Get the details and call it in. That way she can focus on stabilising the casualty.'

Jadyn closed the call with Jen, then called in the information she had given him and was told someone would be in touch as soon as they had anything to tell.

Staring out through the windscreen, he saw the lane disappearing off in front of them, and far off, the rear lights of the vehicle they were now chasing.

BACK IN THE house above Marsett, Harry was putting two and two together and coming up with not a damned thing. His frustration was so vivid he could almost hear it buzzing in his ears.

'We're thinking the same thing, aren't we?' he said, looking now at both Liz and Jameson.

'That you don't believe in coincidences?' said Liz.

'Exactly.'

Jameson said, 'If it's this Nicholls who broke into that house your officer called about, then I doubt very much that he has anything good planned for us. And I say that with the weight it deserves.'

'I agree,' Harry said. 'Whatever they did at the house Jen's headed to, it sounds and looks like it didn't go according to plan. They've ended up here by accident, their numbers down, one of them badly injured. And not by a vehicular accident either. My guess is they thought they'd hole up here for an hour or two, get themselves together, then disappear in the storm. But now they know we're on to them—'

'They can't really let us walk away, can they?' said Jameson.

Harry shook his head.

'No,' he said. 'And all of this means that right now, whoever Walsh is, and wherever he is, and whatever he's up to, I can't say that I really give a damn. Either of you have a problem with that?'

'Not in the slightest,' said Liz.

Harry was impressed with the steel in the young PCSO's eyes; she was clearly as terrified as everyone else, including him, but she was still managing to stay calm.

'So, what are we going to do?' Jameson asked. 'We can't make a run for it, and neither can we take them on and try to overpower them.'

'We can't even call for help,' said Liz. 'Not that anyone can get here, but they have our phones and radios, remember?'

'Did you get anything on that vehicle they turned up in?' Harry asked.

Liz shook her head.

'I was waiting for a call back on that, and on Walsh or Setton or whoever he is.'

Harry noticed an itch starting beneath the scars on his face, a sign that his mind was troubled. Not just by the recent events either, but by Walsh, by the missing kid, by what he'd seen, but also not seen, outside the house.

Stepping away from Liz and Jameson for a moment, he closed his eyes, forced himself to think, to try and see now in his mind's eye what he hadn't seen then.

'The Jeep ...' he said, his voice a whisper.

'What about it?' said Jameson.

'When I was outside,' Harry explained, 'I knew something was off. I couldn't work it out, because everything was covered in snow, and then I knocked my leg against Walsh's tow hitch. But that's what it was, the Jeep; that's what I noticed.'

'How do you mean?' Liz asked.

'I mean,' Harry said, 'that everything we do always boils down to spotting things that should be there, but aren't—'

'And things that aren't, but should be,' Jameson finished for him.

'Exactly,' Harry agreed. 'And the Jeep, which should've been out there where they parked it, wasn't.'

Jameson and Liz stared back at him wide-eyed with disbelief.

'That's not possible,' said Liz. 'That thing's huge.'

'Exactly,' said Harry. 'No way I could miss it, is there? So, I didn't see it, because it wasn't there. The snow was in my face, and walking around out there, you're half blind.'

'But how can it not be there?' asked Jameson. 'And if it isn't, then just where the hell is it?'

'Walsh could've taken it,' suggested Liz.

Harry shook his head.

'No, he was gone before they turned up,' he said. 'He had something else planned, no doubt about that.'

Harry was then very aware of the dull ache in his leg from where he'd knocked it when he'd been outside.

'The tow hitch,' he said, something else falling into place, though he wasn't quite sure what.

'What about it?' asked Jameson.

'Who the hell has a tow hitch on a brand-new Porsche?' Harry asked.

'Lots of people, surely,' said Liz. 'Though obviously ones with more money than sense.'

'But it's an extra, isn't it?' said Harry. 'Which means that Walsh had it put on, probably by the dealer he bought it from. It's not something that comes as standard.'

'You're losing me,' said Jameson.

'And me,' said Liz.

Harry said, 'Walsh had this weekend, this whole elaborate escape, planned for months, yes? So, why would he buy a new Porsche and have a tow hitch fitted? He doesn't exactly strike me as the kind of bloke who fancied a bit of caravanning.'

'You think it's to do with what he planned, then, is that it?' Jameson asked.

'What I think is that Walsh didn't plan to just walk out of here,' Harry said. 'Not for mile upon mile, anyway. He had an exit strategy and right now my gut is telling me that whatever it was, he towed it here behind that Porsche of his, parked it up close enough to walk to, and that's where he went.'

'I see where you're going with this,' Jameson asked.

'After what we've heard from tonight, what everyone had to say as to why they were here in the first place, I think he knew people were on to him.'

'So, he decided to get the hell out of Dodge, right?' suggested Jameson.

'But that doesn't exactly help us with Nicholls, does it?' said Liz.

'Yes and no,' said Harry. 'Walsh's escape isn't relevant, but the Jeep is. Why? Simple: someone must've taken it.'

Liz said, 'Maybe Nicholls moved it.' Then added, 'No, he can't have done, can he? We've had eyes on him and the others ever since they arrived.'

'So, who, then?' Jameson asked.

Harry looked over at the group. They were gathered at the bar. Some were eating bar snacks Jack had found for them. None of them were drinking. They all looked cold.

'The reason I was outside,' Harry said, 'is because, having searched Walsh's room and found it turned over, I spotted footprints in the hall. Only they hadn't come from the stairs, but from further down the hall.'

'From one of the bedrooms, you mean?' asked Jameson.

'No,' said Harry, then told them how he had ended up climbing out of the window into the storm, and down an old fire escape.

'You think someone came in from outside, then?' said Liz. 'But who? Everyone's been in the house with us, haven't they?'

'All I know is that someone did,' said Harry. 'And it's the who that's bothering me, because by all accounts, and like you've just said, everyone was being watched, weren't they?'

'They were,' said Jameson. 'All of them. Never took our eyes off any of them.'

Harry thought back over everything that had happened, trying to see if there was any point where someone could have popped out without being noticed. But then, even if they had, they certainly wouldn't have had time to move the Jeep. It just didn't make sense.

'You find anything in his room?' Liz asked.

Harry pulled out the envelope and showed them what was inside. Looking at it again, realisation sparked in his mind. He knew then exactly what it was, and what it meant, and he was about to say something when a shout from over by the bar caught his attention.

Looking over, Harry saw Tony jabbing a finger at Jack's face, demanding a drink. Jack was trying to fend him off, his arms raised, a packet of cigarettes clutched in his right hand like a tiny shield. There was anger in Jack's eyes, Harry noticed, like he was ready to thump the man. The rest of the group was attempting to intervene.

Harry walked over.

'Tony,' he said.

Tony snapped around.

'I just want a drink, that's all,' he said. 'Don't think that's too much to ask, do you?'

'You said no drinks,' said Jack, looking at Harry.

'Actually, that was Jameson,' Harry said, 'but I stand by it just the same.'

Tony shook his head, made to turn from the bar, then launched himself across it, reaching for a bottle of whisky.

Jack, taken by surprise, swiped at him with his right hand, cracking Tony across the temple, and dropping his cigarettes in the process.

Tony skittered off the bar and tumbled to the floor. Scott reached down to help him get to his feet, then guided him over to one of the sofas and sat him down forcefully enough to make sure he wouldn't think about moving again any time soon. Harry's attention, however, was somewhere else entirely.

'Jack?' Harry asked, having just picked something up off the floor. 'You mind throwing me a packet of crisps?'

Jack did as Harry asked, and Harry caught the crisps without taking his eyes off the young chef.

'So, you're right-handed, then,' Harry said.

Jack frowned.

'I am?'

Harry threw something at Jack, who caught it in his right hand.

'Yes, you are,' said Harry. 'Instinctively so, it would seem.'

Jack shrugged, looking at what Harry had thrown at him.

'Thanks,' he said, holding up the cigarettes.

Harry's mind was working fast now, pulling everything together as best he could. It didn't quite make sense, not yet, but getting it all out, that might help. And even if it didn't, it would be good to empty his brain a little; it had been a busier-than-average Friday night, that was for sure, and his mind was close to leaking out of his ears.

'When I arrived earlier,' he said, his eyes on the chef, 'you were with the others, if you remember. And you were on your phone.'

'I was?'

'Yes, you were,' Harry said. 'You were holding it in your left hand, if I remember correctly. Which I do. It's a small thing on its own, for sure, but when you put it with everything else ...'

'I use both hands,' said Jack.

'Everyone does,' said Yalina.

'I don't,' said Rasheed. 'Can't write with my left at all. I kick with my left foot though, which is a bit weird, isn't it?'

'Most people can use both hands to a greater or lesser degree,' said Harry, 'but usually the dominant hand is quicker when it comes to typing. And, when I first saw you, in here, you were tapping away at the screen with your thumb. Quickly, too, which makes me think that's how you do it naturally. Remember?'

'Yeah, I remember,' said Jack. 'We were in here and I was on my phone. I'm not sure what you're getting at. It's not a crime, is it?'

Harry leaned on the bar.

'No, it's not a crime,' said Harry. 'But what I'm getting at is this ...' He held up his left hand to count through each point he was about to make, finger by finger. 'One, that when I first saw you, you were using your left hand to type a message on your phone.'

'Okay,' said Jack, with a shrug. 'If you say so.'

'Two,' continued Harry, 'that we weren't in here at all, but in the dining room.'

At this, Harry noticed a flicker of concern zip across the young chef's eyes.

'And three ...' Harry held up his three fingers for just a little longer before speaking, drawing attention from everyone in the room, '... as far as I know, there's bugger all phone signal up here. So, whoever it is you were messaging, they were close by. Bluetooth connection, I'm guessing, and that's usually around ten metres.'

The flicker of concern Harry had seen in the chef's eyes grew just enough to cause the corners of his mouth to turn up. Fear was there, Harry could see that, but there was something else, too; confidence.

'What are you suggesting?'

Harry shook his head.

'Right now, I'm not too sure, but I'm onto something, aren't I?' he answered. Then he smiled and asked, 'First, though, why don't you tell me where the real Jack is?'

CHAPTER THIRTY-THREE

JADYN ONLY REALISED HE HADN'T CLIPPED IN HIS SEATBELT when the Suzuki hit a particularly nasty dip in the lane hidden by the deepening snow. His head slammed into the roof, dazing him momentarily.

'You alright, over there?' Matt asked, not bothering to turn to look at the young constable, his eyes fixed on the road ahead, and further ahead, the vehicle they were now chasing.

Jadyn quickly clipped himself in, then rubbed his head, as a call came through on the radio.

'We've found him. I repeat, we have found him, over.'

Jadyn looked over at Matt, went to speak, but Matt hushed him with a stare as he buzzed in a reply to the call.

'This is Dinsdale. Copy that. How is he, over?'

'Cold,' came the reply. 'But he's okay. His quad bike ran out of fuel. Don't think he actually checked it before nicking it from his dad. Ended up digging himself a snow hole in a drift to get out of the worst of the weather. Did a decent job, too, if you ask me. Could've seen the night out easy, what with the sleeping bag and mat that he's got. Over.'

'He's bloody lucky,' Matt said, shaking his head. 'Parents informed? Over.'

'Yes, copy that. They've been told. Glad it's not me dealing with them. Taking him off the hill now and to the hospital for a proper check-up.'

There was a pause, then the voice came back again.

'There's something else as well. Over.'

'What?'

'You're probably not going to believe this, but he's ... well, he's drunk. Over.'

'Drunk?' said Jadyn, looking at Matt. 'How's that even possible? He's fifteen and sitting in a snow hole in the middle of nowhere!'

Matt was on the radio again.

'Can you repeat that, please? Did you say he was drunk? Over.'

'Yes, the lad's drunk,' came the reply. 'Like I said, had enough sense to take a sleeping bag and mat, he's wearing warm clothes, plus he's a few packets of biscuits and some chocolate, but he's also carrying a bottle of ... well, I don't know what the hell it is. Smells like you could use it to clean out your radiators. Over.'

Matt asked, 'Any idea where he got it? Over.'

'He says he nicked it from his parents. Doesn't smell like anything you'd buy in the shops though, if you know what I mean. Over.'

'No, I don't,' Matt said. 'Can you repeat that please? Over.'

'Matt, this is homemade,' came the reply, and Jadyn heard real concern in the voice. 'The kid's lucky he's not poisoned himself.' There was a pause, then, 'Over.'

Matt stowed his radio and Jadyn heard him mutter a few swear words to himself as he drove on.

'That doesn't sound good,' said Jadyn.

'No, it bloody well doesn't, does it?' agreed Matt.

Ahead, the vehicle they were following was now heading towards lights not too far off in the distance.

'That's Stalling Busk,' Matt said, pointing out into the night. 'And that's Marsett, just to the left. Not hanging about, are they?'

Jadyn was thinking about what they'd just heard on the radio.

Something had floated to the top of his mind, a note that Harry had jotted down on the board back in the office.

'Liz found bottles of booze out in the woods,' he said. 'In the den Thomas had made.'

'That'll be what he was necking, then,' said Matt.

Jadyn frowned, rubbed his forehead as though that in some way would help him think.

'I know,' he said, 'but there's something else, I'm sure of it.'

'What?' said Matt, then added a sharp 'Hold on!'

With so little warning given, Jadyn was swung violently to his right as Matt heaved the vehicle around to the left.

Matt said, 'Yep, he's heading towards Marsett.'

Jadyn wasn't listening. He had his eyes closed now to help him focus. He could see the office, Harry by the board. He imagined walking towards it, worked hard to bring it into focus, which wasn't easy seeing as Harry's writing was hard to read at the best of times. He saw notes on what had happened at the farm, something about a gun, a detail about Mrs Cowper shutting a door (like she was hiding something?), a dog on a chain, the hallway filled with pipes and urns ...

The door, he remembered; Harry had noted something about a cupboard behind it, that he'd seen jars filled pickles and bottles filled with beer.

Jadyn opened his eyes.

'It's not beer ...'

'What isn't?'

'In the cupboard,' Jadyn said. 'The one at the farm Harry saw filled with pickles and everything else. It wasn't beer.'

'You've lost me, lad,' said Matt. Then added, 'Wait up, he's slowing down ...'

Matt swore.

'What is it?' Jadyn asked.

'They've bloody well disappeared, that's what!' said Matt. 'Must've switched off their lights.'

'Bit dangerous, isn't it?'

'Not so bad down here as it would've been up on the fells,' said Matt. 'Lights from the houses will help him navigate.'

'So, where are they, then?' Jadyn asked, leaning forward, close enough to the windscreen to see his breath on it, staring out into the snow.

'Well, they can't have gone far,' said Matt. 'Best we can do is just roll on slowly and see if we can spot them. But at least we know what it is they're driving.'

'We do?' Jadyn asked, having no idea at all himself.

'Don't see many of them round the dales,' Matt said. 'But the closer we got, the clearer it became, and I'd recognise it anywhere.'

'You would?'

'Yes,' Matt said. 'They're driving a Jeep.'

LEANING ON THE BAR, Harry clasped his hands together and stared at the young chef. He heard a short laugh of disbelief and looked to his left to see Kirsty staring at him.

'What are you talking about?' she said. 'He's there, right in front of you, isn't he? That's Jack. Tell him, Jack, tell him it's you.'

Harry stared at Kirsty for a second or two longer than either of them expected. When she pulled away, Harry was dragging something else up out of his mind, another connection.

'He is, and he isn't,' he said, turning back to look again at the chef. 'I'm right, aren't I?'

Jameson came over.

'Mind letting us all in on what you're thinking?' he said.

Harry pushed himself up from the bar.

'No harm in that,' he said. 'And I don't think our friend here is about to do a runner, are you?'

Stepping away from the others, Harry walked over to lean back against the desk, stuffing his hands in his pockets as he did so, and in both his hands touched on something suddenly very important.

'There's been a lot going on,' he began, 'and little if any of it has made much sense, mainly because it's all been so cleverly hidden, which was the point really, I guess. Not just by Walsh, either, I might add. But anyway, seeing as we're dealing with something a little more urgent, now, than where the hell Walsh is, I'll get straight to the point.'

'Please do,' said Hazeem.

Harry stared at the chef.

'When we arrived, you were using your phone with your left hand, not your right, like I said. The fact you just said you thought we were in here rather than over in the dining room, confirmed my suspicions.'

'And what are they, exactly?' asked Kirsty.

Harry wanted to say something to Kirsty, but that could wait a little longer. He was thinking on the hoof now, the pieces clicking into place barely moments before he was giving voice to them.

'That Jack here, I'm guessing, is a twin,' he said, 'and that the reason he's here, just like everyone else, is to bring Walsh down.'

'What are you talking about?' Kirsty said.

'I don't follow,' said Hazeem.

Yalina, Scott, and Tony all just stared.

Harry continued.

'Back when the people who've locked us in here turned up, Jack was the one who protested about them using a room upstairs, suggesting the reading room. I didn't think anything of it at the time, not until I went upstairs to have a nosy round Walsh's room and found that someone had turned it over, clearly looking for something. Not sure what that was, but I found something while I was up there. Anyway, that person had managed to get into the house through an old fire escape at the side of the house, which comes out at the end of the hall upstairs.'

Harry paused, still trying to get it all in order in his head, his hands now playing with what was resting in his pockets.

'If you remember, Jack went out to his van for a first aid kit, right? But, what I'm saying, though, is that it wasn't him who came back inside. They swapped.'

'Who swapped?' Yalina asked. 'What the hell are you talking about?'

'Jack and our currently nameless friend here,' said Harry. 'That's what, or who, I'm talking about.'

'Assuming any of that's true,' said Scott. 'Why? What's the point?'

'I think, that when Jack learned that Walsh was dead, he was so shocked that he wanted to see for himself,' Harry explained. 'But Jameson here wouldn't let him enter what was now a crime scene. So, he texted his brother, who was outside in his campervan, and told him to climb in through the open window and check the body.' Harry now turned to stare at the chef. 'Which is what you did, didn't you? Only once you were in the lounge, you found the manikin, not Walsh. So, you panicked, headed back into the snow and up the fire escape to see if you could catch him in his room. But he wasn't there, was he? And that's when you realised that he'd bolted. So you ransacked the place to see if you could find clues as to where he might be headed.'

Harry paused. The room was silent.

'My guess is that you've done this before, swapped around, pretended to be the other brother. Perhaps you were going to do it all weekend, play a few games with Walsh, spook him a little, before you went for the big reveal? Except you couldn't because he'd already got the jump on you and bolted. I can imagine you weren't too happy when you found out.' Harry paused, then added, 'Can't say I know what your end game was, exactly, or if there was one at all.'

The room was silent, with everyone hanging on Harry's words, like they were sitting at the feet of a master storyteller.

'I'm going to assume that, when he went out to his van, Jack spotted Walsh's tracks in the snow. He went to follow them, saw that the keys were still in the Jeep, and took that. I mean, he couldn't take the campervan, could he? It would just get stuck. So, your job was to come in here and keep up the charade, while he did his best to try and track down Walsh.'

'But I'm Jack,' the chef said, his eyes flicking between Harry and, to Harry's interest, Kirsty. 'Like she said.'

'If that's the case, then where's your belt?' Harry asked.

The chef instinctively checked his trousers.

'You see, that was something else I noticed when I arrived; Jack was wearing a shiny belt buckle. And you're not, are you? Seems odd that it's now missing, doesn't it?'

Harry pushed himself up off the desk, at the same time revealing something from his left pocket.

'And then, of course, there's this ...' he said and held up an evidence bag.

'That's a cigarette butt,' said Yalina.

'It is,' said Harry. 'I found it next to what I thought was Walsh when I was having another look around. But here's the thing: it's in none of the photos PCSO Coates here took of the crime scene when we arrived. So, the only conclusion I can draw is that it was dropped at some point after, wasn't it? And, seeing as the room was locked, the only way for it to get in here at all was for someone to come in through that already open window and drop it.'

'This is making my brain hurt,' said Jameson.

'Same here,' said Liz.

'Anyway,' said Harry, looking at the chef, 'now that I've managed to get all of that off my chest, and because I'm not about to go running off into the snow to look for Jack or Walsh right now, I need to ask you something ...'

'What?'

'First, your name, because I can't go on calling you Jack when I know that's not who you are. And second?' Harry turned to look at the rest of the group. 'I seem to recall someone mentioning something about there being a shortwave radio ...'

CHAPTER THIRTY-FOUR

'I'M OLI,' THE CHEF SAID. 'OLIVER.'

Harry smiled, seeing Oli's shoulders sag a little with resignation as he finally gave up on trying to maintain the lie.

'Good to meet you, Oli,' he said.

'I don't know where Jack is, though,' Oli said. 'He just raced off, said he was going to find Walsh, and told me to come in with the first aid kit. I told him he was an idiot, to just let it go, but he wouldn't listen. I guess, after all the work we'd put into being here, he just, well, you know ...'

'On that,' Harry said, and pulled something out of his other pocket. He then looked over at Kirsty. 'What you told me about your friend, that was clever.'

'That's because it's the truth.'

'It is, in a way,' Harry said, and handed over the envelope from the bedroom.

'What's this?' Kirsty said, staring at the envelope.

'It's what's on the inside that matters,' Harry said.

Kirsty pulled the note out from inside.

'It took me a while, but that's your writing, isn't it?' said Harry, leaning in and pointing at the writing on the paper. 'The numbers and the dates? It matches your notebook.'

Harry watched as Kirsty stared at the note for a moment, then handed it over to Oli without a second thought.

'Those water marks you can see, they're not snow,' Harry said. 'My guess is those were from tears shed a long time ago because you couldn't pay Mr Walsh. You were young, had two young children, the debt wasn't going away. In fact, it was just getting worse, wasn't it? As to what's happened between then and now, I've not the faintest idea, but here you are, years later. And with your two boys, right?'

'You don't have to say anything, Mum,' Oli said.

Kirsty smiled at that.

'I ran away from home,' she said. 'I was just a kid, and I was pregnant, and I was terrified of what my parents, my dad, would say, what they would do.'

Harry said nothing, just allowed Kirsty to talk.

'I couldn't go to them for anything, so I hid. I needed money, and Walsh was there, wasn't he? He wasn't called Walsh back then, though.'

'John Setton?' Harry said.

Kirsty shook her head.

'No, but that's one of the names he's used over the years.' She looked at Yalina, then continued, 'Back then, he was Reggie Matthews.'

Harry noticed that Liz was writing in her notebook, jotting everything down.

'In the end, with the debt growing and growing, I just couldn't take it ...'

'Mum,' Oli said, reaching out a hand. 'No ...'

Kirsty held it.

'I took an overdose,' she said. 'I rang my parents, gave them my address, said goodbye, and took the pills. They found me and my boys, which was why I told them where I was. They also saved my life, which wasn't what I planned, but I'm glad they did. Then Dad ... he went after Reggie.'

Harry frowned at this.

'Sounds like your dad wasn't someone to be messing with,' he said.

Kirsty smiled, and Harry saw darkness there, and fire.

'If Reggie had known who my dad was, his reputation, he might have thought twice about doing what he did, but he didn't.'

Harry was already reading between the lines.

'Would I be right in thinking, then, that your dad was the kind of person Carl, I mean Reggie, would have had every right to be afraid of?'

'He owned a few nightclubs,' Kirsty said, 'dealt in various grey areas, if you know what I mean. When he found out some small-time shark had caused his daughter to try and kill herself, he had everyone looking for Reggie. He had plans for him, I know that. He never told me what they were, but they would've been ... horrifying.'

Harry found himself briefly wondering if Kirsty's father was still in business.

'He nearly found him, too,' Kirsty said, 'but that slippery bastard just disappeared. Then, a few years later, Dad died, and everything he'd been involved with, his businesses, it all just faded. But I didn't give up. I couldn't. I knew that what Reggie had done to me, he had done to others. He had to pay.'

'How did you know that Carl was Reggie?' Jameson asked.

'That ego of his,' Kirsty said. 'Though it was luck, really. I was at the doctor's with Jack or Oli, I can't remember which one, and I picked up a magazine, and there he was, staring at me from the pages. Older, fatter, richer, but I recognised him. He has a face I'll never forget, more's the pity.'

'He carries something with him,' Oli said. 'That's what we really want. That's what all of this was about, to get it off him, use it against him instead. I was looking for it when I was upstairs in his room. And I know it was a long shot, but I thought he might have Mum's ring as well, the one Gran gave her. Maybe he'd kept it as a souvenir or something? It wasn't there though.'

'The jewellery you said your friend tried to use to pay him off with,' said Jameson.

In answer, Kirsty gave only a sorrowful nod.

'What does he carry with him?' Harry asked.

'A file,' said Kirsty. 'Back when he was a loan shark, it was this book, with all these notes in it, photos he'd taken, stuff he had on everyone he dealt with. It's probably not that now, but I bet he's still got it in some form or other.'

'That's what we wanted,' said Oli.

Scott laughed.

'He knew, didn't he?' he said. 'He knew who we all were, set everything up just to rub our faces in it. If he wasn't such a bastard, I'd almost be impressed.'

'Have you heard from Jack since he took off?' Harry asked, his eyes on Oli.

Oli shook his head.

'He said he'd be in touch, but I can't even check my phone now, can I?'

'The radio,' Harry said, and noticed Jameson staring at him.

'No, it's too risky,' said Jameson.

Harry shook his head.

'No, risky is staying in here not knowing what the hell's going on, or how Nicholls and his little gang will react when they realise that Oli's brother has buggered off with their transport.'

'Around back, there's an outhouse with a freezer in it,' explained Oli. 'You can't miss it. Radio's in there.'

'Harry ...' said Jameson, caution in his voice. 'Think about this.'

Harry was over by the window. He paused, turned back to face the group.

'The manikin,' he said, and walked back over to the sofas, pointing at the one with its back to the door. 'Sit it there, next to Tony.'

Scott grabbed the manikin and did as Harry instructed.

Harry pulled off his jacket, swiftly swapping it with the one worn by the manikin.

'If someone comes through that door, all they'll see is seven of you sitting, chatting,' he said, jogging back over to the window.

'That's not very convincing,' said Hazeem.

'It's close enough for jazz,' said Harry. 'Won't be long ...'

Not waiting for an answer, Harry was out of the window and back in the snow. The first thing he noticed was that the jacket Walsh had used for the manikin was somewhat on the small side. He tried to pull it tight across his chest as he turned into the wind and snow, but it was no good. So, he hugged himself as best as he could, and made his way down the side of the house and around towards the back.

When he came to the outhouse, he pulled out the torch that Jameson had found in the cupboard under the stairs. He placed the fingers of his left hand over the lens and switched it on. The beam shone through the cracks in his fingers just enough to allow him to see where he was going, but hopefully not bright enough for anyone who might be looking out of the windows to notice.

The door was held shut by a bolt. Harry pulled it open, momentarily glad he wasn't having to deal with a padlock holding it shut, and walked over to the radio, sat down, and switched it on. Red lights shone out as he grabbed the handset, and adjusted the volume so that it was just loud enough to hear the squelch as he held in the side button.

Harry knew that the frequencies used by the police were encrypted, for obvious reasons. So that meant his only real hope lay in someone else listening.

While he had been running through everything about Jack, his brother Oli, and their mum, Kirsty, Harry had also been thinking about everything else that had been going on that day. Not just with him, but with the rest of the team. He knew that Matt and Jadyn were out with the mountain rescue and that the search party would be communicating with handheld shortwave radios. He had no idea what frequencies they were on, and was fully aware that what he was about to try was a massive long shot, but it was one he had to take regardless.

Torch off, Harry started to scan through the channels on the radio.

'This is Detective Chief Inspector Harry Grimm, can anyone hear me, over?'

Cloaked in darkness, Harry was all too aware of the cold. The wind was howling around beyond the door to the outhouse. He knew he had to be quick, but he also knew that he had to give this his best shot, not least because he hadn't come up with anything beyond using the radio. Beyond that, the only option right now seemed to be to barricade the lounge door and hide behind the bar, which didn't strike him as all that sensible.

Harry tried again and again, going through the channels and back again. Then, just as he was wondering whether it was too risky to give it another go, a voice came back to him on the radio.

'Boss?'

Harry stared at the radio. Was he hearing things in the wind?

'Boss, is that you? Over.'

'Jadyn?'

'Boss! What the hell ... I mean, what are you doing on here? I didn't know police radio linked up with the mountain rescue ones. Jen's been trying to raise you. Everything alright? Over.'

Harry knew he didn't have much time and had to get back to the lounge.

'Jadyn, listen to me ...'

'All ears, Boss,' Jadyn replied.

Harry took a moment to think what he was actually going to ask Jadyn to do.

'We've a situation at the house up past Marsett,' Harry said, and was about to explain everything when Jadyn interrupted.

'We're driving through there now, actually,' he said.

'What?'

Harry heard Jadyn go to answer, but his voice was snatched away by the sound of a scuffle, then another voice spoke to him.

'Harry? It's Matt. What's going on? You still up at the house?'

'Jadyn just said you're in Marsett,' Harry replied. 'I thought you were out looking for Thomas Cowper?'

'We were,' Matt replied. 'He's been found, and he's on his way to hospital for a check-up. He's bloody lucky, I can tell you that for nowt. Not just from the cold either; the lad's pissed, would you believe? Pissed! In a snow cave!'

'What the hell are you doing in Marsett?' Harry asked, remembering the bottles Liz had found in Thomas' woodland den, and the ones he'd seen back at the family home, sitting on shelves in a cupboard Jane had been a little too keen to shut the door on.

'You wouldn't believe it if I told you.'

'Try me.'

Matt said, 'Jadyn spotted lights, so we followed them, thinking it was young Thomas. Turns out it wasn't, as he'd squirrelled himself away in a snow hole further down and was found by someone else. Pretty clever if you ask me.'

'What was it, then?' Harry asked. 'The lights Jadyn saw?'

'Crashed quad bike and its rider,' said Matt. 'Unconscious, not just from the accident either; looked like he'd taken a proper beating.'

Harry lowered the handset for a second and stared into the darkness as more things fell into place.

Lifting the handset again, he said, 'Any ID?'

'No,' Matt said. 'It's a bloke in his fifties, no idea what he's doing out here, if I'm honest. Must be mad.'

'What does he look like?'

'Cold,' Matt said. 'Beaten up, too.'

'No, I mean describe him,' said Harry.

Matt did just that.

'That's Carl Walsh,' Harry said.

'And just who the hell is Carl Walsh when he's at home?' Matt asked.

'Carl Walsh is our victim,' Harry said.

'What? How can he be? That doesn't make any sense at all!'

'Long story, and it'll have to wait.'

Matt said, 'Well, someone knocked him off his quad bike, and that's who we've followed over to Marsett. I thought we'd lost them; they turned off their lights when they got close to houses. Found them again, though.'

'Where are they?'

Matt was silent for a moment.

'Matt?'

'Sorry, I was just checking with Jadyn to confirm.'

'Confirm what?'

'They've parked just down from where you are right now, Harry.'

Harry said, 'Whoever's with Walsh, they need to keep an eye on him. He needs to be put under arrest.'

'I don't think he'll be putting up much of a struggle,' said Matt. 'He's not in the best of shape right now. Anyway, why are you on the radio? How did you find this channel? What's going on?'

Harry was about to tell Matt everything, when a metallic click sounded in the darkness behind him.

CHAPTER THIRTY-FIVE

'Harry? You still there?'

Harry ignored Matt as something cold and hard pushed into the back of his skull, pinching his skin.

'Nicholls found the dummy,' said a mean voice from behind him. 'So, why don't you turn that off and tell me what you've done with our truck.'

'Harry?' said Matt, his voice cutting through the dark from the radio.

Something hard struck Harry over the back of his head.

'Turn that off. Now.'

As Matt came through on the radio once again, Harry carefully squeezed the trigger on the handset, silencing him, but keeping the channel open from his side.

'There,' he said. 'It's off.'

'Good. Now turn it all off. All of it, right now.'

Harry kept the trigger held down on the handset, hoping Matt was still listening.

'Pointing a gun at my head isn't a great way to get on my good side,' he said.

'The radio,' the man said, ignoring Harry. 'Switch it all off, or I'll switch you off. Permanently.'

Harry said, 'There's only four of you and one of you is injured. As for that mean-looking black Jeep you turned up in, I haven't the faintest clue where it is.'

The sound of the gun being fired so close to Harry's ears sent him off the chair and onto the floor. Ears ringing, he looked up to see that the radio was now very much dead, the person in the darkness with him having taken it out with a single shot.

Harry looked up to see a man's silhouette in the doorway, behind him snow spun in the dark like ticker tape at a parade. He knew the man was speaking, but it sounded like he was talking underwater, the words dull and muffled.

Harry shook his head, then pushed himself back up onto his feet, his hands up in submission, waiting for his hearing to come back. His eyes, however, were focused on the silhouette in the doorway.

'You should've stayed on your knees,' the man said, and he raised the barrel of his gun. 'Then I wouldn't have to stare at that fuck-awful face of yours as I put a bullet in it.'

In one simple move, Harry twisted his torso to the right, striking out at the pistol with his open left hand, and leaning his body out of the way to his left. His palm hit the metal and he kept on twisting, gripping the barrel and forcing it out of the way, thrusting forward and down, stepping in towards the man, forcing him backwards. The pistol went off, but the round went wide, and Harry was already well out of the way.

With the pistol now firmly pinned against his assailant's stomach, Harry pressed on, driving the man backwards, at the same time striking him once, twice, three times across his face with his elbow, hard enough to break bone. He reached down with his right hand to join his left, gripped the pistol, and gave it a violent and vicious twist, into the body of his attacker, and up. The pistol came away, and judging by his attacker's scream, so had the finger on the trigger, ripped away by the trigger guard.

Harry field-stripped the pistol in seconds, throwing everything but the barrel out into the snow. Leaving the outhouse, he pulled the door shut behind him, silencing the groans from the man inside. He slammed the bolt home, and used the barrel of the gun in place of the missing padlock to jam it shut. Then he raced around to the front of the house.

Jack was running up the drive.

'Jack!' Harry called, waving his arms and pointing away from the house. 'Go back! Now! Go back!'

The wind snatched Harry's voice from his throat, twisting it to nothing.

Harry kept on running.

'Jack! Get the hell out of here!' he called. 'Jack!'

Jack stopped, stared at Harry.

The front door to the house opened. In the light spilling out onto the snow, Harry saw a hand extend into the gloom. Clasped in its fingers was the sawn-off shotgun. Fire blasted from one of the twin barrels.

Harry saw Jack fall to the ground with a yell.

The barrel turned then towards Harry, and he took a desperate dive to his left as the gun fired once more.

Harry heard the door slam shut, then pushed himself up out of the snow, spitting slush and gravel out of his mouth.

For a moment, he couldn't see Jack, but then he spotted him, half running, half limping, back the way he had come. And hopefully, into the waiting arms of Matt and Jadyn, Harry thought.

Thankful that Jack was at least alive, if not also now hugely confused and disorientated by what had just happened, Harry turned his attention to those still in the house, hoping that what he had done with the radio before his attacker had shot it had been enough for Matt to at least be able to call it in. Now, though, Harry knew that the only card he had left to play was to stall for time. And he couldn't do that freezing his arse off outside.

Cold, wet, and with his ears still ringing, Harry walked over to the front door. Calming himself with a slow, deep breath, he raised his fist and hammered it against the wood.

The door slipped open to reveal Nicholls bathed in the soft glow of the hallway light behind him.

'Where is he?' Nicholls asked.

'Who?'

'You know bloody well who.'

Harry shook his head.

'Honestly, I've no idea what you're talking about,' he said. 'Seem to have gone a bit deaf.'

Nicholls lifted the shotgun and pointed the barrels at Harry's chest.

'Try again,' he said. 'I sent someone to find you. He's not come back, and here you are, right as rain.'

'Look, I went to get help,' said Harry. 'Police, remember? I slipped out through the window. Didn't exactly get far, as you just saw yourself.'

'Who was that, then?' Nicholls asked. 'Who was that I just saw in the snow? What did you tell them?'

'Not a damned thing,' said Harry.

'You're lying.'

'I'm not. You winged him though, you know that, right?'

Nicholls stepped back.

'In,' he said, his gun still raised.

Harry, his eyes on Nicholls, stepped out of the snow.

'You know you can't get out of this, don't you?' he said, a shiver rippling through his words.

'Watch me.'

'I aim to,' said Harry.

Nicholls waved his shotgun not at the door to the lounge, as Harry had expected, but up the stairs.

'Had to move everyone, I'm afraid,' Nicholls said. 'Didn't want anyone getting the same idea as you and disappearing out into the snow to get help.'

Harry thought back to what Liz had told him about the break-in Jen had been heading to. .

'Come on,' said Nicholls, frustration in his voice. 'Don't make this any harder than it already is. Move!'

Harry said, 'There was a survivor.'

'What?'

'At that house you visited before ending up here, I mean. I've no idea what that was all about, not yet, anyway, but I'm going to guess that whatever it was, it didn't go according to plan, did it?'

'Plans change.'

'And the dead keep their secrets,' said Harry. 'Unless they're not actually dead, of course. Bit remiss of you not to check, really. Shoddy.'

'You talk too much, you know that?'

Harry said, 'I'm also going to guess that despite all your strutting around, you're not the boss. Someone sent you and your friends to do a little clean-up job. That's what it sounds like to me, anyway.'

'All very interesting,' said Nicholls.

'I've been in this job long enough to spot something like that,' said Harry. 'Long enough to know that witnesses aren't part of the deal, and that trying to get out of a shitstorm like this with baggage just isn't possible.'

Movement caught Harry's eye, and he looked past Nicholls to see the other man from his little crew walking down the hallway from the reading room. He was wiping blood from a small knife with his shirt.

'Is it done?' Nicholls asked without turning around.

'It is,' the man said. 'She put up a bit of a fight, but—'

Nicholls swept around with the shotgun and pulled the trigger.

CHAPTER THIRTY-SIX

AT SUCH A SHORT RANGE, THE BLAST FROM THE SHOTGUN was devastating and the headless body dropped to the floor like a sack of bricks, the air briefly filled with a faint, pink mist.

Nicholls turned back to Harry.

'You were saying something about baggage,' he said.

For a moment, Harry was lost for words. He heard screaming from upstairs, then someone was beating against a door.

Nicholls dropped down beside the body and removed a pistol from the dead man's belt.

'Harry?' Jameson yelled, his voice distant, but clear enough for Harry to hear it, the sound of his fist hammering against a door. 'What the hell's going on? Harry!'

'Go ahead,' Nicholls said. 'Answer him. Tell him what's just happened. And maybe, just maybe, that'll have you and the rest of them behave long enough for me to get out of here. What do you think?'

'Oh, I reckon it's probably best if I keep what I think to myself,' Harry said. 'But you're on your own now, you know that, don't you?'

Nicholls frowned.

'Just one more to deal with,' he said. 'He'll be back soon enough once he's given up searching for you.'

'No, he won't,' said Harry.

'You lied, then.'

'I just don't take kindly to being sneaked up on in the dark,' said Harry.

Nicholls gave an almost-approving nod.

'You did me a favour, then,' he said. 'Saved me the trouble of doing it myself.'

'You can't kill us all,' Harry said. 'There's no chance of that now, is there?'

'You know, you're absolutely right there,' said Nicholls. 'All I need is one willing volunteer to play hostage just long enough for me to disappear. And by willing volunteer, I think we both know what I mean, don't we?'

Once again, Nicholls lifted the barrel of his gun.

'So, I'm going to give you a choice, Detective. Live now, come with me, die later. Or die now, I take someone else, they die later. Your choice. What's it going to be?'

Harry had already taken a huge risk with the man out in the shed. He was fairly sure that if he tried the same move again now, the odds wouldn't exactly be in his favour.

'I make a terrible hostage,' he said.

'You killed one of my men,' Nicholls said. 'A lot of people would say that makes you a terrible police officer.'

From outside the house, the distinctive sound of a distorted, amplified voice broke the tension.

'This is Detective Sergeant Dinsdale ...'

Harry saw anger burn behind Nicholl's eyes.

'Looks like the choice has been made for you,' Nicholls said. 'Friend of yours?'

'I have a lot of friends,' said Harry.

Nicholls smiled beneath cold, dead eyes.

'Best you introduce me to him, then,' he said, and pointed at the door.

Harry stepped back.

'After you,' he said.

'Oh, I don't think so,' said Nicholls, then waved the barrels of his gun. 'Move.'

Harry opened the door.

Outside, the parking area was flooded with light bright enough to have Harry instinctively shield his eyes. Then from behind him, the sound of a pistol being fired had him open them again.

'Kill the lights!' Nicholls shouted. 'Now!'

The lights dipped and Harry could see. In his mind, he'd expected to find Matt behind the wheel of a police car, but instead, he was standing behind the open door of a small, red Suzuki 4x4. Which made sense, Harry thought; a police car would have been absolutely useless for the rescue he had been involved with earlier.

On the other side of the vehicle, Jadyn was standing behind the open passenger door.

Matt lifted a megaphone to his mouth.

'Throw the guns away and place yourself on the ground, arms out in front.'

Nicholls laughed.

'Looks a bit cold to me, all that snow,' he said. 'So, here's what we're going to do.'

'Put the guns down,' Matt repeated, emphasising each word deliberately.

Harry wasn't sure whether he was witnessing bravery on the part of Matt and Jadyn, or blind stupidity. It was probably a mix of both, being so close to someone with a loaded gun or two.

'You're going to step away from that vehicle,' Nicholls said. 'And you're going to give me the keys. Then you're going to come over here and let me lock you inside the house with everyone else.'

'There's no way they're going to do that,' said Harry.

'Don't be so sure,' said Nicholls, then he lowered the pistol to point it at Harry's feet, and pulled the trigger.

Fire exploded in Harry's right foot with such violence that he didn't even hear the gun go off. He roared in pain, dropping to the ground with it, nausea racing through his brain, twisting his stomach. He retched, his vision blurred, and the pain just kept growing.

'Bastard ...' he hissed, squeezing his eyes shut, then opening them slowly to see just what kind of mess his foot was in.

'Harry? Harry!'

'Stay back!' Harry yelled, worried then that Matt and Jadyn would race over to help him. 'I'm ... I'm fine.'

'He shot you!' Jadyn shouted.

'I know!' Harry hissed. 'But ... just stay there, okay? Do not move.'

The pain was like someone had rammed a hot poker into his foot and then hit it with a sledgehammer. The snow was pink with blood, spots of it spattering in a long, wide arc.

Just then, a shout from behind them burst into the moment.

Harry looked over his shoulder to see the man from the outhouse coming around the side of the house.

'Another lie?' Nicholls said.

'Can't help myself,' said Harry, rolling over onto his hands and knees.

The man from the outhouse started to jog over. Harry saw that he was holding his hand tight against his stomach with his other arm.

'That bastard, he took my finger!' he yelled. 'Ripped it right off!'

'Don't ...' said Harry, looking up at Nicholls.

'In for a penny, right?' Nicholls said, and lifted the pistol.

The man stopped dead. Behind him, Harry saw movement, a figure racing towards the man: Jack ...

'What are you doing?' the man called out.

'What I have to,' Nicholls replied, and fired.

Harry launched himself from his left foot, driving his head upwards hard and fast. He crashed into Nicholls, knocking him as he pulled the trigger. His head connected with something hard, there was a muffled shout, and he was falling. He landed hard, but Nicholls' body broke his fall. All too aware that the man, though momentarily dazed, was still armed, Harry didn't give him time to recover, and quickly flipped him over onto his stomach, then dropped hard onto his back, winding him enough to cause him to let go of both the pistol and the shotgun.

Harry slapped both weapons away.

Nicholls struggled, but Harry wasn't going anywhere.

'Cuffs!' he yelled. 'Now!'

Matt was over in a beat, Jadyn with him, and together they quickly clipped Nicholls' wrists behind his back.

Harry rolled off into the snow as Matt ran over to the man Nicholls had fired at, returning with him a moment later, also in cuffs. Jack was with him as well.

'Hello, Jack,' said Harry.

Matt looked at Harry.

'You know him?'

'I do,' Harry said, looking up at the young chef. 'Thought he'd winged you earlier; looks like he missed.'

'He did,' Jack said. 'Only just, though; I heard the pellets zip past my head as I jumped out of the way.'

'You were limping.'

'Landed badly on my knees; my left leg was dead.'

The man Matt was holding let out a faint, pained cry. Harry turned from Jack to see a faint splash of blood on his sleeve.

'The bastard shot me!' he said.

'And if Jack here hadn't knocked you out of the way, you'd be dead,' said Harry. 'So, why don't you count your blessings? Though you'll have plenty of time to do that where you're going, I'm sure.'

Harry held a hand up to Jadyn, who reached down and helped pull him gently to his feet. Pain lanced through Harry like razor wire. He reached into his jacket pocket and pulled out the keys to the police Land Rover. It felt like that had been days ago, yet it had only been a matter of hours.

'Here,' he said, handing the keys to Jadyn, 'lock those two up in the back. And take their shoes; should make them think twice about trying to make a run for it with all this snow around.'

He then looked at Jack, thinking back over what Matt had told him on the radio about how they had found Carl Walsh, John Setton, or Reggie Mathews—whoever he really turned out to be.

'You could've killed him, you know that, don't you?' Harry said. 'Chasing after him is one thing, but ramming him and then giving the man a good hiding?'

'He had it coming,' Jack said.

'That I don't doubt,' Harry said, as exhaustion hit him hard enough to force him to brace himself against the bonnet of the Suzuki. 'Doesn't make it right, though. Did you find what you were looking for?'

A look of confusion swept across Jack's face, not because he didn't know what Harry was talking about, but because he did.

'Thought so,' Harry said, and held out a hand. 'Give it to me. Right now.'

Jack hesitated, then pulled a small, thin, orange box from his pocket and gave it to Harry.

'A hard drive,' Harry said.

Jack said nothing, his head dropped forward.

Stuffing the hard drive into his pocket, Harry said, 'I've met your brother, Oli, by the way, and your mum. You really are identical, aren't you?'

'Close enough to make no difference,' Jack said.

Harry called Matt and Jadyn over. He directed Jadyn to cuff Jack, not that he expected the lad to run off.

'Put him in the dining room,' Harry said. 'When you've done that, you'll need to find something to cover the body in the hall, then head upstairs and let the others out. Actually, it's probably best you and Matt do it together,' he added. 'You'll need to grab Jack's brother as well, and their mum, Kirsty. Keep them separate so that we can get all sides of whatever it is that they had been planning. I think I know most of it, but better to be sure.'

Without asking for his permission, Matt and Jadyn each took a side and carried Harry around to the back of the Suzuki, opening the door so that he could sit down.

'Thanks,' he said.

'Best I get that foot looked at now,' said Matt, and reached behind Harry to grab a small rucksack. Opening it, he pulled out a first aid kit.

'No,' said Harry, and took the first aid kit from Matt. 'I've bandaged myself up for worse than this, believe me. You need to get on with everything else.'

Matt hesitated.

Harry opened the first aid kit with his teeth.

'Go,' he said.

A few minutes later, and as Harry finished cleaning then bandaging his wounded foot as best he could, he saw a low shadow come around the rear door of the Suzuki. It sat down in the snow and looked up at him, head cocked to one side.

'Hello, Smudge,' he said.

CHAPTER THIRTY-SEVEN

'Here you go,' said Dave Calvert, and plonked down a pint glass in front of Harry. 'And there's more where that came from, I can assure you.'

Harry reached out for the glass, the cool surface biting his skin a little as he lifted it to his lips. He took a long, deep draft, then carefully rested the glass back on the beer mat on the table.

'Well, that's half a pint gone,' laughed Grace. 'Thirsty, then?'

'A little,' Harry said, fully aware that he was smiling.

They were sitting in the bar of the Fountain Inn, the small room bathed in the warm glow from the open fire at the far end. The beer, a pint of Butter Tubs, named after the limestone potholes that lay at the side of the road over to Thwaite in Swaledale, tasted cool and bright.

The bar was busy, but not heaving, with a happy game of darts going on, and a few folk at the other tables enjoying each other's company, a few ales themselves, and some well-filled plates of steaming food. A few days had passed since the Friday night up past Marsett, though everything was still very fresh in Harry's mind, and would be for a very long time, he thought.

'So, how are you doing, then?' Dave asked, staring at Harry over his own pint glass, which was already close to needing a refill.

'I heard from Matt that the Cowper lad was brought off the hill safe and well.'

'He was,' Harry said. 'You know the Cowpers, then?'

'I do,' said Dave. 'Jane, she's lovely. Which makes you wonder how she ended up with someone like Brian, doesn't it?'

'Not sure it's for me to say, really,' said Harry.

'Well, allow me, then,' said Dave. 'That man is ... well, he's a git, isn't he? And a maggot-faced one at that, if you ask me. Not that any fish I'd want to catch would be tempted to go in for a nibble of that mangey pillock dangling off a hook.'

'You don't like him, then?' said Grace.

Dave raised an eyebrow at Grace and drained his pint.

'What gave you that impression?' he said, then stood up and asked, 'Same again?'

Harry finished his pint and handed the glass to Dave.

'Not for me,' said Grace. 'I'm driving old Hopalong here, and I've an early morning tomorrow; never good with a headache.'

Dave headed to the bar.

'About tomorrow,' Harry said. 'You sure about it? I mean, you don't have to, you know that, don't you?'

'I'm not doing it because I have to,' Grace said. 'I'm doing it because I want to. And because it's the right thing to do.'

Harry leaned back, stretching out his leg, his foot throbbing still from where he had been shot. Luckily, the bullet had really only grazed him, taking out a decent chunk of flesh, but managing to avoid damaging any major blood vessels, bones, or ligaments.

'Not sure his dad would agree with that,' Harry said.

'Oh, I know he doesn't,' said Grace. 'But my opinion of him matches Dave's, just with more swearing. Which reminds me; when I was out at Marsett earlier today, to chat with Thomas, Brian asked me to tell you that he's really not happy at all that you not only took his gun and his licence, but also all of his homebrew.'

'It wasn't homebrew,' Harry said. 'It was rocket fuel.'

'And he wants his still back, if you could,' Grace added.

'He told you that as well?'

'Oh, Brian loves to talk,' said Grace. 'Though by talk, I mean complain. About everything. You mostly now, I think.'

'It was Matt and Jim that went over to remove it all,' Harry said. 'Plus, all the spares he had lying around in the hall. If they hadn't done that, he'd have just built another one.'

'It's illegal, then?' Grace asked.

'Anyone can own a still,' said Harry. 'Nothing wrong in that. What you can't do is use it to make alcohol.'

Grace laughed at that, and Dave returned with Harry's beer.

'But that's what a still is for, isn't it?' Grace said.

'It's just a case of the government protecting their interests, that's all,' Harry said. 'He'll have to pay a fine. Thomas had actually been down in the cellar messing with his dad's still when it blew up. Pat next door heard it. He's bloody lucky he wasn't injured.'

'So, what are you up to tomorrow, then?' Dave asked, looking over at Grace.

'I'm taking Brian's son, Thomas, out,' she said.

'You are? Why's that, then?'

'He's got two loves in his life,' Grace said. 'Music and ferrets.'

'Didn't know you played an instrument,' Dave said, but Harry saw the smile.

'I don't,' Grace said, 'but I know plenty about just how good ferrets are for clearing out the rabbits. And with Dad getting on, taking on an apprentice might just serve to have him finally hang up his shooting stick. We've been in touch with the school and they're happy for him to take the day as work experience.'

'Anyway,' Harry said, deciding to turn the conversation back to Dave. 'What is it you wanted to talk about, then?'

They were in the Fountain not just because Harry had needed to get out for a couple of pints, but also because, before everything that had happened Friday, Dave had been in touch, asking Harry to go out.

Dave fell silent, suddenly very focused on the pint in his hand

and the crisps he'd also brought to the table, opening the bag very carefully so that they could all dip in and grab some.

'Dave ...?' Harry said.

Dave looked up, glanced at Grace, then at Harry.

'You promise you won't laugh?'

Harry looked over at Grace, then back at Dave.

'Why would we laugh?' he asked.

Dave picked up his beer, drained half of it, then set the glass back down.

'You see, I've been working offshore for years, like, saved up more than enough. So, I can afford to do something else, can't I? With my time, I mean. I don't need to earn much. Plus, there's my goats. So, I've been thinking, I can do something useful, can't I? Does that make sense?'

'Well, it would if you got to the point,' said Grace.

Dave picked up his beer, finished it, then held the glass in his hand, staring into it like a crystal ball.

'Two things,' he said.

'And they are?' Harry asked.

'Cheese,' Dave said, then before Harry could interrupt, added, 'and I'm thinking of becoming a PCSO.'

LATER, and back in his cottage in Gayle, Harry was sitting back in his sofa, his foot resting on a cushion, up on the coffee table. Grace was busy in the kitchen preparing her lunch for the following day. Smudge and Jess were on the rug on the floor together, curled up in front of the fire, along with their new friend, the still-unnamed Whippet Grace and Jadyn had found. The dog was being picked up tomorrow by the man Jen and Jim had helped out at the traffic incident over on the Buttertubs Pass. His visit to the vets with his own dog had been a final one, but now, quite by chance, he was soon to have a new four-legged friend.

Outside, the world was still hiding beneath thick snow, though the roads were grey now, the main routes through the Dales cleared by the ploughs then turned to mush with grit. Leaving the Fountain to climb into Grace's old Land Rover, Harry had been struck by how quiet Hawes was, the snow deadening the usual sounds of the night. The air was still cold, though the wind had died at last, bringing to a stop the slow migration of drifting dunes of snow across the fells.

Closing his eyes, Harry cast his mind back to everything that had happened over at Marsett. That Thomas had been found was a relief to all, and he was fairly sure that anyone who knew his father at all, would be happy that the man no longer had his gun, or the means to lace his veins with his own liquor. And now that he knew the police were watching him, Harry hoped the man would look to changing his behaviour a little. Not that he would ever bet on it, though.

As for everything up at the house, as investigations went, he doubted very much that he would ever again be party to something so wholly bizarre. He certainly wasn't looking forward to all the accompanying paperwork, that was for sure, never mind the interviews still to be had with everyone who had attended the weekend. Right now, he had no idea who would be charged with what, but what he did know was that Walsh's hard drive was a gold mine, and that the man was going to end up behind bars for a very long time indeed. But that was really only a part of the whole, wasn't it? Harry sighed to himself. So much else had happened that it was hard to keep a track.

While Harry had been dealing with everything up at the house beyond Marsett, down on Blean Lane, Jen had somehow managed to stabilise Marina White. And what they had learned since then about her husband, Harvey, led back down south, and all the way to London's own violent crime scene.

From what they had discovered so far, Harvey had been trying to find a way out, had used information to his advantage, and had hoped that on leaving prison, he and his wife could just disappear. He could not have been more wrong, and his past had still caught up with him.

Much like Carl Walsh, Harvey had learnt the hard way that some people have long memories. Their arrival in the Dales had opened a door into a world where very bad things happened in the dark hours, as well as the light, but then the same was true everywhere, wasn't it, Harry thought? Some criminals were caught, while others got away. Marina was now under full police protection, and where it would all end for her, particularly after everything that had happened, Harry couldn't even guess.

As for the hare coursers Grace had spotted, they had disappeared, and with little if anything to go on, the only hope was that they would turn up somewhere else and not be so lucky.

Harry yawned, a wave of tiredness sweeping over him so heavy that he felt himself sink deeper into the sofa.

Grace returned from the kitchen, lowering herself down beside him.

'You heard anything from Pete?' she asked, picking up the remote for the television and switching it on.

Harry didn't answer straight away, instead sitting up to reach for his mobile phone, which was on the coffee table next to his foot and resting on top of a postcard from Gordy who was clearly having the best of times with Anna in the snow up in Glencoe.

He unlocked the phone, saw a message waiting, and read it.

'Yes,' he said.

'He's okay, then?'

Harry read the message, shook his head.

'Not sure okay is the best word to describe how Pete is, not right now anyway,' he said.

Grace turned to stare at Harry, confusion in her eyes.

'And what kind of nonsense is that?' she said.

Harry held up his phone for Grace to read Jameson's message.

'So, what does that mean?' she asked. 'He's taking your advice? To do what?'

'You wouldn't believe me if I told you.'

'Try me.'

So, Harry did.

Find out what lies in wait for Harry and the team in the shadows of
Middleham Castle in *Silent Ruin*

JOIN THE VIP CLUB!

SIGN up for my newsletter today and be first to hear about the next
DCI Harry Grimm crime thriller. You'll receive regular updates on
the series, plus VIP access to a photo gallery of locations from the
books and the chance to win amazing free stuff in some fantastic
competitions.

You can also connect with other fans of DCI Grimm and his team
by joining The Official DCI Harry Grimm Reader Group.

Enjoyed this book? Then please tell others!

The best thing about reviews is they help people like you: other
readers. So, if you can spare a few seconds and leave a review, that
would be fantastic. I love hearing what readers think about my
books, so you can also email me the link to your review at dciHarry
grimm@hotmail.com.

ABOUT DAVID J. GATWARD

David had his first book published when he was 18 and has written extensively for children and young adults. *The Dark hours* is his thirteenth DCI Harry Grimm crime thriller.

Visit David's website to find out more about him and the DCI Harry Grimm books.

 facebook.com/davidjgatwardauthor

ALSO BY DAVID J. GATWARD

THE DCI Harry GRIMM SERIES

Grimm Up North

Best Served Cold

Corpse Road

Shooting Season

Restless Dead

Death's Requiem

Blood Sport

Cold Sanctuary

One Bad Turn

Blood Trail

Fair Game

Unquiet Bones

Silent Ruin

Printed in Great Britain
by Amazon

18943014R00173